THE TEMPTING:
SEDUCING THE NEPHILIM

January 2015

Published by

BroadLit ™
14011 Ventura Blvd.
Suite 206 E
Sherman Oaks, CA 91423

ISBN 978-0-9905156-3-0

Produced in the United States of America.

Visit us online at www.TruLOVEstories.com

*This book is dedicated to
my children for their love and belief in me.
My sisters and friends for their faith in me.
My friends and publishers, Nancy, Barbara
and Cynthia and the BroadLit team.
And to all the women who have been taught
to want the happily-ever-after dream, but
courageous enough to face reality and still be
willing to fight for true love.*

THE TEMPTING:
SEDUCING THE NEPHILIM

by D. M. Pratt

A BROADLIT BOOK

Chapter One

Eve Dowling left Thibodaux Hospital and never looked back. After surviving thirteen months in a deep coma she'd returned to consciousness unable to remember huge chunks of her recent past. She remembered her childhood, her parents and relatives, her home in Chicago, high school, college and moving to New Orleans for her dream job at *Southern Style* Magazine. Her most recent and last memory was of a fabulous party at her favorite estate outside of New Orleans on a lush romantic night dancing sensually with a seriously handsome stranger. That dance led to the greatest seduction she had ever experienced in her life and ended with an orgasm so intense she was told she arched back and hit her head hard enough to give herself a concussion, which left her unconscious and in coma for over a year. When Eve finally awoke, she was greeted by the amazing, intelligent and seriously handsome man with whom she'd danced at the party.

If there was such a thing as love at first sight, she knew the moment she saw him she was his. Like Cinderella at the ball, he had pursued her, found her and stayed by her side during her dark sleep. Like Sleeping Beauty, when her eyes fluttered open, he was there, waiting and wanting her. To her utter surprise, he wanted to marry her and take her into his life with their beautiful ... son; Philip: Okay, that was a shocker she hadn't expected, especially because she'd slept through both the pregnancy and her son's birth. The nurses had insisted jokingly that after being pregnant and going through the birthing process themselves while conscious, she should count herself very lucky. They had pumped her breast milk three times a day while she slept, fed her son and cared for her sleeping body.

Eve was convinced she was experiencing some type of fairytale syndrome, but her psychotherapist, Dr. Lisette Honoré, with her mountain of blonde hair and lizard green eyes, tried to convince Eve that her feelings were normal reactions to a set of very, very unusual events. As for Eve's struggle to remember events from her life before the coma, Dr. Honoré said, "That's just your mind dealing with the gap of time you spent in a coma. Sounds enter your subconscious while one is in an unconscious state. The conversations of visitors, television programs, radio shows that play in another room are carried into the mind through auditory nerves and translated into memory. Even smells picked up through the olfactory nerves can stimulate the mind and be translated into memory. Our brains try very hard to make rational sense of our lives, especially after this kind of trauma."

"This kind of trauma?" Eve thought. She sounded so annoyingly logical. Eve had awakened into a ridiculously perfect life and, despite the rather scary missing pieces and the occasional flashes that came in shadowed and bazaar images that woke her from her sleep drenched in sweat, Eve told herself she shouldn't care. She was happy. Right? So happy she promised everyone, especially the police, which the sordid details of her 'accident' were of absolutely no importance to her ... and mostly that was true ... mostly.

Beauregard Gregoire Le Masters was kind and patient during the months Eve was kept at the hospital for observation and physical therapy. Her muscles had severely atrophied and despite all those damn years at the gym doing classes, weights and yoga, she had literally gone to mush. Beau was there every day, encouraging her and cheering her every victory. In between the medical tests and the mental and physical therapy, he courted her, winning her trust, getting to know her and she him. They shared stories like two teenagers dating. In the afternoon he'd pushed her around the hospital grounds in her wheelchair and they had as many meals together as he could. He was dealing with "family matters," the details of which he wouldn't discuss with her until she was better. More often than not he had the finest chefs in New Orleans prepare and deliver gourmet meals featuring Louisiana's most decadent cuisine: etouffé or gumbo or crawdads boiled in Cajun spices, creamy rice and sautéed mustard greens with sweet iced fruit, bread pudding with whisky sauce. Beau had fine French cheeses flown in from Paris. Her favorite was accented with figs and laced with apricot jam. Linen table cloths, flowers and candles were the finishing touches for these unforgettable evenings that made her fall more and more deeply in love with him every day.

Once, even though he got into trouble with the hospital that night, Beau filled her room with sterling silver roses of the palest most delicate lavender color she'd ever seen. Their scent caught the night breeze and made her pleasantly light-headed. He hired a mariachi band to entertain everyone on Eve's hospital floor. The patients and staff enjoyed the show before the harsh reprimand from the squinty and slightly cock-eyed senior medical advisor ended the performance. When the medical advisor finished fussing at them like naughty school children and left, Eve and Beau turned to each other and burst out laughing so hard they thought they would never be able to stop. Beau was funny and charming, wonderfully loving and romantic, smart and amazingly down to earth. Eve loved him and in turn, Beau seemed totally captivated by her and told her he was happier than he could ever remember.

When he finally kissed her for the first time since her re-awakening, it reminded Eve of an innocent and gentle kiss between two twelve-year-olds and the night she lifted her bedcovers and invited Beau into her tiny hospital bed, the chemistry that had drawn them to each other the night of the party, came flooding back. The sensual rush of discovery reminded Eve why she'd let this stranger seduce her in a garden during a party without even first asking his name. He was both strong and gentle. When his lips found hers, he took her breath away.   Beau explored her entire body with leisurely, meaningful kisses; his lips brushing every inch of her face, her mouth, her neck. When his hands found her breasts, her nipples were already erect, anxious for his touch ... his mouth and kiss. Every caress, turn of his tongue, each kiss and delicate bite woke her body from another kind of sleep: the kind that shuts down when a body is left unloved. Still, a strange little voice in the back of her head kept whispering to her, "None of this makes sense." How could she have fallen so easily for him? She was Eve, the original wall flower when it came to men. Okay, yes, the physical attraction was off the charts, but from what she could remember of her past, she was beyond cautious when it came to men. She had meticulously placed so many walls around her heart, letting anyone, especially a man inside was akin to cracking the fire wall into the CIA. Yet, from the moment she woke and looked into Beau's eyes, he seemed to have an instant place so deep inside her heart it had to be true love. He belonged there, as comfortable and right as if they had been together in another life and found their way back in this one. There was no question her body wanted him to make love to her again no matter how many times the little voice said, "What's wrong with this picture?"

Dr. Honoré insisted they could not have intercourse until Eve regained her strength, which inspired Beau's creativity. Each night he slipped into her bed and found new ways to bring her to the brink of orgasm, only to stop and whisper that they would have to wait until the doctor said it was safe. He promised her delights and bliss beyond her wildest imagination.

"My imagination is pretty wild," she said with a lascivious smile.

"Good," he replied. "I'm counting on it."

'Once they were allowed to return home' was the mantra from hell from the senior doctor, the one she hated most. Frustrated and sure Beau was as well, Eve tried to give Beau the same exquisite pleasure with her hands and mouth. He gently refused with a smile, kissing her sweetly.

"I'll have my turn when we can climax together."

When Beau was gone, her time was spent cooing and talking and playing with her beautiful little boy. It wasn't hard to fall in love with him. Like his father he was perfect. Now and then the little voice whispered that he was "too perfect," but Eve brushed it away like a few strands of loose hair.

Upon her release from Thibodaux Hospital, Eve and their amazing son Philip were piled into a limo. They rode, wrapped in each other's arms, through the vast expanse of Louisiana countryside, and after what felt like a thousand hours arrived at the family estate. Upon seeing the main house again, its commanding beauty and expansive, architectural grace almost took her breath away. Beau handed Philip to the nanny so he could lift Eve into his arms and carry her through the massive double entrance doors of the Gregoire Estate mansion. On that day her husband-to-be, Beauregard Gregoire Le Masters, gave her a six carat, D, flawless white, pear-shaped diamond set in platinum and asked for her hand in marriage. Eve felt the rush of warm salt tears swell in her eyes as she whispered, "Yes." She had never felt such complete joy.

From that day forward she, Beau and Philip began the quiet process of settling into the life of a too perfect, happy family. Eve was doing her best to ignore the little voice that kept getting incrementally bigger, bringing with it the relentless, gnawing feeling of terror that pulled at her when she was alone or drifting in and out of sleep. Despite her haunting fears, all of which she kept secret from Beau, the little family moved into the guest house just off the west wing of Gregoire Manor. From there they were close enough to keep involved in the daily progress of the restoration, but far enough away to avoid breathing the clouds of plaster dust and paint fumes, which was a Godsend.

Ten months passed in the blink of an eye. Beau insisted on waiting for the title to the Gregoire Estate to be transferred out of the trust and back into his name before they officially tied the knot. The legal transfer process was finally nearing completion. Because of his parents' complicated will and his grandfather's relentless attempts to override the legal provisions when he thought his grandson was dead, Beau found himself buried in a quagmire of legal details that needed to be addressed by an army of attorneys. His legal problems and the day-to-day responsibilities of the estate created a layer of tension in the house. She could see Beau did his best to leave his problems at the front door so she did her best to make their home a respite from the troubling reality. Eve had met Beau's grandfather, Millard Le Masters, the very day she woke from her coma. From the moment she laid eyes on her grandfather-in-law-to-be, she didn't like him. More importantly, she didn't trust him. Yes, Beau had left right after college. He did run away and disappear for twelve years. Because no one had heard from Beau for eight years, as Millard explained, in the pain and grief of losing his only grandson, he declared him dead and went on with life and the responsibilities Beau had apparently walked away from.

Occasionally, the hint of a deeper, uglier truth reared its head and triggered horrible fights between grandfather and grandson. The clashes left Eve feeling trapped in the middle. One part of her wanted no part of the sordid details behind the Gregoire family secrets, but the ever curious journalist inside her wanted to know everything. Why did Beau's parents block Millard's access to Beau and the estate in the first place? Why had Beau run away and disappeared? Both subjects were taboo when Eve asked questions. In good old Southern tradition, no one would speak about what had happened all those years ago and what legacy Beau needed so desperately to escape from living. Clearly Eve would not be getting any answers, at least not until she was officially a member of the family. The wedding was still months away so Eve channeled her attention to the needs of Beau, baby Philip and the mansion. So much still needed to be done to redecorate the main house in time for the ceremony, so Eve set to work sweeping away the thick layers of dust, sadness, real and historical cobwebs that clung to the paint, wood and stone that was the Gregoire Manor. Most of all Eve wanted to eradicate the past memories that clung to the tattered silk wall fabric, Persian carpets and brocade curtains. Even after they'd all been pulled down and carried away, the aromas lingered to taunt her olfactory senses each time she stepped through the front door. There were days when she felt like an unwelcome intruder as the house fought against the changes she wanted to make, but day by day it released its hold, somehow knowing she wanted the best for it, and with a creek and a windy sigh it finally let her win.

Beau told Eve her job, if she chose to accept it, was to breathe new life into the grand, old house. Beau wanted her to keep the bones that had stood for centuries, but rip away the past that covered them like a loved outfit of fine, but outdated and musty, old clothes. She was to design an elegant look for every room using her favorite colors, fabrics, wood and stone, all the new things that would someday have meaning only to them. The renovation in the house moved laboriously slow and all the wedding details ate into the precious moments she wanted to spend on her newest and favorite job: raising their new son, Philip.

Beau and Eve were the loving parents of a smart eleven-month-old who was very busy joyously navigating the countless halls and rooms of the estate's west wing on two wobbly little legs. As Eve entered the makeshift guest house nursery every morning, the sight of Philip happily playing with his fingers and toes in his crib made her smile. The soft, pale blue chiffon curtains that draped over his crib hung from a brass ceiling hook that always glowed in the wash of sunlight that spilled in through the window. The light appeared to give Philip's body its own aura, a magical spirit from another realm, Eve thought. Just looking at him made her smile. Loving Philip and Beau were the greatest gifts she could have imagined receiving. Her heart swelled with love as Philip pulled himself up to his feet by the crib bars and stood smiling with arms outstretched for her to take him. She gathered him into her arms, sat on the soft cushions of the rocker by his crib and offered him her breast. His mouth on her nipple made the world and all its problems and responsibilities, save for him, fall away. Philip was an amazing baby and Eve adored him.

Eve looked at her son and, as he stared back at her with those deep, mysterious, unreadable dark eyes—not hers, not Beau's, but somehow she didn't care—she'd lose herself in their silent communication and his unflinching and often unnerving gaze. She didn't want to admit it, but sometimes he frightened her. Eve closed her eyes and held her breath, fighting against a crushing sense of terror.

Those moments and that tiny growing voice that screamed in her head something is very wrong... but what? Those moments of sweat-drenched terror were followed by violent headaches that stabbed her like a knife piercing through her skull. They came at irregular, random intervals caused by seemingly nothing, but they always came and carried with them flashes of blinding images. At first the image was always the same; a long hallway with a door at the far end she could not open when she finally had the courage to get there. She pressed her ear to the hard wood and could always hear voices on the other side saying things she couldn't understand, speaking in a low, persistent whisper as harsh and hissing as an icy winter wind relentlessly rushing as it passed through a slivered crack in an almost but not quite sealed window pane.

Today was different. Today the images expanded into a barrage of indiscernible faces and frightening events that made no sense. Places she'd never been to yet she knew them as well as if she had gone and done and seen them a thousand times. The images surrounded her and closed in on her. Eve held her breath, opening her mouth to cry out for help, but no sound emerged only more images. These pictures in color and black and white were even more frightening than the last. Eve knew the longer she stayed in this terrifying nightmare, the more horrifying it would become.

"Wake up," Eve heard herself say in a voice so distant no one else could possibly hear her. Wake up from what was the question that echoed back to her. Again and again she commanded herself to wake from the hellish nightmare, to push past the wild swirling and very confusing images that held her captive inside their strange, funnel of meaningless information.

These tortuous terrors now came every night. Always fragments of images that were becoming more and more complicated and twisted. Some were new and whole, some the same broken and shattered: flashes of events, people, places, pieces of a broken puzzle that didn't fit together. And the voices, whispering and insistent, a jumble of words that were not quite understandable, too muffled to be coherent, but never completely silenced. Eve opened her mouth to scream, but the more she tried to call out, the more she couldn't. Now even the air from her lungs stopped flowing. Finally she screamed and with her desperate scream the visions retreated and all she could see was Beau rushing in to hold her.

Her scream still echoing in the room, she watched, trembling as

Beau switched on their bedroom light. Eve's feelings of hopeless misery and helpless fear slipped away as he bundled her into his arms. He held her and kissed her tears away, stroked the river of honey hair that had grown luxuriously thick since her time in the hospital. Beau would bury his face and hands into her curls. He loved to forage through her silken forest of hair to find and gently kiss her flesh until she calmed, relaxing into his embrace. His kisses warmed and melted her until she surrendered to his touch. Then, she would softly whisper, "Make love to me."

He made love to her as only he could do. His touch, his lips on hers, his hands caressing her skin would conquer all her ghostly fears, driving them farther away with each kiss. Then he would slip slowly and methodically inside her again and again, until she was wet and wanting all of him. Beau rode into her with the force of a hundred gentle waves sliding into shore then retreating again and again into the ebb and flow she loved so much. Together they fell into the ever building rhythms of a sensual tide and with each stroke he would carefully bring her back until the present was all she could think about and all she could feel. Her husband-to-be, her son, her home, her friends, and her world came rushing back around her. They were real, warm and safe tingling through her as Beau quickened his stride, pushing in and out of her until he masterfully brought her to orgasm and commanded Eve back to joy.

Her euphoria would last a few days, sometimes even a week, then her scattered memories rushed back in and brought the inky blackness of night's prison. They held her captive until the dim shadows of morning's first light crept back across her bedroom floor. Even then, fragments of her lost memories seeped into her mind once again, filling her with dread that something dark and scary was hiding deep inside her. This mental fog clouded her dreams, both her daydreams and her nightmares. It lingered, waiting, billowing with an inaudible yet urgently important message, too foggy to see clearly. Eve thought of these days as shrouded time, cocooning everything in a cowl of stormy clouds that rolled across her world, blocked the sun and pained her every thought.

"It's all the stress," Beau kept reminding her. "Just like a storm, darlin'. It'll pass." But something in her throat clenched and made her catch her breath. To make it pass she knew she needed answers to questions she was afraid to ask. Eve made it through the days by staying busy with Philip and the house. Philip would giggle and squeal and fall into her arms and make the world right again. At night she learned to watch her open-eyed visions in silence as the rush of images bombard ... her mind finally faded and stopped. Eve would make herself go back to sleep allowing the last of the strange mental pictures to drift away like clouds blown by high winds as she tucked herself into the safety of Beau's arms ... until the next time the headaches cracked her thoughts and flooded in.

There was no way she could handle these "attacks" alone, but neither Beau nor Cora, Eve's very best girlfriend, were capable of understanding. She returned for sessions twice a week and shared with Dr. Honoré some of the images from her strange nightmares and even the occasional auditory hallucinations that plagued her. Dr. Honoré said that post-coma patients did experience both auditory and visual hallucinations sometimes.

"The release of endogenous dopamine could be a residual of the trauma to your head," Dr. Honoré explained.

Eve could consider haloperidol-based drugs and cognitive therapy if the hallucinations became more prominent, but at the moment she wanted to keep nursing and her doctor felt they were unnecessary. Ultimately, it was about time: allowing the brain to heal and allowing the love of her family to surround her and take away her unfounded sense of paranoid delusion. Her doctor's words sounded all too logical until a headache gripped her and the flashes of incoherent, violent images sped past her mind's eye, showing up when she caught a reflection moving through a mirror or an unnatural shadow wriggling on a wall. Eve promised herself she would learn to live with it until whatever it was in her brain went away. In her heart she simply prayed she could survive.

Chapter Two

Every day the Gregoire mansion waited for Eve to arrive. The painters, wood workers, masons, and fabric hangers, who Eve's friend, Cora had insisted on her hiring were coming closer to finishing the massive list of requested changes in the main house. Together they had transformed the mansion room by room. They had re-plastered the faded blue and painted the walls a warm, soft cream done in a faux texture with a hint of mustard gold. The color was finished with the slightest kiss of lavender all blended under a Venetian sheen that suggested the first hint of summer dusk.

Cora had been a Godsend. Decorating was in her blood and the air she breathed. She had them strip the years of paint off the plaster crown moldings and patch and refinish them in a rich, bold white the color of ivory clouds. The moldings framed the silk moray fabric that stretched along the entry stair walls and into the master dining room. The wainscoting that lined the entry, lower halls and climbed the curved stairway, Eve matched to her molding, but in a shade warmer to enhance the hues that flowed up from the grand, travertine floors of the entry. The stone was buffed flat to look raw, muting the shine to a dull haze. The house seemed to come alive under Eve's touch and Cora, with her whirling energy, iron fists with the workers, hilarious wit, laughter and a few bottles of great French wine from her extravagant cellar, made it fun. Everything fell together as the house awoke into modern life.

Once or twice when the headaches got her, Eve tried to share what she was experiencing with Cora, but Cora laughed and asked only that she please share whatever psychedelic drug of choice was making her trip like a bad sixties movie.

"Better still, I don't want any unless we can get you to make it into a happy high and have much more fun, Suga." Cora said and focused them both onto the task at hand. "Now I won't hear another word. Promise? There is much too much to do."

"Promise," Eve replied, knowing she would try to get Cora to help her figure out the Gregoire mystery.

Cora had been Eve's best friend since she moved to New Orleans from Chicago. They met on a double date, got crazy drunk, dumped the guys and partied the rest of the night. They also almost died in a speed boat on Lake Charles, but Eve pulled Cora out and saved her life; a fact that bonded them for life. Cora was a seriously old moneyed, TFB (Trust Fund Baby) and had never worked a JOB a day in her life, but Eve knew better than most that, her dear friend was the hardest working woman in New Orleans' old family, high society. Cordelia Belle Bouvier, Cora to her friends, had twelve generations of southern history flowing in her veins. She and Beau's family bloodlines were among the oldest and most respected in the state. Cora sat on the Board of Directors of six charities, two banks, a liquor company and two universities. She was smart, beautiful, young, and very rich and she loved Eve like the sister she never had.

"You, you northern hussy, need to buy yourself a wedding dress. I'm taking your ass to Paris for Fashion Week and we are goin' to go crazy! You better warn Beau you need his black American Express with no limit," Cora told her.

"I could never max out a black card," Eve said.

"That's the point of it being black and bottomless. No one can max it out. However, I'll teach you how to give it a workout, suga," Cora replied making them both laugh so hard they cried.

Today Eve was alone. She found herself in one of the mansion's four attics. Vast rooms inside pitched roofs with round windows covered in dust. There she'd found stacks of old paintings of Beau's family covered with tattered, muslin cloth. Some paintings dated as far back as the seventeen hundreds. Each told a story about his family history. Their faces looked austere and stern to Eve. The men looked strong and determined to live life to the fullest in a world long forgotten. There was a powerful, cruel edge in the eyes of the men and a frightened plea in the eyes of the women that disturbed her. As she dragged the muslin off the largest painting, Eve covered her mouth and coughed from the haze of dust particles that danced on the sunlight around her. She gasped as she found herself staring face-to-face into the azure eyes of Pearlette and Gofney Lafayette Gregoire, Duke and Duchess of Maurice, dressed in the lace and velvet, gold and pearls that symbolized their wealth in both the old and the new world. There was a cold timelessness about their features she found disturbing. She found an ancient bible and looked on the page that listed the marriages and christenings. A handful of pages were torn out at the beginning and, on a rag of a page, she saw what looked like the name Gremoire. It was hard to read and had been scratched out and changed to Gregoire. She Googled them both. She found no reference to Gremoire, only a variation on the name found in some of the earliest writings in France that had something to do with dark, demonic magic. Eve was sure that was a mistake so she moved on to Google Gregoire, but here she discovered only snippets of their history, much of which had been lost to time or destroyed thanks to the fires that devastated their sprawling French chateau during the height of the French Revolution. They were harsh landlords feared and disliked by the people of the region. They were listed as killed by guillotine, but here they were... proof they'd escaped and come to America. They changed their destinies by fleeing the bloody blade of the guillotine to become the matriarch and patriarch of the Gregoire American lineage.

Eve could see their character and resolve in the set of their eyes, the tilt of their chins and the strength of their broad, erect shoulders and the same cold stare in Gofney's eyes. Philip had his eyes, the eyes of a conqueror. Eve vowed Philip's eyes would never be cruel... never. There was no question these were brave and strong adventurers who left their French chateau and vast lands in France to come to America and settle in the new world. Her son came from strong, noble genes. Eve ran her fingers across the ancient oil, cracked with age, and wondered what their journey from France must have been like; months across the turbulent Atlantic, into the gulf where they would change to a barge. The first glimpses of the wild, primordial bayou, filled with snakes and alligators, Indians and pirates, slaves and free blacks. Finally, up the Mississippi until the bustling frontier city of New Orleans unfolded like a blossom~exciting, deadly and beautiful. They'd bought land titles from Louis the Sixteenth long before the revolution, perhaps trying to help save France, perhaps visionary enough to see the inevitable demise of the aristocrats and the coming blood bath of the guillotine. Then, once in America, they fought charlatans, Native Americans, weather and bouts of Yellow and Scarlet Fever. They built the first wood and rock frame version of the mansion and carved out a life for themselves and their seven children with the ten thousand acre deed that would set their wealth for generations to come.

One Sunday, when the workmen were gone, the house was silent. Beau had taken Philip for a drive, so Eve returned to her secret adventure in the attic. This time she searched for the weathered old leather trunk with an arched lid and brass hinges and handles. It contained a treasure of old books, letters and papers. Most had fallen apart over the years from neglect, but a few of the books, maps and the antique bible that had caught her interest were still readable. Her French was modern, yet she could still make out who was who on the opening pages, which revealed the Gregoire family genealogy dating back to the twelfth century with detailed records mapping the family lineage. There was one more mention of the oldest lineage that tied to the name Gremiore. Again, the name was scratched and torn away. Every family book she looked into, dating back before the sixteenth century, always ended with the remains of the tattered pages, torn out and intentionally removed.

Eve brought the Bible down from the attic to show Beau, but, once again, he acted a true Southerner by saying he cared little about the past. Eve saw a flash of anger pass across his face before it was replaced by a sweet smile.

"This is the past and it's done...unchangeable," he said. "Let's lay it to rest and live life here in the present. Please."

He kissed her and she promised, but in her heart she knew she couldn't. Family history meant something to her and besides, rummaging through the attics distracted her mind from the haunting images that plagued her. As a matter of fact, the headaches never came when she was up there among the historical treasures. The Gregoires have what she never did, a written chronicle of their family's evolution. It was the history missing from her family. Her mother was an orphan who never knew anything about her real parents or their past, so these fascinating, ancient family histories of Beau's had a very special meaning to her... her son would have the history she did not.

She read passages from some of the letters she found to Philip while he nursed or when he was falling asleep, sharing with him the names of his six times great grandmother and grandfather, aunts and uncles, cousins and on and on and their trials and tribulations, triumphs and joys. There were letters that detailed how many of their children had died, some as stillborn babies, some killed by raiders, pirates and Native Americans attempting to re-claim the land stolen from them. Some of their children were lost in the American Revolution and some of the next generation in the War of 1812. Then, there were years of peace: weddings, births, deaths, until mother nature intervened and brought droughts that destroyed the cotton and food crops and then, when things looked their blackest, kindly gave them long periods of abundance once more. They bought more land and in hard times sold thousands of acres. The Yellow Fever in 1830 and then again in 1850 took so many sons and daughters, mothers and fathers. Eve could see the tears Suzette, a pale-skinned, fair-haired slip of a girl, wept as she wrote. Suzette's tears dried deep into the page, smudging the ox blood ink and leaving tiny concentric circles splattered like raindrops: sad stains etched by time onto the page forever. Eve brushed her fingers across the sepia-colored paper. She could feel the kindred soul of the young woman they once belonged to sadly watching those she loved die of the fever and being left behind, cursed to live and carry the family name with her brother and sons. Suzette said in one letter she accepted the burden of what she had taken on when she married into the Gregoire family, but she learned about the truth too late to change what had been destined.

"Had been destined," Eve whispered to herself, pondering the meaning as she ran her fingers across the words.

Beau and Cora insisted she keep her focus on the job at hand and again Eve promised, but Eve found herself compelled to return to the attics and dig through the dust-covered past every chance she could get. There were answers there to questions she wasn't sure how to ask, but her journalistic mind drove her along with the whispers and images that haunted her thoughts. It seemed to her that being in the attic and digging through the past quelled the dreams as if to say, *we will be still if you keep looking for the truth.*

The central attic held memorabilia left from the Civil War. The war claimed the lives of Maurice De Cuire Gregoire and four of his seven sons. A tattered piece of the red, white and blue stripes and stars of a flag, the thread-worn fabric faded and frayed, made Eve realize that two of the brothers had fought on the side of the North. One son and one daughter were all who were left to his wife Claudette. She, with her two children, picked up the pieces of the remaining lands and spoiled crops and rebuilt. They survived, lifted their heads, and carried the Gregoire name into the future. Maurice had saved them by opening bank accounts in the North. When the South fell and the Confederate dollar became worthless, Claudette loaded her eldest living son into a buggy, rode to New Orleans, caught the paddle ferry up the Mississippi River, and finally boarded a train to New York to retrieve their northern cash, which would allow them to rebuild, buy seeds and land and pay workers.

The attics held many other wonders: old clothes, hats, paintings, and photo albums with tintypes and black-and-white photos of happy times, trips to Europe, China and Egypt. An entire album was dedicated to a safari in Africa with too many pictures of dead elephants and lions. That cruelty had made her put the books away and stay out of the attic for weeks. But one cool day she found herself in the west attic amid remnants from the First World War, the Great Depression, and the Second World War.

Over the centuries the Gregoire family had also known a few scandals. The most interesting she found in the north wing's attic. The greatest scandal of them all involved Beau's grandfather and the Le Masters side of the family. From the letters Eve found in the north attic, buried in a pile of papers stuffed into an old wood and silver letter box, she learned that none of the Le Masters were liked. In fact, they were downright hated.

Millard made numerous attempts to come by with gifts for his grandson, flowers for Eve and heartfelt peace offerings for Beau, but as their legal case became more and more tangled Beau finally asked him to stay away. He'd screwed things up so royally it would take an army of attorneys and a small fortune to undo what Millard had done. Eventually Millard stopped trying. The last gift he sent Philip was a little, sterling silver bracelet that looked as if it had been in the Le Masters family. Beau told Eve to please send it back. Instead she placed it in a cedar keepsake box and hoped for better times and forgiveness.

She'd brought some of the more current photo and picture albums downstairs to share with Beau. Again that flash of anger clouded his usually tranquil blue eyes as once again she explained her need to know him and his family because she had no history of her own. Beau stared at the books for a long time before he released a long sigh and crossed to sit next to her.

"I won't do this if it pains you, Beau," Eve said.

"Yes you will," he said with a sad smile. "You'll do it until you understand whatever it is you're looking for in my family's history. So, perhaps if I can help you find it we can let this all go and move on with our lives. I need you to be okay and comfortable with who you're marrying and all that comes with it. So open the pages and ask me what you want. I'll do my best to answer," Beau said. "If you don't trust me completely, this won't work."

Eve looked at him to understand the subtext of his words. He'd agreed so she opened the first album.

She'd found the photos from the seventies and eighties when Beau's mother, father and younger sister were still alive. They looked to be a very happy family. Until his sister's death in an odd accident Beau described as "the fall," they had been happy. Then time seemed to stop. There were no more pictures of birthdays, holidays, trips or happy occasions. He told Eve the loss of his younger sister left a dark cloud over the house that sucked the joy out of everyone and everything - especially the Gregoire home.

Then, even more mysteriously, soon after that dark time of his sister's accident, Beau's parents' unexpectedly died in a car accident. Their deaths killed the heart of the house and made living there unbearable. Beau's grandfather, Millard, who'd never been welcome when his parents were alive, stepped in to raise him. They looked at a few snapshots of a sad little boy of twelve being sent off to Europe to attend a prestigious boarding school in Switzerland. From there only a few awkward shots at Beau's graduations, both from high school and then from Oxford University were stuck into the pages of his high school year book. His grandfather was there, but the pictures were clear evidence of the distance that loomed between them; never touching or even standing too close, like a sharp knife cut the air between them. In every picture Beau kept his distance, obviously wanting no part of his past or the vast fortune he'd been bequeathed by his parents or his Grandfather, Millard Le Masters.

After University, Beau told her how he'd traveled and worked in Europe until one day he just walked away. He vanished for eight years exploring Africa, New Zealand and South America. Until a letter from Beau's oldest and dearest friend, Augustus Valentine Lafayette the fourth, aka A.V. came with the knowledge that the family estate, the only home Beau'd ever known, was about to be lost to him. A.V.'s letter convinced Beau to give up his freedom and come home. Beau explained to Eve that he'd called A.V. and together they called the estate's lead attorney. Lincoln Bryant, senior most partner of the prestigious law firm and Beau's father's friend and attorney, told him he'd all but lost everything because he'd been declared dead by his only living relative, his grandfather so he'd better get his ass back to New Orleans. Mister Bryant and A.V. started the paper work to raise Beau from the dead, but his presence would be needed in court as proof of life.

"That's when I came back," Beau said, explaining that he'd told no one except A.V. he was returning. Unannounced, he arrived at his family's mansion the afternoon of that fateful summer night they'd met. He'd come home, gone into his old room, uncovered the dresser and bed, crawled under the covers and fallen asleep.

"When I woke it was dark and the party was in full swing. I showered and dressed, remembering only then A.V.'s letter said the house was being used for a gala to raise money for the Southern Belles Charity."

"A.V. Lafayette adores you," Eve added.

"He's a good friend and a great attorney. He'd suggested I wait an extra day before I came back, but I'd gotten the dates turned around and somehow came in the day of the event," Beau said.

Beau never told Eve that A.V. had been in love with him, wishing Beau would see him as more than a friend, a wish that blossomed when they were pubescent boys, or what had transpired between them the night of his parents' death.

"I remember you dressed in that crisp white shirt and blue slacks," Eve said.

"I found them in my closet and that old blue jacket somehow still fit well enough to finish off my ensemble."

"That jacket fit tight as a kid glove and you looked like Adonis descending." Eve said with a smile and held an old photo of a much younger Beau. "You definitely filled out from your days as a slender youth."

Beau smiled and they shared a kiss.

"I'm glad you liked what you saw," he added.

"I never had a chance. I was smitten from the moment I laid eyes on you," Eve said.

Beau talked about how he'd found his way down the curved entry stairs and stepped over the velvet rope put in place to keep the lookie-loos from exploring the upstairs. He had been starving and in search of food and drink. A passing waitress flirted and made it her business to keep him satiated with his favorite poison; a glass of scotch, neat, that went straight to his head. He talked about foraging the buffet tables for food, nibbling from the delicious display of Southern delights he'd missed so much in his travels. Their scents, spicy and sweet, ignited his olfactory nerves and had his mouth watering. He'd made sure to sample everything.

"I never tasted a bit," Eve said, remembering her terrifying entrance with a laugh. It was good for her to remember those last hours before the coma. She liked talking about them and so did Beau.

"I'd been gone a long time and I certainly didn't look like the twelve-year-old boy who left New Orleans. I watched as several women eyed me like a steak dinner on a plate and whisper between them about who would get first bite."

"They were wondering who you were," Eve added.

"One or two of the bold ones sashayed up and did their best to say clever things about the night or the house, blatantly flirting, but none of them got the satisfaction of discovering who I was, where I came from or why I was there," Beau explained and laughed.

"You are a wonderfully wicked trickster. And, I have to say, I like your lack of humility," Eve said.

"Hey, I was looking for you. I just didn't know it," he replied.

Again they kissed.

"So, how did you say you found me?" Eve asked, knowing the answer.

Beau smiled as he told her again how he'd found a shaded corner near the entrance to the main living room between the large, exotic plants the decorator had brought in for the party. They stood majestically and filled the space and gave just enough covering for him to sit, eat and drink undisturbed, allowing him to watch the night unfold from the shadows.

"The same men, ever Southern pompous and arrogant, and the women with too much make up bored me. Add to that the scotch, great Louisiana cooking and the fatigue from my jet lag and I was so relaxed I was falling asleep in my secret hideaway. That's when I gave up, dragged myself to my feet and was just about to head up the stairs when I saw an awkwardly adorable and very beautiful stranger with a river of long, honey hair standing at the entrance trying to convince herself to find the courage to enter the room," Beau laughed.

"I wasn't talking out loud," Eve said, horrified at the thought.

"Your honesty radiates like the sun and you become a piece of glass, so transparent I can see your every perfection, my darling almost wife," Beau said.

Eve melted into his arms. He'd told her the story a thousand times, but each time she heard it, it made her smile.

They kissed and talked about how the music from the DJ changed to a slow, sensual ballad called "Will You Remember Me?" by Brenna Whitaker. A title they each thought appropriate in hindsight - a song that had become *their song*.

"It was the music that pushed me forward until my arms slipped around your waist," he said. "I wanted you from the moment I saw you with power that defies explanation."

"You know you touched me and the room and everyone in it disappeared," Eve added.

"And when we danced, we floated across that room," Beau told her, cuddling and kissing her neck.

They each recalled their versions of dancing gracefully out onto the veranda and into the garden or when it was she'd lost her shoes.

"I felt as though I was holding living, breathing electricity," Beau said. "Somehow I captured this ethereal, energetic light; beauty and grace inside of one being and I wasn't ever going to let it go."

"I felt the same," Eve said with a nod. "You held me in your arms and when your lips touched mine and it turned into that first kiss –

so sweet, gentle, innocent and yet... Fireworks."

"No, it was the second kiss I gave you," said Beau, "That kiss made me feel like I was a God being driven by some insatiable, indefinable hunger. You made time stand still and the world melt away."

Tears of joy welled in Eve's eyes. She told him how when her mouth met his, she had no choice but to give herself to him, surrendering with utter abandon was her only option. Clothes fell away and they made wild, passionate love surrounded by the thick foliage of the garden's hedge maze.

"How many hours did we make love?" he asked.

"There is no time when I make love to you. That's what you do to me."

"Good," Beau kissed her.

He slipped his fingers inside her and felt how wet and ready she was to be taken. Eve's eyes glazed over as he fondled her breasts with his other hand and kissed her mouth. It hung open, suspended in the shape of a tiny, perfect 'o' beckoning him to slip his tongue inside. Her hands found his cock, each stroking motion making him harder and harder.

Between the kisses, sucking and strokes, Beau whispered about how they built up the I-can't-get-enough-of-your-passion, almost coming over and over, again and again, but holding back until they finally climaxed together.

She moaned, uttering between his kisses how in that final, sensual thrust of passion, she'd somehow known the exact moment when he'd given her his child.

"Tell me. You knew the instant Philip was conceived?" Beau asked.

"With all my heart I believe so. What I didn't know was that he was a Gregoire with hundreds of years of history flowing into each dividing cell," Eve recalled breathlessly. "But, my fiery master of love, at that moment you could have been a Troglodyte for all I cared."

Beau's fingers worked in and out as Eve's breathing escalated, matching his.

"I exploded from the inside out," Eve said

"You were magnificent. Your arched back, bare tits to the sky," Beau said.

"And slammed my head on the statue and knocked myself out," Eve said laughing.

Beau threw her back and slipped inside of her.

"I thought I'd killed you," Beau said.

"Best sex I ever had in my life," Eve said.

The story made them both laugh until they cried tears of embarrassment and joy. Beau climbed on top of her and slipped inside. They made love and kissed, holding onto each other as they always did when they shared their story. They made Eve's favorite kind of love; the mad, passionate, ride me until I scream with breathless delight and bring me to our highest climax kind of love. Spent, they fell asleep in each other's arms.

Hours later, Eve woke. Tangled in his arms and legs and exhausted, she held Beau while she stroked his hair thinking how excited she was to be his wife and to be part of a family. Her thoughts went to Philip. The Gregoires had married and repopulated through the centuries, their children born with thick black ribbons of curls and azure blue eyes ... until Philip.

Eve had seen the evolution of his features, each detail memorialized in oil, painted on ancient canvases, held captive in the gilded frames that displayed them. She had explored the paintings and letters and photos and all the dust-covered memorabilia and found the line of genetics that carried his features and those impossibly dark eyes. Sadly, she knew her family didn't have his nose or eyes or hair. She could only see Beau in him. Beau had his mother's eyes. None of it mattered. She loved her son and she felt certain she would forever be unconditionally in love with his father.

Restless, she untangled herself from Beau and walked down the stairs. Eve meandered around their guest house. It was small and sweet, but she'd made enough changes in the antiquated décor so it felt like home at least until the big house was complete. She raided the refrigerator in the tiny kitchen and ate cold, fresh picked peaches, hungrily biting into them and letting the sweet juices run down her chin until it made her smile. Then, having made a mess of her face and her night gown, she headed up and into her bathroom, dropped her clothes on the floor in a heap and stepped naked into the warm water of her shower. The shower spray tingled and caressed her body, still electric from making love to Beau. His scent hung on her skin, his taste still lingered on her lips. There was no question, she loved him and he made her very happy.

Her hands mindlessly soaped her body as Eve enjoyed the slippery bubbles as they lathered up in between her fingers. She washed her face, then her breasts. They felt fuller because of Philip's nursing and Beau's reverent attention to them, but the rest of her body was tight. She'd lost the baby weight. The long walks along the back forty made her muscles feel lean, firm and strong. She let her fingers slip down her stomach, across the tuft of blonde hair and between her legs. As she touched herself she thought of Beau again. She wanted him again. He had that effect on her. Eve smiled imagining her hands were Beau's hands caressing her, arousing her, loving her. The water seemed to beat harder as she fingered her clitoris. She stepped closer, straddling the shower's lower body jet. It had just the right amount of force and pushed right at her G spot. Eve stepped closer and closer until the rush of water pressed against her mound. She massaged her breasts and fondled her nipples as the water did its magic. Her breath quickened. Her head fell back, arching her spine as her erect nipples brushed the cool of the tile shower wall. The steam of water from above swirled over her, moist and hot. Eve turned up the water pressure until the sensation felt unbearably delicious and, just as she climaxed, her fingers slipped inside.

Her eyes closed. She gasped with pleasure when suddenly an explosion of wild images filled her mind. At the same time, something physically grabbed her filling her, inside as if it were trying to possess her body. There was only blackness. Eve's arms reached out to push the invisible force away. The harder she pushed the more it pressed in against her, holding her as she struggled. Whatever it was she could feel it all over her body, grabbing her breasts, sucking on her nipples, licking at her clitoris. It was inside her, huge, thick, hot pumping in and out and in a matter of seconds she erupted in orgasm. The fire of her orgasm pulsed in her inner walls and seized her in spasms so powerful it weakened her legs and sent her crashing down to her knees in a prayer of pleasure and horror. She knelt on the tiles in the rush of cascading, hot water, panting and wanting more of whatever surged inside her. Part of Eve wanted it to stop; the other part spread her legs, as it plunged deeper, pressing her into the floor. She opened her mouth to cry out for Beau, but a huge hand covered her face, leaving her in silent blackness.

"Beau," she whispered in her mind hearing only the echo of her helpless cry. Useless words swallowed up by the crash of water flailing against her on the shower floor.

She called again for Beau to come, to protect her from the blinding, senseless images that crowded into her brain. It was as if they were pushing her toward some bottomless pit of erotic insanity. The images pulled her deeper into spiraling depths of pleasure so overwhelming she knew, if she gave in to them, she would disappear forever and never find her way back. There, on the shower floor, trembling, she made her mouth open and she screamed.

"Stop!"

In an instant the vision stopped and the simple sound of water falling was all that filled her ears. Unable to move, Eve allowed the water to cascade down on top of her and wash the fear from her mind. Lying on the shower floor, she grabbed the shampoo and scrubbed the attic dust from her hair and the strange feelings off her skin. She scrubbed so hard she thought her fingers would bleed. She was attempting to banish the thoughts and images she feared could only be the first signs of ...what...insanity? Was she losing her mind? Was what happened a hallucination or was it real? Her body ached. She tried to shift her focus to all the responsibilities that awaited her. Trembling, Eve struggled to her feet, rinsed the soap away and stepped out of the shower. She held the wall as she sank to the floor, still weak and drained. Something caught her eye and when she looked up she saw Beau standing in the bathroom doorway towering above her, naked with his erect cock jutting into the room. It looked more like a weapon than a penis to Eve. When she could tear her eyes away from his raging erection, she looked up into his face. His expression was dreamlike and placid as if he were sleepwalking.

"Beau," she whispered.

He didn't look at her. He just stared wide-eyed into the room. Hearing his name, his erection melted and he turned and left without saying a word. Eve turned off the shower and listened as Beau's footsteps padded down the hall and descended the back stairs. *What the fuck* was the only thought that passed through her head.

She reached for a plush towel, gently dried herself and applied pear-scented lotion on her skin. Every inch of her skin ached as if it had been bruised, but there were no visible marks and the simple act of lotioning her body calmed her. Her hands vibrated with the slightest tremor like an old woman with weak muscles struggling to do the most mundane of tasks. Eve brushed and braided her hair into a long single plait. Her first step made it clear her legs were still weak. She dressed in a simple, pale green shift dress that gathered at her waist and had her favorite bone buttons running up its front. Carefully, she walked from her room, through the guest house second floor and down to the nursery. She suddenly felt concerned for her son's safety. The look in Beau's eyes haunted her. First she would take care of Philip, then she would deal with Beau.

Philip's room was peaceful and warm. Streams of soft yellow light reached through the window, flickering from harsh to soft, illuminating the chiffon curtains as they danced on the warm breeze that slipped in to fill the room. His nursery was the color of a summer sky with voluminous ivory clouds painted on the walls and ceiling. The color deepened into a periwinkle as it reached the bassinette and the clouds faded, allowing a tiny constellation of stars to splatter across the ceiling above her baby's head. Eve tip-toed closer and looked down at her son with his black satin curls. He looked up at her. His eyes were the darkest brown she'd ever seen, the color of pure, bittersweet, dark chocolate found in the best Swiss candy. Sometimes, in low light, she would gaze into Philip's eyes and feel as if she were drowning in two dark, shimmering pools of liquid velvet. His eyes seemed to pierce her soul. He knows I am losing my mind, she thought. His knowing stare held her. No matter how hard she tried, she was unable to look away. Again, she felt a rush of fear as she fell into her son's eyes. He knew and then he would gurgle and smile and reach for her finger or pull her hair and the icy feeling of fear melted away and Eve fell in love all over again. Philip smiled up at her and Eve reached into his crib and gathered him up into her arms.

After her strength returned, she and Philip would walk in the gardens and orchards surrounding their mansion, breathing the soft air of spring, then summer, and now the chill of fall. The unseasonably frosty nights had destroyed any fruit still left on the trees and turned the leaves from light green to a dark emerald and jade forest. It wouldn't be long before the deciduous trees, the sycamore and elm, did their dance of color and turned to shades of gold, orange and burgundy, before dropping to the ground so she and Philip could play, roll around, and throw them into the cloudy blue sky and laugh as they watched leaves drift, caught on the swirl of an autumn breeze.

Noticing the changes in weather reminded Eve of the many arguments she and her journalist friends had had about global warming. Eve suddenly realized she had not had a single thought about her career as a journalist since her prince charming had awakened her from her sleep. She felt a traitor to her feminist side and for a long moment she missed her job and *Southern Style* Magazine. Eve pushed the thoughts from her head. *I'll think about that tomorrow*, she shrugged. Eve started to laugh out loud when she realized she was emulating a very famous southern belle. The Gregoire mansion could never be her Tara. She was not a southern belle, nor would she ever be. It went against her northern nature and for that, she was actually grateful.

Eve wiped away her tears, smiled and kissed Philip's head. "Your mommy is a very silly mommy," she whispered.

Chapter Three

Eve's best friend Cora Bouvier had given birth to a beautiful baby girl she named Delia, short for Delia Jacqueline Bouvier. The fact that Beau was the father and about to marry Eve was, in true southern tradition, not discussed. Most days Cora and Delia would come to the estate, Cora to help with the decorating and Delia to play with Philip. The children were young, but both had a keen and urgent awareness of one another that Eve could not help but feel seemed well beyond their age. When Eve would sit in the tree swing on the back lawn while Delia and Philip explored the warm sun to play with an array of toys scattered around them on soft blankets, she would find herself gazing at Delia's head of dark black curls and look into her eyes, which were the exact same sky blue as Beau's. She would shake the thoughts of how Delia looked more like Beau than Philip. She wanted to feel betrayed, but no matter how hard she tried, she couldn't. Cora was her best friend in ways Eve could never explain and that she and Beau sought refuge in each other's arms the night her doctor told them Eve would probably never wake from her coma was somehow forgivable. It was, according to both, only one night. And what if she had died? What then of her soul mate, her son and her best friend? Mostly, Beau and Cora having loved each other was a good feeling. Mostly.

Now and again though, something about this awkward gothic romance novel—absurd and melodramatic—reality involving her husband-to-be and father to her best friend's child upset her stomach and made her head spin. Because she loved them both, Eve asked them to search their hearts, to make sure their love and their life together wasn't what was supposed to be. They'd had months to get to know each other and she'd had only one dance. Eve felt she had a mysterious déjà vu with Beau, while Beau and Cora had actual time on their side. Eve wanted to say she would step aside. She wanted to say she understood their bizarre circumstances were unprecedented and who was she to stand in the way of their love. But she couldn't force the words past her lips. Both Beau and Cora had insisted that their coming together was because they both loved her so much. When faced with the idea they were losing her, they had comforted each other once and from that union, Delia was conceived and born.

Eve saw the sincerity in their eyes and believed their words, which gave her some peace. Yet, it was hard to see them when they looked at each other or hugged hello or good-bye, laughed or shared their little girl as she played with her half brother ... how could she not wonder about what feelings still lingered in Beau or in Cora? Even more unnerving was the feeling Eve experienced when she looked into Delia's eyes; some unexplainable connection that made her want to cry. *Hormones*, Eve thought, *fucking hormones*. Then she would push the fears away, give Delia a hug and set her down to play on the blanket, happy to watch as she crawled to grab Philip's hair and make him giggle with delight. *Hormones* she'd remind herself again and again, but months had passed and that excuse was wearing thin.

Mornings would come, nights would go and her world was by all who looked in, perfect—and it was, except for those raw snippets of demon-filled nightmares that as of recently had found their way into bizarre daydreams carrying with them shadowy details that repeated in the terrifying nightmares she'd fought so hard to hold at bay. For months she had been winning the battle on her own, refusing to take the narcoleptic medication that would have prevented her from breast feeding Philip. Her therapist, Dr. Honoré, suggested she face her dreams head on. She'd offered hypnotherapy, but Beau insisted Eve not even consider such an idea.

"No drugs and no hypnosis," he all but pleaded.

Dr. Honoré smiled pleasantly and told her the offer stood if Eve ever wanted to reconsider. In some hidden recess of her mind Eve knew she needed to face the demons in her dreams especially if they meant she might be going insane. That possibility frightened her; a need no less powerful than the need of an alcoholic to taste that next drink was her hunger to understand. Dr. Honoré said the day would come and when it did, understanding it could free her. Her fear was that understanding too much might push her over the edge from which she might not easily be able return. It turned out today was that day.

Eve stood impatiently in the main kitchen, the smell of fresh paint and wood oil polish filtering in from the main house. The combination suddenly made her feel dizzy. The room shifted, moving around her like the horizon on a ship at sea. She laid her hand on the cool granite counter and reached for her glass of water, dabbing a bit on her neck as she watched the installation of their cumbersomely large, brand new Traulsen freezer and fridge, a monstrous, yet beautiful pair of monolithic, stainless steel boxes, the fridge with glass doors and industrial shelves. The freezer was simply a wall of stainless steel. The workmen finally finished hooking up the ventilation system and filter, connected the electrical plugs, and fired up the motor of the mechanical beast. The motors added a low hum to the room making their presence known to all who entered.

Job done, the three burly men turned to face her. Each man was tall, well-built and fit, each smelling of sweet spice and tart musk, each sweating rivulets through the dirt that stained their faces and very muscular arms. Their similar skin coloring and the shape of their eyes and noses made Eve guess they were brothers or cousins. First and second cousins had been marrying each other for generations in Louisiana so the possibility of a little inbreeding played itself out in their features. Skeeter, the youngest of the three men, couldn't take his eyes off Eve, especially her full, ripe breasts. He'd had an erection bulging beneath his jeans since she walked into the room. Eve politely ignored it and his lascivious stares. She gave them water, signed the paperwork, tipped them generously and started to say good-by as they stepped out onto the back sun porch. The other brother walked away, but Skeeter turned.

"Thank you, gentleman. You have a great day and ..." Eve started.

Skeeter interrupted her, "Uhm ... Ma'am," he started to say.

It was that Southern term, Ma'am, that made her feel older than she was.

"... well, I just want you to know, if you ever need some help with anything at all, you can call me direct. It would be a real pleasure to help someone as lovely as yourself ... well ... do anything."

"Well, thank you," Eve said, pretending she didn't remember his name. "You just call me... I'm Skeeter and I'll come right over and ... fix you up. You know?"

He smiled with a horny eagerness that almost made her burst out laughing. Eve couldn't help but notice how young he was ... sixteen or seventeen at best. And the already extremely large bulge rising in his pants said everything his words and eyes did not.

"I do understand, Skeeter. I'll remember your kind offer if I ever need anything fixed," she said, smiled graciously and closed the back door, making sure she turned the lock hard enough to be heard.

Finally they were gone. Still woozy, Eve walked back inside and crossing the kitchen, found herself staring curiously into the fridge's empty shelves. *Have to keep that organized, bummer,* she thought. That's when she noticed her reflection in its thick green glass doors staring back at her. She look tired, more tired than she remembered ever looking before. Eve pushed loose strands of hair back from her face and tucked them into her rope of honey hair. She touched the dark rings that hung like little grey ghosts beneath her eyes and sighed.

"Cora, how can you always look so damn perfect," she mumbled to herself.

Just as she was about to walk away, her image shifted, wavering like heat rising from a street on a hot summer day. It faded, blending into ... into... Cora standing on the stairs in her house in New Orleans; no... not standing... running, panicked, terrified, racing through the upper hallway of her house. Cora, her eyes wide with terror, tore down the curved stairway that anchored the house. The fear etched across her face intensified as she glanced back at what was chasing her. Eve stepped closer to the glass as if to look deeper into this other world. A shadow, large, dark and foreboding, pushed out of the darkness that cloaked the upper floor. It leaped on top of Cora, wrapping around her, dragging her into its folds of blackness. A huge hand with long, sharp fingernails jutted out, tearing the stairwell wall fabric with the preciseness of five, perfectly formed razors wielded with superhuman strength. Eve watched as it tore at Cora's body, her arms, her neck, her face. Blood gushed from Cora as she screamed and fought for her life.

Eve struggled to pull herself out of the daydream. Was it a wish? A prophesy? A memory? Was this real? No. Impossible! Had it been real Cora would have been left horribly scarred.

"Miss Eve, are you alright?" a young woman's voice said, piercing through Eve's vision, startling her. Eve screamed, knocking her glass to the floor with a crash.

"I'm so sorry. I didn't mean to give you such a start but ..." the voice stopped. "Oh, my, Miss Eve, you should sit down."

Eve gasped, feeling the girl's hands guide her to one of the oak

Windsor chairs that circled the kitchen table.

"Let me get you some water."

Eve looked at her savior, but a dizzying haze covered the details of her features. She turned back to look at the fridge. It too was now a haze of grey. When she looked back again she saw Aria reaching for a glass and pouring water from a pitcher that sat on the counter.

Aria was the young nurse from the hospital. Eve had known her mother, but for the life of her Eve couldn't remember why or from where—just only that she had. The young girl handed Eve the water. Her smooth features and long tight curls were braided into two braids that hung down to her shoulders, making her look even younger than she was. Aria could see Eve's hands were trembling as she handed her the glass. Eve drank, taking long, deep swallows, feeling the cool liquid wash down her throat and soothe her body. When she stopped, she gasped and caught her breath, forcing herself to slow down. She held on to the wooden arm of the chair with one hand until the trembling slowly subsided.

"Better?" Aria asked.

Eve wanted to say, yes, and shake away the images she had just witnessed, yet she also wanted to remember every detail. This was the most complete version of the terrifying fragmented visions that kept plaguing her thoughts day and night since awaking from her coma. Again, she turned back for one last look. There it was, a glimpse, wavering in the glass, of the shadow's hand cutting through the air and ripping into Cora's face. Eve squeezed her eyes shut and drank another series of long sips. She sat back and steadied herself against the smooth wood of the oak table. Aria looked from Eve to the massive refrigerator.

"My, my, it's pretty gigantic for a fridge, but if you don't like it, I say send it right back," Aria offered, her Louisiana accent thick and slow, as she continued her study of the Traulsen that seemed to be the focus of Eve's tormented expression.

"It's fine," Eve said.

Eve touched her own neck and thought of the small scar on Cora's chin and neck. She'd seen it. Of that she was sure. When she first awoke in the hospital she had noticed the wisp of a scar crawling out from under Cora's chin; a jagged piece of some forgotten past, but she couldn't remember if Cora ever mentioned where it had come from. It battered Eve's memory. Desperately, she tried to blend the visual of the terrifying images that skittered across her refrigerator with a piece of a memory. A time and place that didn't fit anything she could remember doing. Eve struggled to focus on the truth of what happened to her when she hit her head. Getting knocked out wasn't what came to mind. She woke in the garden alone, she thought. But how? When? How could she determine the correct answers when she didn't even know which questions to ask? She'd tried more than once to talk to Cora about her visions, but Cora said she had no idea what Eve could possibly be talking about, waved her hand as if to brush away an unwanted fly, abruptly ending every such conversation. Beau responded to Eve's questions in essentially the same way. Eventually, Eve stopped asking questions and focused on her ridiculously perfect world of pre-matrimonial and motherhood bliss and prayed she wasn't losing her mind.

"Miss Eve? We better be getting back to Philip. He'll be waking up any minute," Aria said. "He'll be hungry. That boy of yours is always hungry."

"Philip?" Eve asked.

Aria smiled. "Yes, Philip. Remember? Your rambunctious son, who you hired me to nanny? Good thing you did 'cause that little boy is a demon of energy. I've never seen anything like him in my life. And growin' like a weed, that handsome little one."

Eve watched as Aria spoke while busily grabbing a bottle of chilled breast milk Eve had pumped from the second fridge in the pantry. Suddenly, Eve felt a rush of moisture release from her aching breasts.

When she reached up and touched her blouse, it was soaked with mother's milk. Aria saw and handed her a kitchen towel.

"Guess nature calls and you're on duty," she said with a smile. "Unless you're not feelin' up to it? You have two bottles stored and I could get the pump for you now."

Eve shook her head as she stood, straightening her wobbly legs under her.

"I'm fine, Aria," Eve said. "You put him down in the nursery?"

"No Ma'am, he's in the garden house with Miss Cora and little Delia."

Suddenly she could hear her son's cry from the backyard, distant, but strong.

"Will you get a bath ready for him?" Eve said.

"I'll have it ready by the time you're done with the feeding," Aria said.

Eve looked one more time at the refrigerator. She wiped her bodice with the kitchen towel, crossed the kitchen and exited out the back door.

Stone steps led from the back sun porch to the patio. The still flowing milk from her breasts, trailed down her stomach, staining the soft green cotton fabric of her dress as she walked. Still carrying the towel, she wiped again. Eve smiled as she looked in the direction of her son's screaming. His cry demanded she hurry to fill his empty belly before she spilled all of his lunch from her breasts. There was a real messiness to motherhood. Yet her aversion to pumping, which made her feel like a cow, was clearly superseded by the pleasure she took in giving her son nourishment and life.

Eve stopped. A chill ran up her spine the moment she felt someone's eyes on her. She turned and saw him: the slightly rumpled, but very handsome Detective from the New Orleans police force with the sad, worried eyes. Detective Macklin Blanchard had been trying to build a rape case against her soon-to-be husband. After all, he'd reminded her more than once, she had been a guest at a party who ended up raped and pregnant. All the evidence made a compelling case: young woman taken into the bushes, knocked into unconsciousness and found to be pregnant. There had been a rape kit taken at the hospital without her request and, well, there had been Philip. She had no boyfriend and admitted to surrendering to Beau's seduction willingly. When Eve woke from her coma, Beau fought hard to keep Detective Blanchard away from her. She and the detective had spoken and, to the detective's frustration, Eve had refused to press charges. The impending wedding muddied the waters even more.

Eve's eyes connected with his as she stepped from the shade and the heat of the warm morning sun pressed down on them. Eve was hit by a feeling of déjà vu. Of course this wasn't the first time he had come to the house, not to mention all the times he had tried to speak with her while she was still in the hospital. Eve liked him. Something about him made her even trust him. There was an easy kindness he exuded. Cora and Beau didn't like him at all. As a matter of fact Beau vehemently hated him. Cora insisted repeatedly that Beau was jealous—always saying it in that coquettish, playful, Southern belle way she had when she wanted to make a point while avoiding making anyone mad. But Eve never felt jealousy coming from Beau—just immense concern that played itself out in southern hostility. After the last interrogation, Beau had demanded Mac leave her alone.

Once she refused to press charges everyone thought Detective Blanchard would go quietly away. Beau asked her to promise never to talk to him again and Eve had agreed. After all, she and Beau were getting married and, whatever the circumstances of the case Mac was trying to build, she had forgiven Beau his passionate indiscretion that fateful night. After all, she had been a willing accomplice to his seduction and every day that passed she found herself falling more and more in love with him. She was moving on to a bright new future. But there Mac stood, a walking red flag warning her of some danger neither he nor she could articulate. He was staring directly at her, obviously wanting to probe her for more answers to questions she knew she didn't know how to answer.

"Eve, I mean Ms. Dowling ...," Mac said.

"Detective Blanchard?"

"Mac, please, you promised to call me Mac," he replied. He stood there watching her, waiting for an invitation to speak to her despite the palpable tension between them.

"You shouldn't be here. My fiancé has asked you not to come here or talk to me, detective. The case is closed," Eve said.

She moved to pass him, but Mac blocked her.

"I know. It's just . . . This isn't about police business exactly . . . I . . . have been... and please don't think I'm crazy until you hear me out. I have been having ... these dreams... nightmares is a better word. You're in them a lot. They're so real and I... I was wondering if you ..."

His words stopped her. She looked into his eyes. He knew and worse, he knew she knew. Eve could tell he knew from the flash of horror that flushed her face and turned her cheeks red. He knew she understood exactly what he was talking about: dreams and visions from another time and place that made no sense. Eve fell silent, but her heart screamed, pounding in her chest like a frightened, captive bird desperate to escape its cage.

Yes, I'm having dreams too, nightmares, daydreams, fragments of images that don't make sense. Horrible dreams that wake me from sleep and block my eyes and fill my mind with dread and fear that something happened I can't remember. That something very wrong is happening. She wanted to say all of it out loud to Mac, but Philip's screams cut through the air. He wanted his mother and he wanted her now!

"I ... I'm afraid I don't know what you're talking about and I have to go to my son. Please leave, detective."

"I think you do, Eve," he said as he pressed his card into her hand. She felt a rush, a connection that calmed her. "I know you know,

Eve. Call me when you you're ready to talk. Help me help you before it's too late," he whispered.

Eve backed away. Her heel caught a stone and she began to stumble. Mac caught her, his arms circling her waist. He pulled her close, lifting her off her feet. Face to face, their breath mingled and she could smell the scent of aftershave, leather and clove breath mints. His arms were strong and she felt amazingly light in his embrace. For a moment, Eve actually felt something she realized she'd not felt in a very long time ... truly safe.

Eve twisted from his arms and pushed away. She headed to the summer house. Her head spun, a new, strange, light-headedness made her dizzy again, but this time pleasantly so. She quickly glanced down at the card in her hand. A voice inside her said, *tear it up and throw it away,* but she slipped it into her pocket and followed the sound of Philip's cry.

Chapter Four

As much as he hated the conventionality of corporate wear, Beau always looked good in a suit. It wasn't just that his tall frame and broad, square shoulders filled the Armani Black Label suit; it hugged his body in all the right places. He knew how to choose the perfect ink blue color, the one that looked like a night sky over the bayou, to punch the blue of his eyes. It was the way he carried himself: the calm certainty, the tilt of his head, the regal but never snobby presence he could exude. There was something rare about him. He sat in his pale blue shirt and mustard gold tie that seemed to pick up the flecks of amber in his eyes. Those amazing blue eyes could capture the warmth of a summer sky and brighten a room when he smiled or flash a chill as cold as an ice storm. Right now, he was angry ... very angry. His eyeballs ached. He'd been reading over legal documents all day. He'd started at ten in the morning, sitting with seven pinched-faced, cold hearted, viciously calculating lawyers; two of whom belonged to the oldest legal firm in New Orleans, the prestigious firm of Robb, Gallagher and Grant and were trustees of the Gregoire Estate; two belonging to his grandfather, Millard Le Masters, who had declared Beau dead so he could sue the Estate and overturn the will. It all started when Millard learned not only was he not sole executor after

Beau's death, but that he'd not inherited any portion of the Estate itself or even a small part of the vast family fortune. Instead, the entire Estate had been bequeathed to the Avery Charitable Trust. The two Avery Charitable Trust representatives were very, very unhappy at the possibility of losing such a grand gift. Their sadness doubled when Beau returned and they were told everything was to revert back to the original heir. The seventh attorney, the only non-pinched-faced member of the legal clan, was Beau's attorney and childhood friend, Augustus Valentine Lafayette the fourth, aka A.V. to his friends, of which Beau was and always would be listed as his best. A.V. was movie-star handsome with sandy blonde hair, wicked green eyes and beautiful full lips that anyone would love to kiss. He was smart and tall with a quick wit that could give fifty lashes with a single quip. If he had a fault it was that he liked to drink very expensive cognac and make love to anything that caught his fancy.

Beau watched the proceedings with burning eyes, exhausted from the hours of arguing over the Gregoire Estate and its sizable fortune. The Estate encompassed an enormous amount of rich Louisiana land, multiple homes, multiple farms, cotton and pepper plantations and the, as yet, untapped oil and gas fields. That treasure trove Millard had planned to crack open like a case of vintage Lafitte Rothschild, circa 1947. The Trustees blocked him based on the wishes of Beau's parents, which were that after their death nothing was to be done with the property until Beau came of age and could, with the Trustees' guidance, decide how he wanted to run the Estate. Millard has waited patiently for his grandson to get through high school and then college and even suggested that he take a year off to travel and see the world. Beau's last credit card bill and passport visa came six months later from Tibet. After that, there was nothing for eight years. At exactly seven years, without any word from Beau, Millard hired a series of investigators to find proof of Beau's life - or death. By the end of the eighth year Millard filed to declare him dead.

Once Millard had Beauregard Gregoire Le Masters declared legally dead, Millard assumed, as his only living relative, he would inherit, uncontested, the Estate. He demanded the codicil of the will that related to Beau's death be read and implemented. Upon learning that his daughter-in-law, with the consent of his only son, had left him out of their will, he went to war to overturn the will. The fact Philip Gregoire senior and his wife Geraldine had left the entire Estate to the Avery Charitable Trust made the situation even more complicated. Then, to top the entire fiasco off, Beau showed up, very much alive, and the real legal nightmare began.

The small hand of the fine antique, grandfather clock that dominated the main conference room of Robb, Gallagher and Grant chimed seven P.M.

"Enough, gentlemen," A.V. said.

A.V. raised his eyebrows signaling Beau to get up as he gathered his stacks of papers, phone, iPad and computer and stuffed them into his monogrammed, don't-fuck-with-me, oxblood leather Versace briefcase. He closed the sterling silver latches of the case with a final gong that signaled to all the meeting was over. He and Beau stood.

"There's not a goddam thing anyone can say that hasn't been said since this shit hit the fan. Ergo, I and my client are leaving and we will see you in court."

"Ergo?" Beau whispered an aside.

"Beau, son, let's work together on this. I don't see why you can't grasp how deeply invested the Avery Trust and I are in these new gas and oil fields, not to mention all the restructuring I had done on all the land and property rights," Millard repeated probably for the thousandth time.

"You didn't own it and, since I'm alive, neither does the trust. If you all hadn't been such greedy assholes, perhaps we could have come to some kind of an agreement of joint tenancy," Beau said.

"You need me," Millard said.

"I don't need anything from you, I never did and neither did Mother and Dad, so get over it, grandfather," Beau said.

Millard rose to his feet.

"You ran away from the Gregoire legacy and that's bigger than anything that's laid out on this table, Beau. You have no choice because no one else understands the truth about your family. You know that as well as I do and you will accept who you are, Beau. The question is will you accept my help?" Millard asked with an icy tone that Beau alone understood.

"You chose to sell your soul. I didn't have that luxury," Beau said with a cold last look.

Beau and A.V. left the room. They walked in silence down the two-hundred-year-old corridors and out into the main entry to the glass elevators that anchored the center of the atrium. Beau looked around at this architectural marvel that perfectly blended the old and the new. It had been tastefully modernized when they knocked out walls and floors and added a grand Plexiglas and wrought iron stairwell and elevator that screamed French Quarter 21st century. Yet, somehow, the designer managed to maintain the staid feel of *we're the oldest, richest and finest law firm in New Orleans and don't you forget it.* Beau was fuming. He felt suffocated standing inside those thick, hallowed walls. He could smell the tucked leather furniture and feel the glare of the gleaming brass as it reflected the fine Persian rug that graced the floors. Every wall in every hall and room they passed was accented by an array of stunning classic oil landscapes capturing the stodginess of the fine old south.

The elevator door opened and Beau and A.V. stepped in, rode in silence, then stepped out. They walked together for a long time. They were friends and words between friends were often not needed. But the biggest secret between them was that Beau was A.V.'s heart. He had been since they were small. As teens they'd played football and tennis and been inseparable, but the night of Beau's parent's death, A.V. had been the only one who could console his grief. Beau, lost in fear, loneliness and anguish had wept on his friend's shoulder and in the sadness they had crossed a line and explored love for the first time. Millard found them naked and spent, tangled in each other's arms. A.V., to this day, had never found a way to fill the void Beau left in him. That night remained unspoken. In Beau's mind it was a memory of a one night, boyhood experience, never to be repeated. After Beau's parent's funeral Millard shipped Beau off to boarding school in Europe. A few letters and emails went back and forth between them in the beginning and then ... nothing from either. Years went by, life went on and then, word of Beau's death came. The news of Beau's death hit A.V. harder than he thought it would. He even went to their old club house deep in the bayou, a tiny shack they'd built together a thousand summers ago as boys. It sat inside the arms of an old banyan tree. He wept and drank several toasts to Beau and hoped his ghost was in a better place. Beau never shared the dark secret of his family legacy and his fears that he would succumb to the curse he didn't understand.

A.V. cried for his lost friend, but his love for Beau was a truth he never shared with anyone. The tears flowed again at the service Millard held. Millard looked at A.V., blaming him for his having to send Beau away. Millard knew what no one else did.

When Beau came back from the dead and Eve .... well... happened, A.V. stepped in, stepped up and stood by him. He never left his side. Their friendship picked up and just kept going without a single hiccup. Yes, secretly, A.V. kept a candle of hope Beau would see him as he saw Beau, until the day Eve woke from her coma. When the call came, A.V.'s heart broke again. He thought, though beautiful and smart, Eve was not worthy of Beau's love or trust. He didn't trust her, just some "gut somethin' southern lawyers have," he told Beau. Beau said he loved her from the first moment he laid eyes on her and that was that. A.V. never said another disparaging word about Eve or about his deeper feelings for Beau. He was asked to be the best man at the wedding and, after the wedding, to stand Godfather to Philip along with Cora as Godmother for the christening. Friendship was his fate and he accepted it to keep Beau in his life.

As they stepped out of the building and into the street, they were assaulted by the sweltering air that made everyone move slower. It was why the south was the south: that unbearable humidity could suck the sweat out of you and leave you limp, lazy and soaked. The tiniest breeze rolled off the river and cooled their wet faces, giving a small respite from the heat of the late afternoon. It felt good and carried the sweet smell of chicory coffee and freshly fried beignets covered in a thick dusting of powdered sugar. Beau could see A.V. was as tense and angry as a caged tiger.

"What the hell was that legacy bullshit about?" A.V. asked finally.

"Let it go," Beau said. "I have. All of it."

A.V. started to pursue the line of questioning, but one side glance from Beau stopped him in his tracks.

"Well, fine, because this whole cluster fuck is an exercise in futility. They can't win. You know it, I know it and those arrogant old toads up there know it," A.V. said.

"At five hundred dollars per lawyer, per hour, they'll drag this out and earn enough to satisfy their coffers," Beau said.

"Not if I can help it," A.V. said.

A.V. breathed in the air. He filled his lungs, letting out a huge sigh to expel all the frustration from the day. Beau followed his lead and visibly relaxed. He rolled the last of the tension off his shoulders with a shrug.

"You got time for a drink or a coffee?" A.V. asked as they walked.

"I do, but I want to go home and see Eve and hold my son. Remind myself of the reasons I'm staying in New Orleans and fighting to get my life back," Beau said.

"Back? You know, you never told me where you were all those years

Millard was looking for you."

"I know and I am grateful you never asked," Beau said.

"You must know I'm curious as hell; have been since you showed up."

Beau stopped and looked at A.V. for a long time. Perhaps he was sizing him up or considering if he should share some part of "the lost years" as A.V. jokingly referred to them.

"Let's just say I was doing all the things we promised we'd do and then some," Beau said.

"That sounds ominous," A.V. said.

A.V. looked at him. Beau knew by his even stare that A.V.'s "lawyer gut feeling" was twisting around inside his stomach, in turmoil from a thousand unanswered questions.

Beau had always been a bit of a mystery, even as a kid.

"It is," Beau said with a laugh as A.V. rolled his shoulders and continued walking.

"I have a couple of buddies who did a few tours in Iraq and Afghanistan. They say the same thing." A.V. pointed to Beau's eyes. "They have the same look in their eyes when they say it too. Seen stuff you wish you hadn't and can't erase the images from your mind."

"Let's just say I promised I wouldn't tell and it's very important that I keep that promise," Beau said.

"Let's just say, whatever it is, when you're ready to share, I'm here to listen."

"I know and thanks," Beau said.

"We'll get through this bullshit with Millard and the Trust too. I'll make sure the Gregoire Estate is yours, Eve's and Philip's. Hang in there."

Beau and A.V. shared a hug. A.V. turned, walked away and in a moment, disappeared into the crowd that filled Royal Street.

Beau watched him go. Millard's threat gnawed at him as he

headed to the sanctuary of the one place he knew he should never have come back to.

Chapter Five

That night Eve sat at her vanity and brushed her hair. It was a ritual her mother had taught her. Eve found it relaxing. Each stroke seemed to pull away all the stress and left her to relax in the moment. She looked at herself in the mirror. The dark circles seemed more evident this evening than at any other time. She hated wearing makeup, but tonight she wanted to look exceedingly pretty for Beau. He had been in New Orleans most of the day arguing with the lawyers, fighting over contracts and trying to undo what his grandfather had done. He'd missed both dinner and his most favorite ritual of putting Philip to bed. Eve heard the sound of his car driving up their gravel driveway. There was a long pause before the car door slammed. She wouldn't be able to hear Beau arrive once they moved into the big house. She wondered what it would be like living in the monstrously large main house of Gregoire Manner.

Eve dabbed a little concealer on the dark circles under her eyes and pulled out her favorite scent- a small blue crystal bottle of pear and amber oil from Egypt that Cora had given her. She dabbed her finger and traced down her long neck and into her décolletage, letting the oil ride in between the cleavage of her breasts. They were high, full and pressed against the tight bodice of her cream-colored nightgown. She listened to the noise downstairs in the small study just off the parlor as Beau uncapped a crystal decanter and poured himself a glass of single malt scotch. It must've been an incredibly stressful day—he wasn't a drinker. A few moments later she heard his heavy steps coming up the stairs. She tied her hair back into a long braid and tied a small ribbon at its end. It was loose enough so that if he ran his fingers through her braid, it would tumble apart. She knew that playing with her hair was one of his pleasures. Eve stood and lit scented candles. She dimmed the lights in the room. She felt his presence at the door before she turned, the match still between her fingers.

"How was your day? We missed you," she said.

Beau barely looked at her as he crossed the room while pulling off his clothes and headed into the bathroom.

"I've had better," he answered.

The next sounds Eve heard were his shoes and pants falling to the floor. The metal on metal of the shower curtain being pulled back blended with the squeaky turn of the handles inside the shower and the sound of falling water. She peaked through the crack in the door and watched the steam billowing up as the hot water from the shower clouded the room. She stood and watched the wet, bare shoulders of her husband-to-be glisten in the dim light. He had a broad, muscular back that curved into his high, firm ass, all perfectly balanced on two, long powerful legs. Eve liked how thick and strong his thighs were. She liked his body. She loved his hands. She wanted very much to make love to him tonight. The twinge of guilt from the attraction she felt when she and Mac spoke was still gnawing at her. Eve didn't want to lie to Beau, especially after his long day dealing with the flock of legal vultures, but she didn't want to stir up any paranoia he might have either. He didn't like Mac and jealousy always seemed to rear its ugly head whenever the detective's name, and even worse, his presence, arose.

Eve slowly pushed open the door of the bathroom, stepped inside and closed it behind her. She studied Beau: an Adonis with his hands pressed against the shower wall, his head lowered, eyes closed and his mind obviously in deep contemplation. She slipped out of her nightgown, stepped into the shower and gracefully slid under his arm. Beau looked up. His eyes met hers. She could see in his eyes a pain and sadness so obvious it hurt her heart. She pressed her lips to his gently; once and then again. She felt the warm water run over her as she took the slightest bit of soap gel and lathered his chest and arms. With each slow circle she kissed his lips again and again. She soaped her own breasts pressing them into him, rubbing her soft mounds against him, slowly sliding from side to side until she could feel her nipples become erect. Her hands traced down his rock hard stomach before separating just above his patch of thick black hair. She moved slowly down each hip until her hands captured his penis, which hung thick and semi hard until the moment of her touch. Like a soldier called to attention by its general, his cock became rigid. Beau was a big man, well endowed, and he knew exactly what to do with all his attributes. For the moment, he did nothing except allow her to take him. Eve rubbed and washed him, running her hands up and down his legs. She turned him around and stepped into him, pressing flesh against flesh, using her body to wash his back as high as she could reach while her hands guided the water. She took the shampoo and lathered his ebony curls, then soothingly pulled his head back into the spray of warm water to rinse the thick suds away. He slowly surrendered as her hands washed every inch of him. With each caress she heard his breathing both gradually relax and deepen.

He kissed her and slid his tongue into her mouth. His hands cupped her breasts, squeezing them just gently enough to make her moan. He kissed her lips with purpose before moving down the side of her face onto her neck, gently biting her flesh until he found his way to one ear. He sucked on her ear lobe and slipped his tongue inside its tiny orifice, tracing up to the edge of her ear. It tickled her and made Eve moan with pleasure. She felt beautiful in his arms. He let his face drift lower. She could feel his tongue wrap around hers. His kisses traced their way along her shoulder. He bent his body as he lifted one breast into his mouth; a kiss, a suck, a gentle bite sent chills through her entire body. She felt her libido ignite. Her hand closed around his cock, rubbing sensually up and down its shaft. She kissed him hard, a kiss filled with pure passion. She pulled from his grasp and slipped down his chest. Eve licked his nipples, playing with them as he had done to her. Her face moved down his stomach, kissing and caressing every inch of his torso. She loved his skin. It was taut and smooth with small, well placed, silky patches of dark hair. She felt her hands slide against the small dimple of his back and cup around the high, firm arc of his ass. Eve closed her eyes and squatted as her mouth found his cock, hot, hard as steel and wet from the flow of hot water that ran over them both. Her lips parted and he slid in. She sucked on him like her favorite new candy pop. He moaned a sound she'd never heard from him. She moved her head back and forth, pressing gently down with her lips. She traced up and down each side of his shaft using her tongue; she teased and licked and sucked on the sensitive head that was starting to throb. Eve heard a deep, guttural moan, a sound so primitive it sounded as if it came from another person ... from another place. Eve glanced up into the shadows to see his head drop backward in pleasure. She took him deeper into her throat. His hips moved in and out gently, ever so gently at first. In and out again and again he rocked. His fingers wove into her hair to hold her head as he pumped his manhood between her lips and down her throat. His pleasure built with each plunge until climax was only a stroke away. Eve closed her eyes imagining him loving the pleasure she was giving, but the face wasn't Beau's - it was Mac's. She was making love to Beau, but fantasizing about the Detective. As much as she wanted to shake the image from her mind, the fantasy of taking Mac turned her on.   Beau stopped her, reached down and, catching her under her armpits, lifted her to her feet and into his arms so she could straddle him.   Eyes shut tight she envisioned looking into Mac's eyes.   He parted her legs and stabbed himself inside her.   Eve held onto the shower curtain with one hand and latched her arm around his neck with the other.   He lifted her up and down again and again and again.   She placed one foot on the rim of the tub for balance as he grinded and twisted inside of her.

God he was strong.   One hand grabbed under her ass and lifted her up.   She wrapped both her legs around his hips and held on.   She was lost in her fantasy and he was lost in their pleasure – experienced animals, wild and unfettered.   It was freer and more erotic love making than she had ever remembered.   It was a feral kind of passion, exploding and building as they released all inhibitions and unleashed a new level of their passions.   She rode him like a wild horse set to the rhythm of the pounding water.

A rush of guilt shook her.   Why was this fantasy so incredible?   Eve forced herself to open her eyes to look at Beau.   He was there.   Her lover.   Her husband-to-be, but he did not look back.   His eyes were closed.   Was he imaging someone else?   All she could see was that he was beautiful.   A haze of swirling shadows encircled him.   She could see his eyes.   They suddenly looked as dark as Philip's.   His expression was one of someone lost in the throes of erotic passion.   Suddenly, Beau's brow furrowed more and more with each thrust inside of her. The intensity was building, driving him harder, faster, stronger and deeper.   Beau was there and yet he was someplace deep inside himself. It was what she'd seen when he stood naked in the bathroom with his fierce erection.   He pushed her feet down from the step and turned her around.   Eve held onto the wall.   His cock slammed up inside her.   He pounded into her harder and faster.   Her hair in his hand bending her back, her face forced away from his, she felt each thrust like a jack hammer, filled with what felt like anger, meanness, a rage she'd never felt from him before. Eve tried to rationalize what was happening. Did he know she had a momentary fantasy of another man? He crashed into her harder. Eve braced herself, taking each thrust, feeling the guilt of her unspeakable sin. She took the pain as a kind of penance for her thoughts of Mac. Her mind raced. Maybe it wasn't Mac. Maybe it was just all the frustration of everything that was happening in his life suddenly being released inside this act of violent sex. He whipped her around to face him and pulled them both down to the floor of the shower. He crawled into her, his body pressing onto hers. He was crushing her, jamming into her. The harder the stroke, the deeper his cock went, the bigger he felt inside her. Somewhere inside the pain she felt orgasmic waves of a very different kind of pleasure. Did she like his anger? Did she like the throbbing flashes that vacillated between pleasure and pain? She didn't want to like it. She wanted him to stop!

Beau stood up, towering over her and snatched her up into his arms; lifting her, wet, dripping with water, he carried her into the bedroom and dropped her down on the silk comforter.

"Beau —" Eve started to protest.

He dove onto her, slamming himself inside. Beau, on his knees, pulled her hips up, pushing and thrusting his cock into her. He grasped the brass bed frame above her head for leverage. Eve moaned beneath him, taking the rhythm of each stroke. He kissed her, his tongue probing her mouth. Deep gasps of air echoed in the room as the pleasure her body wanted and her mind's fears fought each other. His hand moved to her breast and he squeezed hard enough to make her arch up. His mouth went to her nipple. He sucked and licked and with each action there was a counteraction below until she surrendered. She came, exploding in a rush of silken fluid that flowed over his cock and down her legs, hot and wet. Her wet, throbbing cunt aroused him more and he responded, his hips moving faster and faster, his cock swelling bigger than she'd ever felt him. The pleasure was insane and horrifying. Eve bent her head back, her eyes closed. This time she slipped her hand down and cupped his testicles, fondling them faster and faster. She wanted him to come before he ripped her apart. He erupted with the force of Vesuvius and Krakatoa combined. A sound so primal, so lost in pleasure, bellowed from his throat and Eve opened her eyes. What she saw looming above her in the dim, shadowy light made her close them in disbelief. Something else was over her or was this some wild imagining too. She felt a rush of terror.

"Beau!" Eve called out in a helpless whisper.

Her body tightened, but he didn't, couldn't, wouldn't stop. He pushed deeper and drove himself into her harder and faster. That sound ... that primal sound filled her ears and she felt a searing, burning fire between her legs. She was passing out. She wanted to look, to open her eyes, but his mouth covered hers, his tongue inside of her, his hands everywhere. Eve twisted her face away and opened her mouth to cry out.

"Beau! Stop! Stop! Please! You're hurting me!" She screamed, sobbing through gasps and tears.

Everything stopped. Beau stopped. The shadowy haze that swirled around him stopped and faded like a ghostly mist running away into the dim light. He hovered over her, confused, breathless and panting.

"Forgive me," he said, gathering her into his arms. "I don't know what happened."

Eve was trembling. She wanted to push him away. She stared around looking into the shadows of the darkened room and then back at him. Inside a slim sliver of light that fell from the window she could see it was Beau ... only Beau, worried for her, not a horrific monster that had tried to rip her to shreds... only her beautiful Beau.

"You make me crazy. I lost myself. You know I would never hurt you."

Beau kissed her face and arms and fingers. The gentle stroke of his hand traced across her body.

"Tell me what you need me to do?" he asked.

Eve shook her head and curled up into his arms.

"Hold me. Just hold me."

She felt like a child waking from a nightmare and those she loved had come to encircle her. He felt warm and strong, but he didn't feel the one thing she desperately wanted to feel at this moment ... safe and that frightened her more than the pain throbbing between her thighs.

Chapter Six

Cora was having a very bad day. She had purchased the deluxe kit of *Teach Your Baby to Read* by Dr. Glenn Dorman and faithfully, every day, had done ten flash cards over 30 seconds of spoken and visual words, number dots, and famous paintings. Delia listened and looked, but to date refused to speak. On this element of child development, she and Philip had taken a strange code of silence, pointing to what they wanted, but never verbalizing their needs or demands. The two children would play together and sit or lie in an almost Zen state staring at each other as if communicating telepathically, a fact Cora was certain of since she first noticed the strange eye contact that held them spellbound for minutes at a time. However, nothing she said could convince either Eve or Beau that baby telecommunication was a feasible possibility.

Today, Delia was extremely irritable and unfocused. After the first set of cards she stood up, went to Cora and, placing both little hands on the cards, pushed them to the floor with a look so defiant it actually frightened Cora. Delia then opened her mouth and started screaming in full-on tantrum mode. The day nanny, Zamara, was about as plain a woman as Cora could find after the last two cute young nannies found their way into her extensive, black label, couture-filled closets and helped themselves to her clothes under the bizarre assumption that was acceptable behavior. Zamara, on the other hand, was a healthy muscular size 14, in her late forties, Latina, a trained nurse and an avid reader. When she didn't have Delia, she had a book or a reader in her hand. Zamara rushed into the room as a stunned Cora reached out to embrace her daughter in an attempt to control her temper. Delia flailed, arching her back and kicking her feet. She whacked Cora in the face with such force she left a tiny red hand print on her mother's cheek. Zamara stepped in.

"Let me have her, Miss Bouvier," Zamara insisted.

Zamara lifted Delia into her arms and whispered something into Delia's ear. Silence fell, leaving only the echoes of Delia's voice ringing off the marble surfaces in the atrium.

"What ... what in tarnation did you say to her?" Cora asked, rubbing her cheek.

Cora noticed there was blood on her lip as well.

"Nothin' really, Ma'am," Zamara responded.

"Nothing? A thirteen-month-old, in a full out nuclear tantrum shuts up and stills when you whisper in her ear and you choose not to tell me what you said? Seriously?" Cora said, glaring furiously at her nanny.

"It's not the words, Miss Cora. It's deep inside the breath that carries them."

Cora stopped, completely stunned. Her daughter was not only calm and quiet, she snuggled into Zamara's arms and buried her face in the nanny's neck.

"It's an art with children my Mamacita taught me. I could show you if you like?"

"I would like very much if you showed me how to do that, please," Cora said.

Zamara lay Delia down in the cradle, gave her the warm bottle of milk she was bringing up anyway before the sounds of infant

Armageddon broke out, and crossed to Cora.

"The key is to be as still and calm as you can be in the middle of such chaos," Zamara explained.

"Well, that's the first challenge, suga'. I can't be still and calm when the world is in utter chaos," Cora said with a roll of her eyes.

"Then it won't work, will it?" Zamara said, her voice even, her tone pointed. Zamara tipped her head and arched her eyebrow as if to say, "Do you want to do this or not lady?"

Cora took a deep breath. "Okay. Okay. I'm calm."

"Good. Now, take a deep long breath," Zamara said, doing it as she explained.

"What?"

"Breathe. You don't breathe right. You breathe from your chest, not from your abdominal muscles and back. If you breathe deeper, you will be able to calm yourself in a stressful situation. Now, breathe," Zamara commanded and took a breath with her.

"The second thing you have to do is lock your arms around her, like this."

Zamara came up to Cora and put her arms around her. Cora didn't realize how much taller Zamara was than she until that moment. She felt the strength in Zamara's arms press in on her so tight Cora's breathing was actually constricted. Not enough to make her panic, but certainly enough to make her aware she was being securely held. Then with a soft, gentle breath Zamara blew, using her nose, into Cora's ear. The result was instantaneous. Cora's entire body relaxed, every ounce of tension released and her body turned to Jell-O. If she'd wanted to speak, she couldn't. It was the second breath Zamara blew into her ear that made Cora melt in a way that shocked. Cora felt her nipples become erect and her vaginal juices flush as if she'd just had the most gentle, most sensual orgasm she ever experienced in her life. Cora released into Zamara's arms, her head dropped to Zamara's shoulder and in those few moments Cora felt as calm as she'd ever felt in her life.

Slowly Zamara released the forcefulness of her grip and somehow navigated Cora to the glider. Zamara's hands, strong yet as smooth as silk and velvet combined, lay on Cora's skin and the connection sent waves of pleasure through her.

"This is what happens to Delia?" Cora asked, whispering the words.

"She relaxes. What happens is what you want to happen," Zamara said.

Cora was mush, a human pudding. All she could do was look into Zamara's eyes. And that too was strangely erotic. Her eyes were the color of sable with flecks of gold. Cora studied her, peering at her perfectly smooth, olive colored skin. Zamara had full lips and a keen nose, high cheek bones and bone straight black hair that had to have Native American in its DNA. Zamara was strong, beautiful and commandingly sensual.

"I ... I don't understand what just happened. What's still happening," Cora said, almost unable to speak.

"It's important you put her down right away. That lets her understand the feeling and learn to recreate it for herself. That way she doesn't need me or you to calm her."

"Uh huh," Cora said, speaking from some out-of-body space.

"Keep breathing and I'll put Delia in her crib and get you some water. Let your mind take you where it wants to. Enjoy," Zamara said.

Cora heard her pick up Delia. Her footsteps moved away from her down the hallway. There was a moment of relaxed silence, a long slow breath and her eyes opened. Cora saw Zamara standing in front of her. Cora watched as Zamara knelt down in front of her, parted her legs and let her, hot, smooth and very gentle hands slide up her thighs. Cora wanted to gasp, to cry out, but only a long, slow hiss of a moan came out as her lips parted. One of Zamara's hands slipped slowly under her dress and caressed her breast. The other hand slipped deeper between her legs and snapped the lavender silk ribbon of her La Perla thong like it was a piece of spider web. Cora couldn't move. She sat motionless as Zamara unbuttoned Cora's dress and pushed the bra down allowing her left breast to lift itself out with the turn of a single finger. A gentle pinch of her nipple and Zamara's face leaned in. She brushed her lips against Cora's erect nipple and at the same time slipped a very wet finger into her. Cora closed her eyes. Zamara's warm tongue traced around the hard flesh and then her mouth attached and gently sucked on her nipple. Her free hand massaged Cora's breast, slipping sensually over the flesh between every third or fourth squeeze with velvet perfection. Between her legs, Zamara's finger seemed to swell as it slipped in and out and in and out, again and again in motion with the glider chair. The rhythm seemed to fall into slow easy, gentle motion, unhurried and oh, so good, giving her wave after wave of pleasure. Then Zamara's full lips slowly kissed their way up Cora's décolletage; tiny, hungry kisses and little licks with gentle bites that traced up her neck and into her ear where her gentle breath flowed out like honeyed smoke that slipped into Cora's ear. The warm feeling curled into her body with the warmth of a hot summer rain on naked flesh. Cora felt Zamara's fingers coaxing her pulsing pussy into opening and closing and sucking on the flesh that stroked inside her. The whispered breaths in her ear stopped as if Zamara knew to continue would bring Cora to orgasm. Zamara's lips brushed across Cora's face until they reached her mouth. The kiss sent waves of passion through her and Zamara's fingers inside her swelled again. All of it at once filled Cora in a way that she had only experienced once before ... Beau. That one night they had succumbed to each other wrapped in grief. The night the doctors were sure Eve was going to die and they wept in each other's arms. Their grief led to kisses and kisses to desperate passion. They made love for hours, far into the morning and early afternoon.

That encounter came rushing back to her in vivid detail. Cora opened her eyes and looked up ... it was Beau inside her. She wanted to scream, but what she was feeling was beyond pleasure. She was helpless. She couldn't stop even if she wanted to and she in no way wanted to. She had hungered for him for so long. She'd worked so hard to push the feeling she had for him away because she loved Eve. But when Cora looked into his eyes and ran her fingers into those perfect curls she couldn't stop. He kissed her, devouring her mouth, as hungry and desperate as she was. He stopped and his face dropped down between her legs. His tongue was hot and hard as it vibrated against her clitoris. He slipped one hand under her hips and his finger went inside while his tongue and lips licked and sucked. The other hand pinched her nipple, sending her into a frenzy of erotic passion.

"Beau ... please ... oh God please ... we can't," she moaned.

"Beg me again," she heard a voice say and the ... the orgasm took her.

He lifted her from the chair and laid her on the floor. Both naked, he slipped inside of her and found the rhythm of her passion. He rode her easy, hard, faster, slower. Her body arched and he rode her harder. He sustained the height of her orgasms until her body vibrated with his. He was an amazing lover. She felt as if they blended into one fluid being. When she was spent, she relaxed. He hovered over her, his wet skin taught as it stretched over the perfectly sculpted muscles in his arms, chest, stomach and thighs. Still throbbing inside her, he slowly pressed down, flesh against flesh, on top of her. He kissed her lips and stroked her hair. His face went to her ear and he breathed one last time in her ear. She completely surrendered, collapsing into his arms. Her face found its way into the crook of his neck and there she planted the gentlest of kisses as she felt his arms coil around her. She was happier than she'd ever been in her life.

"I love you, Beau," she whispered and drifted into sleep.

Zamara stood at the door to the playroom holding the glass of water. She crossed the room and sat it down on the floor next to a sleeping Cora, still in her dress and very much alone.

Chapter Seven

Detective Macklin Blanchard stood just inside the closed door of his precinct commander's office. Lieutenant Mitchell Hanover; friend, hero, leader, tough guy and one mean ass son-of-a-bitch when he needed to be. A collection of qualities that could make him turn from friend to foe in a heartbeat. At the moment he was fuming, and, had the situation been a cartoon, Mac was sure he would have been able to see steam shooting from his ears.

"What are you doing?" Hanover shouted. "Beau Le Masters has a court ordered restraint for you to stay off his property and four hundred feet away from his wife. What part of that don't you understand detective?"

"She's not his wife," Mac said.

"Seriously? Did you actually just say that to me?"

"Technically, she's not," Mac added.

"What the fuck is your problem?" Hanover asked.

"She was raped, impregnated with a child that bears little resemblance to the father and..." Mac started to explain.

"Stop! Enough!" Hanover told him. "You have been walking a very fine line. You do understand that every precinct in New Orleans is under the high-powered microscope of the U.S. Attorney General's office?"

"Yes, of course, but—" Mac tried again.

"But what? You don't care because your record's clean? Shit, half the cops in this city are facing charges of excessive force, acts of omission, multiple criminal civil rights violations and a truck load of other major criminal acts including misconduct. They're looking at everything from illegal stops, searches and arrests of individuals without reasonable suspicion and probable cause to police beatings and shootings." Hanover said as he picked up a stack of affidavits. "According to these documents and in some cases videos, they have a fuck load of severe infractions of unreasonable use of force. Far too many to ignore. We're in a state of siege and behind it a tsunami of major reform. So, if you think I have time to deal with your bullshit, voodoo ass, conspiracy theories, you're crazier than I thought. Now do the Goddamn job the city pays you to do and stay away from Eve Dowling."

Mac didn't move. "She's in danger and I want it on the record," Mac said.

"Well, when you can tell me what she's in danger from except being one rich and very powerful lady, I'll spend a micro second being concerned. Until then ..." Hanover stopped talking and reached into his desk, pulling out a card. "You're going into therapy. Call her. Set an appointment. You are now on psychiatric leave of absence."

"Under what ..."

"Under my orders as your commander, so don't argue with me Mac. Eight sessions. Now, call her and get out of my office," Hanover said. "Mac, you're a good detective. One of my best and I need you here, but I need all of you here."

Mac took the card. He knew there was nothing more to say. He stepped out and closed the glass door, heading back to his desk. From the looks of the other detectives, Hanover's voice had carried far enough to draw looks from his fellow detectives.

He sat, looking at the pile of cases stacked on his desk. He knew that's where his head should be. That's where his efforts should be, but his eyes were drawn back to the *New Orleans Post* clipping announcing the wedding of Eve Dowling and Beauregard Le Masters.

Let it go, he said to himself.

"She's not your concern and it's costing you your job," Officer Vantes said.

He was tall and thin and walked with a limp.

"Hey. That loud huh?" Mac asked.

"Yeah, that loud."

"Vantes? How are your legs? I mean have the doctors figured out what started the degeneration?" Mac asked.

"X-rays showed multiple fractures all through my body. They said maybe stress. X-ray technician said it was the damnedest thing he ever saw. He thought I'd have had to been lifting a building for those to come naturally," he responded. "I'm healing. Should be back pounding the pavement in a few months. Don't that just sound like peaches and cream?"

"That's good," Mac said.

"Hey, Mac," Vantes said, his voice dropping to a low whisper. "I want you to know I think somethin's funky with both members of the Le Masters clan. I'd check the old man, if I was investigating. Which I'm not, mind ya."

"No, you're not and technically neither am I," Mac replied. "I'm gonna go get my head shrunk for a few weeks."

"Between my bones and these stupid headaches and weird ass dreams, I need to get in line behind you," Vantes said.

"I didn't know you were having dreams," Mac said, giving him his full attention.

"Yeah, over a year and they're getting worse, not better."

"What kind of dreams?" Mac asked.

"I don't know. A bunch of weird shit that doesn't make sense. I feel like I'm reading a science fiction book and remembering stuff that never happened in the story. Don't tell anyone or they'll think I'm crippled *and* crazy."

"Guess we're in the same sci-fi book," Mac said, pointing to himself. "Headaches and bad dreams for over a year and getting worse. Sometimes I feel like... it's some kind of premonition... like something's supposed to happen and I'm supposed to know. The Dowling woman mentioned weird dreams once when I first interviewed her and then shut up."

Vantes' body cramped, a rush of pain shot through him and registered on his face like someone took a bite out of him with electric teeth.

"You okay?" Mac asked.

Vantes looked around as if he were being watched.

"No, and neither are you," Vantes said.

There was a wild, paranoid terror in Vantes' eyes as they darted around the room looking for something that wasn't there.

"Yeah, maybe we both need a shrink inside our heads," Mac said.

"Maybe. Just watch what you say, Mac. They're here," he says and looks around again. "Myself, I think they're everywhere."

Vantes walked away. His limp was suddenly more pronounced than before, the throngs of some unseen pain digging into him deeper than ever.

"Who's here?" Mac asked himself, as he picked up the card and turned it over to read the doctor's name. Dr. Lisette Honoré.

Chapter Eight

Eve sat in the waiting room for Dr. Cheney Renfroe, New Orleans' finest and most renowned pediatrician. The parents of her clientele, Beau and Cora insisted, were the who's who of not just New Orleans, but of much of the surrounding state. Rumor had it, women drove from as far away as Baton Rouge to give birth and have her care for their little ones. She had brought Philip into the world and managed to induce labor in a comatose woman which, by all medical information Eve was able to Google, was highly difficult and unusual.

Eve held a sleeping Philip, gently rocking him rhythmically back and forth as she nestled in the plush cream couch. Interesting choice for a pediatrician's waiting area, Eve thought to herself, with all those sticky little fingers, snot, puke, pee and well ... she shuddered and decided to stop imagining the rest. Yet, the soft mushroom brown color of the plush sofas and chairs that ringed the office looked as though the furnishings had been delivered this morning.

Eve quietly observed the seven other children waiting with their mothers in the outer office. All of the women looked to be about Eve's age, perhaps maybe a little younger. They were exceedingly attractive with good cheekbones and, curiously, all of them had long hair. Not as long as Eve's perhaps, but even the shortest fell mid-back between the tanned shoulder blades of a sweet-faced young woman with chestnut curls and an olive complexion.

She smiled at Eve. Eve smiled back realizing she must have been staring.

"How old is she?" the tanned woman asked.

"He," Eve said correcting her. "Eighteen months."

The moment Eve heard the words come out there was a rush of disbelief. She looked down at Philip.

"Tall for his age," the woman added.

The fact that so many months had passed sent a shiver up her spine. He was tall. Even for 18 months he looked more like a three year old than a two year old and that wouldn't be official for four more months.

"Well, I'm tall and so is his father," Eve said.

"Tilly's tall too," she said referring to her daughter. "She's fifteen months."

Tilly had the same thick curls as her mother. Sweet face but her skin looked pale in comparison. *Not as much sun worshiping*, Eve surmised. Still for a girl and fifteen months, Tilly was almost as tall as Delia, and Delia was just a little smaller than Philip.

"Somethin' in the water. I'm quite sure of it," another woman added in a thick Southern drawl.

That fact made several of the women laugh. It was an inside joke because Dr. Renfroe had insisted all the children drink only a special brand of PH water. Eve was fine with it because Philip hadn't gotten even a sniffle since she brought him home from the hospital. No colds, flus, ear infections and Dr. Renfroe had not given any of the vaccinations she'd read about. That fact had been troublesome to Aria, but Philip was her ward, not her child, so she stated her case and backed down.

The conversation woke Philip and he wiggled out of her arms and onto the floor. Eve kept him trapped between her legs, but Tilly toddled her way over and the two children discovered each other.

"Kelly," the tan woman said, introducing herself.

"Eve."

"She's usually not very friendly. I'm surprised she's so curious."

Eve let Philip slip to the floor. The green carpet was soft and clean and looked more like grass than carpet. The two children sat staring at each other when Tilly, who had been carrying a small duck plushy, offered it to Philip.

"Duck," said Philip.

Eve just about fainted. He may have been tall, but until that moment he'd not said one word. Not mama or dada or water or anything.

"Oh my," Eve said with a smile. "That's his first word."

"Duck," Tilly said, as clearly as Philip.

"I'll be dipped in honey and molasses," Kelly said, blurting out the words with a laugh and a smile. "That's hers!"

It was at that moment Eve noticed that all the children had squiggled out of their mothers' arms and were moving toward Philip. She didn't know if she should gather him up and take him away to protect him or leave him to see what he would do. It was then she realized all the babies were girls - except hers.

"My daughter hasn't spoken yet either," another woman said.

"My mother told me that was normal in some cases," a third added.

"My father said just the opposite," a fourth woman said, trying to keep up with her daughter who had crawled next to Philip and plopped down on her bottom.

She stared at Philip like an eager puppy, grinning an adorable grin.

"Duck," Philip said, pointing at the duck.

"Duck," the puppy-faced girl uttered.

Eve didn't know what to do or say. She turned to the mother of the puppy faced girl.

"How old is she?" Eve asked.

"Eight months, and she's done several things that ... well ... aren't quite age appropriate. And, well, now talking. I ... I'm flabbergasted."

Eve looked at her. "Appropriate? What do you mean ... appropriate?"

"Appropriate may not be the right word: unusual. She ... makes pictures with anything she can get into: spilt milk, her little blocks. When we gave her my iPad to play with," the woman stopped and pulled out her iPad, calling up a page and turning it around.

The expression on everyone's faces in the room was shock.

"Tsung is twenty months and she can play the piano. At first we thought she was fascinated by the keys and let her bang, but last week we heard lines of Mozart's that matched from a record playing in her room," a woman with Asian features and a river of straight black hair said.

The room was silent. Eve could tell by each woman's expression that their daughters had displayed some 'unusual' behavior. Though she couldn't explain Philip's prodigal talents, she knew her son was unusually advanced for his age.

"Philip Le Masters?" the nurse called as she opened the door.

Eve looked at the other women in the room. They had shared a moment, something unanswered hung in the air, inexplicable, but very real.

Eve stood and gathered Philip into her arms. He felt heavier than before, as if, since she'd set him down and picked him up he had gained a few more pounds.

The other women said nothing as Eve and Philip slipped behind the door, down the long corridor and into the brightly colored examination room.

The examination room was more kid friendly with black and white and primary colors splattered across one wall for the less developed eyes of infants and bright colors and shapes for the fascination of the toddlers. None of the characters that looked back at her from the walls were fairy tale characters - no Aesop, Grimm, Hans Christian Anderson – the figures looked Egyptian or perhaps older and the symbols were some kind of ancient hieroglyphics.

"Please undress him and lay him there on the scale and we'll weigh and measure him to see where he fits on the growth chart," the nurse said with a warm smile.

"He's tall for his age," Eve added.

"Eighteen months?" the nurse said as she fiddled with an electronic chart on the room's computer.

Eve undressed Philip while the nurse gave him a squishy, red rubber ball that went immediately to his mouth. Eve took his shoes and played with his feet, making him giggle the best giggle ever. As she pulled his little jeans and baby blue t-shirt off, her eyes kept going to the walls. She found herself captivated by the images; not Roman, or Greek or even Egyptian, but older. The fact they were done in a kind of modern, animated style made it harder to pinpoint their historical origin.

Philip liked them too. His focus, however, was on the ceiling. Eve followed his gaze and what she saw sent a chill through her bones that actually made her shiver: precise, detailed constellations of stars. At first glance she was sure they were not like the starry skies she'd painted on Philip's walls and ceiling next to his bed. She'd painted them in his nurseries both in the main house and in the guest house. But these star maps were more...real. Eve was sure that if she looked in the night sky at various star constellations like the Pleiades, Orion or the Milky Way, they would match what she and Philip were seeing here in the doctor's office.

"Home," Philip said. He pointed to a star with a stream of light at the far corner of the ceiling.

"What did you say?" Eve asked him.

Eve shivered the second time because, upon closer inspection, the stars Beau painted above his bed, the stars she thought were randomly placed, were here, exactly the same. It was as if he had been an astronaut or an astronomer. Eve stepped closer. There was no question; a small part of this ceiling was an exact duplicate of the ceiling in Philip's rooms at home.

"Hi," Dr. Renfroe said as she stepped into the room and startled Eve. "And hi to you my handsome little man," she added to Philip with a sweet, warm lilt.

Philip lowered the ball, refocused on Dr. Renfroe and smiled.

Dr. Renfroe washed her hands as the nurse checked Philip's weight and height. He was off the scale. She pulled out a small extender to the ruler and typed in the number. The digital chart program calculated on an electronic graph.

"You got all his info from Thibodaux?" Eve asked.

"Yes, we did," Dr. Renfroe said. "We are always very excited to see this young man."

"You are?" Eve asked. Her stomach tightened. "Why's that?"

Dr. Renfroe ran her hands over Philip. Checking his ears and eyes, listening to his heart with a small stethoscope she warmed with her breath and hands before she touched it to his bare skin.

"His birth was under unusual circumstances, don't you agree?"

"Unusual?" Eve asked.

"You were in a coma during your entire pregnancy and when he came into the world. I would call those circumstances highly unusual."

"Right. Yes. Very unusual," Eve said, feeling foolish. "He's alright though, right? My being in a coma didn't affect him, did it?"

Dr. Renfroe stopped her examination of Philip and turned her attention to Eve. Whatever else she was, she had great bedside manner. The attention and eye contact said that as clearly as a welcoming sky on a summer day.

"Eve, I can't tell enough from the records they kept on you both at the hospital through your pregnancy. The fact that you were in a coma and carried a child to full term is highly unusual. Dr. Stevenson helped me induce labor for a vaginal birth and that you two are fine is miraculous and perplexing. I know you received proper nutrients and vitamins, but there is no way to tell from his growth charts what affect your situation had on his development. It may take years to discover if there were any complications to his lungs, brain, eyes, organs or even his emotional development. You understand that, don't you?" Dr. Renfroe asked.

A flush of tears and concern welled up in Eve's eyes. The idea that something could be wrong with her son and that somehow it could be her fault crushed her heart and shredded her emotions.

"He seems so healthy," Eve said, struggling to speak.

"He is a fine, healthy and very happy baby by all I can tell from this gobbledy-goop of fancy software programs. Well, that and twenty years of looking after these cute little people. And by the way, I'm pretty darn good at what I do," Dr. Renfroe said, her face breaking into a smile.

The confidence in Philip's doctor's voice and demeanor chased the elephant that had been sitting on her chest away, but a seed of concern still remained. She could feel it. *Crap, one more thing to torture myself with*, Eve thought.

"Duck," Philip said and bit into his teething ball.

"Alright! Now we know he won't be the strong silent type," Dr. Renfroe said.

She checked Philip's skin, looked at his hands and feet, checked his cute little butt, scrotum and penis.

"You chose not to have him circumcised?"

"I didn't have a choice in the matter I guess," Eve replied.

"Not too late if you feel it will make his life easier."

Eve looked at Philip. *Ouch*, she thought.

"I'll discuss it with his father."

"Go ahead and get him dressed," Dr. Renfroe said before leaving the room.

Eve kissed and tickled Philip. She watched him laugh as she pulled on his t-shirt and diaper, jeans, sox and little shoes. Philip's eyes went again and again back to the walls and ceiling.

When Dr. Renfroe and the nurse were gone and Philip was dressed, Eve pulled out her cell phone and switched it to video. Slowly, she captured the strange images that covered the walls and the stars that were scattered across the ceiling. Through the lens she looked at the hieroglyphs: people and creatures, temples and mountains. They toiled in the fields and fished the rivers, honoring the sun and water. Near the corner of the room, a kind of domed temple stood, priests and priestesses and a larger High Priestess with a golden, winged crown stood in a circle under a shimmering blue arch. Rays of light shone down on an altar where a body lay prone. In the wash of light Eve could see something. She pushed into it, but whatever it was had no form she could discern. She hit pause and stepped closer. There was something there. She switched her camera phone to still and took a picture of the star and the strange beam of light.

"Home? Huh?" Eve said staring at the star before returning her gaze to her son.

"Duck," Philip said, wiggling to the edge of the table.

"Oh, no you don't little man," Eve said gathering him up. "Now, duck is a perfectly fine word, but if you really want to win your daddy's heart say ... Dada."

Philip looked at her and his little hands went to her cheeks. He held her face and stared into her eyes with those dark, limpid pools of chocolate that seemed to drag her into his soul.

"Neteru," Philip said as he turned her face away from his and toward the corner.

The light that rose from the altar moved. It shimmered as if it were real. Eve's heart fluttered. She squeezed her son as tightly as she could. She looked back at Philip and then at the undulating, radiant glow. It peeled itself off the wall and reached toward her and her son. Her heart pounded so hard in her chest she thought it would explode. Philip turned to the beam and reached out his hand. It was coming to him ... for him. Eve stumbled back, grabbing for the door handle with her free hand. It slipped. She turned to grab and open it again. The door clicked open and she stepped out, but the diaper bag caught on the handle. Its strap dug into her shoulder. With a tug she ripped it free and stepped farther back as the door swung shut and the light retreated.

"Are you alright?" the nurse asked.

Eve, obviously frazzled, looked at her unsure what to say.

"Fine. I'm fine," Eve said, trying to control her breath so she didn't sound like a lunatic.

"Well, you better get this cutie home. Looks like a big storm is coming," the nurse said.

"Thanks," Eve said and turned down the hall. Just as Eve stepped into the lobby she caught a glimpse of Dr. Renfroe standing at the far end of the hall outside an examination room. She was staring at Eve, her face looked strangely ethereal, other worldly. Their eyes connected as the door swung shut with a click and she was gone.

A chill ran through her blood. The little voice that whispered it's warnings of danger was back, hissing at her to be afraid. Eve wanted out! She wanted to be outside in the warm sun and breathe the fresh air. She needed to get herself and Philip home. As she crossed through the outer office, she noticed one last, disturbing thing. It was empty. None of the other mothers and babies were waiting there. It felt to Eve as if they had come only to see Philip, to be in his presence with their daughters then, once seen, they were done and gone. Eve needed to know why. She looked at Philip and got out as fast as she could.

Chapter Nine

Several sleepless days and nights passed. Eve somehow charmed the names of the other mothers who'd been in Dr. Renfroe's office that day from the office assistant. After a few calls it was obvious all Dr. Renfroe's patients were tied to Thibodaux Hospital and all the children in her care had been born there. From there she searched for who these women were, who they were married to and how their husbands and families were tied to Thibodaux, but instead of answers, she encountered one wall after another and no one she reached out to at Thibodaux would help. She'd found Mac's card in the pocket of her green dress and almost called him. More than once the idea fluttered in her head, taunting her to call with the persistence of a hungry horse fly, but she had too many confusing feelings about Mac to call. Frustrated, she did all she could to ignore her concerns and live her all too wonderful life.

It was Cora who noticed the stress in Eve's face. Cora insisted they get away from the house and out of New Orleans for a picnic as far away from Gregoire Estate as they could get. After much insistence, Cora won and Eve, Philip, Cora and Delia packed themselves and a scrumptious lunch into the car. Eve got behind the wheel and they took off on a long, lazy drive through the Louisiana countryside.

Over an hour on the road flew by and the warm sun and bright sky made Eve feel liberated. She thought if she just kept driving and never looked back, maybe it would be the best thing for everyone.

"Good heavens, Eve, suga, where in tarnation are we going?" Cora asked. "We've been driving over an hour."

"It's a surprise," Eve replied.

"You do know I hate surprises, darlin'," Cora said.

"You said we needed to get away is all and you are my very best friend so let's get the hell away," Eve said. "Tell me something amazingly wonderful that's happened to you recently."

Cora fell silent, her mind racing back to that very bizarre and very graphic afternoon wet dream of she and the nanny that transformed into she and Beau and the best sex she'd ever had in her life. To this day she wasn't sure if any, all or none of it was real. The thought of she and Beau making love and the fact that she liked it was all that filled her mind. Cora looked at Eve, wanting to tell her and, at that moment, wanting Eve to be anyone other than her best friend for the simple reason she so dearly loved her. Her best friend, who was about to marry the father of her own daughter, Delia. Had it not been so complicated and sordid, maybe she could have shared it and laughed it off with her dear friend, but the reality of everything was still too raw ... too fresh. Even just thinking of it felt sacrilegious.

"That boring, eh?" said Eve.

"Weird fantasies," blurted Cora.

Eve laughed then fell silent when she saw the solemn look on Cora's face.

"Seriously? Me too," Eve said

"Maybe having babies makes you think strange kinky things," Cora said.

"Strange and kinky? Now you have to share," Eve said.

The roadside sign for Thibodaux Hospital whooshed by.

"You're kidding," Cora said.

"Yes. Come on. The picnic grounds by the bayou are so beautiful and the bird sanctuary is something I think Philip and Delia will remember."

"You are a terrible liar, Eve Dowling," Cora said, her face bending into a pout. "Why are we out at this Godforsaken place? I hate Thibodaux."

"Okay, okay, I do have one thing I need to check on at the hospital and because we're down this far, I saw no harm in taking a few minutes *after* our picnic to take care of it. If it's a problem, I'll turn around right now and come back another time," Eve said.

"Lies *and* a guilt trip. Aren't you the northern bitch? You listen to me, sugar tits, I am your best friend and I know all your moves. Now what the hell is this really about?"

Cora stared at her. She wore that southern, I-may-look-dumb-but-I'm-smarter-than-a hungry-fox expression that Eve loved about her. She was her best friend even with all that had passed between them. Eve wanted desperately to talk to her. She needed to share her nightmares with someone not to mention her very real, very kinky fantasies.

"You'll think I'm crazy," Eve said.

"I already do. As a matter of fact, I think you are almost as crazy as I am. I will let you know when you surpass me. Crazy and bitch are titles I relish and will not give up easily by the way," Cora said with a wry smile. "Oh, add to that getting spoiled and about to be wonderfully rich. Suga, you are about to join the club, so get over yourself."

The two women burst into spontaneous laughter. It was the first time in a very long time they had laughed together. It felt good. It seemed to shatter the thick web of tension that had entangled them since she woke from her coma. They laughed so hard tears ran from both their eyes, forcing Eve to pull the car over to compose herself. It took a pleasurable bit of time to calm down. She turned to look at

Cora who was wiping her eyes with the ends of a shared clean cloth diaper. The two women looked at each other and Eve felt the bond of love that secured their friendship. It was strong and good. They turned back to check on a very quiet Philip and Delia and found the two staring at them with wide eyes and very confused little faces. The two women burst out laughing again.

Their laughter finally subsided and they, still giggling and joking like two high school girls playing hooky from the world, decided to make their picnic right where they were. They drove off the main road and down a dirt path and parked the car in the center of a glorious banyan grove. Thick arms of twisted roots crawled around massive grey tree trunks that had, over many years, gracefully split into thick branches heavy with wide, waxy leaves.

They tumbled out, taking kids, carry seats, blankets and the beautiful wheat colored, wicker picnic basket Aria had helped Eve pack. Across the soft moist earth they set out to find the perfect place to have lunch.

"It's a gorgeous day, don't cha think," Cora said. "The sun is warm and the air is cool. How about right over there?"

The place they chose to lay the blankets was near a small, algae-covered lake not too far off the road, but just far enough to make them feel they were on an adventure. Sunlight dappled through the wide leaves of their chosen tree, it's great, wooden arms draped in thick hairy ropes of Spanish moss. The air smelled of magnolia blossoms baking in the warm sun, sweet and pungent. And the sounds of the bayou echoed around them: cicadas, crickets, nutria and a host of birds and other bugs. No mosquitoes had found them, which Eve noticed as a strange anomaly, but ignored as she hung a lightweight mosquito netting. She tossed a rope over a low hanging branch and together they pulled up the bundle of white netting hooked to the rope. Eve double tied the rope into a constrictor knot; her sailing lessons held some benefit. Once free of the bag, a clever, umbrella-like device popped open to form the top rigging. The net draped over the frame, stretched down in all directions and made the cutest little canopy with enclosed sides. They stretched and tied the hem to four stakes like a couple of roustabouts from Barnum and Bailey Circus, then gathered kids and basket and went inside their little sanctuary to feast and enjoy each other and the afternoon. They sat happy and safe inside the thin film of gauze netting that spread over them like delicate angel wings. The fabric let in the sun and the breeze, but kept any unwanted creepy crawlers and critters out. As delicate as it looked it was made of a remarkably strong nylon thread by a company Beau had invested in.

Cora laid her favorite mustard yellow, blue and cranberry tablecloth she'd brought back from Provence between the tree roots that poked above the ground. Eve spread out their banquet: black and green olives, three kinds of French cheeses, hard and creamy and very smelly. One had been supplied by Cora along with a chunk of wickedly delicious duck pâté Eve swore would be her last ever as she savored each delicious bite. There was a fresh loaf of French bread Aria had baked, some slices of honey baked ham, pickles, water and fruit smoothies because both ladies were still nursing. Or so Eve thought until she watched Cora pull out a bundle with little glass containers and start to spoon feed Delia.

"I have everything homemade and pureed for her. Greedy little darling. She loves food," Cora said, shoveling mouthfuls of green, orange and beet-red foods into her daughter's mouth.

Eve was about to say something when Philip, who was just about to settle in to nurse, saw the colorful display and pulled away. He stood, gathering his sometimes wobbly legs underneath him. Balancing on the uneven soil beneath his feet, he walked to Cora and curiously studied what Delia was doing. After a few moments of assessing the situation, he opened his mouth. Cora scooped in the first bite after which he plopped down next to Delia and hungrily waited for the one-for-you, one-for-Delia routine Cora quickly established.

"Well, guess we're done with that," Eve said.

"She still takes my breast at bedtime, but I think she likes the closeness more than the milk. Besides, I am ready for an adventure into my wine cellar!"

After lunch they played learning games. They studied leaves and pointed to the birds and curious squirrels that came closer than Eve would have liked. Patty cake and raspberries on fat tummies made the children squeal and giggle until they drifted off for an afternoon nap leaving Eve and Cora to nibble on the grown up elements of the picnic.

"So, why on earth are we going to Thibodaux Hospital?" Cora said.

Cora spread pâté on fresh French bread and nibbled on black olives, ham and creamy cheese. Eve barely touched anything.

"Eve? Talk to me," Cora insisted.

"I have trouble sleeping and I keep having these horrible dreams ... nightmares."

"Nightmares?" Cora asked.

"They don't come just at night either. I'm having hallucinations, Cora. Sometimes, in the middle of the day, they block my vision and split my head open like an ax."

"What is it you see?" Cora asked.

"I don't know. I can't see anything specific really, nothing that makes sense, but ..." Eve stopped.

A horrendous panic filled her. Her throat closed off. She couldn't breathe. Eve rose to her feet. The world disappeared into a wash of bright yellow and white light. She felt her hand reach out to touch the smooth trunk of the tree. She knew it was there, that it was real, but she wanted to be touching it in case she suddenly couldn't see it. To make sure it was there ... no, to make sure ... she was there.

"Eve, suga, you are pale as a ghost. Sit!" Cora was on her feet.

Cora stepped over the sleeping children and went to grab her friend to keep her from falling.

"Breathe!" Cora said as calmly as she could.

Eve gasped. Tears filled her eyes. A loud ringing filled her ears to the point of pain. She turned to look at Cora, but saw only the slashed face she'd seen in the glass door of the Trauslen, with rivulets of blood pouring out of each gash. Eve was trembling. She covered her eyes with her hands.

"Dear, lord, tell me what is happening," Cora said.

Eve shook her head and pulled away. She stepped outside the thin mosquito veil and felt the full force of the air against her skin. She stumbled down to the edge of the lake, dropped to her knees and splashed cool water on her face. Eve gasped, sucking in huge gulps of air while the ringing slowly subsided and the harsh glare of the hideous light faded.

"Eve? Eve? Can you hear me?" Cora said.

Cora had followed her. She was standing next to her. Eve covered her ears to muffle the sound of Cora's voice. It replaced the ringing in Eve's head. Cora knelt next to her.

"Okay, how long have these ... headaches been going on?" Cora asked.

"I don't know. Since I woke up from the coma, but they're getting worse. Oh, Cora, I think I'm losing my mind. Dr. Honoré wants to put me on medication," Eve told her, still trying to control her breathing.

Cora thought about the using the breath-in-the-ear trick, but wanted Eve to answer her first. This whatever was happening was too important to repress.

"Does Beau know about these episodes, Eve?" Cora asked.

Eve didn't answer. The look on her face said everything.

"Eve, sugar. You have got to tell him about this."

"Not until I understand what is happening to me. Please promise me you won't say anything. Promise."

"That is a shitty promise, Eve Dowling," Cora said with a huff.

"I know and if you weren't my best friend in the world, I wouldn't ask it, but you are and you must promise you won't say a word to Beau. He has enough on his plate with all the legal binds his grandfather put him in. The anniversary of his sister's death is coming; Philip, the house and we have a wedding and a christening. I just can't share this with him until I understand what the hell it is. Please, promise me," Eve said, tears welling in her eyes.

"Alright, alright, I will, but I won't like it," Cora said. "But you have to tell me what you see in the visions. I think that's a fair trade. The truth for a lie," Cora said.

Eve looked at her friend. She felt as though she had to make a confession of these frightening and absurd visions. The words balled up in her mouth, dry and ugly.

"Last two times ... I saw you. Someone was hurting you. They cut you there," Eve said pointing to her face. "...on your chin. Cora, I think they were trying to kill you."

"Sakes alive! Who? Why?"

"I don't know or maybe I don't want to know," Eve said.

"Who did you see?" Cora demanded.

"It's not a 'who' it's some kind of a 'what'," Eve tried to explain.

Cora looked at her and the look said it all.

"Please don't look at me like that. I don't know if I'm going crazy," Eve said.

"You told me once your grandmother died in an insane asylum," Cora reminded her. "I'm not like her. This is real. Yes, it's crazy, but there's a part of this that makes it—me—feel like I'm standing at the edge of a very real sanity. I'm not crazy. Cora, I'm sure whatever it is... it's not human and I think it has something to do with Beau and his family," Eve said.

Cora pulled back from Eve and then her eyes darted away. Cora knew some secret and Eve could see she wanted to share it.

Something in Eve knew it was about Beau, about his family.

"Tell me! Please," Eve begged.

"Oh, Eve. They were old rumors... gossip as old as the city of New Orleans," Cora started to say, when they both heard a deep, primal hiss. Both women turned and there, on the bank of the lake, an eight-foot-long alligator lay motionless, barely ten feet from the children. It was a massive, green-scaled monster with its jaw hinged wide open, staring at Philip. Philip stood staring back through the mosquito netting from the center of their sanctuary.

Chapter Ten

The burning sting of an adrenaline rush hit Eve so hard she didn't even remember getting up and running. She was already in full stride, heading for her son, when logic caught up with her. What she would do when she got there wasn't even a consideration. Save her son was all that rang like a deafening claxon through her mind. Cora opened her mouth to scream, but nothing came out. She was frozen and silent.

The gator attacked, its squat legs moving in a blur so fast it was at the netting before Eve could get there.

"Here!" Eve shouted at the monster.

It didn't even acknowledge her presence. The huge, scale-covered body lunged into the netting. Its snout, front feet and claws stuck in the fabric that by some miracle tangled, caught and stopped the alligator inches from Philip.

In that surreal, merciful instant, Eve was there. She entered through the other side, grabbed Philip and then Delia, who was now standing ... calmly watching as if a happy little puppy was rolling over and over as if to play with them. Both children had the same tranquil air about them. Eve, however, was in full panic mode. She handed Delia to Cora who had somehow found her legs and was standing next to her. Even with the panicked energy exuded by their mothers, the children didn't make a sound. They kept their eyes on the gator as he struggled, flipping and spinning. Eve and Cora, the children in their arms, backed out of the netting.

No more than two feet away, the gator, trapped in the net, flipped over again to its feet and lunged. It ripped the netting, his dense weight snapping the tree limb with a loud crack. The limb fell. It slammed down hard on the gator as he lunged again for Eve and Philip. She stumbled farther back. Cora stuck her arm out and braced her friend. Eve found her balance and with the children in their arms, they ran as fast as they could to the car.

The wet and slippery earth made it harder to run. Cora's foot sunk into the mud and she and Delia were dragged down, she struggled to protect Delia as she slid in the wet slime desperately trying to get her feet back under her. She fell again.

"Eve!" Cora screamed.

Eve turned back to see the alligator, tangled in the netting, dragging the tree branch, clawing through the mud, relentlessly pursuing them. Caught, hobbled, but so powerful even with the limb dragging a few feet behind, it still kept coming.

Eve raced back to help Cora.

"Take Delia," Cora shouted.

"Get up!" Eve shouted, trying her best to pull them all the while keeping her eyes on the alligator.

"I twisted my ankle," Cora shouted. "Get them in the car and get out of here!"

Eve looked up. The alligator was gaining. With Philip in one arm, she grabbed Delia, raced to the car, threw the children in the back and closed the door. Eve raced back to get Cora. She and the alligator were no more than six feet apart. Cora struggled to her feet, hopping forward on one foot, she slipped and fell a second time. Just as Eve reached her, so did the gator. Jaws open, it lunged and snapped. Eve jerked Cora away as razor teeth bit through a sliver of Cora's calf. Both women fell backwards into the mud. The gator advanced again. Eve and Cora scrambled back, desperately trying to regain their footing. The alligator, wild-eyed, with the taste of blood in his mouth, hissed and lunged for them. Eve saw the dragged tree limb catch in a tangle of roots and jerk the alligator back like a wild dog on a leash. It snapped, chomping at the air again and again, inches from the two women, but the net held. Eve was on her feet and pulling Cora. The car was only few a feet away. Behind them, they heard a roar... a howl of excruciating pain along with bones snapping and flesh ripping and then ... silence.

Eve was too terrified to look back. All she wanted to do was get herself and Cora into the car. When she reached the door she saw both Philip and Delia standing in the front driver's seat. Eve jerked the passenger door open and shoved Cora inside. Cora lifted Delia into her lap. Eve raced to the driver's side, scooped Philip into her arms, jumped in and slammed the door.

Breathless, Eve looked out, but she didn't see the alligator advancing.

"Where is it?" Eve said.

"I don't give a shit. Drive, damn it!" Cora shouted, tears streaming down her face.

She looked at Philip and then Delia. Totally calm, Philip climbed up into her lap to look out of the front windshield.

"Please, Eve! Go!" Cora shouted.

Eve's hand reached to start the car. She pushed the button. Nothing happened.

"No! No, no, no!" Cora shouted. "I took the keys because they had the little wine opener on the ring."

"What! Where are they?" Eve demanded.

"Out there." Cora said pointing back toward their picnic.

Both women looked out the window.

"Are you kidding me?" Eve said.

"I'm so sorry," Cora said, tears flooding her eyes. "What are we gonna do?"

"I have to go get the keys," Eve said.

"No!"

"Cora, we have no car keys and no phones. Your ankle is twisted and you've been bitten by a goddamn alligator, which leaves me one option unless you can give me another."

Cora was silent.

"How's your leg?"

"What?"

"It bit you?"

Cora looked down. She was bleeding. It was more like a vicious scrape and tear than a bite, but she was definitely bleeding.

"Hell, my ankle hurts so bad I don't even feel my leg," Cora said.

Eve grabbed the diaper they'd used to wipe their tears of laughter away and gently wrapped and pressed it on Cora's leg.

"I gotta get the key."

The two women looked at each other and then joined Delia and Philip to stare out the window.

"Take the tire iron," Cora said. "Now I know why my daddy always carried a gator gun in his car. And be careful. It's slippery as a mud slushy out there."

Eve nodded. She reached down to flip the latch that released the trunk. Slowly she opened the door.

"If I don't get back ..." Eve started.

"Shut the hell up and just get your narrow ass back here," Cora said. "I will not explain to Beau I let you get eaten by a damn alligator!"

Eve kissed and then lifted Philip up and slipped out from under him. She stepped back onto the soft ground. It was when the mud squished between her toes that she noticed she'd lost a shoe. With one bare foot she limped her way back to the trunk and opened it. Eve and Cora exchanged a look as Eve raised the mat and took the lug bar and the handle to the tire iron. The lug bar felt heavier. She took both.

"Be careful," Cora called out.

Eve took a long deep breath and closed the trunk. Slowly, cautiously, she walked back up a small mound of earth she hadn't even noticed before. She turned back to the car, realizing once she reached the other side, she would not be able to see Cora and the children and they wouldn't be able to see her. Her heart quickened. She turned her face forward and crested the little hill. She could see the white of the netting. It was still, frighteningly still. Beyond she could see the banyan tree where they had laid down their picnic. She moved closer. Her eyes locked on the bundle of netting. Within a few steps, she noticed something about the netting. It was covered in blood. Behind the bubble of white cloth that caught the breeze, Eve could see a lump of blood, guts and bones, flattened into the mud. As she got closer, the alligator's lower jaw, twisted and jutting out of what remained of its skull reached up out of the mud. Eve walked past and looked down at one of its dead eyes. It stared out from the flattened carcass. It looked as if a giant foot has stomped down on the alligator's body with as much force as a human foot decimating a huge bug and squishing it into pulp and goo.

Eve pulled the tire iron and lug wrench closer as she looked around.

"Eve!" Cora's voice called out from beyond the little knoll. Eve stood on her tippy toes and looked back. She could barely see the top of the car windshield. She could see Cora's head and a bit of Delia on the passenger's side. She caught Philip's hair and eyes, standing in the driver's seat, holding onto to the wheel, watching her with that calm expression.

"It's dead. I'm okay," Eve shouted.

"Then hurry, please," Cora shouted back.

She looked down one last time at what remained of the gator's skin, blood, guts and bones, mashed into the mud. She turned to the trail of stuff that had gotten caught in the net and gathered as much as she could putting what she could salvage into the two carry car seats; purses, sunglasses, keys of course, bottles, baskets, toys. She left the food and took the drinks and the basket.

Eve headed back to the car. She slowed to stare in disbelief at the remains of the alligator. For reasons she couldn't explain, she stopped, setting the carry seats down and dug in her purse for her cell phone. Eve snapped several shots from various angles before she headed back to the car.

Her mind kept flashing back to the image of the alligator as she opened the trunk and loaded everything up. She strapped the kids into their car seats then turned her attention to Cora. Her leg was bleeding badly. They exchanged glances in silence, grateful to all be alive. Gathering the keys and her phone, Eve slipped behind the wheel of the car and pushed the start button. The bayou was as still and quiet as if even the wildlife knew something was wrong.

"Was it gone?" Cora asked.

"Not exactly," Eve replied.

"Either it was gone or it was there."

"It was dead," Eve told her.

"Dead? How?" Cora asked.

Eve handed her the phone. A perplexed look of confusion traveled across Cora's face. Cora's leg was seized by a stab of pain so debilitating she dropped the phone so she could grab her leg.

"Owww," Cora moaned as she squeezed her leg to quell the pain.

"We're only a few miles from Thibodaux Hospital. Let's get you in there and get that looked at in case of some weird, nasty gator, swamp infection," Eve said as she drove back to the highway.

"Gator bites are the least of our problems. Sides, alligators have the purest blood on the planet. They have over twenty antibodies. I read they want to use their blood to cure super viruses including HIV," Cora said, babbling to help take her focus off the pain.

"Well, well, Cordelia Belle Bouvier, have you been studying medicine behind my back?"

"I'll have you know I dated two doctors and a Rhodes Scholar with his own pharmaceutical company. Things rub off when you have to talk between sex. Especially when they need recovery time, thank you."

The two women gave each other brave smiles. Cora reached down and picked up the phone. The photo of the gator on the screen stared back at her.

Cora looked at it for a second and then closed her eyes.

"Oh, my lord. What in tarnation could have done that?"

"I don't know," Eve replied. "I don't know."

Chapter Eleven

Eve sat on the waiting room couch of Thibodaux Hospital's emergency room. The children slept sprawled out on either side of her breathing softly, peaceful and innocent. How innocent though were the questions that pricked at her. The way Philip and Delia stood, fearlessly staring at eight feet of flesh-ripping, reptilian beast that would have gobbled them up in one quick bite. But it hadn't. There was the mosquito netting, the rope and tree limb, she and Cora, a combination of luck ... perhaps. But what killed it like that? It had been squashed dead by a ton of invisible *what* crashing from the sky. Eve looked down at her beautiful son. She ran her fingers gently through his curls. What happened was an enigma, one more piece of a puzzle without answers now more complicated and confusing than ever.

Eve was grateful they were all alive. That was the most important thing, wasn't it? They were alive and safe. Perhaps the odd vision of Cora being hurt was a premonition. She was attacked by something that wasn't human and an alligator is definitely not human. Dreams use symbols. Right? Maybe she was a psychic now, the coma awakening some dormant part of her brain. Maybe she had a vision and it saved them. It was sort of good logic although she'd never in her life shown any signs of psychic ability. Today it would have to be logical enough. Why didn't it make her feel better?

Her head hurt again. The headache was coming back. Eve slipped out from under the children's sleeping heads and made them a pillow of her jacket. She covered them with their traveling blankets and stood, reaching up to take a long stretch. Her muscles ached from the adrenalin rush that had slammed her body. She was certain she would feel even worse tomorrow. She'd washed her face, legs and arms as best she could. She found a few scars from the fall and her clothes were still caked with dried swamp mud. There was nothing she could do about that until she got home.

The waiting room was pleasant with pale pink, pastel green and pearl grey swooshes everywhere. The floors carried the same pattern as the walls. The bold design of bright colors shouted *be happy* at whoever was forced to sit for hours waiting for good news or bad. The room didn't care; it made the same *be happy* statement for everyone to see. Across the room, on the far wall, metal windows opened out onto the same quadrangle she'd looked at every day after she came out of her coma. There was grass, flowers, curved concrete walkways lined with smooth river stone, all framed by huge philodendron vines. Their massively wide, waxy leaves grew between the birds of paradise, hyacinths and other colorful, tropical flowers Eve was sure were not indigenous to the Louisiana bayou region.

Eve studied the grounds, doing her best to shift her mind off the past and into the present. Her eyes stopped at a tall circular tower that climbed five stories into the surrounding oak trees. It sat at the farthest end of the complex, jutting off a long, single-story wing of the hospital that stretched along the grounds, unconnected to anything else. It seemed to crash into the tower, offering only one way in, one way out. A chill ran up her spine. Her head starting hurting worse. Eve was certain she'd been inside, but how and when and why eluded her? Perhaps, she thought, it was during all the months of rehabilitation to strengthen her muscles. Her head pounded again, a pounding that seemed to say ... *no, Eve, it was something else.*

"I just heard Eve. I'm glad you're all okay," a woman's voice said.

Eve turned to see her psychotherapist, Dr. Lisette Honoré, looking at the children.

"They are so adorable. What little angels. How are you?" Dr. Honoré asked.

"Shaken. A few scratches. Okay, I guess," Eve said then looked at Delia and Philip. "The kids are obviously unaffected by the whole thing," Eve added.

"They're so young, they probably won't remember a thing especially if they didn't get hurt," Dr. Honoré explained. "Do you remember if they registered extreme fear?"

"No, not really any emotion at all," Eve said.

"Then they will probably have no emotional connections to scar them. How's Cora?"

"She's waiting for bacteria test results from her scratch. Just to make sure she didn't pick anything up from the gator or the swamp mud."

"How about you, Eve?" Dr. Honoré asked.

"I'm fine. My scratches were negative," Eve said.

"Good. Better safe than sorry, right?"

"Right?"

Dr. Honoré looked down at the children. Eve saw her brow furrow. "How old are they?" she asked.

"Philip is eighteen months and Delia is fourteen months," Eve said.

"Really! I would have thought they were into their terrible twos or threes seeing how tall they both are. Amazing," she said. "Your son is beautiful as is Cora's Delia. I would have thought Philip rather than Delia would show more of a resemblance to Mister Le Masters under the circumstances."

The words obviously slipped out from the expression of *oh shit, I didn't mean to say that out loud* that splashed across Dr. Honoré's face.

"Please pretend I didn't say that, Eve," Dr. Honoré said.

"Please, Doctor Honoré, I've thought it myself. You're my shrink, and if you can't say it, who can?"

"Well, we're not in the sanctuary of a session. Forgive me and tell me how you are? I mean, other than this most recent drama."

Eve looked at her. She'd fought Dr. Honoré in their sessions, mostly because she was struggling to remember the pieces of her dreams that made no sense. Eve didn't want to take the medication Dr. Honoré had recommended for her hallucinations. Her life before the coma stopped the night of the party. All of her memories from her past were intact, but the horrible dreams, or pieces of dreams, that caused her the headaches, like the one she was having right now, were disjointed. They came from a time that didn't seem to fit into her life, yet she knew she had to find out when and where the dreams came from because they were more than dreams, they were real past experiences and somehow she believed she'd lived them. *But how? And how the hell do you talk to a shrink about that, especially if you want them to not think you're crazy, put you on psychotropic drugs and lock you away?*

"Eve," Dr. Honoré called her from her thoughts.

"Yes. Sorry. I was just wondering, other than a hospital and a convalescent facility, what else goes on here?" Eve asked.

"A lot actually and not just for my specialty in brain injuries and studies. I know the hospital does a variety of very different kinds of research. I've seen grant proposals for everything from geriatric longevity studies to in vitro fertilization and genetic research. You know how research doctors are. Everyone can be very hush-hush about their work. I understand the hospital has some patients with rare diseases isolated here, but it's a rather large facility that covers over eighty acres and I can't tell you where they are held."

"Why would rare diseases research be here?" Eve asked.

"The bayou is semi-tropical and there have been some outbreaks of Hantavirus Pulmonary Syndrome, rare virus and bacteria. You know as these oil and gas companies drill into the land and poison the aquifer, they wake up all kinds of micro-organisms and strange bacteria and viruses, shaking them from their primitive states of suspended hibernation that would otherwise have kept them buried and forgotten deep in the earth's layers for eternity. If it's something you're interested in, I could ask for more information. You and Mr. Le Masters are the kind of private donor sources we welcome to create grants for research."

Eve's eyes turned back to the window and without thinking, she pointed across the back compound.

"What is that wing and the tower it connects to for?" Eve asked.

Dr. Honoré's eyes followed Eve's pointing finger to the wing and the long corridor that led to the tower.

"I've only been here for eighteen months and have been very focused on my own division so I'm not really sure." Dr. Honoré explained. "And don't you have a wedding coming up?"

"Six weeks," Eve said and gave a perfunctory smile.

"Are you excited?"

"It's ... still a bit overwhelming. I'm so tired and with everything I'm doing, I'm not sleeping very well," Eve said with a long, deep exasperated sigh.

"Then the dreams haven't stopped?"

"What? Why do you ask?" Eve asked.

"That's what you used to say when they were bothering you. Have the headaches and hallucinations come back as well?" Dr. Honoré asked.

"Dr, Honoré, is it possible to ... um ... get 'abilities' from a head injury?"

"Abilities?" Dr. Honoré asked.

"I was thinking that maybe some of the dreams and visions I'm having are kind of ... precognitive."

"Something you're getting consistently?"

"More than once? Yes. Something bad happening to Cora and, well ... maybe I knew something," Eve said, doing her best to explain without sounding the way she felt - like a piece of china cracking apart.

"Well, there are all kinds of studies about cranial facial injuries opening neurological pathways, some negative and some positive. Do you want me to order some more MRIs?"

"No. No more MRIs please. Could we just talk about it more?" Eve asked her.

Eve wanted to trust her, but she worked here and here was the last place she wanted to come back to ever.

"But the dreams and hallucinations have returned? Yes?" Dr. Honoré asked, this time a little more emphatically.

"Yes, they have. I want to talk to you, just not here," Eve confessed.

"I understand. Look, I just took an office on Wednesdays in Algiers. Call my assistant, Gerry, and ask her to give you an appointment for tomorrow. Maybe talking about things will help get you feeling happier about your life, your family and your wedding," Dr. Honoré said.

Eve smiled. "I'd like to feel better, Doctor."

God she wanted that—to be happy, to feel safe and enjoy being alive.

"I promise I'll call and make an appointment," Eve said.

"Good idea. I'll do some research, look over your charts and see, based on the damaged area of your skull, what you may have knocked loose. I'm sure we can figure it out," Dr. Honoré smiled. It was a warm and reassuring smile that made Eve feel relaxed. "Call me."

Dr. Honoré turned and walked back down the hallway. Just as she disappeared down one corridor, Cora's housekeeper, Miss Clarisse, walked in from the other corridor. The panic in her eyes said it all. She was very concerned. Miss Clarisse moved with the speed and stamina of a much younger woman. She looked great for her seventy years and her being there added one more needed layer of security for Eve.

First Miss Clarisse checked the children to make sure they were okay and then she rushed over to throw her arms around Eve.

"You're okay? How's Cora?" Miss Clarisse asked.

"They're running some tests. They think she twisted her ankle, but the bigger issue is the bite," Eve explained.

"Bite!"

"Yes, I didn't want you driving in full panic mode. It was more of a scratch according to Cora," Eve said.

Tears welled up in Miss Clarisse's eyes.

"If anything were to ever happen I—"

"It didn't. She's fine. We're all fine," Eve said as she shifted the embrace to hold Miss Clarisse.

Miss Clarisse pulled back and wiped her eyes, composing herself as best she could.

"Oui, bien sur mon belle. Pardon," Miss Clarisse said.

"Hey, nothing to be sorry for. You love Cora like a mother and she feels the same way about you. We all love you Miss Clarisse."

Miss Clarisse gave a small smile as she smoothed her dress.

Eve hadn't heard her speak French patois or full-on French for that matter in a long time. It came out when she was angry or stressed or feeling very, very relaxed. She and Cora used to converse in it all the time. Eve had learned a few words because Cora insisted and then high school and college French had taken her down the more classic path. But she knew some of the words unique to Cajun patois. The derivations were just home grown enough to have subtle differences to make those who spoke it fit in a special club.

"Miss Clarisse? Can you watch the children for a bit? I want to inquire about Cora and get something for my headache," Eve asked.

"Of course," she said and crossed to them. "You should call Mister Gregoire and give him an update. He was upset you didn't want him to come down."

"I will. It didn't make sense for us all to be down here. I can drive home just fine. Miss Clarisse, I have always wondered why you call Beau Mister Gregoire and not Le Masters?"

Miss Clarisse all but sneered in disgust before she nonchalantly answered.

"He will never be a Le Masters. That boy is a Gregoire, plain and simple, just like his babies. That's just a fact and if you knew the history, you could understand why I think ..." Miss Clarisse stopped herself. "We'll it doesn't matter what I think."

"Yes it does," Eve said.

"You should take the Gregoire name and so should these children. There I said it," Miss Clarisse said.

"But ... why?" Eve asked.

"A name carries the weight of its ancestry and Le Masters is ... well ... you don't want to burden yourself or these little ones with what and who the Le Masters have buried in their closets. The Gregoires have more than enough history to fill a book. Don't ask about such stuff anymore, Miss Eve. Alright? Promise me. Now please go and find Miss Cora so we can get out of here. I don't like this place. Never have. Never will."

Eve knew from past experience that Miss Clarisse had spoken her mind and that was the end of the conversation. She walked to Philip and kissed him gently on the forehead and then gave an extra kiss for Delia. From Miss Clarisse's expression, Eve knew the discussion of the Le Masters name had opened an old and very deep wound.

"Can I ask you one question, Miss Clarisse?" Eve said.

"Of course child," Miss Clarisse responded.

"Do you know if the Gregoire legacy ever had anything to do with something called Grimoires?" Eve asked.

Miss Clarisse grabbed her chest. She blessed herself and mumbled a prayer in Patois. Eve couldn't understand much other than, *keep us safe from the dark spirits* and the final word *Nephilim*. A word Eve knew, but like her shadowy dreams, she didn't know from where.

Miss Clarisse looked up at her with a cold, even look.

"What's a Nephilim?" Eve asked.

"Shush up! You shouldn't even be saying their name!" Miss Clarisse said.

"Please," Eve begged.

"The darkest of the demons, old and steeped in Voodoo. The same black magic that was born out of the ancient Grimoires," Miss Clarisse said.

"Grimoires? I know that..." Eve stared.

"Hesh! Never, ever say the Gregoire name in the same breath with that dark practice," Miss Clarisse said. "Do not even think it, Eve. Promise me."

Miss Clarisse's face flushed and her breathing quickened. A true look of fear fell over her like a dark shadow. "You promise me!"

"I... I promise," Eve said. "I promise."

Chapter Twelve

Eve stopped briefly by the nurse's station to inquire about Cora. The response was that they were still waiting for possible infection test results.

The nurse added, "It'll probably be another half hour."

Eve sighed, walked down the corridor and stepped outside onto the quadrangle. She lifted her head to feel the last of the afternoon sun on her face as she walked down the lovely, stone-lined path. She breathed the air. The beauty of the trees and hedges, foliage and flowers seemed to ease her headache. *Better fresh air than drugs* she thought and walked farther down the path. On her right, the bayou lake that centered the lush beauty of the place sparkled, catching the sunlight in tiny ripples and making the light dance with every passing breeze. The tall, narrow tower and its single wing caught her attention. Eve turned and walked closer. She shook her head remembering the "rare disease research" explanation she had received from Dr. Honoré and stopped, thinking germs were not what she needed today or ever for that matter, if indeed this was the disease research wing. She turned left and moved away when she heard children playing to her right. She felt compelled to follow the sound of the children laughing and playing. *Odd to put the children's playground near a rare disease research wing,* she thought. As she drew closer she could see a small playground filled with children peeking between the rows of fichus trees. The children, some as old as twelve and others as young as Philip and Delia, seemed normal.

There were at least twenty that she could count. The older ones helped the younger ones and a few nurses oversaw their play time. One young woman rushed past Eve, carrying a little boy in her arms who reminded her of Philip. He was a little older, but with the same amazing black curls. The child looked at Eve, smiled and dropped a small stuffed tiger he was holding. From the mischievous smile the child flashed her, there was no question the act was intentional. Eve rushed over and gathered up the tiger.

"Miss? He dropped ... he dropped his tiger. Miss?" Eve called out.

The woman turned. She looked back to see Eve holding the tiger.

"Thank you," she said and she crossed back to retrieve it. When she reached Eve, the little boy reached his arms out to Eve.

Both Eve and the young woman shared a look of surprise.

"Well, that never happens," the young woman said.

"Take me," said the little boy.

"Okay, that really never happens," the young woman said.

The boy reached harder for Eve and started to get upset.

"I'll hold him if you're comfortable?" Eve said to her.

The little boy squirmed and struggled, fighting to get to Eve. The young girl relented and shifted the little boy into Eve's arms. The little boy smiled. He touched Eve's face with such a sense of recognition it baffled both Eve and the girl. Suddenly he threw his arms around her and hugged her as if she was his long lost savior and best friend.

"Aw, well aren't you the sweetest," Eve said and lovingly hugged him back.

"That's just it, he isn't. He won't let anyone hold him but me," the young woman said.

"Well, I am honored ...," Eve said to the little boy, glancing at the young woman as a hint for the child's name.

"Robert."

Eve stopped and turned her gaze to Robert, "Hi Robert, I'm Eve," Eve said and then turned to the young woman. "And you are?"

"Azura. Azura Peete," Azura said.

"Azura. What a pretty and very unusual name. I ... I seem to remember meeting someone by that name ...," she fumbled for the memory. "Huh ... I just can't remember where or when. You even look familiar, but I don't remember where."

"That is funny. There's something familiar about you too. What is your name?"

"Eve Dowling. I was here at the hospital for a long time," Eve said, feeling the need to explain herself. "I gave birth to my son here. Philip is eighteen months, though you couldn't tell by looking at him. He's gotten so big. Robert's four or five?"

"He's two and a half. I thought he was big for his age, but based on the size of the other children here, he's ... average," Azura said.

"Well, Philip's father is tall," Eve added.

A strange look clouded Azura's face as she reached for Robert.

"I'm sure we met in one of the mother sessions or something. I remember your voice. You have a kind voice," Azura said to Eve as she reached for her son. "We have to go."

Robert held Eve tightly.

"No!" the child shouted.

"You better come right now. You have your lessons and you know how upset Doctor—" Azura said and stopped herself, her eyes shifting to Eve.

"No!" the defiant two year old shouted.

"Please let him go."

Eve gently opened her arms, but the child clung on tighter than a monkey to a pole. Azura extracted her son as gently as she could. She whispered something into his ear and the boy relaxed and went obediently into Azura's arms. The shift caused Azura to drop all she was holding. The two women bent down, Eve helping her gather her things.

"There's a school here?" Eve asked.

"If you call it that."

"What kind of school?" Eve asked.

There was a long pregnant pause. Azura studied Eve's face. Eve could see her thinking as she put the last few things inside her bag.

"I'm considering schools for my son," Eve said.

"You have to be ... invited. It's for the highly gifted. Parents aren't even allowed to visit the children once they go in," Azura said. "It's okay though, I guess. He's smart and strong and..."

"Azura!" a man's voice called from across the playground. "You're going to be late. You two need to hurry."

Eve looked up and followed Azura's gaze to a stern man waiting in white. Behind her the last of the children entered the tower.

"Azura, may I ask you a question?" Eve asked.

"We have to go."

"Of course, I just wondered ... if you lived here."

"We all do," she replied. "Come on," she added to her son and turned to go.

"Please take me with you," the little boy said to Eve.

His arms reached out to her and his eyes held a look of fear and sadness that ripped Eve's heart out.

"Bo, behave," Azura said.

Hearing the child called Beau sent a shiver down her spine.

"You call him Bo?" Eve asked.

"Short for Robert," Azura said. "Sounds nice, don't cha think?"

"Azura!" The doctor called out to her again. This time more impatiently.

Eve watched as Azura hurried away and caught up with the doctor who stood impatiently waiting for her. They spoke. The conversation was rapid fire. It appeared to be an agitated exchange and twice the Doctor looked up at Eve. Robert or Bo, never took his eyes off of Eve. In a few seconds they were inside the door, which closed solidly behind them.

Eve's head started pounding. Why did a strange child want her to take him ... beg her to take him.

Eve moved toward the door then thought better and circled around to the lakeside, thinking she might not be noticed as much if she came up around the back.

Once off the path the same mud that had trapped her back at the bayou squished up into the thick grass. The grass started to thin the closer she came to the lake. Eve glanced into the front lobby as she passed. The entry was two stories high, a circular atrium with a black and white floor. A coiled stairway with an oak-railed balcony connected the first to the second floor. She tried the door, but it was locked and a key card was needed to get inside. Eve couldn't help but notice that the key pad was very new.

The sound of the children's voices somewhere in the back beckoned her forward. As she drew closer it was what they were chanting that slowed her pace. They were speaking in Farsi or Arabic, maybe Egyptian. She wasn't sure other than she knew it to be based on one of the Middle Eastern languages. She'd done three articles for the magazine about the Middle East and two interviews with interpreters. She'd even done a quick, three-week intensive on Middle Eastern and Saudi culture when a Saudi sheik came with his entourage to experience Mardi Gras and Louisiana hospitality. The words were definitely some version of one of those ancient languages, but which one Eve couldn't begin to tell. She'd dated a Persian from Iran for a minute, but this was different. Eve listened harder as she inched closer. She felt the light shift and dim as the afternoon sun began to sink low over the lake. It turned the sky to shades of lavender, peach, rose and gold. Each color reflected back to its source perfectly mirrored in the lake. The wind stopped, the water stilled, adding to the eerie silence interrupted only by the voices of the children.

She came to the very last window; French, prewar with metal casings. It had four panes each and curved metal handles that cranked out to open. The metal frame had been painted over so many times, the thickness of the paint made it hard to close. The last window was slightly cracked tempting Eve forward. Carefully, she peeked in and saw seven or eight boys and girls who looked about nine or ten in size sitting in a circle. They repeated the same words over and over again, speaking together and carefully articulating each syllable.

"Body, mind," Eve said, translating two of the words she understood.

The next few words were Persian, but not Farsi or Arabic. They were older, more ancient. She felt sure of it. Suddenly, the last word stuck out.

"... Nephilim ..." the children said.

Nephilim, she thought. "That's what Miss Clarisse said. I know this word."

"What word?" a voice said behind her.

Eve turned and found a thin man in a white lab coat with thinning hair and dead, dark eyes staring at her.

"Are you lost?" he asked.

"I saw how beautiful the sunset was and wanted to walk down to the lake to get a better look," Eve said, lying.

She could feel the nervousness in her voice. She could tell from his icy, even stare, he wasn't buying the lie.

"Really?" he said, turning his gaze momentarily to the sunset. "Yes, it's beautiful."

Another moment of silence and he gestured for her to walk closer to the banks of the lake for a better look.

"Come. We can walk together. Are you a patient here?" he asked.

"Yes, well, not now. I meant, I was a patient," Eve said.

She really didn't want to get closer to the lake. She just wanted to get the hell out of there. Besides his beady eyes, he had a strange smell. She looked at his ID badge.

"What kind of doctor are you, Doctor Schuler?" Eve asked.

"PhD, not MD. I'm an educator," Dr. Schuler said.

"I heard the children speaking ..." Eve stopped.

"Ancient Assyrian," Dr. Schuler said, finishing her sentence. "They're learning Ancient Egyptian, Greek, Latin and Sanskrit."

"Why would they need to learn dead languages, Doctor?" Eve asked.

He smiled at Eve. "These languages are the foundation of the world's greatest modern languages. We have found, when the children learn the basic etymology of these particular languages, it opens a host of neurological pathways and triggers brain waves escalating the ability to learn and retain all information, not just derivative languages, but also math, science, music. The pathways allow access to several of their higher cognitive functions."

"Higher cognitive functions?"

"My apologies, surely I'm boring you," he said.

"On the contrary, I'm fascinated. I would be very interested in learning more."

Again there was a long pregnant pause. He studied her the way a frog studied a dragonfly right before he devoured it. Eve's phone rang in her pocket. She grabbed it and read Cora's name in the screen.

"They're looking for me," Eve said as she quickly sent a text back saying she would be right there.

"I'm sorry. I didn't catch your name?" Dr. Akin Schuler said.

"Eve Dowling," Eve said offering her hand.

"Yes. Eve. A pleasure to meet you," Dr. Schuler said.

He took her hand and Eve shivered as if someone had laid a cold dead fish against her fingers. The iciness made her look into his eyes.

"Please come back again, Ms. Dowling," he said. "Have a lovely evening."

Dr. Schuler turned to walk back into the tower, stopped and faced Eve.

"Please be careful driving back. People can be so reckless on the roads at night," he said, smiling with that same weird creepiness before he went back inside.

Eve hurried back up the path glancing one last time at the gathering of children inside the room, who were now standing. They looked so emotionless.

She crossed the quadrangle and her phone rang again. This time it was Beau. She answered.

"Hi, we're just getting ready to head home," Eve said into the receiver.

"I thought when we spoke you were heading back," his voice said through the tinny speaker.

"They wanted to run a few more tests for infections on Cora," Eve said, talking as she walked. "She just called and they are all done. We're all fine. Let me go get everyone in the car and we'll be home in a few hours. We'll be tired and hungry, but we'll be safely home."

"Drive carefully, but hurry. I need to kiss you and hold Philip and Delia."

"I could use a few kisses myself. Miss Clarisse came down. She'll take Cora and Delia so you'll be stuck with Philip and me," Eve said smiling at the thought.

"Holding my breath until you two get here," Beau said, and hung up.

She opened the door to the main hospital, shaking off the uneasy feeling that clawed at her. She wanted to find her son, Cora, Delia and Miss Clarisse and get the hell out. She wanted to find out what the Nephilim was and what it had to do with the Gregoire line.

Chapter Thirteen

The drive home was long and boring, but the eerily prophetic warning from the creepy doctor heightened Eve's senses so much so, she drove a little slower and a lot more carefully. Along the way she passed a stop sign and saw the aftermath of an eighteen wheeler truck that had smashed into a minivan. The van was crushed beyond recognition and whoever was inside could not have survived the impact. She, like all the others who passed, found herself unable to look away from the carnage and death. For a moment she let her mind race into a "what if" ... *I had been driving faster, might it have been Philip and me?* The thought rattled around her brain for the next twenty minutes, harking back to the incident with the alligator. In the end, she decided that if she wasn't psychic, she was lucky and blessed and grateful for it.

Eve arrived home, her body aching from all the tension and adrenaline of the day. Beau was asleep in the big chair that centered the front parlor a bouquet of sterling silver roses sat in a vase nearby. She loved the romantic in him. Quietly, Eve slipped upstairs, fed and bathed Philip while Aria readied the small, sweet nursery for Philip's repose. Eve touched one of the toys from Beau's childhood. She'd found them stuffed inside old, dust covered trunks and stickered suit cases, some that reached generations back in the Gregoire family. Lovingly, she'd brought them back into the light of the world. Some were so fragile they could never be played with again. There were trains and carriages, trucks and cars sitting with their worn wheels, chipped and missing parts, dolls and animals with faded faces and missing eyes, loved and played with by distant members of the Gregoire family.

Once he was cleaned and dressed in his favorite pajamas, Eve took Philip and rocked back and forth in the glider, smiling at her son as she softly sang a song her mother had sung to her.

"I love you forever. I love you for always. No matter the journey your Mommy I'll be. And when you are sleeping and when you're awake, imagine the magic of all you can be. We'll ride up on ponies and sail on the sea; grow wings and fly into starlight. I'll love you forever. I'll love you for always. I'll love you forever, just as you love me," she sang.

Her voice drifted into a whisper just as Beau slipped into the room. He smiled and kissed her forehead and stroked his son's pale blonde curls. Beau looked into Eve's eyes and gently kissed her lips. He started to speak, but she placed her finger to his lips and nodded to the sleeping Philip. Beau slipped his arms under hers and lifted his sleeping son, gently carrying him over to his crib. Eve stood, stretched and crossed behind him, watching the sweet love and care Beau had for his baby boy. She slipped her arms around Beau's waist as he laid Philip on his little pillow. Together they covered him and gave him one more kiss before they slipped out of the room.

In the hall, he hugged her as he said, "I don't know what I would have done if you hadn't been okay today."

She could feel the love and sadness in his embrace.

"I promise, no more picnics in the bayou," she said.

Eve took him to the kitchen and fixed Beau a bite to eat. They shared the horrors of the day - both hers and his. The lawyers, the court, the problem with the pepper farmer and how he wanted them to increase the yield. Beau said he wished he'd studied agriculture at university. They talked as they brushed teeth and hair and slipped into pajamas. Eve smiled. She felt like an old married couple and decided she wasn't ready to shoulder that mantle just yet. But truth be told, it was a harrowing day and she was so exhausted she fell asleep in the middle of her sentence.

Eve drifted in and out of sleep. The alligator, crawling into her dreams, kept awakening her. Laying in the dark, her mind spinning, she started thinking about the hospital, the children, and the things Azura and the weird doctor had said. And, as for Dr. Honoré, she would make an appointment tomorrow. She couldn't remember going to Algiers. It was just across the Mississippi, but there was never a story assignment or a reason until now. Yet, something deep inside her said, "Yes, you did." She had been there once before. *But when and why?* These were the thoughts that kept her awake the rest of the night. Dr. Honoré told her that her concussion and coma could have triggered "higher cognitive functions" and "precognitive thought" was a possibility. Maybe the crushed alligator was something she did with her mind. After all there were numerous documented stories of mothers lifting cars when their children were trapped inside; "hysterical strength" was one term she'd found.

"Stop," she softly pleaded to herself.

Finally, her mind quieted. In that momentary silence, one word spoken by the group of children at the hospital came back into her mind. *Nephilim.*

"Nephilim," she repeated out loud.

Miss Clarisse had forbad it even to be uttered. She knew that word. But why ... and from where?

Quietly, Eve slipped out of bed and into her cream-colored cashmere robe with corded ribbons of cocoa velvet trimming its edges. Normally she wouldn't have liked such fancy things. She'd always been a cotton, terry cloth and flannel kind of girl, but this felt like slipping into warm, fuzzy fluff. It was a gift from Beau and it always made her feel warm and good.

Eve went down to the front parlor, which she'd converted into her office. From here she managed the day to day details of her life from the renovation to her impending wedding. She used it to oversee the redo of the big house and handle some personal business; things she still needed to get done for herself and most importantly, there was the wedding. Secretly she thought, after the wedding and Philip got settled into preschool, perhaps she'd write some articles or, heaven help her, a novel in her cozy office. Beau, as modern a man as he was, wasn't very keen on the idea of her working. He wanted her to help with the Estate and, of course, more children. She too wanted more children and that the house be filled with the sounds of laughter, family and music. But that was someday. For now her desk was covered with letters, linen invitations and requests to use the house for cultural events from charitable foundations already affiliated with the Gregoire name, family trust and friends. The Estate's "duties" alone were more than enough to occupy her time.

Eve fired up her computer, Googled the word Nephilim and found hundreds of pages of information; references in the Torah and Old Testament of the Christian Bible said they were the *first creations, fallen angels, people of the fire, giants, the bloodlines of Noah and Ham.* According to one group of writings, the great flood was sent to destroy their lineage, but the bloodline survived through Ham's wife and spread through their children and their children's children. Others said the great flood erased them all. The biblical references also described the Nephilim as giant, human-looking, immortal beings, one third of whom defied God and were condemned to hell.

There were multiple passages in the Torah, Bible and Koran that talked about the existence of the Nephilim. She couldn't find anything that described exactly what they had done to incur such wrath from their creator other than a few passages in the Book of Genesis. According to the ancient writings, the Nephilim became obsessed and uncontrollably sexually aroused by the long, beautiful hair of human women - *straight, wavy or curly, black, auburn, red or gold,* it didn't matter. The Nephilim defied their creator and descended to earth so they could interbreed with womankind. It said their offspring became a distinct and separate species; a few to this day still live among humans on earth. Their decedents remain hidden, their powers fading and forgotten, their names and memories torn from the pages of history, their spawn hunted by the Templar Knights until all were erased. Eve sat back and thought of the ancient Gregoire bible. Who were those Gregoire men and women ripped from the tattered and torn out pages and what was their lost legacy?

Eve's computer pinged softly as an interesting scientific article appeared on the screen that referenced ancient pictographs, and scrolls found near the Dead Sea. They told of "visitors," Advanced Beings, who arrived on earth and caused man to evolve from Cro Magnon to Homo Sapien. Scientists tracked DNA in skeletal remains believed to belong to the Nephilim because of their enormous size ranging from 12-to-35 feet tall. Some believed the Nephilim were genetically engineered by these Advanced Beings to interbreed with humans because the Beings were unable to do so themselves. The offspring of the Nephilim and humans were designed to inherit a greater intellectual capacity. Eventually a select few would begin a process that would repopulate the world with a new breed of "advanced" humans who would lead a race of "lesser humans" when the Beings left. Some scientists believed the "lesser humans" were to be used to mine precious metals the Advanced Beings needed for their own world.

Eve read how scientists believed the Beings endowed the Nephilim with shape shifting abilities so they would be pleasing to human women when they seduced them. The Advanced Beings made one critical mistake: they thought they had engineered their creations to be mortal and therefore controllable, an assumption that quickly proved to be false. The Nephilim were immortal and, in their pure form, almost as powerful as the Beings. This fact coincided with the religious writings Eve had discovered. Unable to control their creations, the Beings sought to destroy the Nephilim. The Great Flood was their first effort, but it almost destroyed all of humanity as well. They then attempted to capture and banish the Nephilim by trapping them between dimensions in a void that human mythologies spoke of as Hades or Hell; Tartarus, the deepest cosmic pit of Hades was reserved for the worst Nephilim who ever lived named Kirakin. Eve ran her fingers over the name. There was something familiar about that name.

"Kirakin," she said softly to herself.

She thought she knew it, but she knew she'd never read it in any history, religious or mythology book or class she'd ever taken. Eve read on learning that Kirakin and his kind were to be sealed forever inside this inescapable pit for all eternity. She was surprised to see that these were from the lost writing of Homer and other ancient Greeks. Over the millenniums his name had changed and evolved, but the stories remained the same. Part religious tales, part past mythologies depending on who told the tale. Eve pushed away from the computer wondering if these Nephilim tales were inspiration for Dante's thirty-four verse canto masterpiece, "The Inferno."

Right as she was about to get up, she made the mistake of clicking one last link. It and Google led her down another series of rabbit holes. After several more clicks she found a particularly fascinating site that told how the Nephilim possessed the ability to change the color of their skin and even make themselves invisible to the human eye. Another section detailed the Nephilim's unparalleled sexual passion and the raw sensuality they exuded when they made love. It was determined from the ancient writings that once a human woman made love to a Nephilim, a human man could rarely satisfy them again. Human men became jealous and denied the Nephilim access to women by creating laws and convincing women the Nephilim were vile demons and if they had intercourse with a Nephilim, they and their offspring would be put to death. The Nephilim were banished from the world of the humans. Enraged, the Nephilim left earth, but vowed to return because of their insatiable inability to resist the lure and beauty of human women, the obsessive need to play in their hair, an addition that could never be quelled.

Eve absentmindedly ran her fingers through her hair as she read about the plight of the Nephilim. She turned away from the computer screen and looked in the mirror. Her hair had just enough wave to catch the light and add dimension to its beauty. Beau loved playing with her hair. As far as the Nephilim were concerned and the stories of their superior, sexual prowess, Eve had to smile to herself, knowing Beau had them beat hands down as a lover.

The final site that caught her tired eyes was called, the SECRET OF THE FEMININE; THE COMING MAGI. EVE, First Womankind: Mother of all, sister, daughter, creator. Eve saw her name and clicked on the site.

"Let me say first," the writer wrote, "Earth was paradise. Earth was the Garden of Eden and we lived in peace never needing anything to survive but the sun, the water and the plants that grew from the soil that gave us air to breath. There was peace among all creatures. Mother earth was in balance until the Immortals came and created the Nephilim. Let me also say, Eve, this epitomized version of womankind who lived in the Garden of Eden, did not receive carnal knowledge from the devil disguised as a snake, but from a Nephilim. Ancient writings explained that the snake was a metaphor for the Nephilim and the forbidden apple for carnal knowledge and sexual bliss; knowledge not just of the mind, but of the feminine body and how it could be utilized as a portal through a state of bliss into other dimensions."

Eve's eyes felt tired, but her mind raced, fascinated by the possibility of other beings co-existing in the universe, entering our world through portals and fissures between dimensions that led in and out of other universes. Giants who could shift their shapes to become man-sized at will. The ancient writings were proven to have come from the Dead Sea Scrolls carried into Mesopotamian, Assyrian, Greek, Egyptian, Nubian and Roman stories twisted and retold until they evolved into religions and mythologies that defined the offspring of "Gods," which eventually all pointed back to the Advanced Beings who created the Nephilim. Even recent scientific discoveries pointed to the existence of the Nephilim, including giant skeletons found by more than one modern archaeological team in the Fertile Crest.

Eve combed through every page on the site until she found the "About" page which contained a picture of a women who appeared to be in her sixties. She had long, thick, salt and pepper hair and dark, mysterious, deep-set eyes. She was a timeless, classic beauty with high cheek bones and full lips. The woman was born in Persia's Iran/Iraq region in the Fertile Crest near the place where the first city of the civilized world, Uruk, once stood. It was in what was known as Mesopotamia as told by the reliefs on the Inanna temples of Karaindas. Her bio said she now lived outside of Cairo, Egypt and her name was Dr. Afrine Kasatah PhD. MD. Eve studied her picture wondering if Dr. Afrine Kasatah possessed the answers she was seeking.

Afrine claimed to be directly descended from the true line of humanity's first mother, Eve. Some believe the first woman "Eve" was the daughter of God, whose offspring became Mages and the ancient alchemists of Susa. Afrine's website offered irrefutable proof of her claim and declared she and a few select others knew the location of the last hidden Ziggurats, its city of gold and its secret portals to others dimensions. Afrin hinted that this city was built just north of the mound of Chogha Zanbil thousands of years before the more famous Ziggurat, now in ruins, built by King Untash Huban, ever existed. Her website displayed pictures of the ruins of once great pyramids and hinted that their sister structures lay still undiscovered in the Zargos Mountains and the Golan Heights. Some of the daughters of Eve and the Nephilim became what history called the Amazonian Women. They passed their secrets and sexual mysteries of the feminine down through generations before their cities and culture were obliterated and their achievements were stolen and erased from history. These women, five millennia ago, stood eight feet tall, proof they were the female descendants of the Nephilim. Afrine's site provided historical and biblical references along with example after example of complex ancient carvings and drawings from Sumer, maps of stars, galaxies, nebulas and planets not yet discovered by man. Afrine believed the Nephilim's presence had profound astronomical significance, especially if their ancestors came from the stars.

Eve bookmarked Afrine's web page before she reread Afrine's claim that she was not the last descendant of the daughter of God or Supreme Beings: at least one other, more powerful than she, lived.

Eve felt the weight of the sleepless night close in on her. Her eyes began to blur and sleep called to her demanding she lay down and rest, but in the still of the morning, she heard the first sounds of Philip crying for her. Her body commanded her to find the strength to go to her son.

Eve stood, but looked back one last time at the screen. She focused on Dr. Afrine Kasatah's contact number in Cairo. She picked up her phone and punched in the numbers. The phone rang its strange foreign tone, echoing again and again across the long distance line. A ping drew Eve's eyes back to the computer screen as a thumbnail picture popped up. It was of a square, granite image carved with some kind of ancient cuneiform symbol. A small message flashed below in red urgent letters that read, "Eve, hurry! They are here and you alone know what to do. Remember who you are."

She watched as the image exploded into fine particles, filling the screen with a bright shimmering light that fell like grains of glowing sand down the screen, but not before the pictograph and red words underneath had seared into her brain. Blinded by a light so brilliant, so powerful her whole body began to tremble. She closed her eyes fumbling with the phone to set it back into the cradle. Eve slammed the lid of her computer shut. She tried to stand, but her legs felt like they had melted. Philip screamed louder and her eyes adjusted as the room reappeared around her. Eve looked back at her phone. The number for Afrine was there in the display until the foreign tone abruptly disconnected and the display screen went to black.

It had my name, she thought, *written on the screen*. A message to her? A path to find the answers she so desperately wanted ... needed? Philip cried again.

Chapter Fourteen

The morning dragged into the afternoon and Eve found herself exhausted and irritable, desperately needing to talk to someone about what was happening to her, what she was discovering and how disturbed she felt. She'd called Cora, but Cora said the phone was no place to discuss the old New Orleans's, rumor mill about Beau and his family. She said it was a story she had wanted to share at the bayou right before the alligator attacked.

"Maybe it's time you knew the dark side of the Gregoire history. What the old folks called the Gregoire curse," Cora said.

Cora told her that she and Delia would come by for dinner and before Beau returned, she would share everything she knew.

"But," Cora added, "If we're gonna open that Pandora's Box, we are gonna have to be very careful, Eve. Please, promise me."

Eve wasn't sure what the words meant, but she could hear fear in Cora's tone.

Eve had made the appointment to see her therapist, Dr. Honoré. She tried several times to talk herself out of going, but she needed a session to unleash whatever was building inside her before she had a meltdown. Besides, what could it hurt? She got in the car and drove to Dr. Honoré's inner city office in Algiers. She had so many things to share. Like the fact that it took her all day to find the courage to reopen her computer to look again at what had literally tried to blow her mind. But no matter how hard she looked, Dr. Afrine Kasatah's site could not be found. That and two more nights without sleep were taking its toll.

She'd driven across the Greater New Orleans Bridge, taken the Mardi Gras Boulevard exit and picked up De Armas Street to head back toward the Mississippi River front that faced New Orleans. De Armas Street took her right down the middle of two of Algiers' oldest cemeteries, St Bartholomew's and St Mary's. The raised white crypts and mausoleums caught the glare of the sun. They had been designed to keep the dead above the water table, but it always creeped her out to see the sprawling cities of the dead. At the same time the names, dates and final messages from the living about the dead always fascinated her. As she drove, she stole glances and wondered about their stories, some dating back as far as the seventeen hundreds. New Orleans was rich in a unique history created by a melting pot of people and mysteries gathered from around the world.

Eve reached for her cell phone only to realize she'd left it at the house; a bad habit that made both Beau and Cora crazy. She wanted to ask Cora to bring a bottle of her favorite Bordeaux when she came over for dinner. Eve arranged everything else. She had bought and arranged the flowers and candles, started the crawdad etoufée, instructed the old cook and the housekeeper how to prepare the table and what side dishes to cook. Cora promised to bring Delia, dessert and Zamara. Beau would pick the wine. He liked to do that and Eve liked his taste, but she loved the dark, very expensive Bordeaux from Cora's extensive wine cellar. She'd already let both of them know she'd meet them at the guest house after her appointment with Dr. Honoré.

Eve loved Cora and the three of them always had a great time hanging out. She and Beau were Cora's best friends and now that

Delia had "taken her off the market" as she professed, dating was still awkward. Eve secretly thought Cora still had feelings for Beau, but she'd given them the chance to admit it to themselves and to her and they'd declined. That irksome little ghost of a suspicion and the fact that she was simply exhausted made her secretly hope Dr. Honoré would prescribe some kind of pill to help her sleep and order her home to bed. Eve's other big fear was that Dr. Honoré would declare her crazy, medicate her or worse, lock her up.

The breathtaking view of New Orleans rose between the buildings like a new world. It sat directly across the mighty Mississippi, breathtaking, old and new, tried and victorious. She really did love the exotic nature of New Orleans, its history, architecture, people and the most amazing food on the planet. Algiers had its own history, a little darker, a little stranger. *Must have been all those pirates and Voodoo priests*, Eve thought.

She found the doctor's address and parked her car. As soon as the car door opened, the heat surrounded her like a giant, musty old coat, humid and dank, clinging to her skin. Only the hint of a breeze teased her skin and carried with it the promise of coolness the night would bring. Eve walked up the street peering in the shop windows, appreciating the long, wooden overhang with its intricate wrought iron balcony that gave her shelter from the late afternoon sun. She stopped at the address where the doctor's front gate guarded a small courtyard filled with trees, vines and flowers. The gate had a key pad and security camera to keep unwanted strangers and riff raff out and because Dr. Honoré said she had no secretary. Eve punched in the code the good doctor had given her and, after a moment of silence and a wink of light from the security camera, the gate buzzed open.

Eve entered the fragrant garden. A stone walk serpentined through the meticulously groomed garden like a lazy old snake leading her forward. The door to the office was unlocked and Eve entered the air conditioned waiting room with its peach-colored roman shades kept lowered to dim the brilliant sunlight and keep the heat at bay.   The outer waiting room was small, modern and well appointed.   A soft beige couch and five chairs along with a coffee table neatly stacked with magazines anchored the space.   A variety of plants framed the window and clung to the last of the sunlight as it reached inside through the open spaces that ran along the sides and bottom of the shade.   It made the place feel comfortable and very relaxing.   She took a seat and looked through the stacks of magazines carefully chosen to appeal to both men and women.   Eve heard the sound of a small water fountain in the corner.   It had at its center a smooth stone ball of polished rose quartz spinning methodically as the water gurgled and sputtered peacefully, adding to the tranquility the room commanded.

Eve picked up a *Southern Style Magazine*, her ex-magazine job. She flipped to the contributors' page and saw Charles Delacroix, her Editor-in-Chief's, name and face.   Cora always said he looked like a basset hound, all droopy eyed and ears dangling, which made Eve smile. Before she could turn the page the door to Dr. Honoré's office opened.

"Eve. Good. I wasn't sure you were going to come," Dr. Honoré said.

Eve stood and crossed to her, laying the magazine back on the table.

"You used to work there, didn't you?" she asked gesturing to the magazine.

Eve smiled and nodded in agreement as Dr. Honoré led her into the office.   The therapist looked more relaxed than when she'd seen her at the hospital.   Still professional, but definitely more relaxed.   She motioned to a large ox blood leather couch that looked simultaneously modern and antique.   Eve was sure Freud would have had it in his office had he still been practicing in the twenty-first century.   Eve scanned the room looking at the decor.   The framed Bachelor of Science degree from Tulane University, MD from Harvard Medical, and her PhD in psychology from Oxford filled the wall. *Wow*, she thought. The latter surprised her the most. Dr. Honoré was so un-Harvard and Eve had trouble imagining her at Oxford or living in London for that matter. *Judging people again*, she thought. *Stop!*

The rest of the office was very feminine: French country, cushy chairs and a mid-twentieth century desk with her therapist chair catty corner to the couch. All in all, the place was rather eclectic and nothing like her office at Thibodaux Hospital. Eve let her fingers run over the vast collection of books that filled the ceiling-to-floor oak shelves: psychology books by Jung, Bettelheim, and Freud; the great books of Plato and Socrates and several books from ancient Persia and Mesopotamia by astronomers, mathematicians and scientists; texts on the planets and a numerological chart.

"You like to read, Eve?" Dr. Honoré asked.

"I do. I'm afraid most of these are a little heady for my taste. I do like history," Eve said.

Her fingers stopped on a large, leather bound book. Tattered and frayed, the once pale tan of the natural animal skin had turned a mottled rusty orange and black from age. There was an energy the book exuded that compelled her to open it.

"May I?" Eve asked.

Dr. Honoré nodded yes and Eve picked up the worn book. It was heavy. The title's gold lettering had long ago been erased by the many hands that had handled it. It looked like it read *Gregoires. Impossible*, Eve though. She balanced the book in her hand and opened it to the first page. The title was there as bold and as legible as if it had been drawn yesterday: "The Nephilim."

Eve stared at the word. She wanted to drop the book and walk out the door.

"Where did you get this?" Eve asked, the tension closing her throat.

Dr. Honoré sat for a moment with a perplexed look on her face.

"I ... can't remember. A patient I think. No, she wasn't a patient. It was years ago, an older woman just showed up at my door. Her name was ... huh ... I don't recall, but her face is as present in my mind as if it were an hour ago. She was amazing, old with skin like a piece of dark chocolate and this wild shock of white hair and her eyes ..." Dr. Dr. Honoré said.

"One blue and one brown," Eve said, then stopped, wondering why she'd spoken.

"Yes. Heterochromia iridium. I had to look that up. Wait, how did you know that?"

Eve stopped, surprised that she knew and uncertain as to how.

"I don't know. I just knew," Eve said.

"Then you knew her?" Dr. Honoré asked.

"No, I mean I don't remember," Eve said.

"Well, she showed up with the book and gave it to me with a message, something about someone would come and when they did, I was to give it to ... wait, I wrote a note," Dr. Honoré said.

Dr. Honoré took the book from Eve and carefully flipped through its delicate, rotting pages searching for the note. As the pages were turned they released a scent of bitter oils and dry wood. It made Eve think of going to church on Sunday with her Grandmother – that smoke they would swing around – *frankincense or was it myrrh?* She couldn't remember the name, but the scent memory was as pungent as if it had been yesterday.

"I started to read it, but it's written in a language so archaic," Dr. Honoré said, pointing to the open page. "Look. See. I think this is some kind of family tree. It's written in old English, but I think it was transcribed from some ancient language from these markings. And I saw those symbols on some of the copper Dead Sea Scrolls," she said, pointing at a series of symbols. "I read about a few places, cities and old Ziggurat temples in Persia long before it became Iran. There are names and people from the Middle East. See this map? That's Sumer, pre-Samaria and that's the Euphrates River and the Fertile Crescent and here," she pointed, "...where the Karkheh and Abs-e Den rivers meet. Anyway I am not a history buff and it bored me so I put it away promising to get back to it, but never did."

Dr. Honoré turned another page and there, on her stationary, in her handwriting was a note. She opened it, read and looked at Eve. There was a stunned expression etched across her face as she handed Eve the note.

"Impossible."

"What?" Eve asked.

"She came here two years ago. I ... I didn't know you even existed," Dr. Honoré said.

Eve took the note and read the words. *A woman will come to you. Her name is Eve. Give her this book and tell her ... she is first born and is the key. She alone must destroy it.*

Eve looked up at Dr. Honoré. "I don't understand. Are you saying this book and message was for me?" Eve asked.

"I'm not saying anything. I actually don't know what to say, Eve. I don't know if this is some bizarre coincidence or ... well ... I don't even know if you're the Eve she told me to give it to."

"It does seem rather like a coincidence," Eve said, struggling to make sense of the situation. She remembered the message on the web site under the tiny cuneiform that mentioned her name. *Could these be from the same woman?*

"The entire incident was odd and this book is even stranger," Dr. Honoré said.

Eve turned the note over in her hand looking for more information.

"There's no name or number? Where is she? Who is she? Is there a way to find her? Did she have an accent?" Eve asked, obviously disturbed.

Dr. Honoré closed the book and placed it on her desk. She took Eve's arm, directing her to the couch and guiding her to sit. She poured Eve a glass of water from an oddly shaped glass pitcher, handed it to her and poured one for her. They drank but Eve's eyes were locked on the book.

"Eve, look at me."

Eve's gaze shifted and she looked into Dr. Honoré's eyes. She could feel the fear pounding in her heart.

"Eve, why are you here?" Dr. Honoré asked.

"What?"

"Why did you come here today?"

"Things have been happening, my coma, residual effects that might have come from it, the kids, the alligator. I ... I haven't been sleeping. I've had these dreams and they don't make sense."

"What kind of dreams?"

"We talked about them but now I see people and places and things, horrible things. In the beginning they were weird foggy dreams and then they were nightmares, but now, they happen in the day, visions so encompassing they block my sight and voices," Eve said. The words blurted out desperate to be heard someplace other than as questions inside her head.

"Voices? What do they say?"

"I don't know. I don't understand them," Eve told her.

"Are they in another language?" She asked.

"No. I don't think so. Just garbled and distant. Sometimes it feels like I experienced them ... and it's a memory," Eve explained.

"Things from the past that happened to you?" Dr. Honoré asked.

"Yes! Well, no. I'm not sure. Sometimes they feel like things I remembered happening but don't know when. I know they didn't happen. I can't remember why or where, but they feel like they happened to me."

"Or maybe they haven't happened," Dr. Honoré says. "You asked me about second sight. Prophesy."

Eve sat in silence grappling with the thought.

"I don't know. I can't tell. That's why I asked if maybe the coma brought on some kind of precognitive ability. And then the alligator dying like that."

"Alligator?"

"The incident with Cora and the kids at the bayou.   I told you. Didn't I? The alligator looked like it had been killed by a giant foot. The way you or I would step on a big lizard and crush the ba-jesus out of it—bones crushed, guts everywhere," Eve said.

"You didn't tell me this, Eve," Dr. Honoré said.

Eve felt flustered. A surge of tension rose in her as she struggled to find a logical explanation for a very illogical situation. Eve looked at Dr. Honoré who simply stared at her ... expressionless.

"You don't believe me?" Eve asked.

Dr. Honoré looked at Eve for a very long time.

"Do you believe you?" Dr. Honoré said.

"I don't know anymore what to believe. Am I losing my mind? I mean could all this be in my imagination?"

"I don't know either, Eve.   Why don't we talk about your nightmares and your visions? Maybe I can help you interpret some meaning out of the visuals and the sounds you're experiencing."

"Like Freud or Jung?"

"Dream interpretation goes much farther back than modern psychiatry.   Egypt, Greece, China.   They considered dreams as supernatural communications and divine interventions. We can look at Freudian wish fulfillment of the unconscious as well as Jungian objective and subjective of the animus and anima shadow symbols. We do in dreams what we can't do in life."

"I would never hurt Cora!" Eve exclaimed.

"But you are angry at her for seducing or allowing Beau to seduce her and creating a child?"

Eve fell silent.

"Eve, we can look at the symbolism behind the images you're seeing and that can help you understand what your psyche is trying to tell you. Once you crack that you might be able to know why you're having them."

"And what happened to the alligator?" Eve asked.

"I think the answers are in your head, Eve, not mine."

"And that book and note the woman left?" Eve asked.

"I don't know," Dr. Honoré said, leaning forward with a look of genuine concern. "We can find out together."

"I don't have time for ten years of psychoanalysis," Eve said falling back against the couch.

"Eve, I can offer you one other suggestion."

"What?" Eve asked. There was a tremor of hopeless frustration in her voice.

"It's pretty unconventional," Dr. Honoré said.

"I'm pretty desperate," Eve said, holding up the note from the book. "And this, that book and a message on a random website we haven't even talked about are adding to an already bizarre collection of coincidences," Eve said.

Eve could feel the tears welling in her eyes and the ache in her heart caused by waves of fear. "Dr. Honoré, I have a man I love and a son I adore. I want ... I need to know if I'm insane. Please, tell me what you can do to help me."

Dr. Honoré leaned forward and took Eve's hands.

"Then trust me," Dr. Honoré said. "Let me put you under. Allow me to hypnotize you." Dr. Honoré asked. "You can wake out of the trance anytime you choose. You understand that right?"

Now it was Eve who sat in silence for a long time. With everything that had been going on she had to do something or, if she wasn't already crazy, she'd surely go out of her mind if it didn't stop. For herself, her sanity, for Beau and for Philip, she had to know the truth. Finally she spoke, "Do it. Please. But we have to start today."

Chapter Fifteen

Eve lay on the couch, her eyes closed, her body as relaxed as she could get.

"Breathe in." There was a pause. "Breathe out," she heard Dr. Honoré say. "Breathe in." Again there was a long pause. "Breathe out."

With each breath she released, sinking deeper and deeper into the warm, soft leather of the couch. It felt smooth against her skin and the tucking in the cushions made her feel comfortable and strangely protected. She was Goldilocks after being lost in the woods and she'd found the baby bear's bed and it was just right. Another few breaths and she let all her muscles release. The next long deep breath slid out of her, brushing past her lips and taking with it months of tension. She hadn't realized how much tension she was holding until she let it go. Dr. Honoré's voice was deep and gentle. Each word sounded more distant, as if she was drifting farther and farther away.

"Are you asleep, Eve?" the doctor asked.

"What?" Eve replied. Her own voice sounding as a sleepy child's would right before drifting off into sleep. "Yes."

"Can you hear my voice?"

Eve nodded yes.

"Can you tell me where you are, Eve?" the doctor asked.

Eve's sleepy face broke into a wondrous smile. "How beautiful," Eve said.

"Eve, tell me what you see."

Sunlight fell across Eve's face as she looked around to see she was standing in the center of a beautiful green field with miles of grass stretched out in every direction. A ring of tall trees encircled her, their leaves blowing in the gentle breeze.

"It's beautiful. There are trees and grass and a lake," Eve said in her sleepy voice. She turned her head. "The sun is setting and I hear the birds and smell the flowers, but I can't see where the sound—" Eve stopped. "Oh."

"What is it, Eve?"

"The hospital. I see Thibodaux Hospital."

"What are you doing at the hospital?"

In the blink of an eye Eve went from the grassy field to standing inches away from the front of the door that led to the tower. She reached out her hand and placed it on the brass doorknob. The orb felt cold and as solid and real as if she were right there touching it. She could feel the chill of the metal. Her fingers traced the carved face raised in the metal. The face looked up at her and smiled invitingly. Eve looked at it and turned the knob. She pushed open the door and without taking a step, the room appeared around her. It had its black and white floor and circular stairway that led to an upper balcony. She looked up and saw the windows that ringed the entry filled with afternoon light. Eve walked, listening to the click, click, click of her heels on the hard surface of the floor. In the distance, she heard the voices of children singing a song. She knew the melody but the words were unfamiliar to her. She followed the sound, not climbing the stairs, but turning down a hallway and watching as the light outside shifted. The space fell into darker and darker shadows until the next thing she knew it was night. There, in the play of shadow and light, she could see rows of closed doors, each with a small observation window.

"I've been here before," she told Dr. Honoré. "But I'm not sure when or why."

Eve walked past the third door on the left and heard a voice.

"Get out!" the voice whispered.

Eve turned. She looked through the small glass portal into the room and saw Azura, the girl she had seen that day at the hospital. Azura was sitting with her son.

"Get out before it's too late. It's too late for me and my son, but if you hurry maybe, just maybe, you can save Philip."

"How did you know my son's name? Why are you in here?" Eve asked her.

"I'm here because I have no choice. I'm here for the same reason that you're here," Azura said. "The truth of why they have returned."

Eve looked at her. All she could think of was that she should be afraid, but she wasn't because she was only in her own mind exploring her own thoughts. Eve turned back to the door and tried to turn the handle. It was locked. She heard a sound and turned to face another long hallway that suddenly lay before her on the left. The hall stretched out and as she stared the end of it expanded, extending longer than it had been even the few seconds before. Eve looked up and saw the light from the globes that hung above her; they began to sway as if caught by a tremor or a wind. Their motion created eerie shadows that rose and fell on the floor and walls before her, moving as if each shadow were alive. The lights flickered off, then on. When they illuminated, a man stood at the far end staring at her—waiting for her. He was very tall and muscular with a full head of dark hair, narrow eyes, a broad nose and full lips. She didn't remember taking a step and yet, in the blink of an eye, she stood right next to him.

Eve shared every detail of her journey.

"Ask him who he is," she heard Dr. Honoré's voice say.

"Who are you? What do you want from me?" Eve asked the man.

He did not speak. She watched his face slowly lower close to hers. She felt his breath on her skin and saw his lips press against hers as he ever so gently kissed her. The kiss was long and slow and it had a kindness that made her feel good.

"I'm glad you came," he said, and kissed her gently again. "Do you know why you're here?"

"No, I don't," she replied.

"Who are you talking to," said Dr. Honoré's disembodied voice.

"Remember, Eve. Remember who you are," the man said. "We have all been waiting for you."

He kissed her again. This time the kiss was harder, deeper and much longer. It was filled with more passion than Eve could ever remember from any kiss she had received in her life. Still, she wasn't afraid.

"I don't remember? Please tell me why I'm here?" she asked.

His hands slipped up inside her blouse and in one motion he unloosed and pushed her bra away. He filled his hands with her breasts and squeezed them gently but firmly, leaning down once again to kiss her mouth. His hands were warm and large and his fingers were long. They squeezed, massaged, rubbed and pinched at her nipples until they rose to attention. One hand slipped down her side and under her skirt. He grabbed the inside of her thigh and, slowly gliding up her leg, his thumb brushed her clitoris as he cupped her ass and pulled her into him.

"I want you to stop until you tell me who you are and what's happening," Eve said, her breath deepening with each caress.

He didn't speak. He kissed her again, this time letting his tongue slide, warm and wet, into her mouth. Eve closed her eyes and released a reluctant sigh of surprised pleasure. She put her hands on his biceps; her intention was to push him away and demand answers, but when she opened her eyes she was lying on her back staring up at a light. She tried to move, but couldn't. She turned to look at her hand only to see that restraints held her wrists. Eve lifted her head and looked down, she was naked. Her hands and her feet were tied, her legs spread. Eve turned her head and saw standing in the dim shadows of the room at least six men. All were tall. All were young, fit and handsome, and all were naked. All were about the same size and from their features she thought that perhaps they could be brothers or cousins. The odd similarity made her think they were definitely related. The table or altar that held her was perfectly warmed and made of stone that felt amazingly comfortable and relaxing.

"Where are you?" she heard Dr. Honoré's voice echoing farther away than before.

"I'm in a room with several men watching something happen. I am watching them, but at the same time I think I am watching myself," Eve said tilting her head as if trying to grasp the out-of-body experience she was having. She was observing what was unfolding as if it were happening to someone else.

"As long as you don't feel in danger, watch and see what they show you Eve. Don't be afraid to ask questions," Dr. Honoré's voice told her.

"Why are we here?" she asked the man who had kissed her.

"Let us show you what you can do," he said.

She couldn't move so she calmly watched. The first man gently kissed her. He leaned over her and looked into her eyes. Just as Eve was about to ask another question he covered her mouth with his. Again he delivered a long passion-filled kiss. He pressed his full, firm lips onto her lips. At the same time she felt warm breath against the skin on her chest as multiple lips, tongues and mouths kissed her, sensually covering each of her breasts, her shoulders and stomach with kisses. She could feel the men kissing her flesh, sucking, licking and gently biting her breasts and nipples. Hands were squeezing and massaging her arms and legs, adding wet kisses in between each touch. She felt their lips pinching tiny mounds of her flesh, a half dozen mouths sucking, licking and kissing all over her while she was being artfully kissed on the lips. She felt hands lift her hips and wet, warm fingers tracing and teasing every orifice on her body. The sensation, though erotic and pleasurable, sent a wave of fear crashing over her. Eve tried to move. She could not. She began to struggle. Eve opened her mouth to scream, but her cries were muffled inside the kisses of the first man and with everything that was happening to her body, her cries melted into moans of pleasure. Her body trembled with pleasure as a dozen fingers caressed every inch of her skin. She was being readied, teased, but she could see no one moving to enter her. *Their only purpose is to tantalize me,* she thought. Her breathing quickened more. She could hear Dr. Honoré, but now her voice was so far away her words were inaudible.

Eve turned her head and looked around her as best she could between the gentle kisses on her lips. Suddenly, at the end of the table, a gray mist swirled, transitioning from its formless shape into solid flesh. He was a man, bigger than the others, just as naked and well-built, but much more generously well hung. In the shadowy lights of this now wall-less room his flesh shifted through an array of different colors. He was so tall his face was hidden in black shadows where the light could not reach. He watched for a long time, allowing the others to coax her into a state of quivering passion. His erection was slowly, methodically growing, thickening, and hardening. Her breasts heaved, her nipples, with each lick and nibble, stood up taught and hard. Her vulva swelled, seething hot and wet, holding her in pure pleasure. Finally, the man at the end of the table reached out with his long sinewy fingers to touch her feet. His hands were as hot as if warmed by a great fire and his touch sent a rush of energy that ran from her toes to the top of her head. Her body arched and her breasts filled the mouths of two of the other men. They sucked harder. Another kiss from the first man met her lips. She could feel the big man crawl up onto the table. The men who had been fondling and licking her just outside her clitoris receded, bowing their heads in reverence so the big man could brush his face along the inside of her legs. The energy his body exuded caused the fine gold hairs on her body to stand straight as if to reach for his touch. As he moved closer he kissed, licked and sucked on her from her toes, to her feet and up her calves. His huge hands squeezed her thighs. As he left one area the other men returned to continue their caressing and kissing. She didn't know where one man started and the other ended. She felt the large one push his face deeper between her legs. She wanted to look but she was completely blocked. She felt his hot breath and hotter tongue slide over each part of her very wet mound. His tongue entered inside her and explored, tasting her. Eve shivered as she felt teeth pressing against her, each tiny, tender bite, one more arousing than the next, came from her chorus of men. The fever building in her body heightened. She felt the big man's tongue slip out and his fingers slip in and open her. She felt two more fingers, wet and hot, push inside, slide out. He pushed in again and again and again. A wash of warm wet flooded from her. Eve was in orgasm, but not a single, powerful warp-your-mind orgasm. She was in multiple waves of pleasure that sent ripples of orgasms washing over her entire body again and again, building and vibrating as if a current of raw pleasure had been released. She knew this was only the beginning as each of the men turned up the dial of what was yet to come.

Eve buzzed in a constant state of orgasmic bliss. Her eyes shot open and she saw above her a glowing haze. At first she thought it was a light fixture, until it moved and began to open. A swirling portal expanded, unfolding into a wavering field, shimmering above her, yawning wider with each rush of pleasure that throbbed between her legs. In that moment, she knew, it wanted her.

"No. No. I will not go through that portal," Eve said. "Stop. Stop!

STOP IT! Don't open the portal."

"Eve! Wake up! EVE!" Dr. Honoré called to her, her voice still sounding distant.

What she saw next terrified her. It wasn't human and yet it was. He ... it ... its flesh undulated between flesh color and pure albino white, blue, red and ebony black with his massive erection growing longer and harder as he came out of the light, getting closer and closer, ready to stab himself into her.

"GET AWAY! LET GO!" she screamed. "No. No. NO!!!"

Suddenly, standing behind him an old woman with chocolate skin and a shock of white hair appeared. Eve could see her mismatched eyes flashed as she grabbed and shoved at the big man, knocking him off Eve. With wild waves of her arms she scattered all the other men with what felt like giant blasts of wind. Using the wind that now blew with the force of a great gale, she drove the creatures back into the gaping portal. The old woman spun and slapped Eve so hard, Eve felt three of the restraints rip as she rolled off the altar and crashed onto the ground.

"Evine! Help me!" Eve heard herself say.

Again Evine waved her arms, knocking the men back as they came to take Eve again. Evine grabbed Eve and pulled her up to her feet, breaking her last restraint. She dragged Eve backwards over the fallen men and down into a long dark tunnel. The man from the light, naked and erect rushed after them. He reached out and grabbed Eve, snatching her from Evine. He threw Eve down and mounted her, his enormous cock poised for insertion.

"EVE, WAKE UP NOW!" Dr. Honoré shouted to her.

Eve looked into the eyes of the man, the thing that was about to rape her. They were Beau's eyes.

Eve screamed, "NO! NO!!"

Far in the distance, Eve heard the door to the office break open with a loud crack. She fought to wake from the trance. She saw the face fade from her and felt her body rushing back as the office reappeared around her. She felt arms lift her from the couch. She heard Dr. Honoré's voice: "Don't touch her."

Eve, panting, shivering, drenched in sweat, opened her eyes and looked into Mac's face.

Chapter Sixteen

Eve threw her arms around Mac. She held on to him as a child holds her father after waking from a horrible dream. Her body ached, still feeling the pulse of the orgasm that racked inside her, vacillating between orgasmic pleasure and pain.

"Put her down!" Dr. Honoré insisted.

Mac hesitated, looking between Eve and the Doctor.

"Now!" Dr. Honoré demanded. "You could be doing more harm than good. Please."

Mac tried to set her down, but Eve would not let go. Dr. Honoré came to check her pulse and heart rate. Eve was drenched in sweat. Dr. Honoré ran to get a wet washcloth and a glass of water for Eve to drink.

"See if you can get her to drink this," she said as she handed the glass to Mac.

He sat on the couch still holding her in his arms. Mac took the glass and offered her the drink.

Mac look at Eve and then at Dr. Honoré. His eyes demanded to know, *what the hell happened to her?*

"She's in a hypnotic state. You need to put her down. Let her go and leave, detective," said Dr. Honoré. "Please. I have this under control. She'll be alright."

As Dr. Honoré spoke Mac took the washcloth and gently wiped the sweat from Eve's face.

Mac looked at Eve. She was trembling. The scent of pheromones exuding from her body was intoxicating. Mac got a very instant, very embarrassing erection.

"She is not alright. What the hell happened?" Mac finally demanded.

"I can't share that with you," Dr. Honoré said. "Why are you here?"

"It's Tuesday and the department set my sessions with you, remember?" Mac said. His eyes locked on Eve trembling in his arms; her face, her beauty, her lips, the absolute vulnerability in her body hit a primal vein in him that both wanted to care for and protect her and at the same time make insane love to her on the floor. He looked up for the briefest of moments to connect with Dr. Honoré.

"Tuesday. Yes, of course."

Eve, still trembling, looked up into Mac's eyes. Whatever she saw there, combined with the feeling of his arms around her, generated the same feeling of safety she remembered from the house. She began to calm. Her breathing slowed and finally the realization she was in Mac's arms and still in orgasm hit her. Weak and confused she shifted, pushing from his arms.

"What happened? Am I okay?" Eve asked.

Slowly she sat up and slipped from his embrace. He said nothing. He handed her the glass of water. She drank and held it out to Dr. Honoré for more. She filled her glass three more times and Eve drank. A moment more, a few more sips of water and Eve tried to stand. Her knees buckled under her and again, Mac caught and supported her.

"Hang on there, cowgirl," he said.

He guided her to sit back down on the couch. He too sat, staying by her, holding Eve's waist to steady her. Dr. Honoré got her another glass of water. Eve drank every drop before her color came back. She looked at Dr. Honoré, remembering where she was and what she was doing there. She then looked at Mac.

"Why ... are you here?" Eve asked Mac.

"I had an appointment," Mac responded.

"He was outside waiting for his session when you screamed," Dr. Honoré explained.

"I screamed?" Eve asked.

"Like a banshee. Scared the shit out of me. My cop side kicked in. I thought ..." Mac started.

"He was worried we were in trouble," Dr. Honoré finished. "You two know each other?"

"I'm on her case from the Gregoire estate accident investigation. The incident that knocked her out and put her into a coma," Mac said.

"Yes. Of course. Odd coincidence," Dr. Honoré said.

"I don't believe in coincidences," Mac said.

"Eve, I'm sorry. I didn't realize Lana had scheduled you two so close together that you could run into him," she said.

Eve turned to Mac. "My fiancé has a restraining order in effect against Detective Macklin."

"Another coincidence?" he asked.

"You'll need to leave, Detective. I'll have Lana reschedule. I'm terribly sorry for the inconvenience."

Mac stood. "You're sure you're okay?" he asked Eve.

Eve nodded, her wits finally coming back to her. "Thank you for your concern. It's good to know the cops are there when you need them."

Mac gave a small smile to Eve and a polite nod to Dr. Honoré and left.

Silence filled the room. Eve desperately tried to remember what had upset her and made her scream during the trance. Questions with no answers were all that filled her mind. A walk in a grassy field was all she could remember. She looked at her hands now more worried than before. Finally she looked up to see the furrow of concern etched into Dr. Honoré's brow.

"What happened to me?" Eve asked. "Please, tell me what I said."

"You went under just fine. You started saying you were standing in a grassy meadow with trees and water. Do you remember anything else?"

Eve struggled to remember. She looked at her dress. It was wet as was her hair.

"I'm soaked," Eve said. "What happened?"

"Don't you remember anything?" Dr. Honoré asked her.

Eve shook her head, *no*.

"You really need to remember, Eve," Dr. Honoré said. "That's what this is for ... you to remember."

Eve shook her head while her mind searched for some small piece of what happened after the grassy field.

"I ... said something. Did I say anything? Please Dr. Honoré, tell me what I said. Please."

Dr. Honoré was silent.

"Please. I told you I don't have time to play games over this. I think my life might be in danger."

That statement got Dr. Honoré's attention.

"Danger? How do you mean?" Dr. Honoré asked.

Eve lost it. "Stop asking me fucking questions and tell me what I said! If my life is not in danger and this is a bunch of psychotic insanity, you can drug me and lock me up. If these dreams have been given to me as a way to protect myself from a dangerous event about to happen to me or my family, I need you to tell me what I said," Eve shouted.

"Okay. Calm down. I'll share what I heard and saw," Dr. Honoré said. There was a long pause and then she went on. "You went under beautifully and I asked where you were. You said you were in a beautiful field and then you said you were at Thibodaux Hospital. You said a woman spoke to you. You didn't share what she said. The last thing you said was you were going into a room with a tall man but that you weren't afraid." She looked at Eve. "Do you remember any of this?"

"No. No. I can't remember. That was it?" she asked. "But why did I scream?"

"I don't know. You were quiet and very still for a long time after you went into the room. You talked about several other men that looked as if they could be related. You mentioned they looked young and strong. Do you remember if anyone hurt you?"

"No," Eve said.

"Your breathing got so shallow I came over to check on you. Then your breathing changed, became erratic and your heart started racing. That's when you broke into a sweat. You started struggling, almost flailing. I could see you were trying to wake up. I called to you to bring you out and you didn't answer. You started to shake and fight but you barely moved and then you started screaming something about, 'Not the portal. Get out or off?' I don't remember. Are you sure no one was hurting you?"

Eve looked at her hands. She noticed bands of reddened skin ringing her wrists. She saw a tear in her blouse.

"What were you doing while I was under?" Eve asked.

"Sitting here. Watching and listening," Dr. Honoré said. "Why?"

"And I was right here the entire time."

"Of course. What do you mean, Eve?"

"I don't know," Eve said.

Eve stood and crossed to gather her purse. "I have to go."

"Wait. We need to talk about this, Eve. You're obviously very disturbed by what you experienced."

"Ya think! Except I can't remember what I experienced," Eve said.

"Of course you can. Maybe it was something that happened in the past and your mind is trying to show you a way to access a clear memory of it. We just have to unlock that memory. Whatever it is, I think it will help you to face what is happening."

"What if what I experienced wasn't something from the past Dr. Honoré?" Eve asked. "What if it is going to happen in the future and I've been given a glimpse of it?"

"A glimpse of the future your subconscious mind won't let your conscious mind remember," Dr. Honoré said. "Eve, let me help you through this."

"I have to go. I'll call you," Eve said and turned to leave.

"Eve. You shouted a name. Evine. Does it have any meaning?"

Eve's mind raced. It sounded familiar, but she didn't know why.

"I'm not sure."

"Do you want me to keep the book? It fell when you screamed, as if someone pushed it off the table."

Eve turned. There on the floor, lying open to a picture of one of the world's oldest ziggurats, The Great Ziggurat of Ur, the book seemed to dare her to take it. At that moment the note fell from the table to the floor.

"No! I don't want that book. I want answers! I want to know what the fuck is happening to me and not you or Beau or the police seem to be able to help me, so I'm going to get to the bottom of this on my own and I don't care what it takes," Eve said and vanished, slamming the door behind her.

Adrenalin shooting through her, she felt alive for the first time since she woke from her coma. She stepped outside into the darkening dusk and breathed in the cool air of the evening as if it were the first breath she'd taken in months. Eve knew she had to start this search now. She could see the pearl grey sky that held all the shades of the coming night and with it the answers to the mysteries that haunted her. The street was empty and still, but her stomach twisted into a knot as she walked. The wind blew and on it she heard a voice.

"You are ready, Eve. I'm waitin' for you. Come at me," the voice that had for months screamed inaudible words, whispered to her.

Eve suddenly knew where she had to be. She didn't know why, but she knew she was being called to a place she'd seen in her visions. A place behind the old cemetery she'd been to before, a long, long time ago. Eve's heart raced with excitement as she slipped into her car and drove away.

Chapter Seventeen

Mac sat across the street in his car, watching as she exited the building and got into her car. Eve sat for a long moment before finally driving away. Mac looked at the doctor's office. He could go and ask her questions, but she was under doctor/client privilege, so that would be a waste of time. He watched Eve's car, its tail light vanishing down the street. He knew he shouldn't trail her; he was a cop and he knew the law, but he felt an intense sense of concern for her. He started his car and followed her up the street. They drove a few blocks, stopped at a sign and then a couple of red lights. She was driving just fine. She didn't swerve or stop erratically. He had no excuse to pull her over and talk to her to make sure she was okay. The erection in his pants was raging and he couldn't imagine why bursting through a door to help a screaming woman would cause that reaction. But it wasn't any woman, it was Eve Dowling and he, his Captain and her fiancé knew he had more than a professional concern for her well being. He had been denying it since the first time he saw her at the hospital - the day he was put on her case.

"Stop it, Mac," he said, admonishing himself.

He knew this line of thought wasn't helping the situation. Maybe his concern for Eve was uncalled for, but she had been so terrified.

He felt a sense of danger whenever he was around her, but for the life of him he couldn't figure out why. Perhaps whatever attracted him to her was the culprit behind what he was feeling. He liked how she felt in his arms, strong and yet unbelievably vulnerable. She needed him, a voice kept telling him; she just didn't know it yet. It had been a long time since someone needed him. It had been longer since he desired a woman and never like this. Yes, he liked her but there was more. When she screamed, he could hear the terror in her voice. He'd been a cop long enough to know the sound and feel of real terror. But of what? What had she remembered in her hypnotic state?

Dr. Honoré had offered to put him under as well when they spoke on the phone. Hypnosis was one of her specialties. She said it was a way to help him open up. She called it a path to remembering not only the strange, segmented dreams and scattered pieces of flashback that plagued him since he was put on her case, but even perhaps their root cause. The weird pieces of dreams made him obsessive about Eve's case; too many things didn't make sense. He wanted to, needed to, understand what was happening. His gut told him she was the key.

His mind rushed back into the present when he noticed that Eve had stopped her car between two old cemeteries and gotten out. He watched as she stepped through one of the old gates.

He wasn't afraid of cemeteries and he didn't believe in ghosts or things that go bump in the night and vampires were not in his vocabulary, so entering wasn't an issue. Vagrants and robbers were another story and much more real and dangerous. The black of night fell like a curtain and the full moon crept over the rows of silent, white-washed crypts. It peeked through the barren branches reaching into the sky. The branches were stark metaphors for skeletal arms with boney fingers scratching at the night sky. The images fascinated him for a moment until his gaze focused back on Eve. She walked with speed and purpose. She knew exactly where she was going. He watched as she strode deep into the oldest part of the cemetery filled with marble markers, their names and dates long ago erased, dating back to the late 1600s. Crooked iron crosses, rusted and broken statues of sad-faced angels, their features worn by centuries of wind and rain, watched her pass. She moved, unafraid, to the farthest back wall until Mac saw the center of the wall had crumbled and fallen, opening a path from the cemetery into a thicket of bushes and great old trees of the bayou. Banyan and giant oak trees draped in Spanish moss spilled out over the dry land and into the shallow water.

At the center of the last piece of land bathed in moonlight, Mac could see the remains of an old wooden shanty. As far as Mac could tell, it had been burned to the ground, leaving only a stone fire hearth and chimney and piles of charred rubble overgrown with moss and algae. He watched as Eve stood by a rusted fence. Its gate hung drunkenly open, broken and bent. He watched as Eve slowly pushed it. He listened as the gate screeched, angry it had been disturbed. Eve hesitated before crossing into the front yard. Mac wanted to call out to her; let her know he was there. But she'd been through so much, the last thing he wanted to do was frighten her again.

A movement from the porch caught his eye. A woman dressed all in black stood on the charred floorboards of the portico. In the moonlight he could see she had long, flowing white hair, wind whipped around her face and shoulders. But there was no wind. The woman stood backlit by the full moon with the skeletal arch of the house framing her like a picture. The woman was staring at Eve.

"I don't know who you are or why I came here, but I think you saved me, didn't you?" Eve asked.

"More times dan you know. What matters is you gotta remember ta save you self, chil'," the woman said.

"You know what's happening to me?" Eve asked the woman in black.

"What's happen' to you is your fault. You da one who let dem back in, chil'," the woman in black said. "Ain't no other fault but your own."

"I don't remember," Eve said.

"Dey bend that. You got'em in one world and dey take you to another. Dey made it so you couldn't resist. Da baby took your heart, but you don't know da truth. Dat's when dey got you blind again. You got to stop them that got you. I try to help you before and dey killed me so dead. I can nah come back, cept for as a shade."

Her words sent a shiver up Mac's spine.

"They killed you because you helped me?" Eve asked.

"Dead in your world don't mean dead in mine. You hear me now, Eve. You did da best you could. You got dem two masters banished from dat realm, but dat was all too late. Too late. Dey done what dey came to do, Eve. Now de key is here and as long as it is, dey can come back. You know only you can destroy de key."

"I don't have a key," Eve said.

"Come closer," the old woman said.

Eve walked closer.

Again the wind from nowhere swirled around the old woman. It seemed to whip faster and harder, knocking into a burned pile of wood and tumbling a piece of furniture that rattled and fell by her feet. Mac's gut told him he needed to do something ... anything.

"Eve! Stop," Mac said with a terse calm in his voice. The kind of tone someone would use when speaking to a person on the ledge of a high building about to jump. "Don't go any nearer to her!"

Before Mac or Eve realized what was happening, Eve was lifted from the ground and pulled ever closer to the old woman. She was being gently sucked forward, caught by the force of the wind. It swirled and twisted around the image of the old woman as it pulled and flipped her dress and hair.

Mac ran forward, ready to throw his arms around her and stop her. He could feel the force pulling Eve forward while he was being dragged back. Mac struggled, watching as he was being pushed away from Eve and the old woman. He stopped, suspended by the force of another wind. The gale that now encircled him increased in speed and force; he could feel it reaching over him.

"Stop fighting her and listen. She knows the answers both of us need," Eve said to Mac. Her voice was as calm as if she'd asked him to pass the salt. "I need to know why this is happening and what to do."

Mac's gut told him everything about this was wrong, but he was helpless. He fought the wind that trapped him inside its swirling vortex.

"I don't give a shit what she knows," Mac said.

Suddenly the woman was standing face to face with Eve.

"Look inside the book," the old woman said.

"I know you," Eve said.

"My majeec saved your life in da other time," the old woman said.

"You're Evine. You—" Eve started.

Mac watched helpless.

"What I was and who I am now ain't no importance. Dey's comin' for good. You da only one who can destroy da key afore it destroys you and all de rest. Dis da last chance too," Evine said.

Mac went to reach for Eve, but he could barely move. His arm felt trapped inside a thick goo that bound him and slowed his movements to a crawl.

"Get to de chamber of Danaria. The teacher Kasatah will show you the key into the light. She gon guide you if you can get with her. Dey tried to kill her many time," Evine said. "But she got the old powers and she know you are comin'."

Mac looked at Evine. He could hear her speaking, but her lips never moved. He reached for his gun, a .38 he kept in a holster behind his back. He could reach back a little easier than forward, but even that was a struggle. Finally, he was touching the gun's handle. It took all his strength to get his hand around it and draw the weapon. Time slowed as he tried to move against the force that held him, as if he were helpless in a dream. He wasn't afraid and he knew damn well he wasn't asleep. But was he dreaming?

Evine turned her gaze on Mac. He could see Evine's eyes; one brown and one blue, looking into him, through him, as if he had no skin or bones, naked, stripped to his soul.

"Stay outa dis before you get yourself dead. And you can keep your gun cause you can't shoot what ain't alive," she said to him. Again her lips never moved. "You will be called soon enough."

"Why me?" Eve asked.

"When you know dat you gonna know all de answers. I don't envy what you gotta do. For all of us, I hope you git de courage to do it," Evine said and, in a breath, she vanished.

Eve dropped to the ground with a thud. She'd been levitating as had Mac, who fell a foot away. He struggled to his feet and reached to help her. Eve jerked her arm out of his reach and walked away.

"What the hell was that?"

"Why did you follow me?"

"What?" he said.

"I needed her," Eve said.

"A simple thank you would have sufficed," Mac said. "I saved you twice today."

"I don't need to be saved," Eve told him.

"No, you need to tell me what the fuck that ... thing was?"

"I don't know. I know her name was Evine, but I don't know why the hell I know, I just know. I think she knows about the Nephilim and what they are and what Beau and I have to do with them," Eve said, heading back to her car.

"Wait! Why were you at Dr Honoré's? What happened in there? What was that old woman talking about? Who or what is Kasatah and what the fuck is chamber of a Danaria?"

Eve kept walking. Mac ran after her.

"Talk to me. Please. You're not the only one having weird dreams and illogical memories," he shouted, catching up to her.

"How do you know I'm having dreams?" Eve said as she stopped to face him.

"I didn't until right now. I guessed because that's what's happening to me. You are in my dreams. Pieces, moments, senseless dreams that started happening when I was put on your case. I don't know why, but it is. I think if you tell me what you know and I share what I know maybe the pieces will fit together and we can figure this out."

"You believe that?" Eve asked, walking across the cemetery.

Mac followed. "I don't know what I believe. I thought there was a logical explanation until I saw the fucking wicked witch of the south floating over there, controlling a small cyclone and putting me in some kind of vice grip force field that doesn't fit into any part of my current reality!" Mac shouted.

Eve stopped, turned and stared at him. He was right about everything. She'd thought it, felt it and lived it since she came out of the coma, but she'd never really said it out loud to anyone.

"I don't know why this is happening. It's as if this is the dream and I can't wake up. In this dream the world has somehow changed, but you and I, and maybe a few other people are trying to remember the truth. That's why we are remembering pieces of the dream," Eve explained.

"Is that even possible?" Mac asked.

"I don't know."

Now it was Mac who stared at her. An old crypt bleached white by time glowed in the moonlight behind them. The writing on it was all but faded. Tired, confused and a little scared, Mac relented and sat down. Eve crossed to the crypt and joined him.

"If what's happening isn't real, what is?" Mac asked.

"It's safe to say any logical explanation doesn't apply," Eve answered.

"What about," Mac said and then turned to look back at the porch where Evine had appeared. "... that. Who was that?"

"Evine," Eve said. "I'm trying to remember who and why and where. She saved my life. I just can't remember when or how."

"Does she have something to do with your... dream theory?" Mac asked.

"This is the dream," Eve said.

"Impossible. This is not a dream."

"Then what is it?" Eve asked.

"Good goddamn question. What is Kasatah?" Mac said.

He was frustrated and confused but then, so was she.

"Not a 'what' a 'who'. She's a doctor in Cairo."

"Illinois?" Mac asked.

"I wish," Eve said. "No. Egypt. I found her site on the internet. She claims she can trace her lineage back to the sacred bloodline of the last Amazonian Queen, Danaria the Christ of the first mysteries, wife of Darius the Great King of Susa."

"Christ?" he asked.

"It's not a name, it's a title. 'The Christ' like 'the master'."

"How do you know this shit?" he asked.

"I like history. I like the way it lives and breathes and tells its story no matter how many years pass," Eve said.

"History is real. People may remember facts differently or rewrite it to suit their needs, but there are records and pictures and writings," Mac said. "What I just saw back there wasn't real. It was bat shit crazy."

"Maybe it wasn't. Maybe it was. Maybe it's been there all along and we just never saw it until now." Eve stood up and started walking back to her car. "I need to talk to her."

Mac was on his feet. "Who, the doctor in Cairo? You're going to

Cairo?"

"I can't live like this. I need to understand what is going on and why before it rips me apart. I'm about to get married to the father of my son ..."

"You mean the guy who raped you?" Mac blurted.

Eve's foot was just about to step off the curb next to her car when she turned around, walked back to him and slapped him.

"Never say that," she said and turned to her car.

"I'm sorry. I'm sorry!" Mac said and ran after her. He closed the door, blocking her way. "That was out of line and uncalled for. I'm trying to help. We both know something. Hell, everything about this situation is way off. If we figure it out, maybe the dreams will stop and we can both be normal people again and go live happy lives. I don't want to live like this anymore, either. Look, here's my card." It was the same card she'd taken before; plain, thin paper with black and white lettering and a New Orleans police emblem embossed in gold.

Eve looked at it. She felt tears well up in her eyes. She didn't want to live her life in this haze of terror and confusion, never understanding what or why these horrific, unexplainable things were happening. When she took the card her hand brushed his. She could feel his kindness and genuine concern in that brief touch. She looked into his eyes. There was a connection. He felt it too. It was a fact she couldn't deny.

"What do we do now?" she said, her voice soft and lost.

"We can go somewhere, have a cup of coffee, talk about this and figure out what we both know and what we think we know? Maybe together we can see if your pieces fit my pieces and together they make sense," he said. "If it doesn't, I'll go away and never bother you again. Scouts honor."

"You were a scout?" Eve asked.

"Hell, yes! Eagle," he said with his best smile.

"Not tonight. Another time. We'll talk, I promise. I just need to get home," Eve said looking at the card. It was the third time he'd given her this damn card. She put it into her pocket.

Mac looked at her. "I'm following you to your gate to make sure you get home safely."

Eve nodded thankfully. She turned and looked back across the crypts and gravestones that formed the white city of the dead one more time to see if the ruins that had once been Evine's house were visible. So many questions pricked at her brain and Mac had just added a thousand more.

Eve got into her car. Mac slid into his. She listened as he started his engine. Five hundred horses of gas guzzling power echoed off the headstones and crypts and reverberated into the night. Eve started her silent engine. Mostly, she loved its silence, but sometimes she wished it would make a sound, something to say to the world, "I'm here and I'm powerful so don't fuck with me." Eve looked one last time at the full moon as it started its nightly march across the sky. She pulled out with Mac behind her and they drove away.

Chapter Eighteen

Cora looked out the window while Beau paced. Delia and Philip had been put into Philip's crib. Zamara and Aria were off in the servant's quarters. The dining table had been set for the three of them. It held plates of uneaten food. Dinner had gone cold waiting for Eve's return.

"You're sure she was going to see Dr. Honoré?" Beau asked.

"That's what she told me. She hadn't been sleeping and she was getting those wicked headaches again," Cora explained.

Cora went into the dining room, got the wine bottle and poured them both another glass of the dark Bordeaux. It was full bodied and dry, aged perfectly, with a hint of flowers. The alcohol content was high and it always when straight to the head. Beau drank, thinking only of his concern for Eve; it was his fourth glass and Cora's third. They stood by the fireplace filled with burning candles, drinking and listening to some old songs by Radiohead.

"Drink. I hate for this to go to waste," Cora said.

"Why didn't she tell me?" he asked.

"She didn't want you to worry, suga. You have a lot on your plate," Cora said.

"She never talks to me anymore. She's been so busy with Philip, the house and preparations for the wedding and I guess I've been caught up in this insane legal battle ... Maybe it's me? Maybe I've been ignoring her or making her feel pressured by everything. She's been so curious about the Gregoire family history. God forbid if she's heard any of those ridiculous old rumors."

Cora looked away. Beau didn't notice the guilt flushing her cheeks because she was the one who was planning to share the old story of Gofney Lafayette Gregoire's curse. He was lost in thought as he took another long drink from his glass.

"She's been through so much," he said as he took yet another swallow. "Did she talk to you about going back to work at the magazine? Does she need that? I just want her to be happy."

Cora took Beau's hand and sat him down next to her on the couch.

"Sure, but she's not. Please stop worrying. She loves you and the house and being a mom. She's excited about the wedding, Beau, and she truly loves you. And as for going back to work, hell, I've told her for years doing 'something' for a living was way overrated," Cora said with a wry smile.

"That's because you have never 'done something' in your entire life," Beau said with a small smile, teasing her.

"Not true! I do lots of things. I sit on boards and host charities and plan major social events and I spend hours and hours shopping and I work very hard at being beautiful. You think looking this fabulous is easy!" she said with a laugh.

It made him laugh for the first time in a long time.

"And I get to be a mommy and I love that the most. If I didn't say thank you for that ... thank you. I know we aren't supposed to talk about it but ..."

Their words fell away into silence as the song ended and an awkward, empty void filled the room. They drank another glass of wine and listened as the lyrics to *The Game of Love* by Daft Punk rushed in to fill the emptiness and wash over them.

"How are you, Cora? I never ask. Are you dating?" Beau asked.

"I've gone out a few times. Collin Selaway for an entire three months. Then Cap. Things were hot and heavy with good ol' Cap. You remember Cap."

"Caspian Deveroux? Doctor, right?"

"Mostly he travels, flies his jet and drives his Vantage too fast for my taste."

"How is it going?"

"It isn't. He's far too arrogant for my liking and when he decided I needed to get my nose done, that ended the relationship. Hell, if he didn't like the package, why give him the surprise inside. Right?"

"Your nose is perfect," Beau said.

"Thank you, suga. Besides, you, my dear friend, are a very tough act to follow," she said flirting but not meaning to ... not really.

Cora looked up and stared into Beau's eyes. Her heart skipped a beat. She didn't want it to, but there it was. That spark of whatever had attracted them in the first place. Both of them felt the rush and then, both turned away. She stood to get the wine and pour herself another glass.

"Maybe I should call her again," he said, pulling his cell phone from his pocket to hit speed dial.

"Well, suga, if you do, the only thing that's gonna happen is that little ol phone she left over there on the table will just ring again and annoy the hell out of me," Cora said.

"Who walks off and leaves their cell phone?" Beau said, shutting down his phone.

"Oh she used to do it all the time. Made me crazier than a bug. I fussed at her, but did she listen? Never. You, darling, as soon as you get that ring on her finger, must train her in instant communication etiquette."

"Train her," he said adding a chuckle.

"Absolutely, Beauregard Gregoire Le Masters. Make that little renegade of your understand that the days of the electric leash are in full swing!" Cora said.

Again they laughed. She made him smile. She liked that she could do that. He had been looking so sad the past few times she'd seen him. She set the bottle down and walked to the little desk, sipping and thinking. There was no question Cora cared about him. They'd become friends because of this whole situation with Eve. They were both bred, born and grew up as members of the New Orleans social elite. They had a number of mutual acquaintances and a few good friends in common. Beau was a few years older than Cora, but by the time age difference didn't matter he was off in Europe and lost to her and her world. Somehow they'd never really talked until the night of Eve's accident. Then there were all those months in the hospital. Days and nights sitting by Eve's bed waiting for her to awaken, looking like some sleeping beauty who just needed a good goddamn kiss. Then one night the doctor said Eve was deteriorating and both she and her unborn child would die. Cora and Beau sat together in the waiting room listening to those dreadful words.

It was too much to accept. She and Beau wept in each other's arms for her dearest friend and the one woman who, in an instant, made him want to change his life and start over—with her. He told Cora that he and Eve were kindred souls. From the first moment he saw her he knew she was the one he'd searched the world to find. How ironic to discover her literally in his own backyard. Beau got angry about how unfair the world had been to him, taking his sister, mother and father and now he was about to lose Eve and their unborn child. He told Cora he had never felt more alone. Saying the words made him weep harder and the thought of a world without Eve in it made Cora weep with him. She held him and he held her. Neither one could remember the precise moment it happened, the moment their tears turned into gentle, loving kisses, which built into desperate, hungry waves of passion neither could or wanted to resist. They surrendered to each other completely.

They made love in the empty guest room on the third floor where families were allowed to spend the night. It was summer and humid hot the way only the bayou can be. The window hung open and the cool night breeze carried on its back the sweet scent of gardenias and night blooming jasmine from the hospital garden. The cool air covered their nakedness with sweetness and kindness and love, not for each other but for Eve. They made love first through the sadness and tears and then through the anger of losing her. Cora could feel his anger in every thrust and it took her pain away and gave her pleasure. They made love again and again. Their sad desperation transformed them into ravenous animals, devouring each other in a feast of unbridled passion that for the next four hours took them away from everything but pleasure. He needed to be loved and kissed and caressed as he fantasized about the memory of his and Eve's one night together. The past had happened and could not be erased. Delia had been conceived. Eve had lived. Eve came back to them and they had been loving and honest friends and together grown past their one indiscretion, vowing never to succumb to each other again. But here they were, warmed by the wine, vulnerable to each other. His hands touching hers made Cora realize that right now, she needed one more kiss. Her friend would understand. What was one kiss?

Cora wanted him. The memory of their one night of passion weakened her self-control. She knew her life was dull and painful without him, but would never have admitted it to anyone, especially herself. She wanted to stop herself, but the wine mixed with the scent of flowers blooming behind her on the table, ignited her senses. Their scent changed from light and sweet to heavy, spicy and tantalizingly pungent; red peppers, cooking in the hot summer sun, blended with exotic spices and mixed with warm honey. Their seductive aroma mixed with the wine swirling in her head. Combined with his touch the room blurred. Cora turned from him in a desperate attempt to get away. She reached out for the arm of the couch to steady herself, but as she did, she slipped forward and began to fall. With the tears that stung her eyes, the wine and the sadness, she didn't care if she fell into an abyss until his arms caught her; strong, warm, powerful. This wasn't the past memory; this was the present and she was in his arms once again.

"Cora! Are you okay?" Beau said.

He lifted her to the couch and sat down next to her. She looked away, tears flowing in crystal rivulets down her face.

"I'm so sorry," Cora whispered. "I need to go home."

"No you don't. You're staying right here," Beau said taking her glass and setting it down. He wiped the tears from her cheek. "Talk to me, Cordelia Belle Bouvier."

Her name sounded like music when he said it. Her mouth began to water as Beau lifted her chin and turned her face to his. Their eyes met. The spark she'd felt that first night, that first time they had surrendered to each other, shot through her entire body and for the first time in a very, very long time she felt alive.

"Sometimes I can't help but wonder what would have happened if we'd met first that night," she whispered, the words spilling from her lips. Her breath mingling with his.

She saw a hundred emotions flash in his perfect, azure eyes.

"I ... I love Eve, Cora," he said.

"So do I," Cora said.

"It's the wine and ..." he started to say.

"I know," she said.

The song *Have You Ever Really Loved a Woman* wafted through the Bose speakers. The intricate Spanish guitars played and its sweet, lilting melody washed over them while the lyrics whispered in their ears, "And when you find yourself lying helpless in her arms, you know you really love the woman."

The space between them vanished. Their lips met. Cora's body was no longer hers to command, it belonged to the moment. She felt his lips against hers, his breath mingling with her breath. She parted her lips and his tongue slipped inside. Her hands moved under his shirt. She'd forgotten how hard his pecs were and ripped his stomach was. His hands slipped under her blouse. The chemistry, the energy, the rush and flow of emotions swirled around them. His hand pulled her breast from her bra and his lips searched for her nipple. Cora felt her legs spread apart as her hand slipped down inside his pants. Her fingers wrapped around him, long, hard as blue steel and smooth as hot silk. His erection pushed against her. She heard him speak, but the words didn't make sense.

"We have to stop," Beau said, but he didn't.

He pulled her underpants off with one hand and opened her blouse and popped her bra off with the other. He knocked the lamp to the floor. It shattered behind the back of the couch, plunging them into darkness except for the light from the entry hall and the last of the candles.

They slid to the floor in front of the couch as the wine, the music and their passion blended into one. Their bodies intertwined and their clothes fell away as if some spell of passion possessed them and carried them into bliss. In a few breathless moments they were naked. Flesh touched flesh and with each caress, each breath, each pulsating moment their sensuality heightened and every nerve sparked in waves of passion that surged through them. His mouth covered hers in a myriad of blistering kisses, each one more passionate and fiery than the one before. His hands caressed her breasts and his tongue flicked against her nipples. She stroked his cock and the electricity of her touch made him harder. He kissed his way down her chest, over her belly until he found her clitoris. He licked and sucked until it was as hard as his cock and rose erect and throbbing against his tongue. He lunged up and forward. His hands scooping under her ass and lifting her as if she weighed nothing, he parted her legs wider, lowered her, wet and hot slowly down onto his cock. He was on his knees with her legs wrapped around his back. He lifted her up just enough so that the head of his cock licked her clitoris. He sucked on her nipples and lowered her down, pressing himself deeper into her. He brought her up and slid her down repeatedly, each penetration slow and deliberate; each thrust more scintillating than the one before.

Time vanished. It could have been hours or seconds; the pleasure kept building. Cora unwrapped her legs and pushed him back on the floor. She straddled Beau, twisting her hips, slowly grinding him into her. She rode him, cupping and scooping her hips with the grace of a rider on a finely trained stallion executing a course of graceful high jumps, but with much more pleasure. She rocked him into her opening and relaxed her muscles around him. Each time he pulled out she tightened herself, clamping down around him, sliding herself down harder and taking him deeper. Beau moaned, losing himself, losing control, losing his mind. Faster, harder, sweeter. At that instant before orgasm, when he couldn't take another rush of pleasure, he twisted and flipped her over onto her hands and knees reinserting himself into her from behind. Now it was Beau riding into her. He grabbed her hair and hips and drove into her with a wild, fierce abandon. His entire body shuddered in waves of pain and pleasure. Cora's body followed. One body became the other, neither knowing who was whom ... neither caring as the flood of perfect rapture bound them together in passion ... lust ... total abandonment.

Cora pushed back, meeting his every thrust with a hunger that defied words. Again their pleasure grew, exponentially intensifying with every motion. Cora and Beau merged into one entity. Their emotions, minds, their very physical bodies blended and transported them to a place beyond time and space. In a single graceful movement, he flipped her back onto her back. The room seemed to vanish. There were no floor or walls - only a hot, pulsating pleasure that surged through them, piercing every pore and vibrating every cell of their collective being. Suddenly, she was fucking him - hard. His cock was hers and each thrust she pounded into him gave her pleasure. He could feel her nipples as if they were his with wild sensations coursing down into his clit and stimulating the muscles that wrapped around her cock. Everything that was his belonged to her and then it was his and then it was not. The rhythm of their love making spiraled into a throbbing, hot, sweating, creamy wet, volcanic frenzy and just when they thought they couldn't stand another second of pleasure, their eyes met and in a gasping cry of pleasure they exploded in a rush of orgasms that built into feral convulsions of unadulterated bliss. This wasn't animalistic eroticism; this was the godly rapture, perfect ecstasy. Even if they'd wanted to, they couldn't stop. They didn't want to. Beau took her again.

Chapter Nineteen

Eve stood at the door to the parlor, purse and keys still in hand, watching. What she saw in the play of dark shadows, caught intermittently inside the wide streak of light from the hall that stretched across the floor, was not human. She watched horrified and captivated, unable to move or look away, both terrified and exhilarated by this ... *thing* writhing on her floor. It twisted and rolled over and over, undulating and moaning as it rose and fell upon itself. It emitted guttural sounds of erotic pleasure so primal they called to her as Sirens must have called to the sailors on the Argos. Eve knew its voices weren't human yet she thought she'd heard it before, a distant memory from another lifetime. It's provocative, haunting voice bellowed to her and she felt her body being pulled uncontrollably forward. Eve watched mesmerized, unable to look away.

Eve was captivated by the creature's undulating movements and how its skin shifted between shades of pale gold and flushes of burgundy. It was hard to see details of the form that moved before her in the dim light. She stepped closer and thought she could make out a head, arms and legs and even a tail ... no two tails, wrapping around the *thing*, stroking and caressing its body sensually again and again. To her surprise, a vibrating rush of pleasure surged through Eve. Her body was resonating in harmony, feeling the rhythm with what was happening on the floor. Waves of energy wafted across the room and washed over her again and again as gentle and caressing as a warm, easy sea might lap over her body as she lay naked on a beach. She felt her nipples become erect, her skin tingle, aching to be touched. Another rush of warm wetness released between her legs. Eve's breathing changed, deeper and faster, matching her breath with the breath of the creature on the floor. It commanded her to walk in for a closer look ... to touch, to become one with whatever was writhing on the floor.

The voice that lived somewhere deep in her mind screamed at her: *NO! STOP! TURN AROUND AND RUN BEFORE ITS TOO LATE!* The words hit her like a bucket of ice water and slammed her back to reality. *Philip.* Her first instinct was to get her son out of the house and then to find Beau. But as the creature moved itself into the light, she could see glimpses of Beau in the creature. Beau was part of "it."

Eve stepped back. Her heart ached. Everything in her wanted to deny what was happening, but it was there and it was Beau. She slowly and quietly stepped back away from the parlor room door and tip-toed across the polished wood floor of the entry. Just as she made herself turn to sneak up the stairs, she looked back. In that moment she understood why Lot's wife, Ildeth, looked back that one last time on Gomorrah as it fell. Again, she saw it wrestling with itself in the shadows. The view from the stairs changed her perspective and, as she watched, the *thing* divided and transformed into Cora and Beau naked on the parlor floor screwing each other's brains out. What she was witnessing took her breath away and she felt it rip her heart from her body. Seeing them, the man she loved and her best friend, locked in passion, weakened her knees and made her eyes well with tears. *No. He couldn't. She wouldn't. This... is a hallucination. It's not real.* She thought. *Which part?* The voice in her head whispered back. She looked again at the thing that had become Cora and Beau and watched as it melted back into and out of two *things*: one dark bloody red and the other deep gold.

Eve grabbed the banister and pulled herself up, leaning on the wall to steady her feet. Step by step she made herself climb. She didn't know what to believe; she didn't know what she wanted to believe. Could it have actually been Beau and Cora? Her fiancé and her friend? Or was there some unearthly entity in her house? She moved past the room that she and Beau shared. It was dark and empty. *Maybe he was out,* she tried to tell herself. She shook her head knowing the truth. She needed to get her son and get out.

Eve slipped out and down the hall into Philip's room. She grabbed the big diaper bag that was always ready for any situation and crossed to the crib. What she saw made her heart ache. Delia and Philip lay together sleeping, which could only mean that Beau and Cora were here ... somewhere in the house ... together. *If they were in the parlor then ....* Eve heard another low moan bellow up from downstairs. Her body responded with a rush of desire that flushed through her and made her head spin. It was calling to her. The primal side of her desperately wanted to respond, to race down, rip her clothes off and join the rapture of pleasure that pulsed inside the room beneath her.

What the fuck is this feeling! she thought with a shiver. Eve shook her head and ran her fingers through her hair, pulling it to rip from her mind the insane thoughts and erotic sensations that beckoned her. She needed to focus on the children. They slept next to each other: peaceful angels, best friends. Even in the dim glow of the little unicorn night light that shined over the changing table, she could see the children had grown. It was as if over the five hours she'd been out the two had become four year olds. *How was it possible? How could they have physically changed ... aged in a matter of hours?* Before she finished her thought Philip and Delia woke. Delia put her arms up for Eve to pick her up. Eve put down her purse and keys and threw the strap of the diaper bag over her shoulder and lifted Delia up into her arms. She could feel the weight of this little girl to easily be twenty-five pounds.

"Come on Philip," Eve whispered.

How could she carry both of them? Philip looked into her eyes and smiled his mysterious enigmatic, Mona Lisa smile and suddenly Delia weighed nothing in her arms. It was as if Eve held a pillow with a cute sleepy face. When she took Philip's weight into her arms, he too weighed no more than a pillow. Eve heard the moans from downstairs. She closed her thoughts to it and raced out of Philip's room. Once in the hall, her only thought was to get out, but not down the front stairs; that was too dangerous. The servant's stairs were at the far end of the second floor hallway. They led down into the kitchen and from there she could slip out the back door and take Beau's SUV from the garage. As she took her first step the sounds from downstairs fell silent. She held the children tighter and took another step praying that the old boards of the upper hallway wouldn't creak and give her away. With each stride that followed, she held her breath. Finally, Eve and the children reached the top of the back stairs. She started down, careful not to let the old, oak boards creak under her weight. Just as she reached the bottom she saw Zamara, Cora's nanny, and Aria standing in the kitchen. They both turned and just as she was sure they would see her they turned back to look at each other.

"Did you hear that?" Zamara asked.

"Yeah, I did," Aria said.

Eve looked at Philip. Again he smiled the same inexplicable smile and touched her face.

"It's okay, mommy," he whispered and touched his finger to his lips as if to say shush. "They can't see or hear us anymore."

Eve looked for what should have been her and the children's

reflection in the kitchen window. Philip was right, nothing was there.

"I don't know what I think I'm hearing," Zamara said.

"Sounds like raccoons mating under the house again," Aria said.

"Is that what it is? Raccoons," Zamara repeated.

Whatever Philip had done she would ask him later. Right now Eve knew she needed to take advantage of it and get out. She moved with the children across the kitchen. She felt as though her feet were walking on a cushion of air. The trio reached the back door.

"They can wait. I'll call the gardener tomorrow. Right now I wanna' go finish watchin' this impossible show I can't stop watchin' before you have to take Delia home," Aria told her.

"You think it's really about George's secret affair?" Zamara asked.

"Anything is possible," Aria said.

Another moan echoed through the house and they both looked toward the parlor door.

The two women showed no expression. Eve was certain they knew. Without another word they took their snacks and headed back into the servant's quarters.

Eve waited until they were gone. As she was trying to figure out what to shift in her arms to open the door, it slowly swung open. Again Eve looked at Philip.

"You're gonna have to show mommy how you do that, okay?" Eve whispered to Philip.

"Okay," Philip whispered back.

He did it again as they approached the Escalade. All the car doors clicked and swung open ... Philip smiled. She placed the diaper bag in the back seat and leaned forward to strap the children into their car seats. They were well over fifty pounds together, but car seats were still very necessary. She reached into the glove box between the seats where Beau always left his key for the Escalade. The key and his Blackberry were stuffed inside along with an iPad mini—Beau was a gadget freak. He kept his laptop, the Galaxy and the IPhone with him, but the Blackberry and the mini stayed in the car. She was glad to have a phone just in case. It dawned on her she'd set her purse down when she grabbed the diaper bag. She looked at Philip's window and for a second thought of returning. She shook her head. Nothing could make her go back inside now. Eve started the engine and pulled out of the garage.

As Eve drove past the parlor window a rush of tears filled her eyes. The possibility that she had lost both Cora and Beau crushed her heart, if indeed that really was Beau having sex with her best friend, Cordelia Belle Bouvier. The thought of losing both of them in one fell swoop was unbearable. She slowed as she drove past the big house and headed toward the main gate and glanced into the rear view mirror. The house looked at her, the way it had always looked at her, commanding her to come home like Eleanor to Hill House. Then she saw, parked out front of the big house, Cora's new Vantage. It was so Cora to have the most expensive, luxury car on the planet along with her elegant life and bottomless trust fund. Maybe it was Cora and her Vantage who belonged there more than Eve and her Prius. The car sitting there—and Delia in the back seat—left no doubt: Cora was there and so was Beau.

Eve felt horribly unworthy. But why? She'd done nothing wrong. It was them. They'd cheated on her. What could she do if Beau was in love with Cora and Cora was in love with Beau? What could she do? She loved them both. The tears wouldn't stop soaking her cheeks. Nothing felt real. She didn't know what to believe anymore. She also didn't know where to go or what to do. Maybe she should go back and confront them? A vehement surge of anger and the treacherous feeling of betrayal choked Eve. *How could they?* She thought. *I loved them and I thought they loved me. How? Why? Why?* Eve slammed her fist against the steering wheel. The sting of pain in her hand was just enough to give her pause. What had she actually seen? Was it Beau and Cora or was it ... *those things. How could they be real? Because*

I've seen them before, Eve thought. *Was it the Gregoire curse, whatever that was? Was it a beast – a Vampire or a demon?* She had to find out. Eve looked back one more time at the guest house shrinking in the distance and darkness. *You saw them, but when?*

As she drove through the gates, Eve remembered the vision she'd seen reflected in the glass door of the refrigerator. The thing ripping Cora to shreds had a human shape, covered in glowing red skin that looked like an insane niacin overdose gone amuck? The other *thing* had been in more than one of her nightmares, but *wasn't its pale skin the color of sand with a blush of blue?*

"That one was gold. That was new," she said out loud. "How many are there? Or are they real at all. They were real. They were real! Dear God, please don't let me be losing my mind."

The words fell from her lips. Prayers to a God she'd forgotten how to believe in since she was a little girl. That was when her grandmother killed herself and her brother contracted a rare disease and died. Eve prayed and prayed and still Ellis suffered and died. Eve wanted to die too even though she was only eleven. It hurt so badly to watch her brother get weaker and thinner, fighting so hard to stay alive only to succumb to the disease and die as she watched helplessly from across the room. Ellis' death march had taken exactly three weeks from the day they got the news of her grandmother's suicide until he left the world. Ellis' death had given her bad dreams too. Eve remembered her grandmother coming to her in those dreams with her brother. She'd felt then as she felt now, that someone was trying to tell her something important, but Eve's grief was too great to hear anything her grandmother said from the grave. Eve feared her grandmother's insanity might be in her blood too and now that fear was scaring her again. She had tried to erase that fear from her mind all those years ago. She was determined to believe the old woman was selfish and didn't want to leave this world alone so she had taken Ellis with her. In the dreams, her grandmother said, "You have to stay, child. You have things only you can do. You will know soon enough who you are."

Eve hadn't thought of those old nightmares in years. She didn't want to think of them now, but perhaps her grandmother knew about this destiny she would have to face. Eve tried to tell her mother about the nightmares with her grandmother and brother, but it only made her parents concerned for Eve and fearful for themselves. Her worst childhood nightmare came not long after Ellis' death. He was standing by the door calling her to join him rather than stay and face what was coming for her. Because they were twins the Doctor said that kind of thinking was normal. *Survivor's remorse or something.* Eve remembered feeling inconsolably sad, frightened and so angry, but the dreams stopped eventually and Eve made her peace with Ellis dying. But those were dreams. Ellis' death was real ... logical. What the hell were these walking, living breathing nightmares and visions out of some demonic horror movie? They felt just as real as anything she'd ever experienced. No hallucinations could affect her like that ... could they? Was this all really part of some curse?

Eve glanced back at Philip and Delia who'd fallen back to sleep. She re-focused on the mystery unfolding around her and the clues she was uncovering. Her last session with Dr. Honoré held a key. The last thing she remembered was the grassy field and trees, but there was a building - a tower. Eve stopped the car.

"I was at Thibodaux Hospital. There was a door," Eve said.

Eve took off her seat belt, locked the car doors and closed her eyes. She made herself imagine the door at Thibodaux she had seen during the trance. Eyes closed, Eve's hand reached out and turned the knob. It had a raised face on it...a man with fat cheeks and small eyes. A click and the door opened. Instantly, she was standing in a room with no walls, watching - herself. The six, naked, beautiful men were there too, caressing her body, tongues licking, lips kissing, hands fondling, fingers stroking and probing, but this time she was the observer, detached from the Eve stretched naked on the table being ritualistically seduced by seven perfect men whose naked flesh undulated from sandy wheat to a plethora of hues in the dim light. But that one, the big one wasn't red or gold or blue, it ... it was only flesh colored. *Wasn't it?* All that had happened to her under hypnosis came flooding back to her. Eve, the observer, looked up and saw the ceiling spiral open above the Eve on the table, but from where she, as the observer stood, she couldn't see what or who was inside the gaping space.

Eve, the observer, felt frightened for the Eve on the table; salty tears trickled down her face and ran across her lips. Eve opened her eyes and saw she was still in Beau's car. She stared back at the dark ribbon of road that led to what was supposed to be her home, then turned, started the car and drove away. For a long time she kept her gaze on the highway. Ahead, a fork in the road made her stop. A flash of lightning followed by a low, foreboding rumble of thunder echoed around her. A storm was coming. Eve looked at the two roads as they stretched to either side of her. Suddenly, as if an answer were being offered, the full moon broke from behind a scattering of clouds and lined up perfectly with the road on the left which headed north away from the Gregoire estate in the direction of New Orleans. She knew people there: a few friends from work, Charles and Kathy Lee, Piper and Victoria Lynn, but they weren't close friends. Cora took up all her free time. Besides, how could she explain what was happening when she herself didn't understand.

She wished she'd taken the ancient book from Dr. Honoré that had been left by Evine. She thought about the doctor in Egypt. How could she help when she was on the other side of the planet? How could Eve get herself and two kids across the Atlantic and into Egypt? She didn't even have her purse.

"Okay that's the goal. Right now I need someone to talk to and a place for me and two kids to sleep tonight," Eve said.

Another flash of lightning was followed by a distant rumble of thunder.

"Detective Macklin," she said and reached into her pocket.

His card was there. His name and cell number stared up at her. Somehow, he already knew how bizarre the circumstances had become. He'd seen Evine floating in the air with her own special effects. Maybe, just maybe, he could help them. Okay, he didn't know about Beau and Cora in flagrante in the parlor ... if that was Beau and Cora. He didn't know the details of her dreams and visions or what was happening to the children including Philip's newfound abilities, but he'd seen Evine. Eve turned the wheel and pointed her car in the direction of New Orleans and her only hope ... Mac.

Chapter Twenty

Beau and Cora lay wrapped in each other's arms content in the pleasurable afterglow of passion and coiled around one another so intimately that one could not tell where one began and the other ended. As they drifted in spent sleep, Beau's skin began to undulate and ripple. It looked as if he were shedding his flesh and from the supple shell, Kirakin emerged, lifting through Beau's skin. Kirakin's skin glowed, pulsating from shades of olive tan flesh tones through subtle blushes of ruby red and deep burgundy. He looked back at Cora and Beau, breathing as one and smiled, pleased by their tranquility. He then looked out the window at Eve's car. Another being, pale with a blush of gold color emerged from Cora. No words were exchanged before the being with the shimmering gold hue to its skin turned to smoke and evaporated.

Kirakin's body floated through the house from the parlor, up the stairs, from Eve's room to Philip's room. He looked into the crib. The children were gone.

She knows, he thought. *But what and how much?*

Kirakin searched for her, but she had always been too strong for him to find her by using his thoughts. He searched for Philip, but the fact that he was with Eve shielded him. And the girl child? She too would be his once Eve surrendered to him.

Kirakin lifted a sweater Eve kept in Philip's room to wear on chilly nights to his face so he could breathe in her scent. He felt his body react. He wanted her, but more importantly, he needed her to exist. He breathed in her scent again and turned to see Zamara standing at the door. Without a word he slammed the back of his hand into her face. Zamara flew across the room. Before she hit the wall he held out his hand, wrapping her in a force field that held her in midair.

Zamara hung, suspended eighteen inches above the ground, her body trapped in the force field. She was being crushed. Her eyes stretched wide, her mouth gaped open in a silent, tortured scream. Kirakin closed his open fist, tightening his grip, squeezing the life from her.

"I ... did ... as ... you ... asked," Zamara gasped.

The words hissed out of her mouth on the last breath left inside her lungs.

Kirakin opened his hand and slowly lowered her to the floor.

Zamara gasped, as though she'd had the wind knocked out of her. To reopen her lungs was as painful as having them crushed.

"I kept Aria away. I did as you asked," Zamara said in a hoarse whisper.

"Silence," he said as he crossed to the window that looked down into the front courtyard.

"What does she know?" he asked.

"I told you, I have never been able to penetrate her mind," Zamara said. "What about Eve?"

"I felt her. She was in the transition chamber with the Brothers. I don't know how or why. The Priests had her, Macon had her, and then she was gone," he said.

"How? When?" Zamara asked.

"It doesn't matter. She was there. It doesn't make sense," Kirakin said.

"You have bent an entire dimension to create this reality. How long can you make it last?" Zamara asked.

"As long as I need it. As long as it takes to get her back," Kirakin said.

"And what of Gathian?" Zamara asked.

The mention of Gathian's name caused Kirakin's skin to flush a burning glow of red. His body grew larger as he turned to glare at Zamara.

"He's searching for this dimension," Zamara said. "I feel it."

"Then we must make sure he never finds it or her and he must never find the spawn. These are my children," Kirakin hissed at her.

"Not until she surrenders to you," Zamara said.

"She has no choice. Her body hears my call. It's only her mind I need to win," Kirakin said. "Deal with the two humans downstairs. They will be tortured by their betrayal and their guilt will keep them vulnerable. Humans."

"It wasn't their fault," Zamara said.

"I know and you know, but they don't," Kirakin said. "Use them to find her. You will not fail me, Zamara."

Kirakin faded from the room, leaving the scent of spices and honey to linger, thick and pungent. The scent was so strong it almost choked her.

Zamara wrapped her arms around her body and rubbed herself. She ached from the bone crushing force field he'd held her in. She knew Kirakin could have crushed the life out of her, but he needed her and that had kept her alive. She could handle Cora and Delia, but she hadn't quite figured out Aria. There was something about that young girl that made it hard to get into her head. The children had always been a distraction, perhaps even a barrier. Maybe Aria had her own shield, but if she did it was so subtle, so invisible, Zamara could not perceive or feel it. Perhaps with the children gone at least for the moment, she could find out why Aria was able to block her out.

Zamara stepped into Philip's bathroom and looked at herself in the mirror. She looked tired, more tired than she could ever remember. She was only thirty-eight-years old and yet she felt a hundred. She wiped blood from the corner of her mouth while her thoughts once again went to Aria. *The pouch,* she thought. She always wore that leather pouch. Her mother's Grigri, she'd called it. Zamara didn't know what was in it, but perhaps it held powers: strong powers. Zamara knew Aria had come from Voodoo royalty and that her people dated back two hundred years. She'd let slip how as a child she'd watch them gather together to perform their dark rituals, singing chants and making charms. She said she liked the smell of powders her mother used when she made jujus, grigris for her spells. Aria said she cut herself off from all of that and never looked back, but the pouch was her last connection to her mother.

An innocent? Zamara thought. *Or was she?*

Chapter Twenty One

Zamara Estrada was a lovely blend of African and Latina Spanish, Cuban to be exact. Her ancestors came from all over the Caribbean, anywhere slaves were taken by the Spanish, and their bloodlines blended with Africans, islanders and Spanish. The black magic called Santeria had come over from Africa. It protected them over the centuries and it was still strong in Cuba.

She, like Aria, had come from her own Latin line of magi. It had been years since her possession, but she would never forget the man who gave her soul away: her father, Keke Estrada, headed a Black Latin splinter religious group called the Santeria in the jungles of Cuba. She closed her eyes and could still see Keke's face as he leaned into the dim light of his study: ancient, leathered, olive skin, sagging around two sparkling black eyes and a sliver of a mouth that opened to accept a cigar. Keke had a river of wild white hair that fell to his shoulders and framed his eerie face. He was old. Zamara had no idea how old. She suspected he was over a hundred when she was born. He always dressed in white, especially for the holy rituals where white chickens and doves were sacrificed. As far as the Santerias were concerned, Keke's father and grandmother were big medicine from Cuba. Even before the "rising" had happened, their reputation drew people from all over the island of Cuba. At the height of his power, just as the revolution started, he was asked by the elders for protection. He performed the blackest of the dark rituals to build a special army, one strong enough to fight against Castro—an immortal army of men and women raised from the dead and turned into living zombies by the powers of the Santeria's dark magic. They would fight against the armies that took their food and land and called it freedom. He summoned these dead men and women from their graves to rise and walk and fight, but he did not have the power to control or lead them against their enemy. They rose, half bone and rotted flesh from the dirt and turned on Keke's and twelve other villages. They attacked the military and, at first out of fear, the army stayed away from the jungle people, but then the zombies, ravenous, turned on the villagers. They were strong and relentless; undead monsters with ghostly grey eyes and blank, vacant stares, killing and eating all living creatures in their path.

To save the village her father performed an ancient ritual with a name she'd never heard before or since. He drank the most powerful of the South American holy hallucinogens, Ayahuasca. Under its influence, he sent his spirit from this world into one of the other worlds. Because of the fear that filled his heart, the journey led his soul into the darkest of the realms. Zamara saw the flames rise up and engulf his body; how they turned a bloody and fiery red but never burned his flesh. She watched as first his breathing stopped, then his heart and finally, his entire body vanished. What happened next, only Keke knows for sure. When he returned, nine hours later, he wept, telling Zamara he'd made a deal with a dark demon named Kirakin and she was the price of their salvation. The people of the villages were to cover their windows, mark their doors with menstrual blood and stay inside. Kirakin kept his word; he appeared inside a great black mist and the Zombies fell. Their bodies were taken by the earth, sucked down into the dirt to rest in silence until the final resurrection came to take all who didn't know the great mystery of how to never die.

Zamara, once young and beautiful, had hoped her father would make her Oya keeper of the ancient secrets and the mysteries. Now, she was no more than a slave to be taken and used at the will of Kirakin and his dark demon children who roamed the earth as incubi and succubi. She escaped from Cuba, running from her past, running from Kirakin, but he found her in Florida and sent her to Louisiana.

Zamara was sent to live in a house in the Latin Quarter. She filled it with colorful candles that burned in even more colorful glass jars, each laced with scents—lavender, oregano, myrrh and frankincense. There were plastic and porcelain statues of the great ancient master, Jesus the Christ, his wife Mary Magdalene and his Mother Mary. There were a host of Saints, so many she had forgotten their names, but she prayed to them every day to free her from the bondage of her curse. The walls of her bedroom were covered with velvet paintings, a dozen frightening African tribal masks and thousands of crosses. Her room was her sanctuary. The one place Kirakin hated, but it wasn't powerful enough to keep him out if he chose to defy her. Each night she would look up at Jesus the Christ bleeding from the crown of thorns that pierced into the skin above his tortured eyes and ask him for help. At the far end of the room, draped in shadows, the glow of incense swirled into curls of ghostly smoke that danced in the candle light. It gave her peace and let her drift into sleep, where she hoped he would not come to take her.

He'd left her alone since she'd started working for Miss Cora ... mostly. There was the time in Delia's room when she showed Cora the trick of how to calm her daughter that he slipped beneath Zamara's skin and took Cora for his pleasure. He planted in Cora the passion that would be her undoing. It was easy for Kirakin to open her when he stepped inside Beau to seduce Cora. When she resisted, he sent one of his golden demons into her and she could no longer deny the pleasure that took over her.

"I need to weaken her for what's to come," Kirakin had said.

Zamara shuddered at the thought of what that meant. She felt the fear rush up her spine and grab hold of her heart. Zamara shook it away. Fear was what made her most vulnerable to him. She knew that and so did he.

"No," she said out loud. "I won't fear you. I'll hate you and someday ..."

Zamara stopped. She dare not speak the words out loud or even think them. He could hear her thoughts. So she pushed them deep inside the way her father had shown her and waited for the day when she would exact her revenge.

Zamara knew what she had to do next. She had to go downstairs and wake Beau and Cora. She had to tell them that Eve had come in and seen them in their passion. Zamara would watch as their feelings of guilt destroyed their love for each other, while their remorse would crush any small ability they might have left to resist Kirakin when he finally came for them. Worst of all, she would tell them their children were gone, taken by Eve. Zamara wasn't sure if Eve was strong enough to stop what was coming or Aria was powerful enough to help her. She knew only one thing – she needed to *survive, prepare, and be ready for the final shift*, Zamara thought. She straightened her dress and left the room.

Chapter Twenty Two

Mac had taken her call, given her directions and opened his home to Eve and her refugee children, who had stolen away in the night and sought sanctuary from a storm of confusion and unearthly things; unspeakable things Eve had still not yet wrapped her mind around.

Inside the small, wood-frame house just off the seventh district on Granville Street, Eve was given a short tour of Mac's old family home. The little Victorian had three tiny bedrooms and one bath on the second floor with a small entry, parlor, dining room, wonderful kitchen and an added half bath off the back mud porch. The third floor was an oddity found only in older homes. It was a single room with its ceiling and walls in the shape of a coffin. Eve had heard about, but never seen, this strange morbid little room where in years gone by families gathered to mourn the loss of loved ones and hold funeral services. The tiny room had one window that faced the neighborhood church and the shadow of the steeple and cross, when the moon or sun aligned with it, reached into the room and fell precisely on the center of the floor where the coffin would be placed. It would sit on velvet covered saw horses with just enough room for a few chairs around one side and for people to come, sit, pray, weep, file around and say their last good-byes. Now it was only an oddly shaped room filled with dusty boxes and old cloth-covered trunks. Eve wondered what kinds of family treasures and memories left over from the past lay inside.

Mac said the house belonged to his mother's family and he'd inherited it when she and his great grandfather, Papou died. The pictures that sat on the parlor mantle, hung on the walls down the wood-paneled entry hall and climbed up the stairs, told the stories of multiple generations of Macklins who'd lived, loved and died there. He'd changed very few things since their passing, but he'd added the few creature comforts he could on his detective's salary. The minute changes made his home feel like it was his. Eve found it very male, with its ox blood leather chairs and tuck-pointed couches. Dark stained cherry wood tables and chairs filled the dining room. He was the neatest bachelor she'd ever met.

When Eve and the children arrived, he asked no questions. He could see she was upset. He led her to his room where she undressed the children down to their undies and tucked them, upon his insistence, into his queen size bed. Eve lay with them until they fell into a sweet repose obviously unfazed by their new surroundings. The bed felt comfortable, soft and welcoming. It seemed to make her problems melt away and for the first time in a long while she relaxed. Just as she drifted off, she felt Mac standing by the door, watching over them like some guardian angel. His presence filled her with a kind of peace and that same feeling of safety she had experienced at the hospital when she and Mac first talked, then the day he came to the estate, in his arms at Dr. Honoré's, and finally earlier that night at Evine's. That was the feeling of tranquility that enveloped and lulled her into a welcomed, dreamless sleep. *Safe*.

Chapter Twenty Three

Beau and Cora woke, stilled tangled in each other's arms, flesh against flesh, her hair blossoming into matted curls across his chest. Her vulva ached, her nipples became erect as the scent of their passion filled her nostrils and seeped from their skin. She wanted him again. His taste lingered on her lips as sweet as expensive wine laced with honey. They should have languished in the warmth of a thousand suns glowing powerful enough to unwind time and make the world fresh and good and new. Instead, the realization of what had happened turned her world black. Shame rushed over her, dragging her into the present. In silence they slowly unwound themselves and like Adam and Eve in the Garden of Eden after they'd eaten the forbidden fruit, they covered their nakedness in abject embarrassment. Unable to look into each other's eyes or speak a single word, they gathered their clothes that lay in colored puddles around the parlor and dressed. She and Beau had fallen from grace; fallen into the depths of forbidden, carnal knowledge. They realized that because they had sinned, they would forever be punished and exorcized from paradise. Cora found and slipped into her dress. Her legs trembled, weak from the intensity of their intercourse. Unhinged, both physically and emotionally, she wept. She let out deep sobs, the kind a child experiences when something precious dies and is lost forever. She wasn't sure if her tears were for the treachery of betraying her best friend or the sadness that she could not ever allow herself the pleasure of loving Beau again.

Beau, tormented by the sound of her sobs, turned to look at her. He wanted to console her. He too was feeling this same deluge of emotions that pummeled her. In her heart of hearts Cora knew he didn't dare cross the room. She could see him through the tears that blurred her vision as he turned away. Beau gathered his things and dressed.

"The children are gone," Zamara said from the entry. "So is Miss Eve."

The words stabbed into Cora's heart. Beau rushed from the room and raced upstairs to search for his son as if Zamara had been lying and he alone could find them. Beau rounded the door to Philip's room. It was empty. His future wife and baby son gone! She had seen him with Cora. *She saw. She saw.* How could he explain?

Downstairs, Cora was having the same thoughts. *How could this unthinkable thing have happened? How can I explain my own actions to the woman I trust and love and call my friend? Why does she always win?* Cora thought.

They had been concerned for her, just like the first time they had slipped into each other's arms. *The first time,* Cora thought and now this had to be the last.

"Where's Delia?" Cora asked as Beau came down the stairs. Her voice raspy, dry from the tears that rung her out and left her parched.

"Gone," Beau said clinging to the wall as if it held him up.

Cora didn't remember crossing the room or stepping into the entry, but there she was facing Beau as he stood halfway down the stairs.

"What do you mean? Where?" Cora demanded.

"She took Mister Beau's car, Miss Cora. Miss Eve's car is out front," Zamara said.

For the first time Beau and Cora looked into each other's eyes. *She knows.*

"I called her cell phone a hundred times," Aria said stepping in from the kitchen.

Beau and Cora turned to Eve's phone, mute on the desk in the parlor ... the battery dead ... forgotten ... abandoned.

"She took my car. The Blackberry's in it," Beau said.

He crossed to his phone, picked up and dialed. They held a collective breath while it rang and rang and rang.

"She's upset. She'll calm down and call us. Right?" Beau asked Cora.

Cora had only been on the receiving side of Eve's anger once. Then they didn't speak for three weeks.

"I don't know. She's a northerner. Maybe she doesn't hold anger like ... Beau, she has our children. Is this punishment for ..." Cora stopped speaking, the tears welling back in her eyes, the words choking in her throat.

"Get some coffee," Beau said to Aria. "Please."

Aria and Zamara left as Beau crossed to a distraught Cora. He started to put his arms around her and stopped.

"We'll find her, Cora. I need you to calm down and help me think of where she might have gone. We'll call Doctor Honoré and—" Beau stopped.

"I was her friend. She would have come to me," Cora said.

Tears beat against her eyes, choking her into sobs that caught her breath and strangled her, driving her into a panic attack.

"I would never hurt her," Cora cried.

Beau fought himself. He was a good man. A kind man and her friend. He wanted to go to her and fold her in his arms, to comfort her and for her to comfort him. She had become like the sister he'd lost and yet after last night they'd crossed a line of trust, and almost as an act of incest, they transferred between them the unspeakable. The act of loving one another had corrupted the innocence they'd worked so hard to bend back from darkness. They had held and loved each other because of fearing they would lose Eve that first time in the hospital. They had been honest and truthful and Eve had forgiven them. She'd even offered to step aside and they declined. Together they walked into the light of love and trust and friendship and now it was destroyed. The punishment had been that Eve, in her pain and anger, had taken their children from them.

"Oh, God. Oh, God! Oh God!" Cora shouted.

"We'll find her, Cora, and we'll explain," Beau said.

"Explain what? Do you understand what happened?" Cora shouted through the tears.

"We ... had too much wine and—" Beau started to say, but Cora cut him off.

"Bullshit! I won't lie to myself and I won't lie to you or Eve anymore. I love you. I have loved you from the first time I saw you at the hospital. You have a power over me. I thought I could control what I felt and what I know you felt. Eve saw it. She may not have wanted to, but she saw it. We made her believe we were better and stronger and could hold this tsunami at bay, but we can't. It took us over the edge to a place I never knew existed and I want it. Look at me and tell me you don't love me! Tell me!" She screamed.

Beau was silent. He looked at her. She could see the storm brewing in his eyes that changed them from warm sky blue to an icy gray sea. She could see the emotions flash inside him between anger and sorrow.

"I love Eve, Cora. Yes, I love you, but ..." Beau started to say.

Cora trembled. Rage, pain, sorrow, a barrage of feelings soaked in confusion, ripped through her. She grabbed her purse and keys and stormed out the door.

"Cora! Where are you going?"

"To find my goddamn daughter!" Cora screamed at him. "And you tell that BITCH if she hurts one hair of Delia's head, I'll crush her and you both!"

Cora vanished out the front door. Beau, in a rush of brutish fury, was on her heels. They spilled out onto the gravel and grass car park, Cora striding like a cheetah, Beau, a lion reaching his claws out to bring her down.

"Stop!" he commanded.

Cora never missed a step. She reached her Vantage and ripped the door open. Beau grabbed her and spun her around. There was a moment when their eyes connected and time split. Cora reached up and shoved her fingers into his hair and pulled his face to hers. She kissed him in an act of perfect passion. The kiss was hard and rooted in voracious anger and irresistible lust. They crashed into each other. She felt his body press her against the car. She felt his cock turn stiff. Her hands searched down his pants. His hands dove up under her dress. His touch felt like fire against her flesh. Her nipples shot to attention. He spun her, pressing her forward onto the roof of the car. He pushed her legs apart. Cora stepped one foot up on the car's running board and with a thrust he stabbed himself inside her. His fingers curled into her hair, pulling her head so she arched her ass back and into him. His hips pumped, fucking her with all the anger and lust that twisted between, around them, inside them. They were drowning in their passion.

"No," Cora murmured through her moans of pain and pleasure. "No!"

Suddenly Cora pushed him back. She spun and slapped him. "Stop!"

But it wasn't Beau she slapped, it was Kirakin. He stood where Beau had just been standing moment before.

Stunned, Cora looked back at the house and saw Beau standing in the parlor window talking to Zamara. He walked away from Zamara oblivious to what was unfolding outside. Cora turned back to face the Nephilim and opened her mouth to scream, but his huge, glowing red hands covered her face. He threw Cora down on the gravel and ravaged her.

****

Aria heard the argument in the entry. She heard Cora leave, looked out the window and saw Beau follow her out. Aria froze at the kitchen entry unsure what to do. They stood silent for a long moment listening. She crept closer into the entry. Zamara saw Aria and crossed to see what she was looking at. Aria could see the car, but it was empty.

"He's got her!" Aria said.

Zamara understood instantly what Aria was talking about.

"Check on Beau!" Zamara commanded.

Aria ran upstairs and Zamara raced out of the house and across the car park. She froze when she saw Kirakin crushing Cora into the ground. She wanted to hit him. Stop him. Do something to help Cora. The closer she came, the harder he fucked Cora. Zamara could hear Cora's muffled screams through his fingers as they covered her face.

"Please," Zamara whispered. It was a desperate prayer that fell helpless from her lips.

Kirakin turned his face to Zamara. His features, twisted in lust and rage, made Zamara step back. That's when Aria came out of the house.

"Grab her!" Aria shouted as she strode past Zamara.

As Aria moved past a petrified Zamara, she ripped the leather pouch from around her neck. Tearing it open, Aria spilled the black, red and white powder and small, sparkling crystals out all over Kirakin. They ignited and set Kirakin on fire. The night shattered with his scream.

Zamara grabbed Cora and dragged her from beneath him.

Behind Kirakin the air split open, creating a fissure into an alternate dimension; a gaping hole, whipped by wild winds sucked him inside. Kirakin, furious, fought the devouring wind. The flames licked his skin as he flailed, cursing in pain until the fissure swallowed him whole and sealed itself with a reverberating CRACK.

Zamara stared at Aria as she held a now unconscious Cora.

"Help me," Zamara said.

Aria rushed to her side and together they gathered Cora up.

"Put her in the car," Aria said. "Can you care for her?"

"Will she remember?" Zamara asked.

"I don't know."

They got the back door open and slipped Cora inside.

"What did you do?" Zamara asked.

"It's temporary. He'll be back and he'll be pissed," Aria told her as she gathered the car keys and handed them to Zamara. "Whatever you do, don't leave her alone."

Zamara reached out and grabbed Aria's arm.

"Can you help me get away from him?" Zamara begged. "Please. Please."

"You have to ask me."

"I'm begging you. I know no magic strong enough to protect me or her from him," Zamara explained. "Help me."

Aria reached out her hand and touched Zamara's shoulder. Aria recoiled as if twenty thousand volts of electricity were ripping through her. Aria stepped back.

"What did you do? You gave yourself to him. You're under his powers? How? Why?" Aria asked, the sadness tainting every word.

"Not me, my father. He had to or everyone would die. I was the sacrifice. I just said yes to help my family. I didn't know ... I didn't know what he was asking until it was too late," Zamara said.

"I'm sorry. You are beyond my powers. I might be able to protect her," Aria said looking at Cora. "... and maybe I can save Miss Eve and the babies, but to break a spirit bond, I ... Your father sacrificed you into that curse? With him?"

"He had to. I was all he'd accept," Zamara said.

"Focus your powers on saving Cora. Make it so she doesn't remember what just happened to her if you can. There are acts of selfless courage that can break the bond, but they come with a heavy price."

"Better to die in grace than to live in hell," Zamara said. "What about Mister Beau?"

"His blood is cursed by an ancient family curse. He has belonged to them since his birth and it is only a matter of time before he becomes what he is," Aria said.

"Can't you try to cleanse him of that demon?" Zamara asked.

"It could kill him, but I can try. I just can't do it alone. Right now I need to find Eve and the children before Kirakin finds a way back and gets to them first," Aria said. "Zamara, I need your help."

"Me? You can't find her by yourself?" Zamara said.

"No. I'll have to summon another of the Nephilim," Aria told her.

"Madre de Dios, one as powerful as Kirakin?"

"Gathian. They are the same spirit divided into good and evil. One cannot live without the other. One cannot die without the other - or so they think. Go! I'll call you when I need your help, Zamara," Aria said, looking at Cora, bleeding and unconscious in the car. "Get her home and heal her as best you can. I'll prepare everything for the séance and then I'll call you. Do you understand?"

Zamara swallowed, her mouth turned dry from a surge of fear. She knew all too well what was about to be asked of her.

"Zamara? Do you understand?" Aria shouted at her.

"Yes, God help us all, I understand exactly," Zamara said and tried to bless herself. Her hand twisted into a cramp. Zamara winced with pain.

"I'll wait for your call," Zamara said

Rubbing her arm she got into the Vantage as Aria looked at the empty pouch in her hand.

Chapter Twenty Four

In the early hours of the morning Mac slipped out and drove to the Creole Café. It was a small family-run business that had been there since long before he was born. He bought fresh chicory coffee for himself and Eve and delectable hot beignets dusted in powdered sugar with a glass bottle of fresh cold milk for the kids. Not healthy, but fun and very New Orleans. As he drove home, he listened to Jimi Hendrix singing his favorite blues song. "Hear My Train a Comin'" played an acoustic, twelve string guitar. Mac sang along off key, bobbing his head and letting the words and the passion that Hendrix laid down on those analogue tracks bend each note. Hendrix could make anyone feel like they had the soul to wail. Mac played air guitar on his seat belt as he waited for the light to change. The song ended, but Mac kept grooving until the weather man cut in announcing the heat index and humidity for the coming day, high winds and a coming storm. A big hurricane was brewing off the Florida Keys. The announcer said it was heading their way, but could fade before it reached them. Mac looked up and saw blue skies spotted with voluminous fluffy white clouds stretched above him. Mac inhaled deeply. He could sense the coming storm in the air. It was a gift, his grandmother told him, to know the weather. That gift had saved them in Katrina. His bones ached from the barometric pressure and the wind carried the scent of salt air. No doubt in his mind or his body, a storm was coming.

He reached the house and delivered his treasures. Mac watched a sleepy Eve, her hair, loose and unkempt, falling past her shoulders as she gratefully took the offering and fed both Philip and Delia. They all shared the beignets. Mac smiled as Eve made sure to shake as much powdered sugar off the top of each beignet as she could.

"Nothing worse than sugar-hyped kids," she told him with a smile.

Eve sipped her coffee, talking and playing with the kids as Mac watched. She was a good mother and even with sleepy eyes, strained from whatever event had brought her to him, she was beautiful. He tilted his head in amazement, watching as the sun reached through the window and kissed her hair. Each time she moved the light reflected off it, catching the honey color of her hair and enhancing each strand with the gold of the sun. If this wasn't the definition of smitten, Mac didn't know what else to call it.

Eve finished her coffee and kissed both children before leaving them to play with crayons and coloring books in the kitchen with Mac close by. Eve gathered their clothes, a shirt, pants and dress to wash on the porch. Eve went to get their shoes and as she wandered down the hall, she peeked in the other two rooms. One held an old, oak framed bed and a matching armoire from the eighteen hundreds. The dresser in the second room was from the forties. It was made of a blonde wood with amber handles and a waterfall front. It had a beautiful vanity with drawers anchored together by a large circular mirror. Eve caught her reflection, but refused to look too closely. She didn't want to see how deep the circles under her eyes had become. A small ancient rocker stood by the window next to an old Victorian rocking horse. *The children would like that*, Eve thought. In the corner were several boxes, neatly filled with old clothes and old papers.

Mac was a bachelor, but he was obviously a neat freak. So the place was clean, which she appreciated. Eve went to the bathroom, peed, washed her face and hands and used her finger for a tooth brush. She found a good, boar's hair brush to pull as many tangles as she could out of her tresses. She braided her locks into a rope and let it fall down her back. Eve took one last look at the face in the mirror, stuck out her tongue and grimaced, then returned to the kitchen. Mac sat with the children in the middle of the floor playing with them, surrounded by a pile of pots and spoons he'd spilled before them. He sang while they made a ruckus of clashing sounds as they laughed and played.

"Thank you," Eve said.

"They're amazing," he said with a smile. It was obvious he was having as much fun as they were.

Eve nodded yes, picked up her coffee and stepped toward the back door.

"Can we talk out on the porch?" she asked.

"Sure," he said with a nod.

Eve opened the wood-framed, heavily painted screen door with its layers of colors from years of care, shade after shade peeking through the cracks and scratches. The door swung wide, screaming to be oiled, as they stepped onto the wood porch.

"WD 40," Mac said apologetically. "What on earth did we do before WD 40?"

"Oil," Eve said with a smile. "Can you grab—"

"Oh, right," Mac said.

Turning with the grace of a dancer he grabbed the kids by their pants and carried them outside like two giggling, squealing piglets and sat them on the grass. Their laughter echoed across the small yard. Eve watched as he filled a pail with water, which he mischievously placed on the grass between the kids next to a small mound of black dirt. Eve laughed as she handed each a spoon and some tin bowls that must have belonged to a long gone dog. Mac crossed his arms and smiled as Eve happily mixed dirt, grass and water, showing the children the art of mud pies. Delia got it instantly. Eve cupped her hands into the water, scooped and splashed enough out to wet the dirt. Delia stabbed her delicate little finger into the mud and with an expression of joyous amazement made her very first mud pie. Philip was more studious, feeling the grit of the wet dirt between his fingers. He tasted it and made a face and held his dirty fingers out, uncertain if he liked the mess it made. Delia put a spoonful of mud in his open hand and when the mud squished through his fingers, he laughed with pure delight and dug in full force. The children played and left the adults to drink coffee and talk nearby.

The overhang above the porch sheltered them from the morning sun. She looked at the carved eaves that turned gracefully into fleur de lis at each corner. *So fancy for the simplicity of the house*, Eve thought. But somehow it all fit. People had loved this house for a very long time. She looked at the cascades of lavender wisteria that draped lazily over the large arbor by the back gate. The whole yard was perfectly shaded by a huge, old oak that stood proudly in the center of the tiny yard, allowing just the right amount of sunlight to fall across the ground as delicately as moonlight through a piece of fine Chantilly lace.

"It doesn't have any moss on it?" Eve asked.

"It would if I didn't take it off. Moss is insidious. It'll take over an old tree like that, wrap around its branches and leaves and suffocate the life out of it. It's over three hundred years old, far too beautiful to let die," he spoke of the tree, but his eyes stayed on Eve.

"I know you're busy and I shouldn't have come ..." Eve started.

"I'm not busy and you should have come," he said.

"I apologize for the restraining order. Beau was so insistent, but I don't want to get you in any trouble."

"Hell, too late for that," he said with a laugh. "I've been suspended."

"Because of me? Oh, God, Detective Macklin, I'm so sorry."

"Mac. If I'm going to jail for harboring you, please, call me Mac. Okay?"

Eve nodded and smiled.

"And no, I got suspended because of me. I should have left you alone, but ...," he stopped. "Look, Honoré's office was a coincidence and as for me following you through the cemetery, well, I was worried at how drained you looked. Then I saw that floating thing behind the cemetery and I had to help."

"I'm glad you did. Thank you," Eve said. "I needed someone to witness what I saw."

They sat in the quiet of the yard, the silence broken by the occasional chirping of some birds and giggles from the kids. Finally Eve spoke.

"I have to get to Egypt. Today," she said.

Mac looked at her as if to say, *Seriously? And you're telling me this because...*

"I need your help. We need passports for me and the kids. I have some money in my old account and some old credit cards I think still work," she went on.

"What makes you think all cops know guys who make fake passports?" he asked.

"I don't," Eve said feeling embarrassed. "Do you?"

"Actually I do. If I'm mistaken, you don't have a purse unless it's in the car."

"It's not. I left it at the house."

"Then you can't go to your bank. Look, I may have some money I can lend you."

"I couldn't ask—"

"... and I might even have access to a private jet," he said.

Eve looked at him and blinked.

"Old oil guy with ridiculous money and all the toys in the world. Loves beautiful women and owes me a big favor," Mac said.

"Wow, Detective Macklin, I'm impressed," Eve said.

"It is bullshit until I pull it off, but it's good bullshit," he said. "Are you going to tell me that what we saw floating at the burned out house behind the cemetery has something to do with why we are going to Egypt?"

"She's part of my dreams. I haven't put all the pieces together and I think she's just the tip of a very deep iceberg. The scary thing is, I don't know how deep it goes," Eve told him. "Look, I have no right to ask for your help or put your life in danger, Detect—Mac."

"You don't have a choice. The way I see it, I'm all you've got," he explained. "Eve, I've seen the white rabbit and I'm going down the hole as deep as it goes until I get some answers. Look, I ... I've been having dreams too. They won't stop. They don't make sense and I want to understand what is happening so I can get my life back," Mac said.

"And you're the only person who understands what I'm going through," Eve said.

"Understand isn't the word, but I am aware and something is very wrong with this picture. I'll tell you what, I'll share everything I've been dealing with on this twisted mental frequency of a warped channel that's been pumped into my head since I met you, and you tell me what you remember of your dreams and visions. Fair?"

Eve weighed the offer. He was right and Eve knew it. There was no one else she could talk to except him. They shared a common bond tied into the experience behind the cemetery, proof of something beyond strange, but they both knew there was so much more. Eve took a deep breath. She looked over at Philip and Delia and, as she did, Philip pushed himself up from the ground, his hands and body covered in mud, and reached for her. A moment later, Delia stood too. The expression etched on both their faces belonged on a grown-up's, not on two sweet, innocent children covered in mud.

Philip walked over to Eve and Delia followed; two adorable little mud puppies staring at her with their beatific eyes.

"Oh, Philip, you're a mess. You too, Miss Delia," Eve said with a sad little smile, knowing what it would take to clean them up.

"He can't protect you," Philip said, his eyes locked on Mac. "But he will serve another purpose when the time comes."

"What?" Eve said, perplexed by the words coming from her too young son.

She and Mac exchanged a look, both of them too stunned to speak.

"You need Aria," Philip said.

"Zamara can't know. She belongs to him," Delia said. "So does Mommy."

"How are they doing that and what are they talking about?" Mac said, his voice barely above a whisper.

Again Philip looked at him.

"Time is growing short," Philip said.

"Please tell me you understand what and how they are saying these things," Mac said.

Eve gathered the mud-covered children, once again weightless, into her arms.

"I don't understand the meaning of the words, but I feel the urgency. Beau, Aria, Cora, Zamara and the children ... he ... they are looking for us," Eve said, turning to head back into the house.

Mac was on her heels. "Them? They? Who are they?" he insisted.

"You know them from your dreams, Mac. The Nephilim and they are not of this world."

He opened the door to let her pass through with the children.

"I'll get the children clean." What do you need for the passports and to arrange that jet? They'll need clothes, shoes and jackets. We need to check the weather in Cairo. I'll find a way to pay you back. I promise."

They stepped onto the mud porch where Eve found a towel, wet it and wiped the larger, dried cakes of mud from the two of them. Eve sighed; only a hose down in the shower and full bath would take care of the rest.

"Okay, this... is freaking me out," Mac said, obviously shaken.

"More than Evine?" Eve asked.

Mac stopped. Something inside him whispered, *Trust what you know and share what you are feeling. Hurry or you are all lost.* The words echoing in his mind sent a chill up his spine. The voice belonged to his grandmother.

"Okay. Photos for the passports. No one will believe they're under two, so we'll have to decide how old and what year they were born to be this mature," Mac said.

He picked up Delia as Eve picked up Philip and both headed into the house to run a bath.

"You think at this growth rate we should err on the side of older rather than younger?" Eve asked, looking at Philip who seemed to age in her arms. "Make them size four."

The children seemed to be in a state of metamorphosis, spurts of physical transformation forcing them to grow up at an alarming rate. It made her heart ache. She feared she would never get to teach them things like normal children.

Philip touched her face and sent her a thought in unspoken words to her, *it's alright. You are on a far greater journey, mommy.* Eve looked into Philip's eyes. She'd heard him just as clear as if he said the words out loud.

The children were washed and their hair neatly combed by the time Mac came up with his digital camera and snapped several pictures, checking each to make sure it would work for their fake passports. He took a series of shots of Eve as well. When her eyes looked into the camera lens and connected with his, he felt his heart melt. The camera captured the soul in her eyes, the sensuality of her lips and the way the light danced in her hair. It made the emotions that spun in his heart open to an even deeper place.

Eve told him she would feed the kids and put them down for their naps.

"If they still need naps," she said looking at how big they were.

"I'll be back in a few hours. Help yourself to everything, but I suggest you stay inside," Mac said, as he slipped on an old baseball cap.

Eve nodded. "I don't know how to thank you, Mac."

Mac looked at her for a long time. Silence hung between them as palpable as a warm mist. He read in her eyes that she knew what he wanted to say. She knew he liked her, that much was obvious, and he wanted to believe she liked him. He could feel the words he wanted to say gathering like a turbulent storm in his mind. A visible shiver trembled through her. She stood there looking at him, completely vulnerable. She needed his help and his protection. The worst thing he could do was let whatever it was he was feeling for her come to the surface. So he let the storm subside.

"I'll have to think about that for a while," he said and smiled at her.

Eve smiled; she knew and felt all he was going through in those brief moments of silence. It was easy to read it in his eyes. That's what she liked about him most, that they could read each other's needs almost before the other knew themselves. She was grateful she had him as a friend.

"Mac, be careful," Eve said.

Mac stepped outside and was gone. The wind, growing stronger, caught the screen door and slammed it shut. Eve looked up to see the fast moving clouds darkening from white to gray. A storm was coming.

Chapter Twenty Five

Beau sat motionless on the edge of the bed in their bedroom holding Eve's brush. His expression was blank, his body felt numb. He didn't want to feel the pangs of guilt and betrayal that gnawed at his thoughts. He wanted to talk to Eve, explain, promise it would never happen again, beg her forgiveness, kiss her face and make love to her, but first he had to find her.

He lifted his other hand to his eyes. He could still smell the scent of Cora ... of the two of them on his skin. He didn't want to admit it, but he wanted her. Some wild animal impulse that he had no control over, needed her. Beau stood and crossed to the bathroom. Turning on the water, Beau stripped out of his clothes and stepped into the water. He needed to scrub her off his body, out of his hair, and out of his mind. He caught his reflection in the bathroom mirror, peeking through the billows of steam. Angry red claw marks striped down his back. He hadn't remembered her nails being that long or that sharp, and worse he hadn't remembered her gouging them into him. The memory of them making love made him erect. It had been like nothing he'd ever experienced; present, visceral, immediate, but at the same time otherworldly. It had been a state of pleasurable bliss that defied description. Yet making love to Eve was even better. He needed her. He turned to face the mirror and as he did something inhuman flashed through his image.

Beau's heart jumped into his throat. It had to be a hallucination. He looked again and the image returned – the two reflections mingled into one. They/he/it looked almost human and had several of his features, but the edges blurred as it moved. Their bodies matched perfectly in size, but its skin pulsed, shifting from flesh into an array of shades inside a glow that ended the spectrum at a deep, reddish hue like a bad sunburn. Before Beau could comprehend what was happening, a voice spoke to him.

"It's time for you to remember who you are and why you were born," the voice said.

Beau stood speechless, staring at the image that vacillated between his and someone ... some*thing* else's.

"I am Kirakin. I am you. I run in your blood as I ran in your grandfather and his father and his father before him. I am the blood of the Nephilim."

"No! I broke that curse," Beau said.

"Mortals and fools call it a curse. What you are is a gift, created before time and given to humanity. You thought when you drank the ayahuasca in Peru and the medicine man guided you to dance with the winged women, you were made free. But you know your freedom is impossible. You cannot be free from yourself."

"I made love to the winged woman!"

"You think her powerful enough to break your bonds. Did you erase from your memory that after you fucked her to death, you raped a hundred more women, just as Gofney did when he lived in France and then a thousand times again when he came to the new land. He did as his ancestors did, and as his spawn did. So did you. Just as Philip will when he is called."

"No," Beau said. "I found Eve. I mated with Eve."

"You did what I commanded you to do," Kirakin told him.

"She was why I came home. She gave birth to my son."

"Did she? Or is he mine? As for saving you...until she knows her truth, she cannot save you or herself and I will take her back long before that happens," Kirakin said.

"Then I'll wake her! She will save me!"

"That I will not allow. You hid from me for eight years, but you came back because you had no choice. You are weak. You betrayed her. She saw you seduced. It's far too late for you and Eve, Beau, and now, I will bring you into my world. Once I have you here, it will be by my will alone that allows you to return," Kirakin said.

The red in his skin deepened, the glow that emanated from Kirakin's eyes intensified. There was something in his eyes Beau had seen before, but he couldn't figure out where.

In the mirror, Beau saw his own eyes lift, move up, a spirit ascending from flesh. He could see the ghostly shape of his transparent image drift out of his body and be dragged toward the mirror. His ghostly image looked back helpless at his body, a motionless, empty shell, waiting for Kirakin to step inside. Beau began to fight. Struggling, he used all his strength and pulled his spirit form back from the mirror and into his body. He commanded his feet to step out of the shower, each step feeling as though he moved through thick molasses. Beau stepped out of the bathroom and slammed the door. The pressure released. Naked, wet and weak from the transformation, he leaned against the door.

Beau looked across the room. Kirakin stood staring at him from the bedroom mirror. In the dim light Kirakin reached through the reflecting glass. Beau felt himself, spirit and body, drifting apart again. He dropped to the floor, grabbing pants and pulling them on as he crawled as quickly as he could out of the room. Beau looked down the hall. The walls held three more mirrors. Each began to glow and pulse. Beau darted into Philip's empty room. He grabbed every cover, sheet and blanket he could find and hung them over the glass, windows and mirrors to hide his reflection.

"You think you can escape me?" Kirakin said from behind one of them. "You can't Beau. You are me and I am you, just in your true form."

Beau, half naked and alone, once again felt himself draining away.

"That's a lie. None of this is real," he shouted. "Whatever you are, get the fuck out of my house."

"This is very real so either stop fighting me or I will crush you and bring you into my realm painfully broken!" Kirakin said.

Beau could hear Kirakin's anger intensify with every word.

Beau stumbled down the hallway, his body weakening with every step. Every uncovered mirror pulled on him with the force of a gale wind. He made it to the top of the stairs. His mind spun, he felt weak and disoriented as he stumbled. He tripped, tumbling down the stairs and splattering across the entry floor. He felt the lights fading, as if someone was turning down the sun. As the room darkened his strength drained from him. He looked up into a swirling open portal. He could see that at the other end was Kirakin's world. A long tunnel spiraled into it, narrow at his end and opening wider and wider at Kirakin's end. He saw glimpses of a purple, grey sky with harsh, jagged rocks that jutted up from a barren, desolate landscape. Kirakin stood at its center, enormous, powerful, at least twelve feet tall, waiting to crush him.

Beau was moving toward Kirakin. Beau clenched his fist. He fought to hold his ground. He would fight Kirakin with his last ounce of strength. He thought of Eve and Philip. He had to find a way to protect those he loved from this monster that was somehow part of him. If he could destroy Kirakin, maybe he could be free. He looked back as he was pulled deeper, closer to the other world.

A strange dusting of grey ashes fell, covering him. Beau looked at his arms and then up at Kirakin. The creature's eyes widened, filling with fury. Beau looked back as the last light from his side became no more than a pin hole and felt arms wrap around him.

"Let him go!" Aria yelled.

Aria threw a large blanket over him to protect him from the vortex that was sucking his life and soul into Kirakin's dimension. Aria was thin and wiry, but she was amazingly strong, determined and very tough.

She dragged him to his feet and got her shoulders under his arms allowing all two hundred pounds of his weight to rest on her. Beau somehow managed to get his legs underneath him.

"I need you to run," Aria said.

It took everything Beau had to move his feet, legs, body. Step after step his body defied him. Still, he pushed forward. Finally he felt the rhythm of her steps and fell into sync with her as they made it across the entry and out the front door. The house began to tremble. Aria knew that Kirakin was furious because she had stolen his prey. Beau stumbled and they both crashed to the hard gravel. She helped Beau to his feet again. The earth cracked and split open behind them. Again they fell. Again they got back to their feet. Together they ran only inches ahead of the opening earth.

Aria changed directions, pushing Beau into Eve's open car door. She slammed it shut and sprinted around to the driver's side. The uneven ground forced her to hold on to the fender. Aria slipped, smashing down into the gravel on her knee. Blood spurted from a gaping wound. The pain bit into her leg and made her eyes squeeze shut and her breath catch. When she opened her eyes her heart stopped.

Curls of crimson red smoke crawled from the crack in the ground, splitting and advancing like smoldering tentacles across the courtyard to get her. Aria reached to her throat to grab her leather pouch. The grigri was gone. She'd used it and its powers to stop him in his own dimension. Weaponless, she had only her wits. Aria pulled herself to her feet. Her leg screamed at her and the pain cut into her. Blood splattered onto the rocks as she somehow got the door open. Beau reached out grabbed her arm and snatched her inside. Aria slammed the door as the red smoke billowed toward them. Aria reached out, *Thank you,* she thought, Eve had left the keys.

The world outside the car boomed and rattled, dust rose from the ground, the leaves quivered as the trees shook in the violent tremors.

"DRIVE!" Beau shouted, looking at what pursued them.

Aria started the car and slammed her foot onto the accelerator. The car lurched forward. The combustion engine roared to life and they took off until—the car jerked to a stop. The engine roared under the pressure of her foot. The tires spun ... held in the clutches of an invisible force. They were captive.

"Go!" Beau shouted, as pressure from the smoke began crushing the metal car.

"My foot's to the floor!" Aria said.

She released the pedal and jammed it down again. The car lurched forward, pulling, inch by inch through the thick swirls of scarlet smoke that cocooned the car. With a final shudder the car broke free and Aria sped for the side gate, gaining speed and precious distance with every second. Beau looked back as the smoke curled back on itself; a red tsunami of trembling energy stretched up above the guest house and with the force of a huge fist, crashed down, crushing the house into oblivion and exploding into flames!

Chapter Twenty Six

Cora woke up in her own bed. She opened her eyes and tried to move. Her body felt as though a train had hit her. It hurt to breathe. Her hair hurt. She looked down and saw the white gauze bandage that covered her hands and felt the bandage on her chin. It was in the exact place Eve told her she had been cut in her dream.

"Hi," Zamara said.

Cora turned her face and there Zamara sat in the rocker next to her bed. She looked exhausted. Cora could see through the drawn window curtains that night and blackness filled the world.

"How long have I ..." Cora started to speak.

"More than a day. It's midnight."

"Delia? Where's Delia?" Cora asked. The tears welled in her eyes as pieces of the lost day flooded back into her mind.

"She's still with Miss Eve," Zamara said.

"Did Eve call? Do we know where?" Cora asked, struggling to get the covers off and get up.

"You need to stay right where you are," Zamara said.

Cora ignored her, forcing her feet to the floor. She grabbed for the headboard to steady herself. Zamara was already up and supporting her.

"We have to find her," Cora said. "She has no right to take my daughter."

"You need to sit down and listen to me," Zamara said.

Again Cora ignored her, pushing her aside and heading to the door.

"Miss Eve is the only hope your daughter has to survive," Zamara said.

That stopped her. Cora turned to face Zamara. "What are you talking about? Where's my daughter and how is Eve going to protect her any more than I can?"

"You need to sit down, Miss Cora, and listen to what I have to say. Drink this water," Zamara said, handing her a glass of fresh water. "Go on. Sit."

Cora reluctantly sank into the rocker and drank the water. It tasted sweet and cold and somehow made the horrible pain that ripped at her muscles fade. Not completely, but enough so that she could bear to move.

"What's in this water?" Cora asked.

"It will help with the pain."

"Why am I in so much pain?"

Zamara let go of a long, sad sigh, "Oh, Miss Cora, do you remember any of what happened last night?"

Memories drifted back into Cora's mind. She could see Beau's face, taste his kisses, feel his touch and the weight of his body intertwined with hers.

"What happened is none of your concern, Zamara," Cora said.

There was no rudeness or even the slightest hint of Cora's usual haughtiness. She was embarrassed and the idea of discussing what had happened with her best friend's fiancé with her nanny was more than inappropriate.

"But it is, Cora," Zamara said.

Suddenly the formalities fell away and only two women faced each other.

"I ..." the words caught in her mouth.

"You fucked Beau Gregoire and he fucked you," Zamara said with a cold slap of reality. "What you don't understand is that neither of you had any choice."

Cora looked at her, trying to get her mind around the hope that what she'd done wasn't her fault. That someone else was to blame.

"No ... I wanted him. I ... want him."

"Do you?"

"Yes. More than I can even understand," Cora said.

"You live in a very sheltered world," Zamara said. "I need you to open your mind, Cora. If you are to survive what's coming and save your child as well as the child you are carrying right now, you have to think beyond what you know."

"I'm pregnant? That's impossible," Cora said, touching her stomach. "I know I should have stopped. Beau should have stopped before..."

"It's not Beau who's the father of this child. The father lives through Beau and the child belong to a new race of humans."

"New race of ... that's preposterous. It takes a millennium of random genetic selections to alter human DNA enough to create a separate race," Cora said.

"That's when you are only dealing with human DNA. In this case, you are not."

"Stop it! I won't listen to this preposterous nonsense!" Cora said.

"I'm sorry, Miss Cora, but I am going to have to show you some things. They are harsh, ugly and frightening. Unless you accept them as another kind of reality, one that co-exists inside and outside our dimension simultaneously, you are going to die. Or worse, you'll live as a breeding machine for a cruel monster," Zamara said.

Zamara slowly knelt in front of Cora. "Look into my eyes, Cora, and no matter what you see, don't look away. Do it!"

Cora hesitated, but she knew Zamara was speaking the truth. Slowly, she nodded. Her eyes connected with Zamara's and she felt Zamara's hands settle on her knees. The moment the connection was complete Cora felt her mind explode with colors, places and events. She was in her house in New Orleans, running. She saw Miss Clarisse and a huge man with skin that seemed to glow a fiery red. He attacked Miss Clarisse and ripped her face off and snapped her neck, tossing her away like a rag doll. The man – thing – demon turned on Cora. She saw herself terrified, trying to run. It caught her and fell on her, viciously raping her.

"No!" Cora screamed, backing away from Zamara and closing her eyes.

Zamara grabbed her face with both hands and turned it back to look at hers.

"Look into my eyes, Cora!" Zamara commanded. "Open your eyes!"

Cora opened her eyes. Tears streamed from them as she looked back into Zamara's eyes. Instantly she felt herself falling into Zamara's liquid brown eyes as she became both victim and observer. Cora watched as she lashed out at the demon. She fought and it fought back, ripping and tearing and shredding her into pieces. She watched herself being raped by this enormous creature. She could feel the terror and the pain as he fucked her until she finally succumbed, unable to fight, only able to surrender. It felt as though this monster had swallowed her soul and dragged her into a place so deep and so black it would never let her go. Everything faded to black. Cora felt the tears fall from her eyes. Zamara stood and stepped away from her, allowing Cora to deal with what she'd seen.

"When ... did this happen?" Cora asked.

"It was another time. Three weeks after Miss Eve hit her head in the garden."

"Impossible," Cora said.

"You need to forget that word. It no longer applies," Zamara told her.

"Please. Stop," Cora whispered. "No more."

Zamara closed her eyes and took her hands away.

"He wants you and the unborn child."

"Can you help me?" Cora asked.

Zamara lowered her head and stood, turning away. "No."

"What about Eve?" Cora asked.

"Aria thinks Eve's a very powerful key to some complex master plan that will not only save you and Beau, Philip and Delia, but all of the children who have been conceived to be the next generation of humanity."

"But ... what about you?" Cora asked.

Zamara's eyes flooded with tears. "My fate is cast. All hope is lost to me. I will be punished for showing you what I have."

"By who? That thing? I don't believe you. Why is it that Eve is in any less danger than I am?"

"She's not like you. That much I know."

"No. She is like me. She's hurt and angry because she saw me and Beau and she's jealous. We have to find her. I want my daughter back," Cora said.

Cora struggled to her feet. "And if you can't tell me how Delia is any safer with Eve than with me then ..." Cora cut herself off and headed across the room.

Zamara saw the transformation. Something inside Cora rose, flushing her skin the color of a rose blush and making her eyes flash with a wild rage. Like flipping a light switch, the waves of concern that washed over her turned from worry and guilt into anger and fury. The demon had her.

"You will help me, Zamara. We have to find Eve and get her to bring Delia to me," Cora said, seething as she went on, pacing the room and thinking. "Aria said she didn't take her phone so we can't trace her. Where would she go? Where would she go?" Cora screamed.

"I don't know and I don't know where to look," Zamara said.

"Liar! You do. I know you do. Call Aria and Beau," Cora said as she crossed to her closet.

Cora entered and pulled a change of clothes from her massive closet and stumbled into the bathroom to take a shower. Cora started the water and ran her hand under it to test the temperature. When the water touched her hand her skin flushed this time even more red than before. She felt the water turn from cool to tepid, warm to blistering hot. She kept her hand in the scalding water, unfazed. Cora looked at the red glow that emanated from beneath her skin. Naked, she came out to face a surprised Zamara.

"Why are you still standing there, Zamara? Go and find Aria and Beau and do whatever you must to find out where Eve has taken Delia."

Cora, stark naked, picked up the phone and dialed.

"Millard, Cora. I need you. Come over, now. NOW!" Cora yelled into the receiver.

"What are you doing?" Zamara asked.

"Shut up."

Cora picked up the phone and this time she dialed 911.

"Hello? Police? Yes, this is Cora Bouvier. I want to report a kidnapping. My infant daughter has been kidnapped by Eve Dowling," she said. There was a pause. "Yes, I'll wait until they come."

Zamara watched Cora's skin vacillate between hues of gold, glowing from deep within her. She was possessed, whether by Kirakin or another Nephilim from his army, Zamara couldn't be sure.

Cora felt amazingly invigorated. She, or whatever she had become, had a plan to get Eve and take her daughter back.

Zamara stared at Cora in abject horror. She'd lost her to them.

"Go!" Cora shouted to Zamara. "Go!"

Zamara backed out of the room. She needed to find Aria. She needed to warn Eve.

Chapter Twenty Seven

Beau and Aria stood huddled from the rain inside A.V.'s office portico. Augustus Valentine Lafayette the Fourth, Esquire was engraved in brass letters on the wooden plaque that adorned the archway to his offices, which was located deep in the heart of the French Quarter in a beautiful, hundred-and-fifty-year-old, two-story house, which had belonged to A.V.'s great grandfather's Creole mistress, Marie De Cuire. She was known to be the most beautiful woman in New Orleans in her time and A.V. was sure his grandfather was their biracial love child, taken in by the family and passed off for white. A.V. was very proud of his possible, secret Creole heritage, and he made no bones of his love for beautiful men and women of color, jazz and African art.

Aria looked down at her throbbing leg covered in dried blood and deep purple bruises. Beau, still weak from the encounter with Kirakin, leaned against the door frame. They waited. Again she rang the bell. It was midnight and the echo of church bells chimed from across the four corners of the city. Beau let the cool, wet night air drip against his skin and help him fight the draining fatigue that beckoned him to close his eyes and sleep. Sleep would be his only chance to forget the horrific events of the day.

They waited. No one came to the door.

"Where now?" Aria asked.

"He's here. I know it," Beau replied and pounded his fist against the heavy wood door. "Ring the bell again."

Aria complied and the distant buzzer vibrated.

Finally they heard a voice echoing down from upstairs.

"I'm comin'. I'm comin'," A.V.'s voice bellowed.

A.V. opened the door, his hair and clothes a disheveled mess, his eyes red and swollen from too much alcohol and not enough sleep. He looked first to Aria with an expression of puzzlement and then noticed Beau. Beau stepped forward and his legs gave way. A.V. caught him. Beau was in his arms, broken and bleeding and desperately needing A.V.'s help.

"Whoa! What the hell happened to you? Lean on me," A.V. said to Beau.

A.V. looked around behind them into the street, which was blurred by sheets of pouring rain. He led Beau inside and nodded for Aria to follow, "Please," he said, always the Southern gentleman. Aria entered and closed the door.

"Upstairs. Come on. I have a medicine chest for that leg. Are you sure I shouldn't be calling an ambulance or the Goddamn police?"

"Not the police!" both Beau and Aria replied in unison.

"We don't need an ambulance either. Not yet," Aria told him.

They made it to the top of the stairs and moved down the shadowy hall connecting several offices. The largest, located at the far end of the hallway, was A.V.'s office with its cream walls, oak wainscoting and chocolate curtains, was a well-designed blend of masculinity, power and elegance. Modern furniture accented the mid-century elegance of the space. A small circular conference table ringed by leather and wood chairs sat in the corner. On the right was a comfortable couch with two swivel chairs that could be turned to face either the couch or the massive, glass desk with cabriole legs inspired by Louis the Sixteenth's furniture. Three wall-mounted flat screen TVs displayed without sound world stock reports, a soccer feed from Italy and some local news feed.

A.V. gently slipped Beau down onto the couch, his eyes lingering on Beau's face. He gently covered him with a throw then watched as Aria sat, exhausted, on one of the leather chairs. She gingerly studied her bleeding leg. A.V. poured them both water from a crystal decanter.

"Drink. That looks nasty," A.V. said to Aria.

"Hurts like hell too," Aria replied.

A.V. went into the bathroom and reappeared with a metal strong box. Inside was anything and everything one would need to handle both small and large emergencies.

"I learned my lesson with Katrina. Be prepared," he said as he ripped open pads, alcohol and peroxide wipes and started to clean Aria's leg.

"I can do it," Aria said. "Thank you."

"I'm sure you can, but I'm gonna start it for you so I can see how serious these cuts are," A.V. said studying the wound. "You're gonna need a few stitches, young lady."

"Thank you," Aria said. "I'm a nurse and if you hand me that tape I can make a butterfly bandage. I'm Aria."

"Good lord, yes, I remember you from the hospital," A.V. said.

"Yes, you came in once or twice when they wouldn't let Mr. Beau see Miss Eve."

"She works for us now as Philip's nanny," Beau said.

"Yes. Of course. I remember. Wait. Where's Eve? Is she okay? Where's Philip?" A.V. asked.

"I don't know. I ... it ... something happened, A.V. and ..." Beau stopped himself. His eyes flooded with tears.

A.V. turned and looked into his friend's eyes. He turned back to Aria.

"What the hell is going on?" A.V. asked.

"Mister Lafayette? How versed are you in the ways of the spirit world?" Aria asked.

There was a long pause as A.V.'s glance went back and forth between Beau and Aria. He finally spoke.

"I don't believe in ghosts, vampires or werewolves. What else is there?" A.V, replied.

"Possession?"

"As in demons? You can add them to my list as well. I am not a believer in heaven, hell, the devil or God. Sorry."

"There are other kinds of possession. Have you heard of the Nephilim?" Aria asked.

"As a matter of fact I have. My Grandmother had a thing for Angels and the fallen Nephilim. She read me bible stuff and I explored the rest. I know there are two schools of thought; one in the religious scriptures and mythological writings that names them as the first children of God. One third of them screwed up and got banished and then I guess humans were created and they—we—are still in the process of screwing up. Guess you could call the Nephilim a kind of failed first experiment banished to ... well ... wherever you banish mythological beings. The other school of thought pertains to ancient aliens who came down to rape our lovely planet and cross-breed with human women to create a new race ... us. I think it was for slaves or something. Giants as I recall. There are even videos and photos I saw on the Internet of giant skeletons dug up in the Middle East. Bottom line, a bunch of salacious bullshit," A.V. added with a smile. "Forgive my language, Miss Aria."

"You know a lot," Aria said.

"I am wildly unhappy and don't sleep unless I am inebriated so I spend way too much time watching the History and Discovery channels. Besides I was not allowed to play with Beau because of the 'curse' his family brought with him. The old folks still gossip, but those of us from the present have moved on."

"The curse is real, but it's more of a genetic pact. His family was bred to be used for a kind of demonic possession and it has been carried for generations in their family blood line. He's a human incarnation of the Nephilim and they can posses him at will," Aria said. "He looks like this because he fought one tonight."

"She risked her life to help me," Beau told A.V.

A.V. looked at Beau and then at Aria. They weren't smiling.

"Please tell me this is all a very bad joke. You all did not wake me from my drunken stupor to tell me this fantasy."

"We should go," Aria said pulling herself up on her feet.

"Whoa, whoa, whoa. You still haven't told me where Eve and Philip are," A.V. said sounding suddenly much more officious.

"We don't know," Beau said. "She left. She saw us... something ... and she took Philip and Delia and left. I don't know where she is."

"Delia? Why would she take Cora Bouvier's daughter?"

The pained expression on Beau's face said everything.

"Fuck, no you didn't. You and Cora? Aw, Beau, that first time, I understood. You thought Eve was going to be a vegetable and grief is when you are your most vulnerable, but why the hell ..." A.V. said.

"It wasn't them she saw," Aria shouted. "It was the Nephilim. It ... they possessed them."

"They?" A.V. asked persisting.

"I think there were two separate Nephilims. They've come back to our world and they need Beau, but most of all, they need Eve. We don't know why, but I think she's the key to open our dimension so they possessed Beau because his family blood line has allowed it for centuries and maybe Cora and they will use them to make her join them," Aria said.

Beau and A.V. looked at her, trying to absorb what she was saying and put it into some kind of logical perspective. There was none.

"So the myths about my family... about me... are true? I'm part of that thing." Beau said, his heart racing in his chest.

"Stop. Whatever you think you saw. Just stop," A.V. said to Beau. He turned to Aria. "And you know this because?"

"That's a very complicated answer and I will explain it if you help us," Aria said. "If not, you need to let us get out of here."

"Answer me. Am I cursed?" Beau asked again.

"You have known the truth of who you are since the day you came of age. Your parents tried to protect you but it cost them their lives."

"And my sister," Beau asked.

"Her death was not an accident," Aria said.

"This is insane," A.V. said.

"What if it's not? What if she's right," Beau said, the desperation rising in his voice. "I saw what I saw and I know what almost happened to me and I won't let him take me." Beau turned to A.V. "Right now we need your help to find Eve and the children before that thing comes back and it's too late for all of us. Will you help us?"

A.V. studied his longtime friend and the young woman with the stern even gaze next to him. He didn't know what to think. He turned and crossed behind his desk to a great mahogany ceiling-to-floor bookcase filled with hand-bound leather law books. He pulled a slender, hidden lever and the center section of ten books folded open exposing a bar filled with crystal glasses, a tiny freezer with ice and several brands of very expensive scotch, bourbon and cognac. A.V. poured from a Croiset crystal bottle, three insanely expensive, Remy Martin, Louis XII cognacs. He took one, shot it back and poured another. He gathered the glasses and crossed to Aria to hand her one. The second he handed to Beau and the third he kept. A.V. sipped as he picked up the phone and punched in a number.

Beau could hear the soft ring inside the phone's receiver.

"Good morning, Sergeant. Can you patch me through to Lieutenant Mitchell Hanover? This is A.V. Lafayette calling. Please tell him it's very important," A.V. said into the phone.

Aria and Beau nervously exchanged a look.

"What are you doing?" Beau asked.

"I'm trying to find your wife," A.V. replied. "Yes, I'll hold."

"You believe us?" Beau asked.

"I don't know what I believe, Beau," A.V. said. "If you've nutted out on me, I'll have the both of you certified later. Right now I just want to help you find Eve and the kids. She's probably furious at both you and Cora and I for one don't blame her."

It was at that moment that Aria looked at the TV and saw Eve's picture.

"Turn it up! Turn it up!" Aria said pointing.

Beau and A.V. saw the SIG alert. Pictures of Eve, the two children, her name and the word 'kidnapped' ran under her photo. Then it cut to the crushed guesthouse at the Gregoire estate. In the rain, multiple emergency vehicles, their lights flashing, surrounded the remains of the guest house.

Beau sat back down as did Aria, their eyes glued to the screen.

"Dear, Lord, Cora has good reason to be pissed that Eve took her daughter, but she did not do that to the guest house," A.V. said.

"No, she didn't. The Nephilim did that when we escaped," Aria told him.

"Hang up the phone," Beau asked. "Please."

Beau could hear a click and a voice coming through the phone. "Hanover here."

A.V. looked at the TV screen and the image of the smashed guest house he'd stayed in many times as a teen. More police cars and fire engines, their lights flashing across the crushed remains, filled the frame as news camera trucks rolled in behind the on-camera reporter who did her best to explain the unexplainable phenomena.

"Hello? Hello? A.V.?"

Slowly, A.V. hung up the phone.

"How'd you get here?"

"In Eve's car," Beau replied.

"Give me the key. I want to pull it into the garage until I can get my head around this insanity," A.V. said.

A.V. took one more look at the image on the TV and the tiniest shadow of belief in what they were saying registered on his face.

"No," Aria said. "We have to go to my mother's house behind St. Anne's Cemetery. I'm going to hold a séance to bring another Nephilim named Gathian in to help us."

"I am already not liking this plan," A.V. said.

"You must understand how dangerous this is Mister Lafayette," Aria said. "Your life is in mortal danger the moment you walk out this door with us."

"I need you, A.," Beau said, his eyes pleading for help.

A.V. looked at Beau. These were the words it seemed he'd waited his whole life to hear Beau say.

"Then, let's do it!" A.V. said.

Chapter Twenty Eight

Eve read to the children from an old copy of Dr. Seuss's *Green Eggs and Ham*. It seemed highly infantile for them, but they seemed happy with the story. She lay with them until she was certain they were asleep. Eve was beyond tired and wanted nothing more than to join them in sweet repose, but she knew she needed to talk to Mac and decide their next steps.

A distant rumble of thunder echoed through the patter of falling rain. The sound relaxed her. She'd always loved the Louisiana rain, especially when it fell in the late afternoon and cooled the hellishly hot days of summer. But this was the beginning of a storm that was coming at them from the Caribbean.

Eve dragged herself out of the warm bed, kissed the children and headed downstairs.

Mac sat at the table with two GoPhone's in case they became separated and needed to contact one another, two glasses and a bottle of scotch. He poured her a drink. They clinked glasses and nodded a wordless toast. In silence they savored their drinks. By the third drink Eve felt the tension in her muscles release. She closed her eyes, let her head fall back, and took her first full breath since she had fled the Gregoire guest house with the children. It ended in a long, slow sigh.

"Well, well. Now I know it takes three scotches to get you to breathe," Mac said with a smile.

"Four shots of scotch sounds about right," Eve said.

"That was only three."

"Are we counting? More important, are we stopping?" Eve asked and laughed, holding out her empty glass.

Mac laughed with her and poured another glass. For a second they were like a young, married couple who'd gotten the kids to bed and were taking a moment for themselves. Eve felt comfortable. Mac's house, filled with simple things that didn't have to be the best, the biggest and the most expensive, felt homey. She appreciated finery, but refurbishing the Gregoire Mansion had been overwhelming even with all Cora's expertise and hordes of decorators. This little house felt like a home: safe ... safe. She looked at him, studying in detail the man who sat before her. How could it be that Mac always made her feel so incredibly safe?

Reality tapped her gently on her shoulder, summoning her back into the moment.

"What am I going to do?" Eve said, releasing another sigh.

"We're living in the present tonight? The past is done. You can't change it and the future has yet to be decided. So, tonight you do nothing. Get some rest. Sleep on it. And no dreaming! We'll discuss options in the light of day. Perhaps the doctor from Egypt will have emailed us back. Let it go, Eve."

Eve looked over at the computer.

"I just checked. Nothing yet," Mac said as he poured her a fifth shot.

"Detective, if I didn't know better, I would say you were trying to get me drunk," Eve said, her speech slightly slurred.

"Mission accomplished. Me thinks you are an easy drunk, Miss Dowling," Mac added laughing.

"I am. And proud of it," she said and laughed.

He grinned and leaned forward, his face close to hers and to her surprise, he kissed her. It was a long, warm kiss filled with the sweetness that swirls inside the innocence of a first kiss. Again, reality tapped her on the shoulder and she pulled back.

"Please don't do that," Eve said.

Before she could finish Mac stood and swept her into his arms. This time he kissed her and the world seemed to fall away. His lips lay gently against her's and she felt the wet warmth of his tongue slip inside her mouth. She struggled through the alcohol to protest, but words failed her. Eve felt Mac's strong hands slip down her arms and encircle her waist. She pulled her face back to tell him they had to stop, but he smothered her neck and shoulders with sweet, gentle kisses. Each slow and deliberate kiss touched her skin as soft, warm and wet as fat, summer rain drops. Mac pushed her hair off her shoulder and left a trail of kisses, tasting his way up her neck, delicately across her cheek and ending on her mouth. He tasted like summer pears mixed with the hint of scotch on his breath.

Mac's kisses were unbelievably delicious. He gently pulled her body into his. His other arm found its way under her blouse. He made a move so smooth and fast, releasing the catch on her bra, her breast was in his hand before she realized it. Gently, he cupped and massaged her, intensifying each kiss, brushing his fingers lightly against her nipple and sending quivers of pleasure through her entire body. She felt her nipples go erect and a warm blush of moisture blossomed between her legs. Her body wanted him as much as he wanted her. Eve could hear his breath quicken. She matched his rhythm. The next thing she knew he had lifted her into his arms and bent forward to lay her on the sofa. In a single gesture he pressed his body against hers. She felt how tight and muscular he was beneath his loose cotton shirt. His groin pressed into hers. His hips twisted as he sensually rubbed himself back and forth, building friction through their clothes. She could feel her clitoris swell. Their kiss broke and they looked into each other's eyes. She had expected desire, lust and passion, but not the tenderness of what she saw. Her expression of shock stopped him along with the rush of tears that welled in her eyes.

"I'm sorry," he said. "Are you not enjoying this?"

"I ..." she started. "I don't want to do this," she said. "... I'm hurt and angry at Beau and Cora and I don't understand this insanity happening around me. I'm running away from something and I don't understand what it is or why. Please, Mac, I can't have you complicate my life any more than it already is."

He was silent.

"I appreciate you Mac and, maybe if things were different I... but they aren't." Eve felt embarrassed by what she had allowed to happen. As good as it felt it was just bad timing.

"I ... I'm sorry," he started.

Mac pushed back, sitting up. He was fumbling, doing his best to pull himself together. He finished and turned to her, deliberating what to say and how.

"Eve, I want you. I've wanted you from the moment I first talked to you. Maybe even from the first moment I saw you at Thibodaux and I want you to want me. Me. Not some anger driven by revenge for what you aren't even sure you saw happening between Beau and Cora or, Heaven forbid, because you think I need to be serviced in order to keep helping you. You must know, I'm not that kind of man."

Eve said nothing. There was nothing she could say. She knew he was one of the good guys. She didn't know what she wanted or what she felt other than she liked his arms around her. Yes, she was angry at the insanity of the situation with Beau. Her mind filled with questions. Was she allowing Mac to seduce her because she was jealous of Cora and feeling vengeful because the father of her son and her best friend had betrayed her? Was Mac right? Was she so frightened and desperate because she needed Mac to help her that she would seduce him to ensure he helped them? She knew in her heart that wasn't true. She could see how good a man he was and she loved how safe he always seemed to make her feel. Right now, at this very moment in time, was it about feeling safe and being loved by someone good who only made her feel better? That feeling was what she needed in her life and Beau, as wonderful as he was as a man, a provider and a lover did not make her feel safe. As a matter of fact, based on what she'd seen and the things that had been leading up to his and Cora's indiscretion, he could no longer be defined as 'good' or safe. Eve needed to know why.

Eve stood, reached under her blouse and hooked her bra. The zipper on her pants was half down, though she barely remembered him moving so fast to get her undressed because it felt as if he was moving so slowly and sensually to seduce her.

"Please, don't be angry with me," he said with pleading eyes.

"I couldn't be angry at you, Mac. I ... wanted you too or I would have stopped you. You must have felt that when I kissed you. It's just ... not the right time," Eve said. "I have too many unanswered questions to add any more. What's happening to me and Beau, Cora, those children and now you have to be solved and solved quickly. Something is happening and I'm going to find out what it is or die trying. I'm hoping the answers are in Egypt, but if they're not, I'll keep searching because I have to. I need you to understand that. Because if I make love to you, I want it to be for the right reasons."

"Then I'll wait and I'll do whatever I can to help you," Mac said.

He took her hand and she pressed his to her cheek in a gesture of thankful gratitude. Eve turned and headed upstairs when a soft ding chimed from the computer. Mac crossed to the computer. He ran his hands though his hair and stood for a moment in front of the screen looking at the alert as it faded.

"Eve," he said. "It's from the doctor in Egypt."

Eve hurried back down as Mac opened the email. They read it together.

EVE DOWLING,

YOU ARE IN GREAT DANGER. SPEAK TO NO ONE ELSE ABOUT THIS. I AM ON THE FIRST PLANE OUT OF CAIRO. I WILL FIND MY WAY TO THIBODAUX HOSPITAL BY EIGHT. I NEED YOU TO GET THERE. TAKE THE CHIDREN AND DO AS I SAY: MAKE A NECKLACE WITH A SMALL LEATHER POUCH AT THE END FOR THEM AND FOR YOU. PUT ANAMU GUINEA HEN WEED INSIDE THE POUCH AND ALL OF YOU MUST WEAR IT. IT WILL PROTECT YOU. STAY IN A SMALL ROOM AND SEAL THE WINDOWS AND DOORS WITH THE REST OF THE POWDER AND DON'T COME OUT UNTIL YOU ARE COMING TO ME. PLEASE BE CAREFUL. EVERYTHING YOU THINK AND DO HAS POWERFUL CONSEQUENCES. MOST IMPORTANT, BECAUSE OF WHO YOU ARE, YOU CANNOT HAVE SEX. THE TIMING OF THE OCHIFURUS MOON HAS ASCENDED AND WILL BE FULL TOMORROW NIGHT. ANYONE HAVING SEX WITH YOU WILL CREATE A SERIES OF PORTALS. DON'T OPEN THEM WITHOUT ME THERE TO GUIDE YOU. WE WILL HAVE ONE CHANCE TO STOP THEM. I WILL BRING EVERYTHING ELSE WE NEED. BRING THE GRIMOIRES BOOK. IT WILL BE OUR GUIDE. REMEMBER ALL I HAVE SAID HERE THEN DESTROY THIS COMMUNICATION. I WILL FIND YOU, EVE. I WILL GUIDE YOU. THE OTHERS ARE GATHERING TO HELP YOU FIND YOUR WAY.

WALK IN LIGHT,

AFRINE KASATAH

Eve and Mac looked at each other.

"What the hell is Anamu?" Mac asked.

"She wants us to make and wear a grigri," Eve said.

"That's Voodoo," Mac said.

"Call it whatever you want. It's spiritual and it's powerful and it is tied into what is happening to both of us," Eve said correcting him.

"How do you know that?" Mac asked.

Eve stared at the letter on the screen. The act of reading Afrine's letter stirred memories of the shattered dreams and nightmares that had been haunting her and driving her mad; memories of the other place and time.

"Mac, that old woman at the graveyard saved me before. That's what she said. Remember? I think she was from the time we keep experiencing in the dreams. That letter's making me remember more of the missing pieces I was seeing in the visions and dreams. Mac, look at the letter. Don't you see it?" She told Mac, pointing at the screen.

Mac sat before the screen carefully reading the words, searching for the hidden knowledge.

"That's what she was trying to tell me," Eve said. "She had given me a grigri to protect me. You and I saw something happen and we are remembering," Eve explained.

"Why us? Why no one else?" Mac asked, his eyes still focused on the screen.

"I don't know. All I know is we have done this before. Please tell me you see what I saw?" Eve asked.

"I don't know. I'm not seeing anything but the letter."

"We have to get the anumu," Eve told him.

"I may not understand this, but I do know buying guinea hen weed to make a grigri is some kind of dark magic Voodoo," Mac added. "I've lived in Louisiana and have enough Creole blood in me to know that messing with this stuff is not a good thing."

"We have to fight fire with fire," Eve said as she typed the substance mentioned into Google to ask what it is. The information came flooding back.

"Look. Anamu is from the rain forests," Eve said as she kept reading. "Powerful herb from Jamaica, South and Central America, Africa and tropical areas around the Caribbean."

"But what does it do?" Mac asked.

She searched deeper and read.

"Increase the immune system, destroy cancer cells, arthritis, aid as a digestive for intestinal ailments and pain relief. I want some for good measure," Eve said.

"Shit, it says it can induce abortions," Mac said reading along.

"We're not ingesting it we're only going to wear it."

"But what does it do against these ... things?"

"She said to protect us. It keeps them from harming us is all we need to know," Eve told him.

"Where the hell do you get it here and how much does it cost?" Mac asked.

Eve's fingers flew across the keyboard. She found an herb store just on the outskirts of New Orleans that carried it. "Here and it's not expensive," Eve said.

Her mind started spinning as to how to get everything they'd need together to prepare for meeting Afrine Kasatah.

"I need to get into my bank accounts," Eve said.

"You left your purse at the guest house," Mac reminded her. "Look, I'll go to my bank as soon as it opens. Then I can go to this herb store and get as much as I can," Mac told her.

"Thank you. I'll call Dr. Honoré in the morning. We'll need to go to her office and get the book of Grimoires she tried to give me. Why didn't I take it?"

"Okay. We'll get everything tomorrow. Get some rest," Mac said, looking one last time at Afrin's letter. "Sex portal, huh? To what?"

"I don't know," Eve said.

"That's got to be the best mental chastity belt on the planet," Mac said.

"You have to delete the letter," Eve told him.

Mac hit delete and the letter vanished into the trash.

"Thank you for believing me," Eve said.

"At this point I'm afraid not to. Get some rest. Take my bed and I'll hunker down here on the couch. Tomorrow maybe we get to find out why this is all happening," Mac said.

"I hope so," Eve told him.

They lingered a moment, the attraction still present between them.

"Thank you again. Good night," Eve said.

As she reached the stairs she turned, glancing back at Mac one more time, grateful that he was there.

Chapter Twenty Nine

Beau, Aria and A.V. drove to St. Anne's Cemetery near the heart of Old Algiers. It was four thirty in the morning by the time Aria and A.V. stopped by her apartment so she could gather all the things she would need to conduct a séance. The pouring rain ceased, allowing a fine, cool mist to seep up from the wet ground and crawl along the road in front of them. Caught in the headlights, it drifted lazily between the cemetery crypts like ghosts rising up to peer at them through the iron fences, an eerie warning as they drove up to the chained and padlocked cemetery gate.

"How the hell are we supposed to get in there?" Beau asked.

"We're not. Turn down the alley," Aria said.

A.V. turned right and drove along the twelve-foot white wall that encased the larger crypts inside the cemetery on a narrow street overhung with moss-covered trees whose branches draped so low they scraped the roof of their car. The scratching of the branches sounded like fingernails on a chalk board and made the tension in the car worse. The street narrowed into a one-lane, muddy path without streetlights. Darkness enveloped them. Only the Tesla's headlights pierced into the dark night. Directly ahead of them was the edge of the bayou.

"I better not get stuck here, or worse, sucked into the damn bayou," A.V. said.

"Shut up A.V. If your damn car sinks, I'll buy you another one," Beau told him.

"You won't do shit if you're dead. What the hell are we doing out here trying to communicate with aliens?" A.V. said as he stopped the car.

Aria opened her door, gathered her backpack, and got out.

"First we're raising my mother from the dead. Then she's going to open a vortex and summon Gathian from his world. And if you have a sliver of doubt in your head or your heart, stay in the car. The last thing we need is the wrong demon to show up because you're a skeptic or worse - standing in fear," Aria said and slammed the door.

"She's right. I saw the thing that tried to possess me. I don't ever want to see it again and trust me, neither do you," Beau told him. "What I don't understand is, why now? How did I not know before?"

"Your parents gave their lives to protect you, but he did not need you until Eve came. Until now," Aria explained.

Beau opened his door and leaned out, looking at the remains of an old house.

For a long moment A.V. sat in the car wishing he had a drink. He got out and stepped into the deep mud ruining his six-hundred-dollar alligator shoes.

"Shit," he said as he stepped next to Beau. "I sure the hell hope whatever this is works."

"Yeah," Beau said. "Me too."

Beau stopped him.

"A.V.? I want to ask a favor," Beau said.

"Yeah?"

"If that thing comes for me, I need you to make sure it doesn't take me. Please," Beau asked. "I won't go there." A.V. looked in Beau's eyes. He knew what he was asking and he didn't like it.

"How about we make sure that doesn't happen?" A.V. said.

"But if you can't stop it... promise me."

"Hush up. We'll stop it. Now shut up and let's go raise the damn dead."

Together they walked to the porch.

The stone fireplace and a skeleton of burnt wood encircled what must have been the main room of the house. What remained of the door hung open but oddly enough they didn't see Aria.

"Aria?" Beau called out. "Where are you?"

"In the main room," she called back. "Ignore what you see. It's only an illusion."

"Looks pretty damn real to me," A.V. said.

The two men stepped up onto the moss-and algae-covered porch. Beau stepped inside first but abruptly stopped so fast A.V. bumped into him.

"Hey, Beau—" A.V. said, his eyes on Beau.

Beau grabbed his face and turned it toward the room. A.V. fell silent as he looked around at the room, whole and perfect. Aria stood by the fireplace that presently held a small fire she had started. She was putting the finishing touches on a large circle around a pentagram she'd drawn in white and red powder at the center of the floor.

"Bring that table and those chairs and set them in the middle. And whatever you do, don't break the lines," Aria said.

The two men carried and carefully placed the table at the center of the circle before going back for the four chairs. Aria then set out a cluster of nine candles in the center of the table – all different sizes and colors. Carefully, she lit them, then meticulously placed several crystals also of various sizes and colors in between them. Finally, Aria removed a solid gold tuning fork from a velvet pouch and set it inside a golden stand directly in the middle of the candles.

"I don't suppose you're going to explain what this does?" Beau asked.

Aria looked at the two men. She needed them to help her. She took a long, deep breath and nodded, hoping that even if they didn't understand, they would at least trust her.

"The candles are to create light and warmth to ward off the cold of evil. The tuning fork resonates to a specific harmonic field and is calibrated to match the electromagnetic energy that flows in this area of the bayou. That resonance is amplified by the precise alignment of crystals and the Ophiuchus moon. We will direct our thoughts to connect to an energy vortex that has existed since the beginning of this planet from deep underneath this house. My mother can be summoned through that vortex and hopefully she can help us save Eve and the children," Aria explained.

"I thought you said your mother was dead," A.V. said.

"In this world, dead is what you consider her," Aria told them.

"So, she's not from this world?" Beau asked.

"Neither are you, especially if you think in terms of eternity. We are energetic forces that can never cease existing. When we are done with these physical bodies, unless some force holds us, we move on to another realm and another existence," Aria said. "However, this realm was created and at the moment we are trapped living in it. Eve is the one person who might be able to get us out and back where we belong in space and time."

"None of this is real?" Beau asked.

"What you are about to see from this moment on, defies everything you know," Aria said. "Beau, I must warn you, when my mother comes through, if she needs my physical body to reinstate hers, she will take it. Hopefully, I get to come back. If not, her name is Evine. Make sure you ask her and she answers to be certain. A.V.?"

"Hey," A.V. said. "I'm just here to go with the flow and do as I'm instructed."

"Good," Aria said with a smile. "Are you ready Beau?"

Beau nodded and the three carefully crossed into the circle, over the pentagram, and sat in the chairs.

"Aria? Thank you..." Beau said. "... for everything. And if anything happens, promise you'll tell Eve, I'm sorry and I love her."

"You'll tell her yourself," Aria said with a brave smile.

"Place your hands face down on the table. Breathe, slowly and deeply, and when I ask you to, we'll take each other's hands. No matter what happens, keep breathing and stay calm. I won't let anything happen to you. Most important, DO NOT let go no matter what you see happening unless I tell you. Promise me."

Both men nodded again and placed their hands palm down on the table.

Aria struck the tuning fork with the thick gold wand before also placing her hands on the wooden table. The sound that emanated from the tuning fork at the center of the table was as tender and sweet as the singing of a violin. It was warm and filled with mystery and somehow the promise of all things good. They could feel the table vibrating gently under their hands. The sound grew louder and stronger, changing with each breath they took. As the volume increased, the flames on the candles grew brighter and the crystals began to glow and the sound encircled them.

"Take hands," Aria said.

All three of them reached out, intertwining their fingers, Beau with Aria, Aria with A.V., and A.V. with Beau.

"Evine," Aria said, her voice clear and commanding. "We are here and we summon you into our world. We ask you to come for reasons you already know, to do things you have already seen. Evine, I, Aria your daughter, calls out to you in love."

The lush tone of the tuning fork began to wane, as if it were falling into a vast canyon far, far away. The sound faded until there was nothing except the thick silence of the room. Not even the night sounds from the bayou penetrated the space. It felt as if time had stopped. The candles glowed even brighter and the crystals levitated off the table. Beau exhaled and saw smoke pass through his lips as he noticed the air around them was freezing cold. Beau looked around the table and saw Aria's and A.V.'s breath flow from their mouths in fine white mist. The crystals hovered for a moment before dropping back onto the table. In unison, the candles extinguished.

Cast by the glow of the tiny fire, a large black shadow fell across the table. Beau and A.V. exchanged a look and together turned their gaze toward Aria. Her color had drained to a deathly white. Even her eyes, blank and open, had no iris visible. She wasn't breathing.

"Don't touch her," the voice from across the room said.

Beau and A.V. turned to see Evine floating before them, her white hair, wild and flowing in the same directionless wind that encircled her when she appeared before Eve.

"Aria," Evine said. "Why have you summoned me back into human form?"

"Kirakin and his demon have possessed this man, Beau, and the woman called Cora," Aria said.

Beau and A.V. both noticed Aria's lips didn't move even though they could hear her words.

"I... got away and now I'm asking for your help," Beau blurted.

"You are blood kin of the Nephilim, damned by your forefathers. I cannot save you," Evine said looking at Beau.

"Then take my life, but save Eve and my son? Please," Beau begged.

"Eve has the power to save herself. But the child, like you, is of the Nephilim," Evine told him.

Shaken, Beau started to stand.

"Don't break the bond!" Aria shouted.

"And this one?" Evine asked, looking at A.V.

"You can leave me out of this," A.V. whispered.

"You will help this man you love? That's why your heart says you're here," Evine asked A.V.

A.V. looked at Beau. They had been boyhood friends and Evine had read his heart correctly. Yes, he loved Beau like a brother. In truth, he loved Beau more than a brother, but long ago accepted his love would never be returned in that way. So A.V. took what he could and remained grateful to be Beau's friend. He'd come to love Eve and Philip as though they were part of his family.

"Will you fight for him?" Evine shouted at A.V., her voice booming across the room.

"Hell yes, I'll fight for him," A.V. blurted back looking into Beau's eyes.

"Will you die for him?" Evine asked.

There was only a moment of hesitation and A.V., his eyes locked onto Beau's, said, "Yeah, in a heartbeat."

Beau squeezed his friend's hand in gratitude.

"If the time comes, keep your promise," Beau said.

"He has the heart of a warrior," Evine told her daughter.

"Hear that. I have the heart of a warrior," A.V. whispered to Beau, proud of himself.

"You will be tested," Evine said to A.V. "As will you," she added, looking at Beau.

"Where is the book?" Evine asked Beau.

"Book? What book?" Beau asked.

"Eve must have the book if she is to stop them," Evine said.

"I don't know," Beau said. "Tell me and I'll get it. I'll get whatever you need to help her."

"Where are Eve and the children now?"

"Gone," Beau said. "It made me drive her away."

Evine could see the sadness in his heart. "Forgive yourself. I can see your heart did not betray her because each time your body was no longer yours."

"Tell me how do I get possession of my body back from that thing?"

"You are blood kin of the Nephilim. Your freedom will come only if you can kill Kirakin. With his death, maybe you can be free."

"Is that how I can protect my family?" Beau asked.

"You will know when the time comes. Just be sure," Evine said.

"Be sure of what?" Beau asked.

"Your freedom comes with a price. You will know when the time comes," Evine said.

With that Evine turned to dense, gray smoke and blew across the room, slamming into Aria. Aria's back arched and she screamed as if in excruciating pain.

A.V. started to reach for Aria.

"No! Don't let go," Beau whispered to A.V.

They watched as the two entities of smoke and flesh blended into one. Aria fell face first onto the table.

The candles ignited into a blaze of flame, the crystals rose, glowing, from the table and began to spin. The tuning fork vibrated, its pure tone getting louder and louder until Beau and A.V. thought their ears would bleed. One of the walls vanished and all eyes turned outside to see a brilliant, beatific light as bright as the sun rising from the bayou. It rose from the center of the water, churning and bubbling and from this ball of blinding light, a man appeared. He was at first huge: ten, perhaps twelve feet tall. As the light subsided, he became smaller, perhaps six and a half feet tall. He was beautiful, muscular with features like an Adonis and his skin glowed with an aura of soft blue. In the next instant, Gathian was standing next to the table.

"Fuck no," was all A.V. could say.

"Where is she?" Gathian asked. "Where's Eve?"

Evine stepped out of Aria, her human form of flesh and blood intact, leaving her daughter whole. Evine stood as real and as solid as Beau and A.V. Aria's body collapsed as she fainted. Beau caught her, breaking their hands.

"You can let go for now. Dis bond ees sealed," Evine said to Beau and A.V..

"We're here," Evine said to Gathian.

"I asked you where she is?" Impatience was ringing in Gathian's voice.

Evine closed her eyes and allowed her spirit to reach out into the night.

"She's headed to da tower temple. Da others are gathering as well. Da good and bad."

"Kirakin is waiting for da full moon. He will be ready for us," Evine said.

Gathian turned to look at Beau and a huge sword appeared in his hand. It was silver and gold with a single large emerald in the handle. He swung it back ready to decapitate Beau.

"Stop!" Evine told him.

"I can sense Kirakin's spirit in you," Gathian said, his sword stilled raised.

"Dis one say he's here to help," Evine said.

"He can't help himself. It's too dangerous to bring him near Eve, especially if she needs to transcend."

Beau handed Aria to A.V. and stood to face Gathian.

"Who are you to tell me I can't go and protect her?" Beau demanded.

"I am Gathian. I'm her protector. Who are you?"

"The man she's going to marry," Beau said.

"Your presence gives her to Kirakin. Better you die here than live as what you will become," Gathian said as he lifted the sword higher.

"Stop!" Aria said to Gathian as she weakly stirred in A.V's arms. A.V. helped her to her feet. "If we can just release the bond your brother holds on Beau, his love for her will be an asset."

Gathian lowered his sword and studied Beau.

"The demon pact that holds this man in his powers was made long ago," he said and turned to Beau. "It allows Kirakin to exist through the males of your family whenever he needs to enter into this realm. You should know too, in my world, Kirakin was chosen to be Eve's husband. She rejected him and came to me. To protect her, I hid her here," Gathian said,

"But not before you fell in love with her," Evine said. "Now she hides from you as well as Kirakin."

"She knows I won't harm her," Gathian said to Evine, then turned back to Beau. "But you are powerless against him. If you stay here inside this field, you might be safe," Gathian told Beau.

"And do nothing? No," Beau responded.

"You won't be doing 'nothing'. You'll be fighting for your life," Gathian told Beau.

"He's right Beau, your only chance to survive is to stay as far away from this fight as you can," Aria told him.

"You're asking me to run away and leave Eve alone for the rest of my life?"

"Not if we win this fight. But understand, if you come, you could open the pathway for Kirakin to have her. Those are your choices," Aria explained.

"Aria is right," Evine said.

Beau paused trying to comprehend the choices he was being given.

"I... won't stand by and do nothing," Beau said.

"If you're going to help Eve, Beau and I are going with you," A.V. said to Evine, Aria and Gathian. "That's the way it is."

Without another word, Gathian, Evine and Aria vanished leaving Beau and A.V. standing alone. The walls and roof that had appeared around them vanished back into the illusion and rain crashed in on them. The storm was suddenly raging. In a matter of seconds they were soaked.

"What the fuck just happened? Where did they go?" A.V. asked.

"The only tower I know is at Thibodaux Hospital. Can you take me there? Please?" Beau asked.

"Oh, hell yeah. This is just getting good," he replied as they raced through the rain and got into the car.

Chapter Thirty

A boiling sun climbed over the city igniting triple digits by eight AM. Blistering heat and mixed with a cold front, signaling the next phase of the approaching storm. Even with the air conditioner on, Mac's house was still clammy. Eve woke drenched and went into the bathroom to splash water on her face. She looked in the mirror and saw in her eyes a weary sadness and still too many unanswered questions. But she was beginning to understand some of what was happening to her and, for the first time, she had a plan.

Eve showered and slipped on the light cotton dress the color of periwinkles Mac had picked for her when he went shopping for the kids. It was pretty and it made her feel a little more human. She stopped by the guest room to check on the children. They were still sleeping, their heads touching. Delia was hugging a plush rag doll and Philip held his favorite little red pick-up truck, which she always carried in his diaper bag. They looked so peaceful.

She quietly closed the door and came downstairs to find Mac sitting at the computer.

"Anything?" Eve asked.

"No. Not yet. Maybe she'll contact us when she arrives," he replied.

"She said meet her at the hospital. She'll know what to do? Won't she?" Eve asked.

"She seems to think you know. Why?" Mac asked.

"I don't know," Eve replied. "The last line of her email haunted me all night. She said the book will tell me what must be done."

Eve noticed a bag sitting next to him marked anumu.

"You've been out? You found it?" Eve asked.

"The distributer opened at seven. They carried the largest quantity available in Baton Rouge. I bought a kilo," Mac said. "I feel like a drug dealer. I wonder if this stuff makes you high."

The wheat-colored powder lay spilled across the table.

"He gave me these. He knew what I needed before I asked," Mac said as he held up four leather squares and four leather strips.

He'd scooped a few tablespoons in two of the squares and then one tablespoon in the other two. The smaller obviously for the children.

"Is this about right?" he asked.

"I have no idea," Eve answered.

They folded the pouches and tied them with the leather thongs. Eve placed one around her neck and one around Mac's. Together, they took the smaller ones up and placed them around the children's necks. Then they spilled a line of the powder along the window ledges and in front of the door.

"Save some," Eve said. "We might need it."

When they finished, they looked around the small room. The scent of the anumu filled the air - pungent and bitter, just like the sulfur from a matchstick that stings your nose when it first begins to burn.

"Now what?" Mac asked.

"Mac, I have to go to Dr. Honoré's and get the book of the Nephilim," Eve told him.

"She's not there," Mac said.

"What do you mean?"

"I mean I called and got a recording she would be out of town until Tuesday," Mac explained.

"That's two days away!"

Eve and Mac sat in silence for a long while. They watched as the children woke and discovered their strange smelling gifts.

"I'm going over there," Eve said.

"And you attained your breaking and entering skills at what boarding school?" Mac replied.

She stared at him knowing she had zero chance of breaking a lock on a door or window and it was obvious there was an alarm.

"I know a little about the art," Mac started.

"So now we're adding breaking and entering to aiding and abetting?" Eve asked.

"Hey, let's not forget going against a restraining order," Mac said.

"What's wrong, mommy?" Philip asked her.

"Mommy and uncle Mac ..." she said looking at him with a smile, "... have to get into a door that has a lock and an alarm and we don't have a key or a passcode."

"Perhaps a little too much information even for a two year old as special as this one. Don't you think?" Mac said.

Philip pondered the words for a while, then reached out his hand and the door to the room blew off its hinges and crashed out into the hallway, slamming down on the wooden floor.

"Could I do that to help?" Philip said.

Eve and Mac exchanged a look.

"How did you do that, Philip?" Eve asked.

"I thought it and then the door did it. Is that good?"

"I'm sufficiently freaked," Mac said.

"That's very good, son. Thank you.

"Philip?" Eve asked.

"Yes, Mommy."

"If you thought about making the lock open and stopping the

electricity to the alarm, do you think you could do that?" Eve asked.

Philip frowned. "How does a lock work?"

Mac jumped to his feet and gathered the broken door handle and lock that lay in the hall.

"Like this," Mac said as he showed Philip how the locking mechanism turned to draw the bolt back.

"And electricity is a kind of energy that flows through wires. Sometimes they look like this," she said picking up a white chord that connected to a lamp. "Could you stop the energy from getting from the wall to the light bulb?"

Eve turned on the light. Philip looked at the cord, the wall, and then the lamp. He scooted off the bed and crossed to take the wire from her hand.

"You have to be very careful, son. Electricity can be very dangerous. It can hurt you so you have to make sure you never touch the wire part, only the plastic covering."

He looked at her and then at the cord. Philip placed his hand around the cord and smiled.

"I feel it," he said with a giggle.

Philip squeezed his little hand and the light bulb dimmed and went dark. He giggled again and released his hand. The light bulb came back on, surging brighter than before until he released the cord.

"It tickled," Philip giggled and smiled.

"You're amazing," Eve said, hugging him.

"You have a very cool kid," Mac said.

"Teach me! Teach me!" squealed Delia.

"After breakfast. First we eat and then we all go on an adventure. Deal!" Eve told the children.

"Yeah!!!" they clapped.

She looked at Mac. His eyes went to Philip and then to Eve. They were filled with concern.

Chapter Thirty One

Eve gazed out the car's front window, watching the last light of day fade into the horizon. Storm driven winds blew and clouds cluttered the sky as dense and heavy as a thick winter cloak. She watched as the billowing mist descended across the broad shoulders of New Orleans and enveloped the spires of the skyline. Rain drops intermittently fell, fat and heavy, onto the windshield only to be cleared by the rhythmic swipe of the wipers. Eve glanced back at Delia and Philip sitting quietly in the back; Philip was looking at a book while Delia was challenging herself with some energy game Philip had shown her. Eve could see tiny sparks flying off her fingers and was concerned how quickly they were advancing. These children, as young as they were, had supernatural powers.

She looked at Mac sitting focused behind the wheel. He'd been the one who insisted they wait for the cover of darkness before venturing out, especially with Cora's Amber Alert still looming over Eve and the children. Cora had been on TV most of the day imploring Eve to bring her daughter back. She said she wasn't angry, just terribly worried. But when Eve looked into her eyes as she spoke into the camera, she saw only rage in their cool blue color and heard only anger underscoring every word. Cora's anger frightened Eve. It was not like her, but then nothing was like it was. None of the reports mentioned Beau and that, compounded by the bizarre destruction of the guest house, worried her. Has she lost him too? Her heart ached. She loved Beau and wanted to believe he was not in control of what happened to him and Cora. The question that haunted her was, *what if Beau wasn't Beau at all?*

The children were different too, still young, but definitely not toddlers. The maturity etched in their young faces unnerved Eve. No matter how hard she tried, she didn't understand this odd reality facing her.

"You okay?" Mac asked, catching her as she wiped away the tears that slid down her cheeks.

"No," Eve answered.

"We'll get to Dr. Honoré and find that book. It'll have answers," he said.

"You really think so?" Eve asked.

She could hear the hope caught in her throat. She was hanging on naive wishes of *please let this work out. Please let my son and Delia be normal. Please let Beau be alright. Oh please ... let me be normal.*

They drove to the bridge that would take them over the Mississippi River and into Algiers. The Amber Alert road block out of New Orleans had been only the briefest delay because when Eve turned to look back at the children, it was as if Philip and Delia read her mind. Before her eyes, they faded, leaving only a quiver of energy that was invisible to the police as they drove by. A beleaguered cop glanced in and waved them through.

"Move on," the cop said, searching for a woman and two toddlers they would never find.

The cops looked hot and tired, getting wetter with each hour as they nervously watched the gathering storm overhead.

Several minutes later, Mac passed through the twin cemeteries that flanked the street of Old Algiers that led to Dr Honoré's. When their car finally arrived the rain was kind enough to slow to a drizzle, but the wind continued to gust. Once out of the car, Mac picked up Philip and Eve gathered Delia and they ran to the house as, the wind beat against their bodies and the rain soaked their clothes. Once inside Dr Honoré's front gate they quickly reached the front door of her office and set the children down.

The porch was lit by a single electric brass lamp that emitted a dull haze of yellow light. Mac looked at Eve's dress, wet and sheer, clinging to her body and accenting the curves he wanted very much to touch and hold. He took off his jacket and offered it to her, doing his best to avert his coveting eyes. Eve smiled at him, grateful, missing the blush of color that flushed his cheeks. She looked at her sopping little entourage, wet and cold, and hoped this wouldn't take long.

Mac looked at the alarm and the camera that went with the security system.

"Philip, do you know how to shut these devices down?" Eve asked, pointing to both.

Philip looked up, studied the two devices, and reached out. Mac lifted him and he placed a small hand over each. He closed his eyes and their LED lights faded to black.

"My turn," Delia said.

"You have to keep practicing," Philip told her. "Here Delia, you open the lock. Make the bolt move back with your mind."

Eve picked up Delia and they all watched as Delia reached out, putting her finger against the lock. She swiped her hand and they heard a soft click. With a push, the door opened. Mac and Eve set the children down and amazed, the four shadows slipped inside leaving the cold night behind them.

"I want you to wait here," Eve said. "If the book's here, I'll find it. I think I remember where she put it."

Mac nodded, placing an arm around each of the children.

"Hurry," Mac said. "We still have to drive to Thibodaux."

Eve reached for the light and flipped a switch. Nothing happened.

"I made it all go away," Philip said. "The energy that makes the lights work."

"Do you want me to bring it back?" Philip asked.

"No!" Eve and Mac said in unison.

"Better not in case it trips the alarm," Mac suggested. He reached in his pocket and pulled out his smart phone. He turned on the torch App and handed it to Eve. "We'll wait here. There's plenty of light from the street. We're not scared? Right?" he asked the kids.

They smiled up at him and nodded, eagerly taking Mac's hands. Eve took his phone and walked forward shining the light through the now opened door of Dr Honoré's office and onto the bookshelf that filled one entire office wall. She ran her hand over the volumes of psychiatric and medical books that lined the middle shelf until she reached the center where the ancient leather book had been only to find a dark, empty space.

Eve turned, remembering that Dr. Honoré had laid the book on her desk. While crossing the room Eve flashed on what had happened the day she left the book behind. Her body began to tingle with an erotic hunger that surprised her. She felt as if hands were sensually brushing her body and with each touch, bits and pieces of what she had experienced came back to her. She remembered the room where she had been held; the people watching as six men seduced her. A cold, eerie chill went up her spine and snapped her back to the present moment. When the phone's little light illuminated the desk, Eve saw it was cluttered, disorganized and not at all the way Eve thought the pristine and organized Dr. Honoré would leave it. Dr. Honoré or someone else had been looking for something. Eve noticed the drawers were opened, pulled out and emptied onto the floor. *Someone was looking for what? The book? Had they found it?* Her thoughts raced as she circled around behind the desk, never taking her eyes off the clutter. Eve looked over the papers that lay in disarray. She saw her name, Eve Dowling, on a file. Dr. Honoré's notes, both handwritten and typed - transcribed, dated and organized chronologically starting with her early days at the hospital were all there. She turned over the file and read the doctor's prognosis: delusional, irrational, shows signs of paranoid, undifferentiated schizophrenic behaviors – possibly due to traumatic head injury and coma. Test for chemical imbalance. *She didn't believe me*, Eve thought. *She listened, but she didn't believe me.* A feeling of panic choked her. Eve stepped back, bumping into something. A rush of terror gripped her as she spun, facing a pair of dangling legs in a skirt. Eve screamed as she shot the light up, revealing Dr. Honoré, dead, in a hangman's noose. Her twisted facial features, protruding black tongue and lifeless bulging eyes, stared out at Eve.

Mac was in the room before she realized what was happening. He jumped onto the desk, undid the noose and somehow managed to catch the body before it hit the ground. He rushed the lifeless body to the couch and checked her pulse. Eve followed, keeping the light on them. Her hands were trembling.

"Someone killed her!" Eve said.

"This certainly wasn't suicide from the destruction in this room," Mac said. "It was recent. She is still warm. We need to get out of here," Mac said. "Are you alright?"

"No! I'm not alright! She's dead! Someone killed her! Why? Why!" Eve shouted, her voice verging on the hysterical.

"Eve, listen to me!" Mac insisted, shaking her by the shoulders from her terror. "Eve! We need to get out of here and get to Thibodaux Hospital right now to meet Dr. Afrine Kasatah. Do you understand me?"

Eve fought back the tears, emotions and fear that pounded in her chest. She wanted to breathe but couldn't.

"She's dead. She's dead," Eve repeated.

Mac pulled her into him. He held her tighter. His arms enfolded her, her face burrowed into his chest. The ferocious trembling that racked her body slowly subsided.

It was in that silence they heard a low hiss of air and a deep moan rise up from behind them. Eve and Mac spun. She put the light on what once had been the face of death and found Delia touching a living, breathing, but weak and confused Dr. Honoré.

"She wasn't very far gone," Delia said as innocently as someone who'd just found a lost puppy and brought it back.

Dr. Honoré choked and rubbed her throat. She tried to speak, but couldn't.

Eve went to Dr. Honoré. "You're going to be okay. Do you understand me?"

Dr. Honoré nodded yes. Again she tried to speak, but only the hiss of constricted breath came out.

"Dr. Honoré, do you know who did this?" Mac asked.

"Did they want the book? Did they take it?" Eve asked.

Dr. Honoré looked into Eve's eyes and shook her head no. She moved her lips to speak, causing another choking spasm.

"My ... ca— in my ..."

"It's in her car," Mac said. "Where are the keys?"

Dr. Honoré pointed to the door. Mac took the light and shined it at the door only to see Philip standing, staring at them. He looked angry and very upset. Eve got up and rushed to take her son from the room. Mac searched the area, found Dr. Honoré's purse and dumped it on the floor, searching until he found the keys. The key ring said Jaguar and had a little silver cat leaping into midair. Mac rushed out of the door past Eve and Philip.

"Are you okay, son," Eve asked, stroking his hair.

"Delia was bad," Philip said.

"Delia? She was helping Dr. Honoré. She saved her," Eve said.

"She cursed her. She belongs to them now," Philip said. "Go get

Delia and let's get away, please mommy. Go now. Now."

Philip was getting upset again.

"Delia!" Eve called out. "Delia, come here sweetie, right now."

Delia didn't come.

She turned Philip to face her. "Philip, Mommy wants you to stay right here. Do you understand?"

Philip nodded. Eve turned back and slowly walked into the now dark room. Even with the light from the street lamp she could barely see. Eve's eyes adjusted as she moved toward the couch where Dr. Honoré and Delia had been. Eve could see Dr. Honoré washed in the eerie glow from the window holding on to a very frightened Delia. Even in the dark, Eve could see the tears that fell down Delia's cheeks.

"Delia, come here," Eve said softly.

"She's hurting my hand," Delia said through her sobs.

"Let her go, Dr. Honoré," Eve told her.

"Are these their children?" Dr. Honoré asked.

"They are my son and Cora's daughter. You've met them before," Eve said. "Now let her come to me. You're frightening her."

"The boy is here? He wants them both, especially the boy," Dr. Honoré said, her voice a growl.

"Let her go," Eve said, stepping forward slowly and deliberately.

"What he wants is you. You have the power to let more of them come in," Dr. Honoré said.

"Let her come to me and we can discuss it," Eve said.

"I can help you. He showed me what you can do. How powerful you are. I told him you wouldn't help him and that's when they tried to kill me and—"

"They?" Eve asked.

Dr. Honoré opened her mouth to speak again, but a loud thud cut her off and sent her to her knees.

Delia ran into Eve's arms. Eve looked up and saw Mac standing above Dr. Honoré holding a small piece of statuary. Dr. Honoré tipped forward falling flat on the carpet. Once again, Mac caught her before she hit the floor. He lifted her to the couch and turned back to Eve. Delia held onto Eve as tight as she could.

"I got the book. Let's get out of here," Mac said. "Something tells me we're running out of time."

"All of us," Eve said.

Chapter Thirty Two

Cora stood stone faced, immobile, staring at nothing. Her house was dark and silent and the only sound that came from down the hall was voices. Cora moved forward, gliding as if on a cushion of air and, as she did, the voices got louder. Cora looked down at her feet; they didn't move. She could see the wall pass by her, but she did nothing to propel her body. As she reached the door to the living room she saw Millard. At his feet lay what remained of Zamara. She was dead; ripped and torn, broken and covered in blood. Cora wanted to go to her, but she couldn't move her arms or legs. Cora wanted to scream, but her mouth wouldn't open.

"She disobeyed me, Cora. This is what happens to people who disobey me."

Cora looked at Millard. He wasn't speaking. From behind Millard stepped Kirakin. He peeled from the shadows that filled the back corners of the room and slowly, he crossed to her. He was magnificent; tall and powerful, beautiful and hideous at the same time.

"If you promise not to scream or run away again and do as I say, I will release you," Kirakin said.

Cora, unable to move or speak, looked at him. Slowly he set her down and she felt her bare feet touch the carpet. Like a melting candle she felt the constricting force release her and the pain that racked her subside.

"There. That's much better. Yes?" Kirakin said.

Cora nodded.

"Yes?" Kirakin said this time more forcefully.

"Yes," Cora repeated. "You said you would help me get my daughter back."

"And so I will, and you will help me get Eve. That is our deal," Kirakin said.

"You don't need her, you need Beau," Millard insisted.

"I have Beau anytime I want him. He will be my portal to Eve when the moon is highest," Kirakin said. "This is the night I take her home."

Kirakin walked to Cora with the grace of a cheetah. His body stopped so close to hers, she could feel the heat emanating through his pours. He reached out his hand and sensually touched her face. Slowly, he leaned in and pressed his lips against hers. His kiss was soft and almost sweet. His hands traced down her neck, dragging over her shoulder and gently down her breasts. It was only then she realized she was naked.

"Get your hands off me," Cora said. "I want my daughter."

"A tigress! I like fight in a woman. So... we can do this nice, and I will pleasure you as you have never been pleasured before, or we can do this rough. The choice is yours, Cordelia Belle," Kirakin said.

"I'm in love with Beau, but you know that. I want my daughter back and when this... whatever this is, is over, I want Beau. Do I make myself understood?" Cora told him.

"Why don't you just leave her alone? We have more important things to handle tonight than you fucking this bitch," Millard said.

A swipe of Kirakin's hand sent Millard crashing against the wall. His body fell, limp and silent to the floor.

Kirakin's face never left Cora's.

"I want Eve, but I will take you and when I'm done with Beau, if there is anything left, you can have him and... the little girl... if you're good. Eve and my son will come with me."

Cora looked at Millard lying unconscious on the floor. She felt Kirakin kissing her back and neck, his tongue tasting her, his fingers sliding down her pubis and between her legs, fondling her clitoris. She looked at what was left of Zamara. She felt his other hand pulling at her nipples and his hot mouth leaning down to suck on them. She felt them grow erect. Finally, she looked at Kirakin as his face lifted level with hers and his mouth covered her mouth. She felt his tongue dart inside while his hands moved down her body and grabbed her ass. He spread her legs apart slowly, as if they had a life of their own. She felt his tail curl around her ankle and twist up her leg. She could feel its firm, smooth round tip peel open, unfolding like a flower in the sun, exposing the undulating, silken tentacles that sensually crawled over her and teased and tickled every inch of her vulva. They were electric; wet and hot. Each follicle fondled her as the rows of tentacles spread her open and the core emerged, hard, thick and long and slid up inside her with a wild, erotic sensation impossible to describe with words. Cora closed her eyes as she released to the Nephilim. She would get what she wanted, but a price had to be paid and she was that price.

Chapter Thirty Three

The drive to Thibodaux Hospital took an eternity—high winds and pouring rain, fallen branches and never ending lightening and distant thunder. The worst of the storm was still to come. The children sat silently, staring out their respective windows, unwilling to share what they were thinking or feeling about what was happening. Mac told Eve that as a detective he knew enough to let them ruminate over the events and assured her that when they were ready they would share. It was a lot for a child to take in. It was a lot to take in as an adult. Mac said he couldn't imagine what they as children must be dealing with and the night was far from over.

So they drove. Two hours passed. Three hours. The rain fell and the wind blew, buffeting harder against the car as the storm outside grew in strength. They listened to the local weather reports, praying the class three storm heading in from the Gulf would grow no stronger. The idea of surviving a hurricane in addition to whatever was about to unfold was unconscionable. According to the news reports, Thibodaux Hospital seemed to lie directly in the hurricane's path.

Eve held the ancient book on her lap. In the glow of the dashboard lights, she turned the time-weathered pages. There were whole sections from writings of Enoch. There were chapters on the language of the Angels, quotes and passages from the Dead Sea Scrolls, and quotes from the Philosopher's Stone along with several pages on the science of Ankh and the Ananuki of Niribu and rituals from the Egyptian Mystery schools. She touched pages filled with symbols of mathematics called sacred geometry: anagrams, tetrahedrons, pentagrams that came together and formed four-dimensional shapes and a host of images and references to the Kabala Tree of Life. The section that fascinated her most contained drawings of what had to be portals; one swirling with light and one a vortex into the dark. They spun on either side of a planet she assumed was Earth.

Chapter after chapter described rituals of ascension, step by step, complete with precise incantations. Only they weren't written in any language Eve could read. Only the drawings allowed her to understand what was to happen. One set of pictures was obviously designed to evoke good and banish evil, the other to evoke evil and banish good. In the end, one word was repeated ... Nephilim. From the pictures she could see they were divided—one side light and good, the other side dark and evil. The last drawing showed in great detail that Earth was at the center of the universe and at the apex of some kind of eternal struggle. "*For what?*" was the still unanswered key question that tortured Eve's mind.

"You must understand the dark to know the light," Eve read aloud.

"You can read that?" Mac asked.

"It's Latin. I took four years in high school," Eve told him. "It looks like it was translated from Sanskrit into Persian and then into Latin."

"But what the hell does it mean?" Mac asked.

"I don't know," Eve replied.

She ran her hands over the last page, tracing the large letters of the final words of the book, which were in English: ABOVE ALL, DO NO HARM. THE REST IS WISDOM.

The car stopped. Outside the wind howled and Eve could hear the crash of metal on stone as the gates rattled before them. The huge arch that loomed above them read *Thibodaux Hospital* and all eyes looked ahead as they entered the gates.

"I'm afraid to die," whispered Delia to Philip.

"Death should be the least of your fears," Philip whispered back to her as Eve listened.

Chapter Thirty Four

The dimly lit road inside the hospital complex twisted and turned through the bayou's forest that surrounded the facility. They reached the main administration building just as the wind and rain fell into a soft lull. Lightning and thunder rang out across the lake that lay on the far side of the facility.

Eve watch the flickering lamps that lined the road sputter as searing streaks of lightning reached out from the cloudy firmament. She counted the seconds after each flash until the roar of thunder reverberated off the bayou, so she could determine how close the storm was to them. In the brief moments of light, Eve could see the trees, whipped and beaten, waving their arms at the sky and bending low in humbled submission in the face of the wind. The car finally stopped in front of the main administration door as Eve looked out the window.

"I feel like I've done this before," Eve whispered, a hint of fear in her voice.

"Yeah, I know," Mac said. "The same but different. Kind of a de ja vu, but different. Ya know?"

They exchanged a knowing look. The quorum sat for a long moment looking up at the administration building when suddenly the large wooden front doors swung open.

"Look," Delia said pointing. "They've come for us."

Aria was the first to come out. Why and how she had gotten there was a mystery to Eve. She was sure the answers would lie inside. She was grateful to see her. Aria raced to the car and opened Eve's door.

"Help me get the kids in," Eve told her.

Mac grabbed the old book that had fallen from her lap to the floor and jumped out. Mac opened Delia's door, doing his best to protect both she and the book from the rain. He gathered the little girl into his arms and they raced for the entrance. Mac glanced back as Aria opened the back door and embraced Philip. She led Eve and Philip as together they ran inside.

They all walked past the outer entry and stepped into the main atrium. Waiting for them was Dr. Afrine Kasatah. There was no mistaking her. She was the mirror image of the photo Eve and Mac had seen on the internet. Afrine was incredibly tall, easily more than six feet, with a river of salt and pepper hair plaited into a loose braid that hung like a rope down her back. Eve tried not to stare, but it was impossible. And those eyes, those infinite, piercing, chocolate eyes made Eve feel weak and joyous just being in her presence. Standing with her was Dr. Cheney Renfroe, Philip's pediatrician, as well as all the women she'd seen that day in her office, and Dr. Stevenson who had cared for Eve and then Philip. All three of the doctors looked worn and frazzled, excited by what they knew was coming. Behind them Eve saw Aria with a warm towel drying Philip's face lovingly.

"Look how you've grown," Aria said.

Philip smiled and hugged her, holding on as if he knew something Eve didn't. She watched them, wondering.

"Are you ready?" Aria whispered.

"I think so," he whispered back to her.

"If you think so, then you are," Aria said with a brave smile.

There were other people, perhaps twenty or so, who Eve didn't recognize, at least not at first. She studied their faces and realized where she'd seen them. Again, flashes of the room she'd entered in her trance when Dr. Honoré put her into a hypnotic state flooded into her mind. This time she saw more details of the place and people who watched the event; the door, walls, altar and the men who seduced and sensually prepared her on the altar for ... what ... what? But those six men were not among these people. These were the people who stood behind the men. The watchers. Two of the younger women rushed forward to close the door and seal out the rain and wind. Eve came over as Mac set Delia down. He watched as Eve dried Delia's and then her own hair. Mac wanted to help, to touch her tresses before ... before ... Eve looked into Mac's eyes embarrassed by what she saw there. Embarrassed and yet grateful. Delia ran to Aria. Mac followed behind Eve and took the towel. He turned her and gently wiped her face. They shared a smile.

"We have to get through tonight. If we do that, all truths will become evident. Does that make sense?" Eve asked.

"Nothing makes sense, but I'm not afraid. Are you?" Mac asked.

"Me? I'm terrified. Maybe a little less knowing you're here. Thank you, Mac, for trusting me," Eve said.

"Get away from her," a voice shouted from across the room.

A chill ran through Eve's bones as she turned and saw, standing in the shadows ... Evine. Taller than Eve remembered her, with her mane of silver white hair and mix-matched eyes, Evine stepped into the circle of light that fell from the central chandelier.

"I talked wit Beau. I did nah brought him, cause he's nah safe to have around you and neetah is dis one," Evine said looking at Mac. "Not cha fault, just the truth. You have your job and ya'll know when the time comes. For now, you stay back from her. No much time left," Evine said. "Ya hear me, Eve Dowling?"

"And that's if you believe you can stop Kirakin," Gathian said to Eve as he strode in from behind Evine. "I will help you as best I can, but you know this war is yours."

Gathian was magnificent: strong, tall, handsome. In an instant he was inches from Eve.

Mac stepped forward protectively, but a rush of energy from Gathian's hands sent a field that stopped him in his tracks. Mac felt as if he'd hit a glass wall.

"Stop!" Eve commanded. "Release him."

Gathian looked at her and released Mac.

"Not him! You need me," Gathian said to Evine.

"You know dat an untruth well as I," Evine said. "You can do notin for her here in this reality. What she needs dis night is beyond your powers. If she chooses you after dis night is over, dat is when you'll have your chance."

"She needs to know who she is," Gathian said.

"Da cause ya know well's I do, she alone da one wit da power. Always has been. You da one da need her. You and dat demon, Kirakin need her to exist and she da one who got to stop him and his kind from crossing in. Now ya stay back. Ya hear me? Ya help us or ya get thee gone."

Gathian looked from Evine back to Eve.

"I don't understand what you're talking about?" Eve asked Evine, her eyes on Gathian.

"Ya'll know soon enough, chil'," Evine replied.

"Together, we can be the keepers of good. I will help you fight this battle Kirakin has raged in any way I can." Gathian said.

"Not this night," Evine said. "This night you will watch."

With that Gathian looked at Evine, bowed slightly and stepped back, joining Afrine. "Her fate is in your hands," Gathian said to Afrine.

"Then it's time we get started. Lead us to your sanctuary," Afrine said to everyone.

Eve and Afrine walked together down the long corridor that led to the back tower. Women stood in every open door watching her as the others followed in silence.

"Who are these women?" Eve asked.

"They have born the children of the future. Whose line they follow is up to you," Afrine told Eve.

Eve looked into the faces of the women. There was hope in their eyes. Somehow she represented their hope.

"I don't understand," Eve said.

"You have forgotten, but this night you will remember," Afrine said.

"Why do I feel I know you? As if I've always known you," Eve said.

"We have met many times, you and me," Afrine said. "You are mother, sister, priestess, goddess, first, last and always. I am your first daughter and sworn guardian of your soul," Afrine replied.

Eve felt frightened and confounded by her words. For the rest of the way they walked in silence. Eve felt the force of people moving behind her, a kind of energy gathering as powerful as the storm that raged outside. Each step felt like she was part of an ensemble about to perform in a well-choreographed dance. Eve looked back as everyone ascended the stairs leading to the tower. There was admiration in the eyes of all who looked at her. She wanted to understand who they thought she was. Mac, ever the cop, was the observer trying to figure out how all these pieces of the puzzle fit together.

When they reached the top-most room, they found standing outside its door a hundred children waiting. The children held glass balls of light and their eyes were filled with wonder and joy as they parted, allowing Eve to pass. Eve could hear their thoughts welcoming her telepathically.

Evine halted the flow of people behind Eve before they entered the room. Eve knew it was to allow her to take in the love the children were offering her. Their thoughts and well wishes gave her strength and she thanked them, connecting to each with her mind.

"You children must wait until you are called. Do you understand?" Afrine asked the children.

"I'll take them until the portals are opened," Aria said.

"No, Aria. Azura will take these children and dress them. Make them ready," Afrine told Azura. "We will need your energy in the room," Afrine said to Aria. "Take Philip and Delia with you as well."

Eve recognized Azura. She was the frightened young woman who spoke to her in the garden of the hospital outside the tower. She had a young son named Bo.

"Will they be alright?" Eve asked, crossing protectively to Philip and Delia.

"That's up to you, Eve," Gathian said.

Eve turned to Philip and Delia and squatted to their height, pulling them to face her.

"I don't know what will happen, but I want both of you to know I love you. Do you understand?" Eve asked.

"I'm not afraid," Philip said. "I love you too."

Eve's arms encircled him.

"Everything will be alright," Eve told him.

"Where's my mother?" Delia asked.

"She can no come and you can no think on her, chil'," Evine said to Delia. "Keep your thoughts only with de oter children."

Eve reached out her arm to invite Delia into their family circle. Delia raced into her embrace. After a good long hug she turned the children to face her again.

"You two promise me you will just think only about each other for right now. Okay? Promise me. Okay?" Eve insisted.

Both children nodded.

"Hurry, Eve," Afrine said, her voice flush with urgency.

Azura took the children back down the stairs to wait inside a specially prepared room. Eve watched as the adults filed inside the first door to wait for Eve. Once inside she faced a second door, taller, darker and etched with ancient Druid symbols and hieroglyphics from ancient Egypt and Tibet.

Afrine reached out to Eve to take her hand. With her touch, Eve felt a rush of pure kindness and boundless love surge through her fingers.

"I can guide you through the ascension if you need me to," Afrine said to Eve. "What happens to all of us after that is up to you."

"Me?" Eve asked. "What are you saying?"

"Give her the book," Evine said to Mac.

Eve turned to face Mac. His eyes were filled with deep concern. He looked from Evine to Eve and came forward, presenting the ancient leather book as reverently as possible. He handed it to Eve and looked into her eyes. His concern and fear transformed into compassion. She could still see hints of worry and she knew it stemmed from not knowing or understanding what was to happen next. Those same thoughts spun in her head and around her heart and yet she possessed a feeling of enormous strength. Eve could see he cared and, as always, he was there to be her safe haven no matter the danger of the storm.

"Eve, whatever happens ... choose me," Mac whispered, gently allowing his hand to rest on hers as the book passed from his to her grasp.

Eve smiled as she took the book from him, allowing the feelings of love and strength from his touch to rush over her.

"Let me hold it until you're ready to read the words," Afrine whispered, reaching for the book.

Eve handed her the old book and watched Afrine take it as if she was receiving a new born child.

"The Book of the Nephilim. I thought I would never again see this wisdom. It had fallen for so many millenniums into the hands of the dark minds. Those who wanted only to control this sacred planet and block the true light for which it was created. Thank you,"

Afrine said. Her voice was grateful, rich and melodic. "We have been waiting for your awakening for a very long time, Eve."

"Waiting for me?" Eve asked. "How is that possible?"

"So long ago you chose to leave your destiny and ignore your calling. Time immemorial has passed and you have erased your knowings, denied your true self. Now, it is with great honor that I tell you who you are."

The rush of fear surged back into her. She knew it was an old fear. One that she had run from a million times and only in forgetting had she found her freedom.

"What if I don't want to remember?"

"You are de keeper of the sacred flame," Evine told her. "You can no forget the truth of who you are."

"You, Eve, are Messiah of the feminine. The soul of power and the spirit of love and peace," Afrine said.

"Me? No, no, no. How is that even possible?" Eve said.

"You will understand when your eyes are fully opened and you wake into the light. Come!" Evine told her.

Eve's thoughts went to Beau. At the same moment a blast of wind slammed into the side of the tower, shaking the stones and windows violently. The sound carried in it threat and danger.

"Wipe him from your mind! Do not let your taughts go to him whatever you do," Evine said. "Tonight, he is your greatest threat. Our greatest threat. Git dat in your head and in your heart!" Evine shouted.

"Your thoughts of Beau have just opened a possible portal for Kirakin. You should pray he doesn't find him. Kirakin would rip through Beau to get to you," Aria said.

"Clear your taughts of Beau Gregoire if you want to stay alive. Tink only of yourself and what you must do to destroy Kirakin forever."

"It's time. Is the room ready?" Afrine asked.

Two of the doctors opened the final doors that led into the centermost room. Eve peeked inside. She could see it was almost empty of furniture except for a large wooden altar, a pulpit and a thousand, burning white candles. Eve could see there were no windows, the walls were of stone and the turret ceiling was made of wood.

One by one they all entered the room. Eve looked back at Aria as she took her engagement ring off. It was her last connection to Beau.

Chapter Thirty Five

The rain blew sideways as the car was buffeted by the violent winds. Lightning flashed. A.V. drove as fast as he could, his eyes focused on the road. Beau watched as A.V. clutched the wheel so tight the blood drained from his knuckles, turning them white.

"Why would they leave us behind?" A.V. asked.

"I'm a threat to Eve and more important to what she has to do. I just want to be there for her when she's done," Beau said.

A.V. glanced at his friend.

"You really love her?"

"More than I could ever even begin to explain," Beau said.

They drove in silence for a long time until Beau noticed a tear running down A.V.'s cheek.

"Are you alright?" Beau asked.

"I was flashing back on the night in the tree house we made..."

"We agreed never to talk about it," Beau said, stopping him.

"I know, but you're going to be with her for the rest of your life so I need to say this now. You know I like Eve. Someday, because you love her I'll love her, and Philip stole my heart the first time he peed on my favorite, four-thousand-dollar Armani suit."

"I wish I'd had a camera to capture your expression. It was

priceless. I couldn't stop laughing," Beau said. "But you changed his diaper and held Philip so gently, I wanted that picture too; my infant son and my best friend. You looked happy, A"

"I was. I just wanted him to be ours," A.V. said.

Again the awkward silence hung thick in the air between them.

"I love you, Beau. Always have. Always will. No one has ever made me feel the way you made me feel and I don't think anyone ever will."

"A..." Beau started.

"Let me finish, and then I promise, I will never speak of this again," A.V. said.

"That night, we were young and inexperienced, but somehow, after fumbling past the first kisses and through our clothes, once we were both naked, you knew how and where to touch me. I can't tell you how many times, when I've been making love to other men and women, I imagine their hands are your hands, stroking, caressing, kissing and sucking on me. What we did was perfection and I thank you for trusting me and loving me enough to give yourself to me. If I could hold you and love you one more time I could die and never care," A.V. said.

Only silence filled the car.

"I know that night will never happen and that's okay. I just wanted to say I will always love you Beau."

A.V. turned to look at his friend. Their eyes met and held. There was deep sadness in Beau's eyes and even more in his heart because he could never be any more than a loving friend to A.V. Beau, about to speak, looked forward.

"STOP!" Beau screamed.

Standing a hundred feet ahead in the middle of the road was Kirakin; huge and powerful, with Cora standing just behind him. A.V. looked forward and his instincts made him slam on the breaks. Between the water and the wind the car hydroplaned and twisted, missing Kirakin and Cora as it sailed off the highway and over a fifty foot strip of land. The headlights of the car cut through the blackness. Beau could feel the car lift up and spiral, turning them upside down and twisting around a full three hundred and sixty degrees before it hit the bayou. A wall of mud broke the full impact of their fall and plummeted the car deep into the seeping sludge that splashed across the windshield. Their airbags deployed, seat belts bit into their flesh, holding them in place. The rear end of the car slammed down and instantly the car began to sink. Beau was shaken but alive. He turned to see A.V. had a gash on his forehead with a river of blood pouring from it.

"A.V.?" Beau asked, lowering the electric windows to get out.

"My head..." A.V. moaned. "Can't see."

The water hit the car's electric wiring, shutting off the power and sending the car into blackness. It stopped Beau's window one third of the way down. It was just enough to let water in, but not enough for two grown men to get out.

Beau got his seatbelt off and felt in the dark for A.V. At the same time Beau ripped at the airbags, bursting one and exposing the glass windshield.

"Beau. No. They'll keep us afloat," A.V. said, his voice fading as he held on to consciousness. "That thing? That was... it?"

Beau twisted in his seat and kicked violently at the side window. A flash of lightening exposed the one thing he didn't want to see. The front of the car was sinking fast as mud and water poured in through the open windows. Beau kicked harder, again and again, until finally, the window shattered. The car filled up even faster. They were completely under and sinking fast. Beau was blind in the blackness that surrounded him. He could feel cold water inching up his chest and lapping at his chin.

"Hold on to me and whatever you do, do not let go," Beau said as the water rushed into his mouth.

He tipped his face up and gulped air. Water filled his nose and covered his eyes. He grabbed A.V. with one hand and felt for the window with the other. Shards of glass bit his palm, but Beau wrapped his fingers around the window frame and pulled himself forward, dragging A.V. behind him. Beau squeezed his own head and shoulders out. Then used his legs to push himself completely out. Bracing his feet on the outside of the door, he dragged A.V. through the window. A.V. was limp and Beau was running out of air. He desperately needed to open his mouth and breathe, fill his lungs, but he was still deep under the water. Beau kicked and pulled, swimming with one hand toward what he hoped was the bayou's surface. One stroke, another, nothing parted the water above him. He kicked again. His lungs burned inside his chest. Again and again he kicked until, miraculously, Beau broke the surface. He opened his mouth and sucked in a huge gasp of air. The light from the full moon, even though it was blotted by the clouds, was still bright enough for Beau to see land. He pulled A.V. to the surface and swam with one arm around A.V.'s neck, dragging him to safety.

Beau felt the slippery mud under his feet. Step by step he made it to solid, though muddy land. Breathless, he dropped A.V.'s lifeless body, turned him over and forced the water from his lungs. Beau flipped him on his back and listened for air. Nothing.

"Don't you die on me!" Beau shouted.

Beau did five compressions, tilted A.'s head back and opened his mouth. Nose pinched, his mouth over A.'s, Beau breathed into him. He repeated the process just as they had learned in Boy Scouts, stopping only to listen for his heart.

"You promised!" Beau shouted at him.

"Pity," Kirakin's voice said above Beau. "Such a beautiful specimen of a man."

Beau looked up. Kirakin and Cora stood watching. The rain fell around them as if they were beyond its reach.

"And he loved you. Pity," Kirakin said.

Beau got to his feet.

"Save him. Can you save him?" Beau shouted, glancing at Cora, who watched emotionless from behind Kirakin.

"I could. But why should I? What would you do for me?" Kirakin asked.

The rain stopped and silence hung like death around them.

"Just save him," Beau begged. "I... I'll do anything you ask."

"He's lying," Cora said.

"Silence, Cora," Beau said.

"He's not that stupid and he knows I'm not either," Kirakin said. Kirakin began to circle the lifeless A.V. and Beau.

"Save him, please," Beau begged again. "Please."

"You understand, if I bring him back... he's mine and so are you," Kirakin said.

Beau looked at Cora. She was terrified.

"Do it Beau. He'll give us back Delia and Philip. We have no choice," Cora said.

Beau could tell Cora was out of her mind with worry and terror. He looked at A.V.'s lifeless body, drenched on the ground. Beau shook his head.

"I... can't let you hurt Eve," Beau said, weighing one life against another.

"I would never hurt Eve. She's to be my wife and our union will open our world with yours and change life as you know it forever. If you agree to let me inside of you, you will be part of this new world," Kirakin explained, extending his hand to Beau.

"Do it!" Cora shouted again.

Beau looked at Kirakin. He hated this thing that he was born to be part of, but in his heart he knew this was not the final battle that would end this war. He would not allow it to be. There was still a chance to save Eve and A.V. and maybe even Cora and defeat this thing. Slowly, against everything he wanted, Beau nodded.

"Say it!" Kirakin commanded.

"I agree to give my body over to you," Beau said, almost choking on the words.

With a sweeping gesture, Kirakin's hand passed over A.V.'s chest. It lifted. His head fell back and water crawled from his mouth like rivers of black worms. A.V. gasped for air as he sat up, hacking and coughing, alive and breathing. He rolled over as Beau bent down and reached for him, helping him to his feet.

"Find her," Kirakin said to Beau.

"How," Beau said, feeling Kirakin's energy soak into him.

"Open your desire for her," Kirakin said.

Beau felt his cock become erect. His whole body wanted Eve as he had never wanted her before. It reached out for her and from some distant place, her body was responding.

"Yes, good. Very good. Now, prepare yourself my little army. It is almost time," Kirakin said.

The clouds opened like severed veins and a torrential rain fell. The wind blew even harder and the sky was electrified by bolts of lightning and the roar of thunder. Kirakin opened his arms and, in an instant, the four of them vanished.

Chapter Thirty Six

The golden glow emanating from the large white candles that encircled the altar was warm and peaceful. The smell of warmed honey, sweet jasmine and nutmeg, all melded together as if under a hot summer sun. Eve walked closer to the center of the room. Draped across the altar were plush furs and intricately woven brocade fabric decorated with patterns in rose and amber colors and trimmed in velvet cord the color of new wheat. Hanging from the rafters, yards of cream silk chiffon formed a semicircle around the altar and plinth.

Afrine placed the book on a podium that stood at the head of the altar. Carefully, she opened it, searching through the pages until she reached a section covered in sacred geometry, detailed images, ancient Druid symbols and writings in Sanskrit. A small, red satin ribbon lay horizontally across the page to mark the passage Eve must read to initiate the ceremony. Several of the women removed their coats. They were dressed in white and gold robes. They stepped forward, each placing a hand on Eve and gently guiding her forward. They directed her to stand between the altar and the podium that held the book.

"I don't know what to do," Eve said, looking to Afrine and Evine and suddenly feeling afraid and vulnerable.

"All you have to do is read the words," Afrine told her. "The rest will unfold as it is written it would do."

Eve looked down at the jumble of symbols and writing hand drawn across the open pages.

"I can't read these," Eve said, looking at Afrine.

"She need her a host. One dat is good of heart, honor and truth," Evine said.

Evine, Afrine and Aria turned to study the people in the room. Men and woman of all ethnicities and ages looked back at them.

"Aria read de auras," Evine said to Aria. "You must choose da one most worthy."

Aria turned and looked at every man and woman in the room.

Again the wind pounded against the stone of the tower searching for a way inside.

"She will need the priestesses to guide her through and back. Look for one who is pure of heart. Find true love. It's here, I feel it," Afrine told Aria.

Again Aria's eyes scanned the room. She saw the colors of truth, kindness, fear, hope, and desperation, but the only one who radiated the color of love for Eve was Mac. He stood out like a beacon in the night, his heart beating for her safety and well-being. He desired her, but it was based in his love for her.

"Him," Aria said, pointing to Mac.

"Come forward," Afrine said.

Mac looked around unsure at first that she was talking to him.

"Come," Afrine said.

Mac approached Afrine and when he stood before her, she studied him.

"I need you to help Eve. Can you do that?" Afrin asked.

"Anything," Mac replied. His eyes connected with Eve's.

"Good. That's very good. Now, undress yourself," Afrine told him.

It took a moment for the words to sink in. The loving expression in his eyes changed to embarrassed panic.

"Here? Now? In front of all these people?"

"Unless there is a coward under your skin and that I do not see," Afrine said. "You have a brave soul."

Outside, the wind rose and beat hard against a loose shutter. The wooden roof of the tower creaked as it shifted.

Mac's eyes went back to Eve.

"What do I have to do?" Mac asked Afrine.

"You must make love to her with your body, mind and soul," Afrine said. "You love her?"

"I..." Mac started

"You do. I can see dat. Now let your body prove it."

Again he blushed as he blurted, "Here? Now?"

"De time is now," Evine said. "Trust my words. Dis will be like nothing you have ever experienced in your life. Dis is the path dat opens worlds."

Mac stood dumbfounded, unable to speak or move. He looked again at Eve. Eve turned to Afrine.

"I... love Beau," Eve said to Afrine.

The wind slammed at the walls and roof.

"Clear you mind of him!" Evine shouted. "Each taught will draw him closer to you and...."

Mac stepped forward and kissed Eve with everything that was in him. When the kiss broke, Eve looked into his eyes. It was what she had seen at the house after that first kiss. Whatever the reason, there was no one kinder for her to trust herself to what must be done.

"I guess I choose you," Eve said.   Her smile was sweet and comforting. "I trust them, Mac. Whatever it is we need to do, I believe that you and I can do it. Help me," Eve said.

Mac's hands trembled until he let his eyes lock onto hers. Her even gaze gave him courage as he opened the buttons on his shirt.

One by one the buttons parted and he pulled the fabric back to reveal a broad chest with taught flesh and defined, well cut muscles beneath.

Eve watched. She had never noticed how muscular he was through his clothes. She'd only felt the hardness of his body when he'd saved her and held her close to him. He opened the zipper on his pants. There was a moment of hesitation, as he allowed his gaze to once again meet hers. He pulled his pants down. Commando. No underwear. She wanted to smile, but Mac was very serious, so she kept her gaze locked onto his. Mac felt a warm rush surge through his body. Just looking at her made him erect. The harder he got, the more the people who stood in the shadows behind the chiffon curtains faded away.

"Now, you must undress her. Do it as slowly and as sensually as you can, so she can feel the passion in your touch and, as you take her clothes and caress her body, she will read the words of transcendence. Then, if she needs you to, you will make love to her. You will love her with all your body, mind and soul. When you climax, you must be ready to release her into the void of the universe where she must go. Do you understand?" Afrine asked Mac in a soft whisper.

Mac didn't answer. He kept his eyes on Eve, crossing to her. He stepped behind her and bent forward to gently kiss the back of her neck. His hand slipped around to gather her breasts as he kissed her neck again, pushing the tendrils of hair away. Eve quivered at his touch-more than she imagined she would. With each small kiss he undid a button on her dress. As the dress fell open he pushed it off her shoulders and placed a hand over each breast, gently squeezing as he nibbled at her neck.

Eve felt a surge of her own passion force her forward into an arch to meet his touch and fill his hands. She grabbed onto the podium that held the ancient book and heard it whisper to her. The voice pulled her gaze down onto the pages. Before her eyes the writings and symbols moved, twisting and turning, reforming into English.

With a few artful motions of his hand, her dress fell away, slipping into a puddle of fabric on the floor. She was naked beneath her dress. Mac stopped and marveled at her beauty. He'd desired her from the first moment he saw her at the hospital, lost in sleep, unable to wake. Even then he wanted his kiss to bring her back into the world of the living. Somehow he was being given that chance now. His heart quickened and he stepped closer to her.

Eve felt the waves of passion Mac was experiencing and it made her look up from the mystical events unfolding on the page. She looked into his eyes, seeing the depth of his strength, his courage and most of all his kindness. She could feel his genuine love for her. Of this she had no question or doubt. Fingers of guilt pulled at her, but she knew she could not allow such thoughts to enter her mind. She reached out and traced the curve of his shoulders, focusing on each sensual detail of his well-defined biceps to distract her thoughts of Beau.

Another gust of wind pounded against the walls and roof. She could not even think Beau's name. She felt Mac lean forward, his breath, hot and moist, followed by his lips as they pressed into a kiss as soft as velvet on her lips. His kiss held an indescribably sweet innocence that was filled with untold promises and passion. Her breath deepened. She was surrendering to him.

"Read the way to us," Eve heard a choir of voices softly chanting in her head.

Mac heard the words in his mind as well and moved around her body, kissing and tasting her.

Eve looked at the words on the page and opened her mouth to speak them, "Humans. Mothers, daughters, sisters of Paradise, I call upon you, the collective spirit of the feminine, to come and bless this union."

Eve read even though her eyes were closed in pleasure and her lips did not move and it was not her voice that filled the room. It was a choir of voices more compelling than those of the Sirens that lured Homer from the sea.

Mac moved behind her back, kissing her bare shoulders and down the nape of her neck. The scent of her body filled his nostrils and heightened even more the sensations his lips and fingers felt as they explored her skin. He followed her spine as it rose and fell beneath his fingers with every breath: tiny valleys and hills under silken skin, taking him on a journey of promised pleasure. The tip of his tongue traced each vertebra that trailed down her back. He lifted his head, stepped in front of Eve and kissed from her pubis, up her belly, tasting her nipples with his mouth and hands, sliding up her neck until he reached her lips. As their eyes met Eve realized as did Mac that somehow she was both naked before him and in front of the book at the same time. They stood between the podium and the altar. He was behind her and in front of her simultaneously. Slowly, he pulled her toward him as he sat on the altar facing her, straddling her. Eve could see him and yet the book was there. The words were coming to her as his face moved to her breasts and his lips found her nipples, tongue darting, flicking, lips open to gently caress and fondle her breasts.

The sensations from his licking and sucking, made Eve moan. She was sure time itself had slowed. She wanted it to slow even more, to stop its ceaseless march forward so she could enjoy every moment of the pleasure he was giving her.

The words flowed up into the rafters and reverberated off the arched wood ceiling, echoing in perfect harmony. Eve could hear other voices harmonizing with hers. The room began to vibrate and glow.

Mac turned her and, placing his hand behind her head, gently laid her on the altar. Eve felt the fur and brocade, soft and warm against her back. Slipping his arms under her, he lifted her and crawled over her. Their eyes connected; he kissed her again. Eve could not close her eyes. She wanted to see him. How he looked at her. So sweet was each kiss, laced with a taste that made her hunger for more. Eve opened her mouth. She let his tongue slip between her lips and find her own. Together, wet and warm, they found each other and danced, sharing love. She felt his hand on her breasts, pinching her and making her nipples more erect than before. He didn't press his body onto hers, but hovered over her, softly brushing his skin against hers as if he were the air. Eve felt his other hand slip between her legs, a finger gently rubbing her clitoris until it plumped and raised, eager for more attention. Mac, responded to her body's call. As he kissed her face, chin and neck she could feel the heat from his breath.

"Pleasure me," she whispered and the voices chanted.

"Pleasure me. Pleasure me. Take me body and soul and make me once again one. Pleasure me. Pleasure me. Become as one. Pleasure me," the voices chanted and the harmony washed over them, heightening the sensations and driving the passion.

Eve could feel Mac moving down the middle of her chest, tasting each nipple, sucking, sucking, sucking on her all the while his fingers played her clitoris like the strings of a Stradivarius violin wailing its song of Desire.

Eve moaned and with her moan, Mac slipped his head down between her thighs, pushing her legs apart and taking her into his mouth.

"There," she moaned.

He found her perfect place of pleasure and dragged his tongue up and down and back and forth, pressing his lips and sucking on her to engorge her more and more. His tongue began a dance that moved gracefully between soft and slow and hard and quick, then back to slow the way a tango unfolds - slowing just enough to stretch to the height of pleasure then a quick surge of pressure fierce and full of hot, wet fire. Her body rose with a rush of tension, then fell into utter relaxation. He took his time, building the anticipation of what was to come.

Again Eve could hear herself reading the words from the book. She could see the symbols in the book meld into each other and blossom into three-dimensional, colorful, geometric images, which became a series of doors opening, one after another, leading her down a long crystal tunnel while, at the same time, Mac was making wild, erotic love to her.

Eve's body melted as she gave herself to Mac and felt him surrender to every command her body drove him to fulfill. She felt no resistance on her part to the waves of pleasure he gave her as he fondled her with his tongue and fingers. With each movement he intensified their passionate dance, stopping to suck and lick and rub his tongue across her throbbing clitoris, until her body vibrated in unison with the harmonic tones that reverberated all around them. She could feel herself quivering a thousand feet in the air as she hung, drifting at the edge of an orgasmic abyss.

Mac rose up from his sumptuous, oral delight and with a smooth, wet thrust, quickly pushed himself just deep enough inside her to drive her wild. He knew how to heighten the frenzy of pleasure yet hold her back from falling into orgasm and himself from full release.

Eve felt a voracious hunger overwhelm her. An animal passion so visceral all she wanted was to devour him. He held her down and pushed his cock ever so slightly in and out and in and out, going further and deeper with each thrust until the slow advance of his smooth, hot, wet entry made her lift her ass and push into him. Mac held her hips as he opened her using his finger and driving her to the height of passion. After teasing her he slipped all his cock inside and gave her all of him, retracting quickly for one last tease; the rapid retraction made her legs go weak.

"Please," Eve whispered.

Mac took his cock and rubbed it around the outside of her moist wet vulva. Circling her again and again, heightening the sensation, readying her for penetration. Smooth, slow, delightful circles, giving her just the smooth head of his erect cock until he could feel her reaching out from inside for him, sure she could stand no more. Then, with a graceful thrust, he drove himself inside her. He was hard, thick and just long enough to fill her to her soul.

"Yes!" Eve cried out.

They fit perfectly, becoming one entity. Mac made love to her. She let him, matching each stroke with one of her own until she could feel his rhythm building. Each thrust topped the previous—powerful, wet strokes as he took her to levels of pleasure that surpassed anything she'd previously experienced.

Eve looked up into Mac's face. He was flushed with pleasure. His only desire was to please her. She reached up and kissed him and as their lips melted together he flipped her over and she became the rider. Eve rocked on him harder and faster. Eve felt her hands grab his ass just as he grabbed hers. They thrust into one another again, and again, and again until their pleasure erupted with the force of a super nova unleashing its energy. Their bodies exploded into each other. They became a single body and solo spirit and from this glowing tangle of passion, Eve felt herself rising. She moved through the tunnel of shimmering portals that hung before her. Eve looked back and saw that she was one being colliding with Mac and at the same time she was outside looking back and watching them in this magnificent state of passion. He flipped her again so he could be back on top. With Mac inside, her body was on fire. Eve opened her eyes to see she was somehow making love and at the same time, alone, moving upward through a spiraling crystal tunnel. It was what she had seen above her during her session with Dr. Honoré. Eve looked up into a portal that could only be described as pure light.

Chapter Thirty Seven

The moment Eve ascended the beautiful harmonic chant quieted to a distant whisper. The storm raged outside, wild and violent. Mac, unfazed, made love to Eve. He couldn't have stopped even if he'd wanted to because his only wish was to pleasure her and all her senses and the more he gave her pleasure, the more pleasure he felt. He was lost, joyously lost, unable to resist the desires that commanded him.

From the blazing candle light that surrounded the altar, Evine stepped forward, taking a place next to Afrine and Gathian. Gathian pulled his tortured, jealous eyes from Mac and Eve and with a wave of his hand created a large glass window and looked outside at the raging storm building with each passing second.

"He's searching for her. Kirakin knows what she's doing," Gathian said to Evine.

"Do you feel it? He has found and taken possession of de man called Beau," Evine said.

Evine looked over at Mac and the glowing ball of energy that was Eve he was making love to.

"Dis human is gifted in the ways of passion," Evine said. "He could win her by da simple fact his love for her is so genuine and pure."

"You know as well as I, if she loves him back that could endanger us all," Afrine said.

"Why? She has from the beginning of time worked to quell de evil in this world," Evine replied. "Even she deserves to rest."

"She's had her rest and she has not brought another forth to take her place," Gathian said.

"She has tried," Aria said, joining the conversation.

"And she has failed," Gathian said. "This is her destiny and she cannot abandon it. Too much is at stake for all of us who know the truth."

"I say free her," Evine insisted.

"She is the only one who can do that and I know her soul," Gathian said. "She needs to defeat the dark Nephilim to be free and to do that she needs to fight."

With a loud crash, the wind pounded against the walls with such force the entire building began to shudder.

"He knows," Afrin said. "He feels her transcendence."

"Kirakin's sendin' dis wind right to her and ridin' on its tail, wild and crazy to have you. He's headin' straight to ya," Evine leaned down and whispered into Eve's ear. "He will tear dis place apart."

"He's not here yet," Afrin said, placing a hand on Evine's shoulder to pull her back.

"Then Eve best hurry and remember who she is and decide what she will do," Aria said

"She right. Or we are all lost. I wish it was not here that she had to make this stand. If I'd had more time I could have taken her to the temple of mysteries and called the Priestesses," a flustered Afrine told Evine and Gathian.

"Der are enough Priestess here. Besides, she's already crossed over," Evine said, pointing to the women in the gold and white gowns.

"You and I both know that is not true Evine. She has crossed over, but she must return before he arrives."

Thunder echoed across the sky, lightning blanched everything as the wind screamed and howled, clawing at the bricks of the tower.

"Close that," Afrin ordered, pointing to the window Gathian had created.

"That won't stop him," Gathian said and with a wave of his hand turned the window back into stone.

Gathian's eyes went back to Mac and Eve in the throes of passion. His color shifted reflecting the jealousy and desire that filled his eyes.

"Get out," Evine shouted at Gathian. "Your jealousy will not help dis night, Nephilim and it will be her death."

At that moment Azura burst in.

"The children are frightened. They feel what is coming. We need to get them out of this tower and we all need to leave as well," Azura said.

"It's already too late. They are here," Gathian said, drawing his sword and turning to face the room.

The next moment Beau was standing in the room with A.V. and Cora by his side.

"Listen to me! He's coming, but I think we can stop him," Beau shouted. "Where's Eve?"

"Beau!" Cora screamed. "Don't do this."

Beau's eyes scanned the room and saw Mac on the altar. He stepped forward and looking into the glowing ball of light. Through the beautiful haze he could make out Eve writhing in pleasure beneath Mac. Tears of pain and fury welled in Beau's eyes. Gathian could see the jumble of emotions flooding through him; profound sadness, anger and jealousy. Beau watched, stunned and helpless.

"Take the children into the cellars and hope the stones hold the bayou back," Afrine whispered to Azura. She then turned to all the people in the room. "Stay or go. The choice is yours."

No one moved.

"Den chant," Evine shouted at them. "Chant for your lives and hers."

Gathian stepped in front of Beau, breaking his sight line to Eve.

"You are his conduit and there's nothing you can do," Gathian said. "What she's doing is for a greater cause. If she returns to you, it must be her choice."

Beau didn't move. Jealousy and rage coursed through him.

"I see you fighting Kirakin." Gathian said as he watched Beau's skin flush red with anger. "He will use your emotions. Control your anger or get out!"

Eve moaned, riding on waves of erotic pleasure as Mac's every move intensified her passion.

Hearing her pleasure was more than Beau could bear. Beau lunged toward the altar, reaching to pull Mac off of Eve. Gathian stepped forward and grabbed him. He pushed Beau back toward the door. "If you love her, leaving here is the only thing you can do to help. Go!"

Beau struggled until a chilling calm washed over him. He stilled. Finally, Beau looked up at Gathian and the look in Gathian's eyes said it all.

"It's too late, my brother, I am Kirakin and you are all about to die," Beau said as his body shifted and twisted, becoming Kirakin. "And she is mine."

Gathian leaped on Kirakin, vulnerable in his transition, dragging him down as the others surrounded the altar, chanting to keep him away from Eve and Mac. A.V. grabbed for an iron candle holder headed straight for Kirakin and Gathian.

Chapter Thirty Eight

Eve transcended through space and time, carried on waves of intense pleasure that kept her vibrating like a plucked string caught in a state of absolute bliss. When she stopped, she found herself standing in a forest made of pillars of light that stretched as far as her eyes could see. Flowing through each pillar were streams of light in shimmering colors that crossed the entire spectrum. The lights stretched up until they all but disappeared from her view then arched backwards, around and down until they bent up again and rejoined as double circles of pure, concentric energy. Each pillar was more magnificent than the next and each was more beautiful than anything she'd ever seen. She felt the vibration of the harmonic lights as they blended with her, in tune with the energy of her continuous orgasms. Eve looked down at her body to see she was draped in a shimmering fabric so sheer and soft she might as well have been naked. She had never felt happier. In that instant, every one of her senses told her the same thing ... she had come home.

"It's been a very long time, Eve," a voice said to her. "We welcome you."

The voice was neither male nor female, but both at once and it came from everywhere and nowhere.

Eve's chest heaved. She could feel Mac suck on her nipple, slowing as he slipped himself in and out of her at the same time she stood in conversation. Eve felt her mortal body urging her to return to indulge in the pleasure that was being created by her union with Mac, but the pull of the energetic field that fed her spirit would not succumb to her body's desire for Mac and his erotic passion.

"Where am I? What is this place?" Eve asked.

"It is the alpha and the omega," the disembodied voice replied.

"The beginning and the end of what?" Eve asked.

"All things. You, me, the Universe. Energy that cannot be created nor destroyed, only joined and released ad infinitum. This is our center. The all, of one. You. Your home," the voice explained.

"Me?" Eve asked.

At that moment one of the pillars of light took the form of a beautiful woman. Her eyes and hair were made of stars and the dress moved as if it were made of liquid diamonds lit by moonlight.

"Walk with me, Eve," the vision said to her.

Together they walked through the rows of pillars that parted reverently to let them pass.

"Dearest, Eve. Where you are and what you are doing was, at first, your choice. You went where we all go to feel, experience and learn ... to live and breathe at the center of our most universal paradise - Earth. You stayed longer, returning occasionally to remember who you are and going back anew, creating and recreating yourself again and again. Searching for something you still think you've not yet found. Then one day you liked life in human form more than here. You didn't want to come back or remember your destiny so you cleared your mind of how much of eternity is embodied in you and stayed there, but in staying you opened the doors for others to return. Others who should never be allowed to return to Earth."

"Why would I leave this place?" Eve asked.

"You said you wanted to come to the epicenter of the real struggle so that you could understand the pull of good and evil. You have been the giver of life in this world, but you could only feel what that meant in the human world. So you became Eve. You are the woman's creator and lovingly, though her, you have held paradise in your arms and experienced life. In the beginning you made this planet perfect until you were visited by Kirakin. He intrigued you and you fell in love with him," the vision told her.

"Kirakin?" Eve asked. "He's a demon bent on destruction. How is that possible?"

"He charged your imagination, gave you access to untold knowledge. He inspired your mind and then he seduced your body. From the very first time, he took you to his darkest places of pleasure and you were fascinated and tempted by his darkness. You didn't understand that it was your union that gave him power. Once you gave him a taste of power and all that you could do for him, he offered you his new world in exchange for your union with him. He understood what you never considered, that if he had you, it would give him access to any worlds. You evolved and realized you didn't need him to attain anything you desired, but he needed you. Then his greed took him into an even darker place and you learned his true intentions. On that day you shunned him and left. Still, he needed you to exist beyond his world and with the power you had shown him he knew he must control you. He found you and did his best to seduce you back into his realm and when you refused him the war between you began. You ran from him and took refuge with Gathian. Kirakin has hunted you through time and space and Gathian protected you as best he could, then he too fell in love with you and his passion for you gave Kirakin a way to find you. That's why you came to Earth. Somehow, in your need to protect who you are and what you're searching for, you've hidden on Earth so long, you've forgotten where you came from and why you exist."

"I came to Earth for a reason?" Eve asked. Her mind was racing searching for answers.

"To find a mate to bring your world and Earth's world together. You wanted to save mankind from their primitive selves and elevate the species. Kirakin knew that if you achieved that feat without him and his kind, he would lose you forever. So, when he found you on Earth, your mind erased and happy as a human, he used his powers to deceive and pleasure you. He had you once and lost you again, because those who love you came to help you. He has bent reality to try again and if he wins you will lose."

"How?" Eve asked.

"Long ago he tricked you into sharing the mysteries of the feminine. You showed him the path to ascension and in it the secrets to controlling all the realms."

"Through sexual pleasure? We have access to immortality and all knowledge through sexual pleasure?" Eve asked.

"The two have to be joined and all is possible. Look," the light said and pointed. "The choice of who you are and how you exist has always been yours, Eve."

The beautiful vision made of light gestured to a series of portals that suddenly wavered around her. "You have the power of your destiny, not the one Kirakin had created for you. Create your future and choose."

Eve turned and looked inside the first portal. She saw Beau standing, handsome and smiling inside Gregoire house, now warm and sunny. Philip, still a toddler, sat in his arms reaching for her, but in the shadows behind them she could see Kirakin looming impatiently behind him. This she knew was a trick. In the second portal was Gathian, he stood, strong and powerful in front of his palace. It was both ancient and futuristic. It existed on some distant other world, but it was not Earth. To his right, a massive army gathered, standing in a vast courtyard, armed and ready to fight by her side. Eve knew this was for a great battle against Kirakin and his dark forces.

"Eve," Gathian said as he extended his hand for her to join him. "We are ready for your return."

Eve turned again. Before her eyes Eve saw a third spiral of energy spin open. It looked down onto the Earth and into the tower at Thibodaux Hospital. What she saw in that portal chilled her, it was all she'd just left, unfolding around her human body as it lay on the altar inside the tower. Kirakin swooped in riding the power of the clouds, rain and wind. He had with him Beau, Cora and A.V. Millard's severed head hung from his belt like a heathen trophy. Eve watched as he ripped the roof off the tower and landed inside. He drew his sword and began to slaughter the people who had come together to help her. Lightening flashed and thunder roared in the sky above them. She could see how all the people divided; half to fight Kirakin, the others to protect her and Mac who still made love on the altar, oblivious to all that was unfolding around them. Gathian stepped forward to battle with Kirakin. Eve looked at Beau.

"Is it true?" Eve said as tears filled her eyes. "Beau belongs to him."

"I can see in his heart he still hopes to defeat the Nephilim and save you."

Eve's eyes went to Cora. Her face seethed with rage as her eyes searched for Delia. Eve looked for her son and Delia and the other children. She couldn't see them, but her heart knew they and especially her son were in great danger. She turned her gaze back to the two Nephilim as they crashed into one another. They fought while she and Mac made love on the altar surrounded by Afrine, Evine, Aria and the others who had come to help protect her as best they could. She understood the vulnerable state she was in during transition and the terrible danger she had placed Mac in by holding him there. She could see Mac writhing above her body as it lay suspended in a ball of glowing light. Inside the light she could see herself making love to this kind man who had risked his life to save her. She knew he was a brave stranger. She cared about him, but there had not been time for her to fall in love with him and now she was asking him to die for her. It was at that very moment that Beau saw her making love to Mac. Beau walked forward past the battling Nephilim toward the altar. His face fell into the pained expression of a man wounded and confused. Eve could see the very second his heart broke and his will wash away. It was in that moment that she saw Beau transform and meld into Kirakin, lost to her forever.

"No," Eve shouted into the portal. "No, Beau. It was the only way for me to find out the truth. Please. This is my fault."

When Beau became Kirakin, A.V. stepped forward to fight for Kirakin. Eve watched as A.V. crossed the room and grabbed one of the tall, iron candle sticks. He lifted it into the air and brought it down with the force of a great battle ax, not on Mac or Kirakin, but on Gathian. Gathian fell – dazed by the blow. He struggled to get back to his feet. A.V. hit him again and again. Gathian swung his arm out and his hand caught A.V. across the face with such force it sent his body across the room. A.V. crashed into the stone wall and fell into a bleeding heap, his body twisted and broken. Cora screamed and raced across the room. She leapt on Gathian who still struggled to get his feet beneath him. She began scratching at his eyes. He pushed her off holding her back as she screamed and kicked at him.

"Give me my daughter!" Cora shouted as she lunged at him again.

Eve turned to the woman of light.

"I have to go," Eve said, feeling the tears fill her eyes and the fear of losing everything overwhelm her.

She raced for the portal that led back into the third realm.

"I have to help them," Eve shouted.

She ran through the pillars of light until she reached the portal. Far inside it, Eve could see Afrine, Aria, Evine and the others. Several had stepped in to pull Cora off of Gathian. Kirakin took the momentary reprieve and rose up from beneath Gathian. He swung his sword, cutting down ten people with a single blow. Kirakin turned to Evine, Afrine and the people protecting Mac and Eve. Evine stepped forward and lifted her hands. Using her powers, she conjured up a great wind and forced him back from the altar. He opened his hand drawing the wind into the palm of his hand. Step by step he made his way closer. Evine summoned up a burning wind with searing flames. Still Kirakin sucked the flames into his hand and kept coming.

Cora turned her attack from Gathian to Mac and Eve.

"No, Cora," Eve shouted.

Eve ran harder, but the tunnel of light seemed to grow longer. She could see in the distance what was unfolding, but couldn't get there. She ran faster. Eve watched as the priestesses and priests who had been protecting her and Mac turn on Cora and ripped her into shreds. Kirakin was getting closer. Still blocked by the fire and wind, he summoned a dozen, black shadow demons to fall upon, Aria and Afrine like oily rain, suffocating them.

Eve's heart filled her throat. She knew only one thing, they were losing the battle that raged around her and Mac and she had to get back. Eve ran deeper into the endless portal.

"Remember who you are and that you have the power to exist in more than one version of your life at the same time," the disembodied voice said, calling to her from the distance.

"Make ya choice, Eve," Evine called out. "Lose all fear and make it quick, chil'."

"I want... I want..." Eve started.

Eve turned back to take one last look at the pillar of light that had spoken to her. Standing with the light Eve saw Philip and Delia. She felt part of her keep on running for the portal while another part of her suddenly stood with Philip. Eve, grateful for the moment, dropped to her knees. Philip ran crashing into her arm. He held her and she held him.

"Oh, Philip. I love you so very much," Eve told Philip.

"I love you too, Mommy," Philip said.

"What can I do? What will become of you? Will I lose you?"

Delia came close behind and squiggled into their embrace. Eve held them both, closing her eyes and giving them loving hugs and kisses.

"We'll find you, mommy, no matter where you go," Philip said and kissed her cheek. "I promise."

"You have to hurry," Delia said.

With that she saw both children abruptly snatched away.

Eve stood, shaken by the sadness of loss, but pulled by the urgency of what she was hearing from the battle below her. She returned to her still running self as she headed deeper into the portal of light. As she ran, she passed all four versions of what she had been shown. She had to make a choice, but first, she had to get back and stop Kirakin.

"Hurry, Eve," the voice whispered. "They need you?" Their time is short and the pain of death takes its toll on the living. Remember who you are and that you have the power to exist in more than one version of your life."

"Make ya choice, Eve," Evine call out from the waiting portal.

Eve could see Kirakin turning back the flames and directing them toward Evine. In a moment she would be burned alive.

Eve felt herself falling forward. She plummeted through space and time back to the realm from which she had ascended. Her journey was scored by a roar of thunder. With a snap, she crashed back into herself and into the heart of the battle that raged around her.

At first she saw only Mac above her. His eyes were closed and his face was in a state of bliss as he passionately made love to her on the altar. She felt his hips twist, his cock, hot and slathering wet in her, joyously increasing their pleasure. She felt herself thrust her hips forward, pressing against his so he could enter her fully. Pleasure rushed over her in hot waves as she tightened around his cock with a velvet grip. Each squeeze and release of his cock heightened Mac's pleasure. He moaned as she sent waves of wild, wet, steaming pleasure quivering through him. Eve felt him surrender as she grabbed his hips and pulled him even deeper into her. Time slowed as their motion sped up, faster and faster and faster until they were ready to explode. Panting in perfect rhythm, writhing, moaning and bellowing in absolute pleasure she released into full organism as she bent her back into an arch of pleasure and pain. Mac exploded, falling into an abyss of pure ecstasy.

Eve could hear him whisper, "I love you, Eve."

"Find me, Mac," she whispered back. "And I will find you."

The next moment Eve found herself standing, naked and sweating in the center of the room. She looked up to see the roof had been ripped away by Kirakin and the pouring rain drenched all who fought around her. Cora lay bleeding, pummeled by the priestesses. A.V. and Afrine were dead. Evine fought Kirakin alone using one hand to hold him back with the wind and fire she conjured and with the other, she did her best to heal the wounded Gathian. Kirakin pounded at both of them, backing them deeper into a corner until the flames were about to engulf them both.

"Leave them!" Eve shouted.

Kirakin stopped. Everyone stopped. The Nephilim turned his gaze to Eve.

"You came for me, Kirakin," Eve said.

"Eve," Gathian shouted and weakly waved his hand.

The next thing Eve knew she was standing with Gathian's sword in her hand, dressed in silver armor and white leathers. These were clothes that came from a different time, but she knew they belonged to her.

When Kirakin saw Eve standing in the center of the room, powerful and more beautiful than he had ever seen her, he swept his hand behind him and sent a force of energy so powerful it knocked everyone back across the room and onto their knees. His next gesture held them motionless in a field so powerful they could not move. Slowly he turned his gaze back to face Eve. He opened his hand and his massive sword of blue steel appeared out of thin air in his palm. Its handle was solid gold and adorned with diamonds and precious jewels.

"I don't want to kill you, Eve," Kirakin said.

"I know what you want," she replied.

Suddenly, the rain stopped falling and the wind hushed to the faintest whisper. Eve looked across the room at the bruised and bloodied faces of all who had risked their lives to save her and who were now suspended in Kirakin's powerful field of energy. She looked at Kirakin.

"Release them, Kirakin. And release Beau from whatever curse binds him and his family to you," Eve said. She spoke softly, but there was no question she was commanding him.

Kirakin smiled. "And what will I receive in return?" he asked.

"I will let you go back to your realm, but you must promise never to return to this or any other world," she said.

"With you?" he replied.

"Release Beau and forever sever yourself from his blood debt," she repeated.

Kirakin studied her for a long moment. He ran his other hand down the side of his ribs and Beau's limp body peeled out though the skin and crashed to the ground. Eve could see Beau struggle to find his strength. She crossed to him and dropped to one knee, gently touching his face. Using his last bit of strength, he lifted himself up to her, searching her face for a sign she would stay with him.

"What happened wasn't me," he said.

"I know that," Eve replied.

"I would have died for you," Beau said.

"Live for me instead," Eve said and gently kissed him.

She stood and turned to face Kirakin.

"Don't go with him," Beau said. "Please."

Eve smiled and laid Gathian's sword at Beau's side.

"Remember me," she told him.

Eve stood and turned to face Kirakin. Her eyes connected to his and she stretched out her left hand reaching to the side. From her fingers, streams of light shot across the room and began to spiral.

"Time to go home, Kirakin," she said.

Taking his hand she led him toward the light. Eve looked back on all those who had guided her, helped her, fought for her and loved her. Mac fought hardest as the force field that held them slowly melted with each step she and Kirakin took closer to the swirling light. Eve could see the four portals the voice had shown her. They spun, each with its own life. Each beckoning her to come and live their version of her life. She looked into each portal one more time. This time there was a fifth portal and Eve saw herself, standing alone wearing the dress she wore the night of the Southern Belles Charity event. She watched herself turn to see Cora, alive, standing down the hall of the Gregoire Mansion, beautiful, happy and laughing. Beyond Cora, coming down another hall, she saw Beau walking toward her. He was more breathtakingly handsome than she'd ever seen him. Eve smiled at the simple human life she had wanted. She turned back to Kirakin.

He stood before the portal that lead to his world. He was tall and powerful, sensual and handsome. She had loved him once and she knew why.

"Are you ready to go home and never come back?" she asked.

"I am ready to go anywhere you say," he replied.

"I'm glad you said that," Eve replied.

She could see by his face that he was excited and ready to return with her into his world, but by uttering the words he'd just said, he'd unknowingly agreed, on his own accord, with her mandate to never return. Eve cocked her head and smiled at him as she yanked the gri-gri bag of anumu powder that still hung from her neck off with a snap. In one graceful movement she split the small leather bag open with her fingers and flung the haze of powder at him. The power exploded, dusting Kirakin just as the sword Beau was holding sailed into his side.

"No, Beau," she said.

It was too late. She shoved Kirakin back into his portal. Eve sealed the portal door and with it, sealed all the other portals but one. She could hear Kirakin's voice as he fell back into his world, cursing her name until his voice faded from her ears.

Eve took a deep breath and felt her body being pulled backwards into the portal that held the Southern Belles Charity event on the night that started it all. This time, she prayed, with no demons to temp her or stop her from living a human life. It would be the beginning of so many exciting possibilities. The beginning of what she had dreamed of all along. She closed her eyes as she fell into the warm blackness of the unknown, letting it wash over her until with a soft pop, she found herself standing alone in the entry way of the Gregoire Mansion, surrounded by a hundred people and wearing a stunning dress that fit a little too tight and made her feel absolutely naked.

Chapter Thirty Nine

Eve felt a rush of absolute panic, but she had done it. She'd come to the party of the year and yet as much as she wanted to be here, she felt completely unprepared for the elegance and wealth that surrounded her. Eve tugged again at the very short, very sexy dress that clung to her curves. She was sorry she'd worn it. At least in her usual belted shirt dress she felt armed, ready to face people, but her best friend had insisted this was the first day of the rest of her life and she needed to put it all out there. So she put on the pale blue silk dress Cora had insisted she wear, added eyelashes and ruby lips and piled her thick, honey-colored hair into a twist on the top of her head. Her hair, people always said, was one of her best features; a river of flaxen, impossibly shiny and thick, which is why it was in a knot just like the knot in her stomach. She had put it out there, nipples first, and the cool air made her not-as-skinny-as-she'd-hoped naked body under the silk shift way more out there than she was used to. The constant thumping of the dance music matched the nervous beating of Eve's heart as she stood, staring into a room full of people and feeling horribly alone. She hung back, motionless, looking and listening, furious she had come and feeling more and more like an ugly puppy left abandoned on the side of a road than a pretty woman at a dance. Eve felt frustrated she was attending yet another party without a date. But what the hell was new about that? She hadn't had a date in more months than she could remember and moving to New Orleans had only made her prospects worse. She was here so WTF!

The swell of music echoed up from a band located somewhere beyond the grand entrance and expansive parlors that defined the infamous Gregoire Plantation Estate, daring her to enter. Each step she took was punctuated by the pounding rhythms and primitive war chants that played around her. The hypnotic melody was designed to entice people through the maze of festive décor, past the food and liquor and out onto the dance floor. She took that dare and walked through the parlor into the dining room. Eve inhaled the aromas of red pepper sauce, Andouille sausages drenched in Cajun spices, and the pungent tang of fine southern bourbon, mixed with something sugary like coke or julep. That was just the southern way: the sweeter the better. Eve ignored the wall of chatter that echoed up from the party, unable to shake the ever-present feeling that someone was watching her.

Eve took a long, slow, deep breath and crossed the wide marble hall. She descended the steps that led into the main parlor of the house, which defined southern elegance. The original structure had been built by Lafayette Gregoire nearly three hundred years before and over the centuries it had expanded into the palatial mansion it was today. It sat on the shores of a lake just twenty miles outside New Orleans. Eight generations of Gregoires had been born, lived, married, divorced, fought and died here. Wars had been won and lost as the house stood, enduring the centuries, while patriarchs and matriarchs ruled the lush lands of the Plantation Gregoire.

Eve had always loved this house. She made her mother bring her here at least once every summer, when they came for their annual visits from Chicago, to walk the gardens that stretched along the lake. But until tonight she had never been inside. If she hadn't been so nervous, she would have been in total awe. She would have let her hand trace the beautifully carved wainscoting that paneled the lower half of the entry, falling in straight lines to meet the fine marble floor. She would have let her feet glide across the smooth burgundy surface that stretched out in a perfect circle in each direction and cascaded down the mahogany steps into the sunken living parlor. Eve glanced briefly back at the grand stairway that curled up from the entry and connected to the second floor. In a better state of mind she would have wondered about each of the ten bedrooms that stood like soldiers down the wide, dimly lit hallway. She would have felt each door staring back in sealed silence, keeping the long-forgotten secrets of those who had once inhabited them. But Eve had no time to let her imagination wander. She was feeling lost and hopelessly out of place. Where was her best friend, Cora, who'd talked her into coming? *Why the hell have I come?* She wondered. *Damn it!*

Eve stepped across the crowded entry, through the sunken living room of the old mansion and out onto the balcony. She couldn't help but feel something else growing beneath her normal nervousness— something beyond the shyness that haunted her whenever she had to face the world. Tonight she felt different, strange, almost excited. The tiniest quiver, gentle yet persistent, coursed through her blood like a fever, hot and sticky as the moist, Louisiana summer night air that wrapped around her. The heat infected not just her body, but also her soul with its subtle, constant reminder that the south in summer was its own special sensation.

Eve sighed and walked forward. She recognized a few notable people who always spent their summers at the lake; snobbish southern belles and handsome blue-blooded men whose families had lived in and around New Orleans for the past four hundred years. The women were porcelain dolls with expensive clothes, perfect hair, X-ray thin and way too over-educated to be the trophy wives they had oft times chosen to become.

Eve turned to look at herself in a mirror. She wanted to make sure she was there. *Yep,* she thought, *I actually came. What a masochist.* Her reflection stared back at her. Her face was well painted to enhance what she had been told were her best features: nice lips traced with a line of ruby red, carefully drawn to enhance the shape and colored-in like the meticulous crayoning of an obsessive-compulsive six year old, heavy color on top, lighter on the bottom with a dollop of tangerine at the center of the bottom lower lip to give just the right effect of a pout. God, did she actually believe the makeup advice she wrote about in her magazine. But she had followed the rules: flushed cheeks against pale skin that accented dark eyes, which were encircled by black, spidery lashes that spiked around her almond-shaped eyes. Eve looked approvingly, thinking her hair was just the right amount of tousled to seem like she had not bothered quite as much as she had. She smoothed the soft, silk dress that clung in all the right places and straightened her back. She was wearing *summer diamonds*; as her grandmother use to say before she passed on, "Some are diamonds, some are not." Eve smiled to think of Maman and her little legacy of faux jewels that she lovingly handed down to her. They caught the dim candlelight and sparkled from her neck and wrist, giving the illusion she was appropriately spoiled enough to fit in with the rest of the guests. She was as beautiful as she could be. So why did she feel so naked and vulnerable despite the cosmetic armor and fashion shield she had carefully donned to protect herself? Something was coming and whatever it was, she was certain she wasn't ready.

"Dance with me," a deep, sensual whisper commanded from behind her. Eve started to turn but hands—no, arms—encircled her and locked her in a gentle but firm embrace. Eve looked down and saw two large, olive-colored hands wrapped around her waist. The fingers were long and sinewy, the kind that belonged to great pianists or master surgeons with smooth skin that had never seen a day of manual labor.

His body felt strong and tall as he pressed himself against her back. Eve could feel each cut of the well-defined muscles that ran down his stomach, flat and firm against her back. He was taller than she by a head. She felt his breath rush warm and moist past her hair as it brushed her cheek. His scent drifted into her nose. This was no expensive bottled cologne; his scent was one of life, mystery and intrigue. It was strange yet familiar, as if she had known him her entire life. Sweet and pungent, it touched her heart with a genuineness that eased her tension and made her all but melt into his embrace.

Eve felt dizzy, giddy, intoxicated by him and that hadn't happened since her first kiss in eighth grade. The band was playing a sensual ballad and with a graceful, fluid motion he took her hand and spun her around. When she came to face him, time stopped.

She blinked and shook her head to clear her mind and her vision. Eve's heart quickened because she found herself looking not at a man, but at what great poets describe as true beauty. He was fine; an Adonis and he was dancing with her. His eyes looked so deep into her it took her breath away. They were as pale and as blue as a summer sky with flecks of silver that had to have come from pure moonlight. His expression gave a gentle warning that seemed to demand truthfulness above all else. *Have I fainted, been drugged, died?* Eve tried to think, to feel the ground beneath her feet, to make sense of the dream she had entered. But there was no question, this was real, and she was very awake.

"You dance as beautifully as you look," he said.

His melodic voice was as calming and tender as a Barry White love song. Again she tried to clear her mind. He smiled at her. His lips were round, full, and smooth and they begged to be kissed. Michelangelo could've chiseled his face from a block of warm, flawless travertine. His curly hair was midnight black and caught the candle's glow, demanding she reach up to play in it.

"You... uh... dance pretty well too," she said, feeling like an imbecile as the words tumbled out of her mouth.

"Do I," he smiled, teasing her. "I think you like my arms around you."

Had he read her mind, felt her desire before she had even felt it herself? The tiny quiver that had been growing inside her since she arrived at the party exploded into a blazing fire that made her certain she would spontaneously combust if she didn't run away. Her body began to tremble with excitement.

"May I cut in?" another man asked, shattering the moment.

"What?" Eve replied.

Eve looked away from her Adonis to see another man. He was handsome in an everyman, regular Joe sort of way. He pulled at the collar of his shirt, looking as boyishly awkward as she had felt only a few moments before. He had incredibly kind eyes, broad I-would-always-protect-you-shoulders and the most adorable smile. Eve looked at the two miracles who glared at each other in front of her. *Oh my God, these men are challenging each other over me!* she thought.

"Mac," the man with the kind eyes said. "And I'd like to have this dance if your husband doesn't mind."

"Oh. He's not my husband, but ..." Eve started.

"But the night is young," my Adonis said. "I'm Beau."

"Well according to the MC ...," Mac said. "...we are supposed to cut in because this is the charity dance and I just paid a week's salary for a dance with the most beautiful woman in the room."

"Really," Beau said.

"Yeah," Mac said to Eve with a very mischievous grin. He then turned to Beau. "For charity then?"

"Just make sure you bring her back so we can finish what we were starting," Beau said.

"It's the least I can do if that's what she wants," Mac said, a sly smile clinging to his lips.

Beau opened his arms and stepped back and before Eve could open her mouth to protest, Mac stepped inside her open arms. His arms slipped around her waist and the strangest rush came over her as he danced her away from Beau. She couldn't put words to it, but it felt wonderful.

"I know I promised to give you back," he leaned close and whispered into her ear. "But I'm hoping we can dance the night away and, under the auspices of the Charitable Belles, make a real change in the world together, you and I."

"Really?" Eve said, smiling up at him. "There's nothing like changing the world."

THE END

ADDENDUM

In a parallel world

Eve appeared on the great stairway having transcended from one world to the next with the grace and glory of a sunrise. She stood as she had stood, time immemorial, draped in the white and blue robes that defined her title as Leader of the Guardians of Paradise. Stretched before her in all directions sat her immortal army of the feminine who had waited for her return. One by one their eyes lifted toward the imposing figure who smiled at them. Her robes and hair tousled by the winds that blew across the courtyard drew more and more of the Amazonian warriors. As glimpses of recognition crossed their faces, they rose and knelt without taking their eyes off of her. A sea of joyous faces looked up at her with gratitude and hope.

Eve lifted her hand and with it a cheer erupted, resounding across the courtyard as it echoed out across the land, sea and sky heralding her return.

"Forgive me. It's time," Eve said. "... to take back the power that has been stolen from womankind and bring peace and tranquility to the sacred Paradise called Earth Mother."

Another cheer, this time louder and more joyous, rose from the women.

Evine stepped from behind her. She looked young and more beautiful than Eve remembered. Her shock of white hair, her eyes, one brown and one blue, held a seriousness Eve couldn't read. The darkness concerned her.

"Will the Angels join us?" Eve asked.

"They are arriving as we speak," Evine responded. "Metatron, Michael and Gabriel have pledged the Arch Angels and Raphael leads the twelve Legions."

"You ascended?' Eve asked Evine.

"Only in this realm," Evine replied. "We, who know, become who we need to be when we need to."

Eve looked over and saw Delia, grown into a strong and beautiful young woman. Delia walked up to her and Eve took her into her arms.

"I'm glad you're here," Eve told Delia.

"I'm glad you came. We were worried," Delia said.

"We are glad you came home, but what you did, splitting realms and coexisting as two entities, is a dangerous and risky choice. Only one other has done such a feat," Evine told her.

"My brother is a great Magi and I know well the danger of my choice, but I needed to be human for this plan to manifest," Eve said.

"I bring with me the Nephilim who believe your coming is just and good," Gathian said as he passed into the realm. He still wore the scars he had taken from his last two battles with Kirakin. He dropped to one knee and placed the palm of her hand to his lips. "I and my legions are yours to command." Gathian rose, never taking his eyes from Eve's.

Eve smiled and they embraced. She was his equal in height and their strength was well matched. He held her in his arms and she could feel his love pouring over her in gentle waves as soft and as warm as summer rain.

"You have other promises to me to keep," Gathian said. "I bring bad tidings."

Eve could see in his eyes, he knew the sadness he carried would wound her.

"Philip. Where is Philip?" Eve asked, looking behind him.

"Kirakin holds him," Gathian said.

Eve's heart sank. She had not protected him. A rush of desperation flooded her face.

"How? When?" Eve asked.

"In the last moments before your split transition, Philip as well as half the children were snatched away. He holds Cora and Zamara as well. You saved Beau for now, but you must know, Beau walks a fine line and when he threw the sword he fractured your promise to Kirakin. The crack still grows. Now, only you can clean his soul and end the curse."

"But my son? What can I do to save Philip?" Eve asked again.

"He is in Kirakin's power," Gathian told Eve.

"Only for now," Evine said. "We will find a way to rescue the boy."

"Kirakin will teach him the powers of the night," Gathian told her. "He is still young and may not know the difference between what is good and what is bad. We will all help you save him."

"Philip knows you are his mother. We hope he remembers that you can teach him the powers of the light," Evine told Eve.

"Can I fight for love in both worlds?" Eve asked.

"That's up to you," Evine said.

"In this matter, I have no other choice. And I will win in both worlds, because of it. I must," Eve said to everyone. "Come and prepare. The time is right. The moment to begin is now."